FOOLSMEADOW
DAYS

A GOODMAN MYSTERY

FOOLSMEADOW DAYS

P T MELLORS

AUTHOR OF **GOODMAN, GIBSON AND PARTNERS**

The Book Guild Ltd

First published in Great Britain in 2022 by
The Book Guild Ltd
Unit E2 Airfield Business Park,
Harrison Road, Market Harborough,
Leicestershire. LE16 7UL
Tel: 0116 2792299
www.bookguild.co.uk
Email: info@bookguild.co.uk
Twitter: @bookguild

Copyright © 2022 P T Mellors

The right of P T Mellors to be identified as the author of this
work has been asserted by them in accordance with the
Copyright, Design and Patents Act 1988.

All rights reserved. No part of this publication may be
reproduced, transmitted, or stored in a retrieval system, in any form or by any means,
without permission in writing from the publisher, nor be otherwise circulated in
any form of binding or cover other than that in which it is published and without
a similar condition being imposed on the subsequent purchaser.

This work is entirely fictitious and any resemblance to persons living or dead, or to actual locations
or events, past or present, is purely coincidental.

Typeset in 11pt Minion Pro

Printed and bound in Great Britain by CMP UK

ISBN 978 1915352 378

British Library Cataloguing in Publication Data.
A catalogue record for this book is available from the British Library.

For Diana, who first pointed the way

PART 1

ONE

LOOSE END

Several of us had dropped into The Crown for our customary end-of-term get-together. And since everyone knew that a student of mine had died violently that year by his own hand, it was hardly surprising to hear the subject come up. I'd been Gordon Verity's personal tutor all year and therefore was expected to know, if not why he'd done it, at least what clues he'd given me that he might be considering doing it. It was the same with the police. I was the person they expected to shed light on the sort of student he was, his mood in the days before it happened, what changes I might have noticed in the guy's behaviour, etcetera. Anything that might tell them why a nineteen-year-old shaping up to be a serious contender for my most invisible student of the year should, without warning, suddenly make a shockingly public spectacle of himself by leaping into the path of an InterCity express train from a crowded platform at the town's railway station. That afternoon in The Crown I was, to be honest, as much in the dark about GV's motive as everyone else.

But like I say, he was my student. As his personal tutor, I was the member of staff who'd had most contact with him, the guy with responsibility, according to the prospectus, for overseeing his progress with his studies and his pastoral care. What was I doing standing by, so to speak, while he took himself off to the station and did the unthinkable? Was it suicide, when all's said and done? He didn't appear to have left a note. These were not questions I had answers to, frankly. Even tutors had days when they couldn't read their students' minds. It wasn't as if he'd taken me into his confidence and poured out his troubles. As far as I was concerned, Gordon Verity was the most inoffensive, innocuous, self-effacing student of Business and Politics I had on my register that year. Top marks definitely for staying off the radar. Colleagues who taught him were agreed on that much. He kept himself to himself, and he kept his nose clean.

'What's this I hear, Adam, about you not taking a holiday this summer? Have the police asked you not to leave the country?'

'That's right, Carl. They're convinced I know more than I've told them.'

Nothing of the kind, actually, but Computer Studies guru Carl Watson nodded knowingly, then tapped one side of his nose. 'A deeply religious young man, I believe.'

Was he? How was I expected to know? My students rarely spoke to me of their religious beliefs, nor did I encourage them in case they suspected I had counter beliefs of my own to peddle. My rule of thumb in the classroom: no sex, no party politics, and definitely no religion, thank you very much. My job as tutor was to listen if students chose to talk to me in confidence about any of the above. As I recall, GV made no such approach and, among his career options, he certainly hadn't listed the priesthood.

'He went to one of those funny back street churches. Sahara Street or something,' Heather from the office informed us. Then added, because nobody reacted, 'Didn't you know?'

Sahara Street? I shook my head. I'd say the principal's secretary had passed on this information to the office junior. Lorna enjoyed ex officio access to anything confidential going on in the principal's study, and that obviously included exchanges between the man himself (JR as we called him, aka Mr Langtree to the uninitiated) and officers leading the investigation into GV's death. 'Where do these revelations come from?' I asked Heather. A purely rhetorical question, since I felt I knew all I wanted to know about GV.

Most of the information originated from the lad's mother, apparently – a woman I'd not had the privilege of meeting, for reasons best known to her. She had had the unenviable job of identifying her son's body, we were told, and had been able to help the police with some of those more intimate personal details a mother would be expected to know but which a tutor could only guess at (if he was unwise enough to try, I mean).

You had to hand it to Heather, the way she gave us all the benefit of her received knowledge of what GV got up to when he wasn't attending lectures or tutorials. For a start, did we know he was gay? Well, she'd been told he was and, according to her, his church had probably disowned him for coming out and that was the reason he'd decided to end it all at the station.

Coming out? How come I'd not been privy to that vital piece of information till now? Simple, now I thought about it. Guided by my own house rules and being the quiet, compliant sort he was, GV had kept his sexuality under his hat, so to speak. In the circumstances I nodded circumspectly and kept quiet. Fine by me for GV to be his own person; I ran a tolerant ship.

The principal, we went on to learn, had asked Lorna to attend the young man's funeral on his behalf, as a mark of respect. She'd told Heather that several members of GV's church had put in an appearance. Quite a crowd of them in fact. Maybe my niece too, according to my friend and colleague, Steve Forrester. Steve went on to name my niece as a member of the same church.

'Seriously, Adam,' he put it to me. 'Without a word of a lie, it's the outfit your Sam belongs to. I'm sure I've heard her talk about Sahara Street. Never gave it a thought, mate. Before today, I mean.'

Samantha, he was referring to. My sister Hilary's daughter. I confess I knew sweet FA about my niece's religious leanings; I'd simply taken for granted she had none. Or else was a lapsed C of E type like her mother who, if she attended anywhere at all, went very occasionally to a service at Saint Michael's, the local parish church. No need to ask myself how Steve had come by the knowledge. These days he visited my sister's farm far more frequently than I did.

Steve had been seeing, if that's the word for it, my sister Hilary for several months. Hilary, let me explain, had been a widow for three years or so and whilst, at forty-odd, she no longer had the looks she'd once had, she nevertheless was a woman of some prospects and eligibility, as they say. For one thing, she owned property. Specifically, a farmhouse of her own, and a good deal of land to go with it. Foolsmeadow Grange, they called it, a former mixed livestock farm, at the end of a winding lane not exactly miles from anywhere but far enough out of town to give visitors the impression it was remote.

Hilary had been a farmer's wife, and now, as a farmer's widow, she'd lost any passion she'd once had for working the land. Correspondingly, she'd no desire to meet another farmer, or anyone who aspired to make farming his career. That suited Steve very nicely. As a colleague of mine, he taught cabinet making and carpentry. He could make good a cowshed door, and re-hang it, I dare say; or build an exquisitely appointed dog kennel. But that was as far as it went. He had no interest in livestock or hanging out in all weathers, and that suited my sister perfectly. She'd already had enough of the farm by the time Philip fell ill, and at his funeral talked of selling the place. Then along came Steve and things were put on hold while they got to know each other better.

Now they had plans to share a holiday. Nothing too lavish, mind. Not where this parsimonious pair were concerned. Motoring round Scotland was proposed and agreed, so that's what the pair of them were going to do this summer, Steve had told me. Not that either of them needed or sought my approval. But I'd nodded all the same, to show the extent of my interest.

'Your niece's boyfriend, he's one of the Sahara Street crowd, as well,' Steve went on to inform me.

'One of them, is he?'

'Yes, mate. I've heard him talk about it. In words of one syllable, mind.'

That would be Luke. Surname unknown to me. The latest of Sam's suitors. Sam's choice of boyfriend had always mystified me. Now, if Steve was to be believed, it appeared she'd met a strong silent evangelical Christian lad who'd got her attending his church and was trying to do the same thing with Hilary. Except he wasn't having much luck. Not with Hilary, at least. 'Not while I'm around, mate,' Steve assured us.

'Are you suggesting religion is bad for people?' Carl wondered.

'It didn't do a lot for Adam's student, did it?' Steve had a point, wouldn't you say?

'Your round, Steve, isn't it?' someone reminded him.

Chris Lambertson, actually. His family hailed from Cape Town, but he seemed happy enough to bury himself in the provincial heartland of the old country. Steve said nothing for a moment, then nodded and disappeared in the direction of the bar. He sensibly avoided being tight-fisted in a crowd like this. Too many witnesses. Any reluctance to put his hand in his pocket seemed only to affect him when the company dropped below three. Hilary had to have noticed this endearing feature about Steve by now.

So what holiday destination, Chris wanted to know, had I got in mind for the summer?

The truth was I had nothing planned at all. For the first time in several years, I'd felt under no obligation to make any plans. My family had scattered that same morning. Gone their separate ways. Julie had been offered a Mediterranean cruise in exchange for the company of her ailing mother and had taken young Charlotte with her. Adrian and his new girlfriend had opted to go backpacking together in the Far East – Thailand, I believe they'd said. Yours truly was for once being left to his own devices, having gone to considerable lengths to help the rest of the family on their way with more than adequate financial support. For the first time I could recollect (I'm talking married life here) I was at a loose end.

For obvious reasons Steve hadn't invited me to join him on his Scottish tour. The two of us had till recently been in the habit of spending odd weekends 'messing about' together in Steve's battered Land Rover. Off-roading a lot of the time down green lanes and over moorland tracks. At other times, paintballing with other guys. Playing like kids, Julie called it. And why, she wanted to know, was Steve still single at his age? And why did I make a point of keeping him company the way I did? Like there might be more to our friendship than met her eye. 'He's just not found the right woman yet,' I explained. 'Is he looking?' she'd asked.

Well, yes, he was, and he'd found Hilary, hadn't he? At a barn dance, actually. Soon the arm-in-arm gave way, as you'd expect, to cosier encounters. And now they'd come up with this idea of touring Scotland together. I was pleased for the pair of them. Hilary had got over Philip's death and in my opinion was far too youthful (she was my kid sister after all) to remain on the shelf for the rest of her days. As for Steve, well, he did seem to act as though Hilary might be the woman for him. He could barely wait to drive her round the lochs and glens, in his trusty Landy. Just one week to go, apparently, before they packed everything into the back of it and headed off.

Chris for his part, we learned, was hosting family members

flying in from South Africa. Next Christmas, he told us, those same family members would be returning the hospitality and he'd be flying off to Cape Town to join them. I don't know if he expected the rest of us to divulge our Yuletide plans too, but Heather put him right. 'I haven't given Christmas a thought,' she proclaimed. 'It's too far away, for one thing. And I haven't paid for my summer break yet.'

Two weeks in Majorca for her, she wanted us to know. With two of her mates, both of them 'girlie girls', (as she called them) for company, in case we imagined she might be sloping off with a not-so-girlie girl, my goodness.

'How nice for you. At least there you can rely on being able to toast yourself all day every day,' said Carl. A bit of a sour note which Heather didn't quite know how to take, but there you go, Carl was Carl.

By the time Steve arrived with a tray of fresh drinks, Carl had asked me if I knew where Steve was going. Not surprisingly, Carl had no more time for Scottish mists than he had for endless Mediterranean sunshine.

'You don't go to Scotland for the weather, mate,' Steve enlightened him.

Steve sat down and took a sip of his second pint of guest beer that afternoon. Unusually for him, he waxed lyrical about the ale on offer lately at The Crown. Funny really, the way Steve's outlook on most things had brightened since getting together with Hilary. You might say he'd become a new man. Whether Hilary had likewise become a new woman, I very much doubted. Hilary was Hilary, and nothing much about my sister seemed to change, ever.

'That reminds me, talking about holidays,' chirped Heather. She remembered Lorna had told her that Mrs Verity had been planning to take a holiday abroad with her son. A trip to the States, apparently, which had had to be cancelled for obvious reasons.

'It seems he preferred to catch a train instead,' Carl observed.

Heather reacted as if he'd slapped her hard across the face. 'That's a horrible thing to say, Carl Watson! If it was your family, you wouldn't be talking in that… that silly supercilious tone, you… you…' She ran out of words to describe the sort of loathsome creature she had in mind, and angrily picked up a beer mat and threw it at him. In dodging it, Carl spilt some of his beer into his lap.

'Now look what you've made me do! I can't leave here without people thinking I've pissed myself. Anybody got a wankerchief?'

Heather shook her head violently and scrambled to her feet. With tears welling up in her eyes, she pushed past me, intent on getting out of our sight as quickly as possible.

'What did I say?' Carl asked after she'd gone.

'You've obviously upset the girl,' Chris told him. 'She's a practising Catholic is Heather, in case you didn't know, and Catholics take suicide very seriously. For them it's the worst form of sin. Definitely not something to be treated lightly.'

I remember wondering if Chris and Heather shared the same beliefs. We all knew Chris loved rugby. God's own game, he used to call it. From time to time someone up there had been known to perform miracles on the field when Chris's team looked in danger of losing a match.

By the time Heather reappeared the conversation had moved on to why Scotland had no great cathedrals – not a subject anyone felt able to enlighten us on, funnily enough. 'Who wants to know anyway?' Heather asked, resuming her seat alongside me, apparently intent on convincing us all that normal service had been restored, she'd recovered her usual poise, she was smiling again.

'Well, not me, that's for sure,' Steve confessed. 'I'm not going to Scotland in search of cathedrals, believe me.'

So, what was he going there for? I don't think Steve had

given it a lot of thought, to be honest. I suspect he liked the idea of Scotland. As a land of remote expanses, empty beaches, lochside castles, lonely single-track roads that lead nowhere in particular. Scotland was so readily accessible by road, too, you didn't need a boat to get there. And it went without saying he would have Hilary with him, to share the fun and help with the small talk. What did they need cathedrals for?

'Sounds to me like you won't be wanting a hotel either,' quipped Carl. 'Got a bed in the back, I dare say. A cosy bunk for two, eh?'

I thought Steve would choose not to hear. But he winked at me. Or was it at Heather? Hard to tell. 'Envious, are we?' he teased. 'I dare say I could find room in the back for another.'

When Chris went on to ask him if he was including the Isle of Skye in his itinerary, Steve said he'd be giving it some serious thought, though obviously they couldn't be expected to call at all these places in just a few days. Chris had a friend on Skye, apparently, who'd recently been on a trip to the States to hear Billy Graham preach.

Carl again. 'That's a long way to go for a sermon.'

'Didn't he come to this country? On a tour once? Or was it twice?' Heather wanted to know.

More to check my mouth was working than anything else, I gave Heather the benefit of my knowledge on the subject. 'He's been here a number of times, surely. Even had an audience with the Queen, I believe. Must be back in the States right now, though.' Chris nodded, so I went on, 'Maybe that's where Mrs Verity had planned to go, with her son.' Well, she would hardly have been taking him to Disneyland, now, would she? Or that notorious Nevada ranch where men go for late-night massages. Come on.

Heather looked impressed and beamed at me. 'You could be right, you know! I'll ask Lorna. She might be able to tell us.'

I couldn't imagine my son wanting to be taken to hear Billy

Graham. The Dalai Lama maybe. You can have a joke with him. As for my daughter, don't make me laugh. But then, my kids hadn't had the undoubted benefit of GV's religious upbringing. Now if Julie had been the devout type, had insisted on a stricter domestic regime, on saying grace at mealtimes for example, on fasting and Bible readings, things would have been different. At times I'd tried picturing GV in his home setting, watching television with his mum and dad, and had ended up wondering what does a family like that watch anyway? Not your typical mundane fare, surely. Maybe Sahara Street had its own TV channel and beamed excerpts from Billy Graham's rallies into the sitting rooms of its subscribers. Hence their desire to travel and experience the real thing when they got the chance.

Carl wondered if Billy Graham objected to gay people coming forward to be saved, and then, while we were on the subject, wanted to know what it was that most of the world's faiths find so objectionable about gays anyway.

'It's all about procreation,' Chris explained. 'Same-sex attraction doesn't do a lot for it, now does it? Certainly not in earlier times, when the human race struggled to survive and reproduce. Not quite the case today, is it?'

Heads nodded philosophically. I think that must have been the moment when Martha joined us, along with her tall, larger-than-life friend Ruth, and the need arose to talk about something else. Golf, in this case, as I recall. Martha was in the running to win a title of some kind. Birdie of the year, I think. That's when I felt the urge to go and find the boys' room.

PAULINE

Steve, I happened to know, would not be paying my sister a visit that evening.

Normally there would have been no question about it –

the academic year had ended, and Hilary would expect him to go over there and put his feet up and share with her whatever the two of them had a mind to share. However, this particular evening Steve was off to pay his dad a visit. The old fella had not been well, and. Steve wanted to make sure he was on the mend. In his place, Hilary had invited me to go over for a chat. She had things to discuss. Important things. I presumed she wanted to hear my side of the GV story, and maybe give me an insight into how she felt about the Scotland trip.

Foolsmeadow Grange lay a six-mile drive away. It had been my sister's home for the best part of twenty years, and I was still asking myself why? Why she had dropped her Fashion Design studies all those years ago to take up with a farmer. Hilary was so not what I would call the hands-on outdoor country type. She'd always hated school trips to zoos and visits to rare breed animal farms. She'd gone out of her way to skip cross-country runs by writing her own sick notes and forging her mother's signature. A headstrong and rather wayward girl – that seemed to be the consensus.

Then along came Philip Pope. Philip was a nice enough guy. Not the easiest to get on with, if I'm honest; but certainly not the poorest, having already acquired Foolsmeadow Grange from its previous owner. He was quite a bit older than Hilary. Too old for her in the opinion of some, but she went ahead regardless and married the guy. I attended their wedding. Soon afterwards she gave birth to Sam, then appeared to lose interest in producing any more offspring, in spite of Philip's wish for a son. When cancer forced him to take to his bed, I got the impression he felt life could have dealt him a better hand.

Visitors often had problems finding the farm. Some missed the turn onto Foolsmeadow Lane; others found the lane and failed to get to the end because a five-bar gate blocked the way. Like me to start with, these people were unfamiliar with the concept of gated roads to prevent stock from straying. Others mistook the first house on the lane (the Wilsons' residence, Foolsmeadow Cottage) for the Popes' farmstead. Not too difficult a name to grasp (a corruption of Foalsmeadow, I was told) and not too hard a place to find, according to Hilary. A few misguided souls did drive into the farmyard expecting the lane to be a through road, having failed to spot the dead-end sign. You got used to it, Hilary told me.

Anyway, I set off in the car that evening under a threatening sky, so wasn't surprised when the heavens opened. Soon I had the headlights on and the wipers in overdrive as the Astra splashed its way along the Old Drovers Road ever deeper into hill farm country. I reckon the old drovers, whoever they were, had difficulty keeping to a straight line by the time they'd downed a few in The Dog and Duck on the edge of town. Hence the infamous Seven Bends, a stretch of the road that was fine for inebriated stock drovers, I guess, but could be a hazard on four wheels, especially when it was raining. The camber was all wrong for a start, and the road verge had eroded into an endless succession of potholes.

It was on this stretch, on one of the bends, that I came face to face with a car on my side of the road, its headlights blazing, and the driver intent on challenging me to a game of chicken. Now, I'm the first to admit I'm much more a rabbit-in the-headlights type of guy, the one who freezes, thinking if he remains still, he stays safe. The impact, when it came, was behind me somewhere and off to my right. The other driver, I presumed, had actually blinked first before taking evasive action and, in missing me, had managed to run out of road and hit someone else instead.

Anyway, I recall my car coming to a stop and feeling thankful I was still in one piece. At least, my hands and feet appeared to work, and look, I could reach out and restart my engine and, if I chose, could put my foot down and continue on my way. The rain still fell. My headlights picked out the stair rods well enough, though I could see the sky starting to brighten ahead.

That's when I asked myself if I felt lucky and sat revving my engine. In the end I resigned myself to the inevitable, switched on my hazard warning lights, and climbed out to investigate.

Through the rain I saw the other car, a Mini, with its nose in the hedge and the driver's door in the process of being pushed open as I approached. A leg emerged, with an ankle boot on the end of it; followed by another; followed by a skirt. Not a guy at all, then. Next thing I found myself holding the door open for this woman to struggle clear, whilst at the same time waving a vehicle past whose driver had slowed down to see what we were up to.

'Are you okay?' I remember asking, as the woman clambered free.

'I think so.' She had a coat of some kind with her and was busy putting it over her head as a hood. 'The bloody thing won't start,' she told me. 'It's been a right bastard, this car, today.'

Not surprising, when you considered the bonnet was well and truly embedded in the hedgerow. It clearly wasn't going anywhere without a tow. I reached past her to switch the lights and ignition off.

'Let's get in my car,' I suggested. 'Out of the rain.'

First impression? Well, she wasn't a young thing, put it that way. More like my old school headmistress, except my old headmistress never cursed, not in my presence at any rate. A rather big broad woman who proceeded to waddle over to my car without another word and got in the front passenger side. I slid in behind the wheel and wiped the rain off my face. 'Nice evening for it,' I quipped. 'Are you sure you're okay? Not injured at all?'

That's when the rain, funnily enough, ceased as suddenly as it had started, and I could actually hear the woman speak. 'Sorry to be such a pain in the arse' were the words I heard. Definitely not my headmistress. Now she gripped my sleeve and told me she was fine and, with her face closer to mine than our short acquaintance warranted, asked if I had a cigarette to spare. She'd left hers 'in the bloody car', hadn't she?

I wasn't accustomed to this degree of familiarity from a total stranger, I must admit. I'd say the woman was my age, give or take a grey hair or two. And she was big with it, as I say, with a big, homely face to match. Not my old headmistress then, but more like the lollipop lady who used to grab me by the collar of my coat. You know the type, you come across them outside school gates every day, they keep the world turning. Now I had one in my car, dripping water everywhere and asking me for a cigarette.

'A dangerous bit of road in the wet,' I heard myself mutter as I reached past her into my glove box. 'Easy enough to lose control, even when conditions are dry.' So take more care next time, you silly cow. You frightened the hell out of me. Look at my hands, they're still shaking. And watch your language, if you don't mind. I happen to be a college lecturer who likes people to keep a civil tongue in their head, even if they are shitting themselves.

By now she'd relaxed her grip on my arm and was ferreting inside the handbag she'd brought with her in search of a lighter. 'Please.' I offered her the flame from mine, and in its glow confirmed my suspicion: I wasn't gazing at a film star nor, I realised, had my hand stopped shaking. Yes, she told me in answer to my question, she'd be grateful if I took her to a phone box. This was before mobile phones had been invented, in case you're wondering. A phone box, or the nearest house with a landline meant, by my calculation, a return to The Dog and Duck. So I found a spot to turn the Astra round and off we went.

Of course, when I thought about it, we could have gone on ahead all the way to Foolsmeadow. But I wasn't thinking straight, was I? I probably needed a cigarette myself, but I never smoked in the Astra. The ban extended to front-seat passengers too, as a rule, but I'd waived it in the present circumstances, and was now regretting it. The smoke was doing a good job of reminding me why I'd imposed the ban in the first place. 'I'm Adam, by the way,' I explained between coughs. And told her I'd been on my way to see my sister.

She, I learned, was Pauline. When we climbed out of the car at The Dog and Duck and walked across the car park to the Lounge Bar entrance, I found that, for a big woman, she easily out-waddled me! She declined my offer to make the phone call for her but wasn't averse to my buying us both a drink – strictly non-alcoholic, naturally – whilst waiting for the knights of the road to arrive.

At the best of times, I found The Dog and Duck to be a shabby, depressing sort of place. It probably hadn't changed much since the drovers stopped drinking here, whenever that was. Okay, they'd had electricity installed since then, though the landlord didn't seem to have embraced the idea that lights, if you go to the trouble of switching them on, can have the effect of brightening up the place considerably on a gloomy evening. I took the drinks from him and went and sat by a window so we might at least see the stuff we were drinking. Three locals playing dominoes in a corner clearly ate their carrots regularly. Pauline soon joined me and offered me one of her cigarettes from the pack she'd just bought. Married, said the ring on her finger. A heavy smoker too, said the nicotine stains.

'You got through okay then?'

She nodded. The tow truck, I learned, would stop at the pub and pick her up on its way to collect the car. 'Always wondered what this place looked like from the inside,' she observed, gazing round to register its attractions. 'A bit of a dump, if you ask me.'

I took it her preference was for a classier spot than this. 'It's a pub with a public phone at least,' I replied. Okay, not the poshest place to take a woman, but hey, we weren't there by choice. And we definitely weren't there on a date, if that's what she was thinking. I was doing the woman a favour, remember.

She could have collided with a serial strangler, though I think he might have looked her over and had second thoughts.

Whatever, I won't deny she shot me glances through the cigarette smoke as she sipped her tonic water. Eyeing me up, basically. Forming a second impression, let's say, whereas I didn't feel the need myself, having already assigned the woman to Category C (the file where I assign the dinner ladies and the crossing wardens, if you're curious). 'You're local, I take it,' she queried. 'I guess you must travel this road fairly often if your sister lives this way.'

'I do, though I wouldn't call it often. What about you?' She obviously knew about The Dog and Duck, even if she'd not been inside the place before.

'I live in town, yes. And I suppose these days I do travel this way quite regularly. Should know it better, shouldn't I? Don't like driving in the rain, though. Not round those bends. They give me the shits at times, I don't mind telling you. Pardon my French.'

I nodded forgivingly into my orange juice. Whereupon she added, 'I have a friend I go and see. Lives on Foolsmeadow Lane. Has a farm there. That's where I was coming back from. Do you know it?'

I fetched an ashtray from another table and put it down in reach of both of us. 'Who do you know on Foolsmeadow Lane?' I asked. 'That's where my sister lives.' And don't tell me this friend of yours is Hilary Pope because I don't recall my sister ever mentioning a Pauline Somebody-or-Other from town among her acquaintances. Certainly not one so liberal with her language. Nor one who drives a Mini like a maniac.

The woman took a long drag on her cigarette and proceeded to confirm my suspicion that she had indeed come from the farm, fresh from Hilary's kitchen, where she quite regularly hung out, apparently. And she wasn't the new cleaning lady either, I gathered. This was my sister's latest confidante, whether I'd set eyes on her before or not.

'You must be Hilary's brother!' she concluded. Smart girl! 'She said she was expecting you. Small world, eh? She talks about you a lot.' And added, with rather a nauseating grin, 'You know, I thought I noticed a bit of a family resemblance.'

A bit wouldn't even be close. Me and Hilary didn't look alike, full stop. She had to be pulling my leg. For a start, Hilary wore a permanently pinched look about her eyes. Like she'd spent the best years of her life in the wrong place, in the wrong company. Maybe that explained her choice of new friend, right? And her nose wasn't my nose; her chin wasn't the shape of mine. In fact, her face was flatter than mine, and her head had a different shape. You get the picture? There simply was no resemblance between us, believe me. 'How long have you known Hilary?' I asked, trying to keep some cheeriness in my voice.

It turned out they'd met at the cancer charity shop in town where Hilary had been doing a bit of voluntary work. Pauline ran the place, apparently. News to me, all this, but then, I was hardly my sister's keeper, was I? Hilary made her own friends, just as I made mine, and here I was, lucky me, talking to the latest addition to my kid sister's intimate social circle.

'I see you're married,' I ventured, with a knowing nod towards the ring. With a grown-up son too, I was told, who had gone off abroad somewhere to make his fortune where he was currently doing bloody well at it, even if she said so herself, in her usual well-chosen words.

She reminded me a second time that I'd been mentioned by Hilary as the older brother. The one who bore a passing resemblance to her. And who had absolutely nothing whatsoever to do with farming for a living. You had only to look at him to see that. 'I hope she's not been too unkind about me,' I probed.

'She said you teach.'

Couldn't fault her there. What else? That I had a wife and two children? That I was at a loose end this summer? That one of my students had thrown himself under a train? No knowing how far Hilary had gone with her revelations.

'She reckons you teachers have far too many holidays. You'd disagree, now, wouldn't you?'

That old chestnut. Hilary had told Steve the same thing. Now whether she'd mentioned Steve at all to this woman was a moot point. Of course, there was the possibility she had already met Steve in the course of visits to the farm. Maybe I was going to hear about that before the evening was out. 'To be honest,' I declared, 'there are quite a few things my sister and I disagree on. We grew up together falling out, you know. Siblings, eh?'

Pauline confessed she had none. But the fact I had a sister and had been on my way to see her that evening did prompt the woman to ask, out of the blue, 'Shouldn't you give Hil a call while you're here? Tell her what's happened to make you late?'

Hil. She called my sister Hil! Nobody ever called her that, surely. Now I wondered what abbreviated form I was likely to become before the evening was over. And how exactly might I be referred to in this woman's exchanges with Hilary. That brother of yours is a right one, isn't he? I sat in the pub with him, and do you know, he couldn't be arsed to let you know he was going to be late. I call that a fucking liberty, Hil, I'm sorry but there's no other word for it. More to the point, how might Hilary respond. Clearly, I didn't know my sister quite as well as I thought I did. 'She won't mind,' I said. 'I'll catch her another time.'

The woman wasn't listening. She'd risen to her feet. 'This'll be him now.'

Too soon for the recovery man, it turned out. A false alarm. She sat down again. It gave me the opportunity, this reminder of why we were there, the two of us, talking and drinking together, to suggest that she might like to get herself checked out fairly soon for bruising, delayed shock, whiplash, all those likely after-effects of a road accident, despite her assurances she felt fine. Mind you, she looked fit as a fiddle to me. She even challenged me to tell her to her face that she didn't look a hundred per cent. What could I say? Sorry, I only do fractions?

I saw and heard the recovery truck eventually arrive, its amber lights flashing in the gloom outside the window. Only after the woman had taken her things and climbed aboard did it occur to me that I hadn't got round to the business of exchanging addresses, vehicle registration numbers, insurance details – you know, all that stuff the law requires you to make a note of at the scene of a road traffic accident.

TWO

HILARY

Pauline who?

It occurred to me the woman might well report a different version of how her Mini came to run off the road and into somebody's hedge. There was the possibility she'd blame me for it. Make out, in the absence of witnesses, that I was the idiot driving on the wrong side of the road, on a bend, in the rain. I'm sorry, but the older I get the less trusting I become. My job may well be to blame, I realise.

Needless to say, I postponed my visit to the farm for another occasion. Back home that evening, in case I forgot them, I jotted down pertinent details: the time, the state of the road, the weather, the fact she was driving a Mini whose colour was black but whose registration number escaped me in the distractions of the moment. That's the point though, isn't it? In taking time out to help this woman, I let her beguile me into playing the Samaritan. Into revealing who I was and where I was headed. Into fraternising with her instead of going straight to the business of exchanging essentials. The woman's name may not have been Pauline at all. She could have been anyone.

Next day I rang Hilary to run a check. Told her what had happened and asked if she knew the woman. It turned out she did; they were close friends; how come I didn't know that? Married name Kendrick. Drove a black Mini. Worked, indeed, at the Cancer Research shop in town. And yes, drove like a lunatic, had frightened the life out of her a couple of times when they'd gone out places together. My mishap on the Seven Bends came as no surprise to Hilary.

'I did wonder what happened when you didn't turn up last night. Neither of you hurt, I take it.'

'Just me.'

A mild case of whiplash, for your information, brought on by braking hard. Something I hadn't noticed till I got up next morning. Quite possibly, Mrs Kendrick had woken up suffering from the same thing. And Mister K, maybe not for the first time, had gone without his morning tonic.

Hilary promised to give her friend a call and check she was okay. But first she was glad I'd rung because – guess what? – we still had those matters outstanding that she'd been wanting to talk to me about. Matters best not discussed over the phone, apparently. So would I drive over there sometime fairly soon, seeing as my term had finished and I hadn't mentioned having holiday plans of my own. Steve, I suspected, had brought her up to speed with details of how empty my diary was for the next few weeks.

So it was that I set off a second time for the farm. The Dog and Duck, I observed in passing, hadn't opened its doors yet, though a couple of cars stood in the car park. The Mini had gone from the hedgerow but left behind a gap big enough for a bulldozer. Clearly, I hadn't dreamed any of it.

Hilary had called her friend, as I knew she would, and got her side of the story. The woman couldn't praise me enough, apparently, for acting as I did to get her to a phone and stay with her till the recovery people arrived. Such a helpful, considerate man, she'd called me. She felt guilty she hadn't shown me more gratitude but hadn't wanted to detain me further. As it was, she had her husband to get back to. I was told Mister Kendrick rarely left the house these days. Boyd, poor guy, suffered from one of those debilitating conditions – MS, ME, M Something-or-Other – that meant he couldn't go out to work anymore and sat about in the house feeling useless. Another thing: he got jealous if Pauline paid other men compliments. Because of it, she'd been reduced to whispering my praises over the phone, in case Boyd's ears were flapping.

'Did she tell you she runs the charity shop?' Hilary wanted to know. 'She's my boss. She's the one who set me on there, as her assistant. Part-time, that's all it is, but it gets me out of the house. Gets me meeting and talking to people.'

Fine by me. Two lonely souls meeting over other people's discarded hand-me-downs – nothing wrong with that. I do understand that a remote hill farm isn't the best place to meet new people. But hey, meeting new people is one thing, taking up with your boss is something else. And taking up with this boss, in particular, could raise a few eyebrows – mine, for a start. However, I kept my views to myself, having long ago vowed to keep out of my kid sister's life. Whoever she chose to befriend was no business of mine, end of story.

However, I must have worn traces of disapproval somewhere on my face, for my sister soon took me to task. 'If I didn't know you better, Adam, I'd say you don't exactly approve of my new friend. I've been seeing a lot of Pauline lately. And yes, she comes here on a regular basis. And we go out places together. Are you happy with that? Or do you find something odd about it? What do you think we get up to?'

Search me. None of my business anyway, what two consenting ladies do to amuse themselves. For all I knew, the woman could be a gold digger, after a share in the farm. Maybe she'd persuaded Hilary to set on a handy man. That young guy out there, for example. The one up the ladder, working on the roof of one of the outbuildings.

'That'll be Luke. I thought you knew. Sam's latest acquisition.'

Acquisition, eh? It sounded very much to me as if Hilary harboured some issues of her own. 'Well, you could do worse,' I commented. 'It looks to me like he's making himself useful around the place.' Some of the farm buildings did need a lick of paint, to say the least. You didn't need to be a master builder to see that.

'Sam asked me if he could be getting on with a few jobs. To earn his keep, sort of thing. For the time being, at any rate. Keeps him out of mischief, you'd think, but there's more to it than that. That's what I wanted to talk to you about, Adam. Well, part of it.'

'I'm all ears.' Forever the older brother, see, always offering to share problems and offer advice. The story of my life when you think about it. Pastoral care. The skill they pay me for. The tireless tutor at work. 'Is there some sort of problem? With Luke, I mean?'

'It's the pair of them. Him and Sam. They make out they want to carry on and work the farm between them.'

'Anything wrong with that?'

'It's a smokescreen for what's really going on. They don't want to farm, the pair of them. They want to take over the place, him and Sam, for the benefit of that church of theirs. They'd like me to hand it over. Let them turn it into something else. Only they're not being honest about it. Do you understand what I'm saying, Adam?'

More or less. I may have screwed my face up, baulked ever so slightly at the idea that somebody could be trying to pull a fast one over my sister. Hilary doesn't miss a trick. 'You are saying they're not being honest with you. How do you mean exactly?'

'You don't have to live here, Adam, and put up with it. Being made to feel it's somebody else's place and not your own anymore. It's no fun, I can tell you.'

I invited her to enlighten me with examples of what she imagined was going on exactly. I gave her an obvious prompt by mentioning Sahara Street by name and asking her what they would want with a farm like hers on their hands. A sensible question, I thought, but Hilary accused me of talking as if the farm had no prospects, no value. Hadn't I heard of farm shops, and farm parks? Apparently, Sam had mentioned introducing rare breeds.

'She talks a lot about the plans they have, but that's just their way of trying to convince me they're serious about it. Can you imagine Sam having an interest in rearing beasts, any beasts?'

I couldn't, frankly. Sam had always had a horror of being around animals, even as a child, in case they licked her face or crapped on her foot. Horrid creatures as far as she was concerned – cattle, horses, sheep, donkeys, the lot. As for breeding them, encouraging them to commit unspeakable acts together in order to conceive young that she would help deliver when the time came, the very idea was so not to my niece's taste, take my word for it. Okay, I couldn't speak for the boyfriend, maybe he was different. What, I asked, did he have to say about rare breeds?

Luke, Hilary explained, was no more a livestock man than she was a lap dancer. Hmm, so much for that idea then. He didn't have much to say for himself, as Sam did most of the talking for him. A guy of few words, as Steve had put it. But he did possess some building skills, apparently, and had been putting those to good use, as I could see for myself. He'd also started taking liberties, said Hilary.

'Liberties? How do you mean?' Not that kind, surely.

'Where do you want me to start?'

At the beginning, obviously. Hilary held up a fist and

proceeded to release and raise fingers as she went through the list. 'He's moved in with Sam without so much as a by-your-leave; he's changed the locks upstairs; he's put new locks on the outside buildings; he's taken my letters off the postman and not passed them on till days later. Weeks even. When I speak to Sam about it, she just shrugs and says that's the way he is. The quiet sullen type, you know.'

I see, those sorts of liberties. 'What's he do when he isn't doing odd jobs round the place? Has he got a full-time job somewhere?'

'Come on, Adam, of course he hasn't. Doesn't seem to have a home to go to, either. No family to speak of, apart from his mother. All I know is Sam met him at one of her church meetings, or so she says. She brought him home and he's been here ever since. Hangs around like a bad smell.'

A trenchant young man, in other words. I recalled GV's connection with the same church. Then wondered if Sahara Street made a point of attracting young men like this to its ranks. Young men like what? The sort my niece would invite to move in with her, as part of some greater missionary work, say? I believe I shook my head at the thought before asking Hilary, 'Steve tells me Luke has been trying to persuade you to join his church. Is he having any success?'

Hilary rolled her eyes. 'What do you think, Adam? Do I look like I need saving? Trust Steve to say a thing like that.'

'Not long now before the two of you push off to Scotland, is it? Looking forward to it, are we?'

Hilary pulled a face and did her best to look coy. 'It'll make a change.' She leaned forward, as if about to whisper a confidence, or ask a favour. 'There's something I wanted to ask you about. If you've no plans of your own, I mean. No holiday plans, that is. You'd be doing me a favour, Adam, if you could be persuaded to stay here for a few days. Look after the place for me while we're away. Everything provided, obviously. No need for you to be out of pocket. I wouldn't ask if it wasn't important. The thing is I don't want to get back and find somebody has moved in, do I?'

'Moved in? Who've you got in mind?'

'Well, that bloody church of theirs, for a start. What do they say about possession and the law?'

Did I imagine it or was my sister slipping into the Kendrick vernacular? Not at all like Hilary to describe a community of people in those terms, especially people of faith. She was serious, I could see that, and maybe even just a tad paranoid. Understandable, I conceded, to want to have someone living in the place while she was away. Sam could be doing that, surely, and Luke would be visible around the place, up his ladder or wherever. Wouldn't I be a bit of a gooseberry? A spare part? 'What's wrong with Sam?' I asked. 'She'd be here. Or is she going away, too?'

Hilary informed me Sam didn't take holidays, except from her day job, and Luke never left the farm except to go to church. 'There's always one of them here. Keeping an eye on me, I guess. Every time I go out, I fear they'll change the locks and shut me out. I trust you to keep the place safe more than I'd trust them, to be perfectly honest. Does that sound awful?'

Like I said, a trifle paranoid. 'And how do you think they'd feel about me being here, even if it is only for a few days?'

'They'd get used to the idea. The main thing is I'd feel a lot happier. Your family wouldn't miss you, surely.'

True, none of my lot would be around to object. Not Julie (far away on the high seas), not Charlotte (accompanying her, as I've described); nor Adrian (abroad with girlfriend, ditto). And it wasn't as if I had somewhere else to be or had more pressing matters to attend to. There was just one other person whose name hadn't cropped up yet in connection with this matter, and it occurred to me to wonder why. 'What about your friend Pauline? Have you thought of asking her? Or is her husband the problem?'

Never mind the husband, Pauline had her job in town to think about, in case I'd forgotten. She simply couldn't afford to take the time off. In any case, Pauline already accepted that when it came down to matters of this nature, family was always the preferred option. If one excluded Sam, obviously. 'There are things I don't discuss with Pauline, you know, and what I choose to do with the farm is one of them.'

Well, what a relief to hear that. I took it I wouldn't be expected to do any serious farming if I accepted. No getting up at dawn to milk cows or spread manure. No major repair jobs to take care of up ladders.

'All I need you to do is sit tight, Adam. As soon as I get back, I'm putting the place up for sale. You're the first person to know about it. Keep it under your hat for the time being.'

I wasn't sure I wanted to be involved in keeping secrets, frankly. I guess I must have betrayed a misgiving or two, for Hilary hastened to assure me she'd be telling Sam the news just as soon as she'd come to a firm decision herself about selling the place.

'If you do sell, what happens to them? To Sam and the boyfriend? Where will they go?'

Hilary shrugged. 'If they're so interested, that church of theirs can put in an offer to buy the place for them. It's a hard world out there, Adam. Let's see where they go with that pretence of theirs. Because that's what it is. A sham, basically. All this nonsense about rare breeds. They pretend they want to revive the farm, but believe me, Adam, that's not what they're after. It's the house and the land they want. Well now, they can take their place in the queue. And don't think I haven't given the matter a great deal of thought.'

Luke, I noticed, had gone from his place on the rooftop, and his ladder had disappeared too. Hilary saw me taking a look. 'Sam and that boyfriend of hers, they don't want the place to fall down, any more than I do,' she told me. 'But right now, they'd rather I wasn't around, so they can hand it over in one piece. Without paying a penny. Don't know what will happen to it after that.'

'Are you really that keen on selling?'

Hilary looked at me like I'd not been listening 'Didn't you hear me say, Adam,' she reminded me, 'they've been making my life here a misery lately? I had a debt collector call on me last week. A debt collector, mind. Said I'd been sent several reminders to pay, and I'd ignored them. Didn't believe me when I said I'd not received any of them, when I told him my post regularly gets intercepted. He as good as called me a liar. You know, I shouldn't have to put up with that sort of thing. Not in my own home.'

Lately, too, she'd spotted what looked like surveyors and architects around the farm, invited without her permission. Going round with tapes measuring things, setting up those tripods and instruments they use to peer through. Unfolding charts and blueprints, making notes.

'Have you asked Sam about that? About what's going on?'

She had, and Sam had told her it was all part of their scheme for 'doing things with the place', modernising it, getting it ready for use again as a working farm. Not such a bad idea if you ask me, but that's not what they really had in mind, according to Hilary. Who, she asked me, did I imagine was paying these people? Their services didn't come cheap, and Sam and Luke didn't have that kind of money. 'That church of theirs is behind it, you mark my words. Why do you think they want me to join?'

Hilary hadn't attended a church in years. Not since Philip's funeral, and Philip, I remembered, was buried in the Pope family plot at St Michael's. As for the Goodmans, I admit we were not exactly a God-fearing clan. Hilary had more or less told the rector that as the Almighty could not be relied on to give her the things she wanted, and since Sahara Street, as she put it, simply 'packaged the same product in a snappier wrapper', then

Sahara Street could 'bloody well look elsewhere for recruits.' More Kendrick-speak, you'll gather.

Where my niece's newfound religious fervour came from is anybody's guess. It hadn't been in evidence on my last visit to Foolsmeadow, but that had been months ago. Now I found myself counting up the changes that had taken place: (1) Sam had a new boyfriend – possibly dodgy; (2) she'd joined a new church – dodgy or what? (3) my sister had taken a job in town – excellent news; (4) she'd made a personal friend of her employer – definitely something dodgy there; (5) she'd agreed to go on holiday with Steve – hmm, we'll see; and now (6) she had decided to put the farm up for sale – hmm, no comment. 'I'm having difficulty keeping up,' I confessed.

'You and me both. Welcome to the club.'

'So what do you imagine Sahara Street would like to do with this place?' I enquired. Monks, I'd read somewhere, once inhabited the Grange and had made a living brewing stuff and selling it to the natives for a while.

'Don't ask me. I did hear they were looking to set up some kind of training school.'

'Like a seminary, you mean?'

Not that I knew exactly what a seminary was, but it sounded about right, and Hilary nodded. It sounded more plausible, put it like that, than buying the place for Sam and her boyfriend to raise rare breeds. Okay, Sam was clearly no longer the freckle-faced schoolgirl who sucked her thumb into her teens. Those years had passed and, as the lyric goes, she had grown up in a most delightful way. She'd taken the job behind the counter at Fletcher's Pie and Pastry shop on the High Street on a temporary basis and was now looking, understandably, for a chance to improve her prospects. Good for her. Nothing wrong with a bit of youthful initiative. I regularly gave it a helping hand, remember, as part of my job.

I put it to Hilary that if she did decide to sell, why not

approach Sahara Street first and negotiate a deal. If they were keen to acquire the farm, they might be prepared to pay over the market price for it. A sound proposition, I thought. And a compromise that, hopefully, would suit Sam and the boyfriend down to the ground.

Hilary stiffened and asked whose side I was on. 'I'm surprised at you, Adam,' she chided me. 'I would have thought, after what happened to that student of yours, you'd be the last person to want to encourage a concern like Sahara Street. An unscrupulous, self-serving bunch of weirdos, if you want my opinion.'

Hmm. I took it Hilary had been reading the papers. They had carried the story and made a lot of GV's church attendance. Or else she'd been listening to Steve. I knew he kept her posted.

When I asked, out of mild interest, about Mrs K's churchgoing habits, Hilary burst out laughing. Like I'd asked a really silly question. I was told that Pauline was far too down to earth to have any time for that sort of nonsense. I should have guessed. However, the woman did dabble, I was informed, in clairvoyance and psychic stuff. Whatever that meant.

'She can sense things, you know, before they happen. Bet you didn't know that, Adam, did you? Full of surprises, my friend Pauline, eh?'

Really? She hadn't foreseen our little scrape on the Seven Bends, though, had she? And don't tell me she'd engineered the whole encounter in order to make the acquaintance of Hil's big brother. I believed as I found, and I remained to be convinced she was anything more than an overweight bad driver and a rank opportunist. But Hilary wouldn't hear of it.

'She not a fake, Adam, if that's what you're trying to say. The first time she came here, she told me she sensed a presence in the house. Up in the attic. Sam's part of the house. And they were out, Sam and Luke, at the time. How do you explain that?'

'She's obviously been talking to mother, hasn't she? You

know mother's convinced this house is haunted. There's usually a perfectly rational explanation for these things, if you think about it. We don't need psychics giving us more mumbo jumbo, do we?'

'Rubbish! Sometimes, Adam, you say the silliest things for somebody with the benefit of a good education and a responsible job. You should try taking Pauline more seriously. Believe me, she's a good friend to have around.'

When I asked her if Pauline was likely to want to keep an eye on me during my stay at the farm, Hilary retorted, 'Why would she do that? You'll have the place to yourself. Apart from Sam and Luke, I mean. You'll soon see how lonely it can be living here. It's up to you if you want to invite anyone. Your visitors will be your business, Adam. You'll be in charge.'

'And Sam and Luke, they'll know, will they, why I'm here?'

'Of course. Leave it with me.'

When it came to telling me how soon my services would be required, Hilary had no date in mind. I'd know as soon as she did – that seemed to be as much as she could tell me. Steve had been equally vague. She would be in touch, she promised.

As I drove out of the farmyard, I almost collided with the nose of Sam's little Fiat on its way in. I reversed to give her room to pass. She nodded, though whether she actually recognised me I couldn't say. Then she waved. Not at me, I realised, but at the guy back on his ladder. He'd leaned it in a different place, out of my sight by the look of it. All I saw were the heels of his boots balanced on a rung up there. I'd get to actually meet the guy soon enough, I thought. And get re-acquainted with my niece at the same time. I took it she was back from a day at the pie shop. But she could have been back from a day at the races, the way she looked. At the wheel, in a fetching white head scarf, the sort you'd wear in an open sports coupe, I must say she looked as well as I'd ever seen her. *Sahara Street can't be all that bad for her,* I thought.

THE JOURNAL

'She wants it returned. Let me know as soon as you find it. Better still, bring it in. Leave it on my desk if I'm not here. Or give it to Heather.'

Lorna's words. She's speaking to me over the telephone. Telling me I have in my possession a folder of some written work handed in by my former student, yes, that student, Gordon Verity, the late GV. Had I anything of his? According to the student's mother, I did indeed. She'd been in touch with JR about it, telling him that the folder included the young man's personal diary which Mrs Verity would like returned. Clearly, it had some value for her, sentimental or otherwise, so would I kindly pull my finger out and start hunting for it sharpish.

Okay but what size and sort of document were we talking about? I recalled some late work being handed in by my students for marking that probably did include a number of loose folders. Nothing unusual about that. I went to the room I loosely called my office to take a look. There a heap of papers and folders lay where they'd been dropped on the floor beside my desk to await attention later. This was work, I confess, that should have been dealt with more promptly and handed back, preferably before the year ended. Clearly, my schedule had come adrift in the turmoil of the term's events, and, in that respect, I'd let my students down. But look at it this way: at least GV's diary would have been spared a reference to his final irrevocable act. Wouldn't it?

JR, Lorna had disclosed, was not impressed. Surely I knew that he hated having to make excuses for his staff. The truth was, let's face it, he was being reminded of an episode he considered did not reflect well on the good name of the college. He had hoped he'd seen the back of the entire incident.

By the time I got back on the phone Lorna was on her way out of the door. I told her I'd found no trace of whatever it was

Mrs Verity was after. Did she, Lorna, happen to know what it looked like – its size, colour, etc? You'd think I was asking her for details of some missing underwear, the way she got all huffy about it and told me she had other things to do with her time than concern herself with students' missing personal effects, as she called them. I caught myself wondering, as you do, by what name Lorna addressed JR when nobody was around to hear. I'd only heard her refer to him as Doctor Langtree. Perhaps doctor was how he liked her to address him at other times too. To me Rufus sounded a tad remote and, if I'm honest, faintly ridiculous. I fancied Lorna might have a nurse's uniform tucked away for use at certain times. She would have made a very passable ward sister.

The matter of GV's journal might well have ended there. I had no reason to expect the subject would be raised again. But then, later that day, I made a discovery. In the bottom drawer of my filing cabinet, where I kept records of my students' progress along with my personal comments, I came across a loose-leaf folder I didn't recognise. It must have dropped out from among the others. It bore the words MY JOURNAL in large capital letters across the cover, and Gordon Verity's name penned in smaller capitals underneath.

Inside was a jumble of loose pages which had been torn from their binding and then stuffed back into the folder. Like a poorly shuffled pack of cards. A bit of a mess, in fact. Every page appeared to have been written on, but as for resembling a diary, well, I certainly wouldn't have called it that. Pages weren't divided up into days of the week, for instance, or months of the year. They weren't really divided up at all. There didn't seem to be any order to it, not even any page numbers, so how you were expected to navigate your way through these pages of endless prose was anybody's guess.

At least the writing was recognisable as GV's scribble and, as I had most pages the right way up, I took the liberty of sampling a few sentences, and then a few paragraphs, here and there. Everything read sensibly enough, I must say, though no way could it be described as a diary. It was more like a collection of autobiographical accounts and musings, some of them confidential, some possibly bordering on libellous, others boorish, a few of them amusing. I could see why Mum and Dad Verity wanted this work returned to their safekeeping. In GV's shoes I wouldn't have wanted them to see it, but it looked like they'd somehow become aware of its existence and now they were reclaiming it.

It soon became clear that one sitting would not be nearly enough to learn if this so-called journal contained any bits I might want to read more closely. GV was my student after all, and that gave me a personal interest in holding on to his work for a while longer. Mum and Dad Verity, I reasoned, could afford to wait. If necessary, I could photocopy the entire manuscript before parting with it. Or it could remain "lost", as far as Mum and Dad were concerned, and be "rediscovered" perhaps in due course, when I'd exhausted my own interest in its contents. One way or another, then, I resolved to hang on to it. I'd told Lorna I couldn't find it, and that's how I proposed to leave matters for the time being.

*

By the time I'd looked through a few pages, I'd decided Mum and Dad Verity couldn't possibly have had designs on turning their son's journal into a posthumous bestseller and retiring off the proceeds. Some of the observations in it were good, but, hey, they weren't that good. And the business of making sense of it as a volume depended above all on putting its pages into a sensible sequence. Numbering its pages, in short, in the way GV should have done from the outset. We're talking here of a document of some fifty or sixty double-sided sheets and a few thousand words at a guess. All this, mind you, from someone I had personally found to be a young man of few words. I guess I was about to find out how wrong you can be in my job.

As I've said, this was not a diary such as you or I might have kept. There were no abbreviations as such, no jottings in note form or shorthand, no reminders of, say, dental appointments or deadlines for handing in work. No, this was your full-on walk in the park, deploying complete sentences and a commendable attempt at paragraphing. It was a revelation to me, I don't mind admitting, though GV's grammar and spelling, as always, left a lot to be desired.

I did have to remind myself, as I read, that this work hadn't been intended for marking. I could readily have reached for my red pen at the sight of the inevitable plethora of spelling errors, suspect grammar, and rubbish punctuation. Force of habit, you know, in my profession. Allow me to cut to the chase and pluck a few morsels at random from off a page here and there. Short extracts, of necessity reaching no further than the foot of the page, as the matter of sorting out an acceptable page order would have to wait for another day.

Well, for starters, the journal had something to say about me. Strange that, isn't it, the way a page presents itself and your own name catches your eye, don't you find? COLLEGE it said, in capitals, set out as a heading. And GMan, would you believe, was how I found myself styled. No mistaking the reference. G for Goodman, get it? It couldn't possibly be anyone else among the staff at the college, take my word for it. Besides, I recognised myself from the context. Let me quote you some of it – minus the spelling and other errors, naturally.

> *'GMan is our tutor. For me and twelve other hopefuls. So am I the thirteenth member of the group? With my name I'm always near the end of the register, but this time there's a Wilson in the group and he has to be the thirteenth.*

> Unlucky for him. Things seemed to happen to him from Day One. He fell down some stairs. Then he got the wrong room for one of his lectures. That could have been me, I suppose, if I'd been the thirteenth name on the register.
>
> 'Somebody said GMan was married with five kids. Must have been one of the girls. They always pretend they know and if they don't, they make it up. As if it matters how many kids he's got. Or how old he is. I'd say mid-forties. I'm here to look after your welfare, he told us. That's what tutors are for. He wrote the words PASTORAL CARE on the board so we wouldn't forget. It's mostly the girls who go to him for advice on things. If the tutor had been a woman, I'm sure the boys would find plenty of things they weren't happy with. Some of the girls think he's dishy, judging by the way they fuss a lot when he's around. I bet GMan has seen it all before and doesn't let it bother him. Being a tutor, that's his job. We're just the latest lot on his conveyor belt.'

Definitely me, this GMan, I can confirm. No other dishy tutors that I know about, and yes, I wouldn't disagree with him, I've seen most of it before. Comes with the territory, you know. Here's more on the same theme.

> 'Sometimes I wonder what GMan was like when he was my age and if he knew what he wanted to do with his life and if he talked about it with HIS tutor. I suppose he's always had that birthmark on his neck. They say you never get rid of birthmarks, you can't shave them off with a razor, for example. I wonder if he ever looked in the mirror when he was my age and wished he was somebody else. Or ever suspected that one day he'd lose half his hair. Will I go like that in a few more years? Garth says to stop thinking about things that might never happen. Not easy

though. I bet GMan worries about other things now – like his pension and whether he'll make it that far. In his job I'd worry I look a fool in front of my students because I haven't done up my flies or something daft like that. I'd worry about saying the wrong thing and making myself sound a complete moron. But that's me, I worry a lot. This place is more grown up than school and if they don't like you here, they can tell you to push off and give your place on the course to somebody who'll make better use of it. I suppose that's another job for a tutor, deciding who stays and who goes, and it can be lonely being on a course like this, having to prove yourself or be told to push off, we don't want you here anymore.

'*Anyway, GMan's all right. He's friendly and he'll have a laugh with you and not try and make you look small in front of everybody. I've heard some in our group complain he takes ages to give you your written work back and sometimes it's not been marked. I don't mind because we are none of us perfect. Anyway, I believe what scripture says about WE ARE ALL EQUAL IN THE SIGHT OF GOD.*'

Hmm, are we? All equal? How about that?

What to make of GV's portrait of his tutor, eh? Well, apart from the slap on the wrist for falling behind with the marking (that could apply to any number of my colleagues, let me tell you), I come out of it quite well, don't you think? Yes, I do have a birthmark on my neck, though I didn't realise it's quite that noticeable. And yes, you would be hard pressed to find a friendlier tutor on campus. Oh, and I did worry about my pension, but never doubted I'd make it one day to a well-earned retirement. Gratifying to know I looked no older than my mid-forties and considered all right in spite of the hair loss. No idea where the five kids came from though. Otherwise, a good all-round egg, this GMan guy, if you took GV's view seriously.

Over the page I found he had something to say about Steve, too. Not very flattering stuff this time, though. A bullshitter, apparently, and worse than that, an SF. A Steve Forrester, what else? The opinions were, to be fair, someone else's and not strictly GV's. Someone called Mo, a fellow student presumably, whose name meant absolutely nothing to me but might have rung a bell with Steve. Here's a flavour of Mo's impressions.

'Mo says SF is a bullshitter who puts him off Carpentry because he likes to think he knows everything about everything. He says SF ought to stand for Stupid Fucker and if I don't believe him says I ought to sit in on one of his classes and see for myself. He looks a bit like Mo's dad, Mo says, and Mo doesn't get on with his dad and that's another reason he doesn't get on with SF. In Mo's place I'd ask my tutor about giving up Woodwork and doing something else instead. Before he REALLY gets picked on, he says. He can't mean that. YOU'RE NOT ME, he says. YOU DON'T HAVE TO PUT UP WITH ALL THE CRAP.'

Hmm. Hard to deny the conclusion Steve hadn't gone down a bomb with this particular student. Steve wasn't the kind to lose sleep over a thing like that, though. Or the kind to let it lie for long. I could imagine his riposte: 'Who does the little prick think he is?' Something on those lines, there being plenty more students out there in the great Sea of Learning who would be only too glad to take Mo's place on the carpentry course.

Over the page I discovered more about Steve. A report of an altercation in the workshop, in the course of which Steve had cuffed a student and sworn at him. Well, that was the allegation. I was minded to find that pen of mine, and write the word "allegedly" in the margin, but couldn't lay hands on it at the time. Mind you, Steve was perfectly capable of forgetting himself in front of a classful of witnesses. His head of department had warned him about it – Steve had told me so himself. All the same, to my mind GV, in his youthful wisdom, had given the incident far greater weight and substance than I believe it deserved. Some students end up on the wrong course. Some can't get on with the person teaching them. Shit happens, as they say.

If I picked up the next page, was I going to find yet more comments about Steve? In the event, I found myself out of luck. I tried several more pages and gave up the search. Instead, I came across a page devoted entirely to the subject of Mo. TEN THINGS TO KNOW ABOUT MO, it was headed. Mo for Moses, would that be? Or Mohammed? The items were set out and numbered as below, except they didn't amount to ten, as you'll see:

1. *'He's Jewish. His family are Jewish. He says that means they expect to put up with a load of crap for as long as people know that's what they are. Mo isn't sure whether he's going to give up being Jewish. How do you do that, give up being the person you're born as? I keep meaning to ask him.*
2. *'Mo doesn't have many friends. I always find him sitting on his own in the refectory unless it's very busy in there. He says the same about me. He thinks we have a lot of things in common, except I'm not Jewish, he keeps reminding me.*
3. *'He looks a bit like Garth. From some angles he does. But he's not like him as a person, in the way he acts. Garth says nobody can HELP being Jewish and you can't STOP being Jewish, but I'm not going to tell Mo that's what Garth thinks.*
4. *'Mo has no idea what he wants to do when he leaves college. When I talk to him about going to places where lots of people are poor and there aren't many*

schools or colleges to go to for education, he turns his nose up. That's not a career, he says. That's charity.
5. 'He thinks I'm a lot more religious than he is. Some people make too much of God and religion, he says. I thought you couldn't be Jewish if you didn't believe in God, or whatever they call their God.
6. 'I showed him a picture of Marti and Mo thinks she is a lot better looking than his mother, only I'd not thought about it like that before. I don't think Mo likes his mother any more than his dad. He doesn't know Marti isn't my real mother.
7. 'Mo smokes too much. He keeps saying he'll quit and never does. He says if he quits, he wouldn't be able to offer me one like he does. He can't remember when he started. I tell everybody I only smoke when I want to and it's not a habit with me, which is true.'

That's as far as he got with his list, no Number 8. Ran out of things to add, presumably. Or he got interrupted and never returned to complete it.

It's Moses, I decided. For obvious reasons. Mo sounded to me like one of the few friends GV had on campus. Steve would recognise who he was, surely, even if the guy had finished his course by now and moved on. It occurred to me that Mo might have a ray of light to shed on GV's state of mind; maybe he'd written a journal of his own and dwelt at length on their friendship. Just a thought. Marti had to be GV's mother, but not his real mother, apparently, whatever that meant. All the same he carried her photo around with him. A foster mother, was she? His stepmother? And was this the same person that wanted to get her hands on the lad's journal? As for the reference to Garth, who did I figure him to be? The lad's father, perhaps? Whoever these people were, I figured the only sure way to learn more about them was to read on.

But how to do that in a meaningful way when pages aren't numbered and are shuffled so indiscriminately? It struck me that maybe GV had never intended his diary to be read from cover to cover, like a novel, and had therefore not seen numbering as vital, or even important. So why bother to write things down at all? Search me. If the diary amounted to a series of reflections, say, without regard for sequence or timeline, then perhaps it promised some insight into GV's state of mind, a clue to why he ended up doing what he did. Maybe Moses drove him to it. Or Marti. Or Garth. Or else it was the teachers at college, if only they'd all been as charming and easy to get on with as GMan. Or it was all of the above, together with the tasteless crap they serve you day after day in the college refectory. I could go on but what's the point? Without reading more of the diary, I mean.

Well, I did turn to the very last page in the bundle, and found it was not much help, to be honest. I came across another reference to Marti. How the two of them had eaten breakfast together before going to church. Very stimulating stuff. Would that be the Sahara Street church? I turned back a page to see what, if anything, he'd got up to the night before. A steamy one-night stand, perhaps? A transgression his church could not forgive? Followed by an ultimatum? Whatever it was, he couldn't talk about it. His very words:

> 'I can't talk about it. People say they believe in God, and you know if they did and really meant what they say, they'd behave differently. If people ask me, I tell them I go to church because it helps me make sense of things. Why we're here on this earth, why there are rich people and poor people in the world, lords and servants, good and evil. It's the reason most people go to church, isn't it? To show God matters in our lives. We might fool ourselves, but we don't fool Him. It's like they tell us, God has His way of seeing inside our heads and knowing what's going

on and it's no good pretending nothing's wrong. GOD KNOWS EVERYTHING. We shouldn't deny Him and turn our backs. Instead, we should be honest and pray for HIS FORGIVENESS.'

Hmm. Not very clear what exactly he was talking about, is it? Can't talk about what? An entire paragraph without telling us much at all. An indulgent perambulation, not to say an annoying distraction, as far as I was concerned. Happens a lot, I find, when students submit essays in which you want them to make precise points, in a precise order, about a precise subject. They hand in a load of waffle. Miss the point. Was this a case of GV attempting to justify his belief in the Hereafter? Or was he just pissed off on finding that not all self-professed believers met his own standards of God-fearing behaviour? Hardly a reason to top yourself even so, I would have thought.

From the evidence of that paragraph there could be no doubting GV's religious conviction. Okay, I confess that in class I'd failed to pick up on it. And in my tutorials, I'll admit we didn't go in for discussing whether Mankind had been created last week or whether the race had evolved over a few million years. Nor, for that matter, did we debate whether prayer is any good at helping you pass exams. No tell-tale signs of his beliefs had shown up in his course work. But here, in his journal, was evidence he did more than attend Sahara Street to please his parents, or to eye up the talent. I remember hoping, as I turned over pages, that after such a promising start this journal of his wasn't going to turn out to be, basically, a piece of work in praise of his Maker.

Several reasons to explain why Mr and Mrs Verity might want their son's work returned to them went through my head at this point. Besides the bestseller theory, I mean. For all I knew, Sahara Street could be crooked in some way, not quite the legitimate community of worshippers it purported to be. I could be holding in my hands, say, a document containing some pretty incriminating stuff on its leaders. Sahara Street could be a front for some rather unsavoury goings-on. Stranger things have happened. Maybe Marti and Garth ran a profitable racket between them, trafficking people to and from various corners of the globe. Whatever it was, I'd only find it if I stuck with it.

As I said, one sitting could not do justice to the journal, there was simply too much of it. And without GV at my side to guide me, the chances I would ever succeed in getting the pages in the right order (i.e. the order in which GV wrote them) looked slim. I doubt the lad would know where to begin himself.

Satisfied that hanging on to the journal for the time being was the sensible thing to do, and intent on taking another look at it later, I put the folder back in the bottom drawer of my desk. And made a point of locking the drawer, too. Just in case. Only recently, so I'd been told, an intruder had broken into the college office, opened the unlocked drawer containing a batch of exam papers waiting to be sent away for marking, and, to put it bluntly, evacuated himself all over them.

You couldn't make it up, could you? That was Heather's conclusion, after telling me the story in confidence. He did a wee-wee on them, Heather called it. She didn't want to go into further detail, see. Too graphic. A part-time colleague of hers wasn't nearly so inhibited.

No knowing then, was there, the lengths to which GV's family might be prepared to go to recover this document they so clearly wanted returned to them?

THREE

BUSINESS IN TOWN

It didn't take my sister long to decide that deferring the sale of Foolsmeadow was not to her liking. Except she didn't put it that way to me. She needed my help, she claimed, over a related matter to do with ownership of the farm. In the same way that she needed me to look after the place for her whilst away on holiday, so she preferred me to accompany her on a confidential errand to see her solicitor. There were things to sort out, apparently, and I was family again, see.

We'd agreed to meet in town outside her solicitor's office. Messrs Leggatt and Fidler had first been engaged by Philip to do the conveyancing when he bought the farm. They had gone on to deal with the matter of drawing up Philip's will for him and had subsequently acted as executors in administering its provisions on his demise. They were the obvious choice for Hilary to retain, to deal with any legal queries she might have, regarding Foolsmeadow Grange.

Normally Hilary was never late for appointments of this

kind. Today, however, her car wouldn't start, so she'd waited to catch the bus. I half expected to hear that Luke had sabotaged the motor when her back was turned but no, on this occasion she blamed herself for not having had the car serviced.

When she did turn up, I saw she'd dressed for the occasion. Well, everyone and their aunt could see she had. In place of the jeans and sweater, she wore a skirt that was frankly too short and too tight in my view for a woman of her years and with her figure. I don't mean to sound unkind, and I'm sure Steve would have approved, but Hilary had long since stopped expecting compliments from her older brother and had likewise stopped giving them. To cap it all, she had seriously overdone the perfume. Not sure what brand it was but I for one must have been on some sort of high as the pair of us were ushered into a panelled room and invited to take a seat.

There was no longer a Mr Leggatt or a Mr Fidler to greet us. Instead, our man introduced himself to us as Bower. Ernest Bower. He had taken over from Charles Fidler, the partner who had previously handled the Pope family's legal affairs and who had now retired. Mr Bower looked to be close to retirement himself and maybe we were his last case before hanging up his briefs, as they say.

'You want to know if there is any legal reason why you can't put the farm up for sale,' he repeated back to Hilary, just to be sure he'd heard her correctly. 'Is there any reason why there should be? It is in your name, isn't it, the farm? Your late husband left it to you in his will, according to the records I have here.'

'My daughter expects me to leave it to her,' Hilary explained. 'Has she any grounds for contesting my decision to sell? Any legal grounds, I mean, Mr Bower?'

Cue for said legal adviser to close his eyes briefly to give the matter some thought, and then, to Hilary's obvious delight, shake his head. 'Not unless she has a tenancy agreement with you, for example. I take it she hasn't signed a lease or anything of that kind with you recently. Has she?'

Hilary put a what-sort-of-moron-do-you-take-me-for expression on her face, clearly not pleased by the suggestion she might have committed something like that to paper. 'I would have run that by you people first, wouldn't I? Before entering into any agreement like that, I mean. This is my older brother Adam, by the way,' she announced, as if inviting me to back her up. 'I asked him to come along.'

I allowed my eyebrows to go up briefly while acknowledging I was indeed my sister's brother and had no objection to shaking a lawyer by the hand.

Bower seemed eager to continue. 'Tell me, Mrs Pope, are you proposing to sell because you have no further interest in farming as such? And would I be right in assuming your daughter takes a different view, and actually wishes to take over the running of the farm?'

How did he know that, I wondered. 'My daughter does have plans for the farm, yes,' Hilary explained. 'She and her boyfriend, they don't want me to sell it, they've made that very plain. That's right, isn't it, Adam?'

Since I honestly didn't know if that was the case or not, I nodded. Bower began clicking and un-clicking his retractable pen as he explained to us that in this case no legal duty was owed to the daughter to provide for her future as such in farming, if that indeed was her choice. He added that any moral or personal considerations were a separate issue on which he did not feel it his professional duty to advise. All the same he did ask Hilary if she'd considered leasing the farm to the daughter and her boyfriend, as a goodwill gesture, as well as a practical source of income for herself. Something to keep all the parties happy. A solution Solomon might have put forward, I heard myself remark (for no good reason I could think of).

Bower smiled wryly at the allusion. Hilary, however, wasn't

impressed. 'Don't you start going all religious on me, Adam. I get enough of that as it is, don't you think? My daughter,' she told Bower, 'is very much into religion at the moment. I don't know where she gets it from. Certainly not from me. Young people these days, eh? It doesn't make her a better person, let me tell you.'

Bower's eyes twinkled as he reminded Hilary that the family name was Pope after all.

'Like my brother here, I'm a Goodman myself,' Hilary retorted. 'At least I was till I married my husband.'

Bower looked at me for a moment. Hard to tell if he had a mind to wink or not whilst listening to Hilary making it clear she had nothing against religion as such, it was what people did with it that led to problems and upsets. 'Anyway, that's by the way,' she concluded, and turned to me. 'Adam here, unless he's changed his mind recently, is another one with no firm religious views. He's a teacher, you know.' A pause while lawyer and teacher acknowledged each other's credentials. 'He taught that college student, you know, the one who took his own life the other month. I forget his name. It was in the papers. You must have read about it. They reckon that was religion for you, behind what he did to himself. Tragic, when you think about it.'

Bower nodded, plainly familiar with the story. And having heard it mentioned, went on to regale us with a tale of his own. About a case he'd dealt with whilst working as a younger man for a practice down south somewhere. A woman had come to him complaining her daughter had joined a religious cult and been brainwashed and as a result didn't want anything more to do with her family. The police had told her there was nothing they could do as the daughter was legally an adult. Only just, but an adult, nonetheless. So the mother wondered if the law could help in some way to get her daughter back for her. By making her a ward of court or something. Getting her sectioned. Declared unfit to be in charge of her own affairs. Anything to get her out of the clutches of this cult which he declined to name for what he called obvious reasons.

I could see Hilary hanging on to his words as if expecting there might be a moral here, a solution in the offing to the difficulties she was experiencing with a similar wayward daughter. But the law didn't do miracles, she learned. Bower informed her he had politely but firmly declined the mother's request to put his signature to a letter making out the daughter was underage and a victim of abuse by the cult leader who was a much older man.

Hilary nodded vigorously and told him he'd done the right thing. 'You can't go around compromising your profession like that,' she told him. 'After all, people trust solicitors to give them honest, sensible advice. Personally, I would expect nothing less.' She went on to explain how, oddly enough, her daughter had likewise been caught up in some kind of cult. Whatever a cult might be. She'd never really thought to ask. To tell the truth, she'd never had to think twice about the word before or ask anybody what it meant.

Bower indulged her, pointing out that, as he understood it, cults exercised pretty much total control over their members – over their money, their movements, lifestyle, thoughts, the lot. Hence his earlier client's concerns for her daughter. Some young people, he felt, seemed to like having their lives controlled for them in this way, especially in today's world where, as he put it, 'anything goes, and hedonism is rife, and the normal constraints of respect for family, school discipline and the like have been sacrificed. If you know what I mean.'

Quite. I saw Hilary nod her head several times before answering. 'I do know what you mean, Mr Bower. There's a lot of it about. How do you cope with it? I don't envy Adam here having to teach some of today's youngsters. Not the sort of job I'd like, I can tell you, but there you go. The girls these days are as bad as the boys, if you ask me.'

I believe I muttered something about the job having its compensations. Whereupon Bower asked me, out of the blue, if by any chance I knew a guy from Capetown by the name of Chris Lambertson, who he believed taught at the college. He and Chris were mates, he revealed, from way back. They'd played rugby together when they were both younger and fitter specimens. That's where Chris had got his bent nose. Bower's face too, when you took a closer look at him, had definitely survived more scrums and lineouts than a few. Nothing like the game of rugby, apparently, for teaching men to live by the rules and have a healthy disrespect for the other side. Personally, I'd have said a rugby field is much more akin to a war zone than a classroom is, but beyond acknowledging that CL was indeed a colleague of mine, I didn't get to put this into words because Hilary intervened with a question about a lease. She'd been wondering about it since Mr Bower brought the subject up. Would a lease or a tenancy, she wanted to know, be transferable? To somebody else? An outside lot, say? If she chose to go down that road, that is. No prizes for guessing which outside lot she had in mind.

'Able to be assigned, do you mean? To another party? Without your consent? That would depend on the wording. But generally, no is the answer.'

'What about a change of use?'

'Of the property? Again no, unless the lease permits it, which in the case of a working farm would not be likely. That would be a matter for the owner – and the planning authority, of course. They would have to be involved. I can let you have a copy of a standard tenancy agreement if you want one. You know, to read through and think about. I could go through one with you now, if you like. No time like the present, as they say.'

Hilary shook her head as if he'd offered her a banned substance. Then changed her mind and decided she would take a copy away with her after all, to give it, as he'd suggested, some thought. 'What do you think, Adam?' she asked.

I gave her the benefit of my long experience in property dealings. 'I think a lease might be the ideal solution. Instead of selling the place, I mean.'

Hilary immediately put that look on her face again. 'I don't know why you say that, Adam. Nothing has been decided yet. My brother,' she explained to the man behind the desk, like this was information he really needed to make a note of, 'imagines he can read my mind before I can. Have you got brothers or sisters like that?'

Bower declined to answer but did offer the firm's services, whichever of the two options Hilary might decide she preferred. He took it she would be instructing a local agent if she chose to sell. One from the High Street. One he would already have had dealings with, presumably.

Hilary stood up with a curt nod and thanked him for his help. Outside in the street she told me she saw no reason not to go after two birds with the same stone, seeing as the nearest estate agent had an office only fifty yards up the street. 'No harm in getting the farm valued, while we're at it,' she declared. 'Though I don't suppose it'll fetch the sort of figure I have in mind. We'll see.'

She refrained from naming the figure or asking me to name one of my own.

*

Dickens and Sharp agreed to do the valuation. They would send someone out to Foolsmeadow in the next few days, not a problem. Then madam could decide if she wanted them to put the property on the market and handle the sale for her. Hilary nodded several times to indicate her consent. On the way out she remarked on what a pleasure it was doing business with people with such high professional standards who didn't start reminiscing about their younger days on the rugby pitch.

Out on the pedestrianised part of the street once more we ran into, almost literally, guess who? Yes, her. Hilary's new friend Pauline, hurrying the other way, if you can call it that. The woman was even larger and broader than I recalled, and definitely bigger in her face; and I can confirm, she waddled.

'Fancy bumping into you two!' she exclaimed. 'What a crazy world, eh?'

Like we were so rarely seen out together, Hilary and I, especially in town, which was true, of course. This was, let's face it, a rare occurrence. One that, where this woman was concerned, called for a celebratory chinwag over coffee or suchlike, and where better to go for it than to Lily's Coffee Shop a few doors down the street? The big woman's treat on this occasion, she wouldn't take no for an answer.

What can I say about my second face-to-face encounter with this friend of Hilary's? Well, like I said, she looked even larger than I remembered her. The short hair, the enormous face, the big voice – they were still there and confirmed I hadn't imagined or exaggerated any of it. How about the tweed skirt and sensible shoes? Sorry, I'm being unkind. Today she was wearing a pair of low heels and a sheepskin coat. When she took it off inside Lily's, I swear I caught a strong whiff of armpit, though I dare say it could have been the curled-up sandwiches displayed on the counter. She wore one of those voluminous flowery ankle-length jobs that make you thankful you can't actually see the size, shape and colour of whatever lies beneath. Not at all flattering, I found.

'Have you had your hair done, Hil? It looks very nice,' she purred.

She's still calling my sister Hil! At school Hilary hated being called Hil. Now she didn't bat an eyelid. Looked rather relaxed about it, to tell the truth.

'Have you just had it done?' the woman went on. 'No? You're kidding me. Well, there's a thing.' And to me, standing there patiently, she said, 'That's usually Hil's reason for coming into town, you know. Her regular hair appointment.'

Fishing, you see, for the real reason we were in town together, older brother and kid sister, and the brother looking, she must have thought, like your typical teacher on vacation who'd not had his clothes cleaned or ironed in months. That was the kind of look she gave me, a quick head-to-toe onceover to see whether, like me, she needed to fine-tune the impression she'd formed of me the other evening. Now she went further and singled out the shirt I was wearing as being identical to the one she'd bought Boyd on the occasion of his last birthday. 'We share the same taste. That must be a good sign,' she concluded.

I resisted the urge to roll my eyes and ventured to ask how the Mini was.

'It's still being repaired, so they tell me. They've lent me another one. You'd never know the difference, you can't tell one from the other, except this one runs a damn sight better. I think I'll tell them to keep mine.'

'Any ill effects after the other night? Any bruises? Any whiplash, by any chance?' Any damage to the old upholstery, in other words? Couldn't see anything amiss myself, but frankly I wouldn't know where to start looking under all that material she was wearing, now would I?

'No. Just a bit of hurt pride and a hole in my bank account, that's all. The excess on the insurance, I'm talking about. I dare say they'll put the bloody premium up, too, next month when I come to renew. You know what the bastards are like.'

Hilary nodded her agreement. She knew exactly what the insurance companies were like. She told us she'd been asked to pay a king's ransom this year to insure the farm. 'I may as well get rid of the place,' she declared. 'What use is it to me?'

Any minute, I thought, she's going to declare her reason for being in town with me. And there's me thinking the matter was still under wraps, nobody outside the family needed to know she'd decided to sell. I'd misunderstood, evidently, how closely Hilary took her friend into her confidence. Huddled round a wobbly table sipping coffee, we became like a gang of three in no time at all, with Hilary holding nothing back where the sale of Foolsmeadow was concerned. I was asked again how much I thought the place would fetch and confessed I'd no idea. The land alone, Mrs K mused, amounted to a sizeable acreage. Throw in the house and the outbuildings and she guessed somebody somewhere would put a figure on it that would attract interested parties. Maybe even the likes of Sahara Street would be interested, I suggested. Toss a pebble in the pool and all that.

She laughed. 'You think they'd be interested in buying, do you? It's an idea, I suppose.'

Hilary felt the need to reiterate her earlier point. 'They're welcome to join the queue. I've already told him that, Pauline. I don't know if he was listening.'

I had a mind to hold my wrist out for slapping but instead found myself passing the sugar bowl to a couple of elderly ladies at the next table who appeared to be talking about Reggie's stroke and what it had done to his bladder and bowels. Voices carry in Lily's, you'll gather. By the time I turned my attention back to my cappuccino, Hilary was explaining to Mrs K how my family had gone off on holiday without me.

Mrs K beamed in my direction. 'They've left you behind, have they? Lucky feller.'

She'd opened a fresh packet of cigarettes but then had second thoughts about lighting up inside Lily's. Second thoughts, too, about inviting me to take one. 'Nasty habit, put 'em away, Pauline,' she whispered to me. Then added, as conspiratorially as she could, 'How did you manage to persuade your lot to go away without you then? I take it they will be coming back home again, eventually.'

Did I want to go into detail about my family's holiday

arrangements? Seeing my reluctance, Hilary decided she'd do it for me, and explained, louder actually than she needed to, exactly who had gone where. We were a gang of three now, remember, so I guess nothing was off limits.

'I see. Left you to your own devices, eh?' The woman turned to Hilary. 'And there's me thinking your brother isn't the type. Let me guess, he's the quiet type, but stubborn with it, the one who does his own thing.' She turned back to me. 'I've heard Steve mention you. He says you're one of the good guys at the college. A tutor or something. Or have I got the wrong end of the stick?'

'Steve's a good friend of mine,' I replied. And added, 'But as yet I can't say I've heard him mention your name. Should I take that as a good sign?'

No, I wanted to, but I didn't add that bit. There were too many people in Lily's. The woman turned back to Hilary. 'I like Steve. He's a good bloke. You know where you are with him. When is it you two go off to Scotland, Hil? Can't be far off, surely.'

I guess I could be forgiven for thinking Mrs K might, just might, get a firmer answer to the question than I'd had. But no, a fly was bothering Hilary. It wouldn't stop trying to land in her hair, despite the arm she'd raised to wave it away. In the end a well-aimed flick from her friend's fingers dispatched it into someone else's airspace. 'There. It's your hairspray, you know, Hil, that attracts them. Surprising how many flies follow customers into the shop. You wouldn't believe the amount of insect killer I've had to buy so far this summer.'

Hilary reminded her they worked in the same shop, swatting the same flies. Wasps, too. All manner of flying insects. She dared say midges would be the problem once she got north of the border. Mrs K nodded knowingly, then turned back to me, wanting to know how long I'd known Steve.

'Longer than I care to remember. He was already teaching

there when I joined the college.' My face, I hoped, conveyed my reluctance to go into detail.

'They used to go off together at weekends,' Hilary explained. Before Steve found other things to do with his time, obviously. 'Orienteering, was it? Or was it local history?'

'Really? How interesting!'

'He's full of surprises, is Adam, believe me. Doesn't say a lot, mind, but you know what they say about the quiet ones.'

'It's true as well, so I've found.'

Really? I was on the point of reminding present company that they were talking about a happily married man, thank you very much, whose family loved him dearly, when a loud growl caught my attention. Definitely a noisy stomach. And definitely hers, Pauline's, no doubt about it. I imagine everyone at Lily's tables heard it. For a brief moment I saw Hilary clutch at her midriff in the belief she was the person responsible, before realising she wasn't and pointing an accusing finger at her friend. 'I thought it was me for a minute. You should hear mine sometimes. You must be famished, Pauline. Shall I get us a cake or something?'

Pauline shook her head. 'I'm on a diet, remember. Cakes are out. No kidding. I have a salad sandwich waiting for me back at the shop. But talking of food, we must have a meal together sometime. At my place. What do you say? I'm sure you can persuade Adam here to come along as well. He can meet Boyd. That's my other half, Adam, in case you're wondering. He doesn't get out much these days. as Hil will tell you, but he enjoys company. And he knows how to talk. You can't shut him up when he gets going. I could strangle the bugger sometimes.'

Bad as that, eh? Sounds a hoot. Can't wait. I'd sadly failed to find a reason to decline the offer by the time Hilary nodded for both of us. 'That sounds great. I'm sure I can persuade Adam to come along.'

'Right. Must get back to the shop. See you there tomorrow,

Hil. Usual time, eh? Nice meeting you again, Adam. See you soon.'

She took the liberty of patting my arm as she collected up her things. As she reached the door, I heard her stomach give a further growl, as if desperate by now for that salad sandwich – for a plateful of salad sandwiches, more like, to fill a stomach her size. Only this time nobody took any notice.

SAHARA STREET

'I'll wait and see what the valuer has to say.'

Hilary's last words to me, I recall, as I dropped her off at the end of the lane. Naturally, I wouldn't hear of her taking the bus home. I offered to take a look at her car, too, but she told me the repair shop mechanic had promised to drop by and sort it. She wouldn't let me drive her all the way to her door. The end of the lane would be fine. The walk from there would do her good. Was she practising for Scotland, I wondered.

Still no word from her about when she planned to head off north of the border. Not a priority, apparently. Knowing Steve, I presumed he'd be doing his best to finalise matters – sorting out routes, reading up on places he imagined Hilary might want to visit. For places in this case, read hilltop burial sites, ancient ley lines, former battlefields, abandoned settlements. Just the sorts of places I suspected Hilary might not be too keen to visit, especially if it rained and the mist came down, and the midges took to the air.

Hilary seemed more concerned with finding a way to accommodate her friend's offer of a meal. 'Think yourself honoured to get invited,' she enthused. 'Pauline's obviously taken a shine to you, Adam. Don't know how well you'll get on with Boyd though. Unpredictable sort. Especially if he's having one of his off days.'

Off days? Boyd's complaint, I learned, took the form of a paralysis of the muscles down one side of his face, a type of palsy, which made him appear to be sneering at people, apparently. The way teachers do, if you like, when asked endless silly questions by their students. The condition had led to the onset of agoraphobia, and such was the man's fear of stepping outdoors that he'd given up going to work for the council's housing department and now lived as a "kept man", according to Hilary. Except Pauline's wages from the charity shop barely supported the two of them, so she'd applied to become his carer. Had they no children? 'Don't ask,' Hilary told me. 'It's a touchy subject. Let's just say the fault doesn't lie with Pauline.'

It was starting to sound as if I would be drawing up a whole list of reasons not to dine with Mr and Mrs K. All right for Hilary, the Kendricks were her friends. Hopefully Hilary would soon disappear up north and the whole business would be put on hold and eventually forgotten. By then I'd be left in charge of a farm up for sale. What was I supposed to do about that?

Quite apart from Sam's interests, there was the guy from down the road to take into account, now I thought about it. Ted Shimwell, I'm talking about. I imagined he might have something to say about a For Sale board going up at the farm. I knew from somewhere that he had grazing rights over some of the land. In his shoes I'd want to know how a change of ownership would affect my livelihood. If anyone currently worked the land, Ted did. He'd taken it on soon after Philip died, to accommodate his expanding business at the time. He had cattle in the fields. He cut and collected hay for the winter and stored it in barns scattered around the farm. You could bet your savings that at some point during Hilary's time away, assuming she did actually go ahead and leave me in charge of the place, I'd run into Ted. So maybe it was Ted and his missus we should be planning to dine with and forget the date with the Kendricks. Just a thought. A fleeting one that I wasn't going to lose sleep over, let me stress. I had more pressing things to attend to.

That afternoon I unlocked the drawer and fetched out GV's journal for another look. I'd decided the last time, as I recalled, that there was a possibility Sahara Street could be a front for shady activities. Hmm. Maybe GV had found out about them, and the discovery had put his life in danger. A bit extreme maybe, but hey, worse things have happened at sea, you read about them regularly in the papers. And religious cults, if that's what we were dealing with here, well, they do tend to attract odd people generally, don't you find?

I guess I wasn't the best person to warm to this guy's way of looking at the world, was I? Much more pressing now, as I opened up the folder and got my mind into gear, was the job of deciding where to make a start. On which page? One sheet offered as much (or as little) promise as another, unless it was a sheet with a title or a heading on it somewhere to give you a clue. Like this one, for instance, entitled MY MARCIE. A girl he'd met perhaps, at college, or church? Something to suggest GV wasn't as gay as Heather would have us believe? I found myself taking a closer look.

> 'She likes it because it doesn't have the big arches and pews and stone floors and things you find in most churches. She's right. It's less like a museum. It's where people meet and share feelings about GOD'S PLACE IN THE WORLD. You don't need the arches and stuff. They don't help you pray any better or sing in tune.
>
> 'She says she's a better person because of Sahara Street. She can see how it gives meaning to what she does so she's not just looking after family all the time and putting food on the table, and washing and ironing and stuff, there's a point to it. She sometimes plays the organ – not one of those huge things with pipes all up the wall like they have

in some churches, just a keyboard and a seat, that she complains isn't very comfortable, so she takes a cushion to sit on. At other times Mrs G plays it. She doesn't always hit the right notes, but nobody seems to mind, and you can't hear her play anyway when the rest of us are singing. We have a book with hymns in it, some of them written by people like us who aren't famous or anything. I think I might have a go myself one day as it can't be all that hard to put your feelings about God into words, though I suppose the music would be trickier.

'*She also helps out sometimes with the flowers. Her and Mrs G. They make the tea as well, between them, and clean up after people. Mr Bartholomew includes them both regularly in his prayers. I can see her looking so proud and thanking him when he says What would we do without the pair of you?*'

A cosy set-up, by the sound of things. Now if you're thinking what I'm thinking, Marcie sounds more like the older woman than the girlfriend. Girlfriends as a rule don't do your washing and ironing for you, not in my experience, they don't. At least not until you've married them. It could be GV was talking about his aunt. Or his grandmother. He'd referred to his mother as Marti, remember. The good-looking woman admired by Mo. I suppose you could argue this was the same person, and that here was a case of GV not remembering that he'd called his mother Marti on another page. Not given us her real name at all, which was probably something like Beryl, or Nellie. The trouble with writing a script this lengthy, I imagine, is remembering what names you've given people, especially if you're trying to conceal their identity or prevent them from recognising themselves, should your manuscript fall into the wrong hands.

It did cross my mind that GV might, at some stage, have come into contact with my niece, seeing as they both attended

Sahara Street meetings. Luke too, for that matter. But how would I recognise Sam or Luke on the page, say, if GV chose for any reason to give them a mention? Would he use their real names, or give them fancy ones?

Over the page I came across something more on the lines I was looking for, under the heading SAHARA STREET BLUES. Something rather less cosy this time. See for yourself.

> 'That was the Sunday J went up in front of everybody. He'd been accused of turning his back on God's ways. That's what we were told. It was his choice to go up there because he didn't want to be kicked out, he'd rather confess and repent. Mr Bartholomew reminded us what it says in the Bible about God not abiding relations that aren't between a man and a woman, and forbidding men to have relations with other men, or to have relations outside marriage. He gave J his Bible and told him to read verses from it out loud that he'd marked out for him and told him to read out the same verses over and over loud enough for everybody to hear. I can't remember how many times, but I know it was a lot. Then he was told to read them out again from memory another lot of times, and J broke down in tears by the time Mr Bartholomew took the Bible off him. And when he went back to his seat, we all sang from a sheet we'd been given, praising God for His MERCY and asking His FORGIVENESS OF OUR SINS.'

Oh dear. A case of don't mess with God when Mr Bartholomew is speaking for him, or you'll be sorry? A disciplinarian if ever there was one, this Bartholomew guy. But was Bartholomew his real name? I couldn't help thinking what a fine job he would have made a few years ago if put in charge, say, of my son's secondary school. Just what Adrian needed at the time. No good asking me the identity of the unfortunate J. You have to wonder if the episode was given prominence because the guy meant something special to GV himself.

Being rather curious about which verses Mister B could have chosen to be read out to his congregation, I went so far as to take my dusty Bible down off its shelf to search for myself. The Acts of the Apostles, would it be? Paul's letters? What about James's Epistle to the Twelve Tribes in the Dispersion? Grab a load of this:

'Let not many of you become teachers, my brethren, for you know that we who teach shall be judged with greater strictness. For we all make many mistakes, and if anyone makes no mistakes in what he says he is a perfect man...'

Hardly germane to the case in hand maybe, but a cautionary comment on members of my profession, wouldn't you agree? But just a minute. Far more appropriate to J's situation was this quote from Paul's Letter to the Romans:

'God gave them up to dishonourable passions. Their women exchanged natural relations for unnatural, and the men likewise gave up natural relations with women and were consumed with passion for one another, men committing shameless acts with men...'

Fine as far as it went, but if I was any judge of Mister Bartholomew, his lesson plan would have to feature recourse to divine wrath and punishment at some stage if his congregation were not to draw the wrong conclusions about where God stands in these matters. I read on a few more chapters and found this:

'Let us then cast off the works of darkness and put on the armour of light. Let us conduct ourselves becomingly as in the day, not in revelling and drunkenness, not in debauchery and licentiousness, not in quarrelling and jealousy. But put on the Lord Jesus Christ, and make no provision for the flesh, to gratify its desires.'

A start at any rate. Not sure about that last sentence. Where I come from, it's wise to include some provision for gratifying the flesh or you have a problem. Even Mister Bartholomew, I presumed, had his needs.

I returned my Bible to its shelf, satisfied it contained more than enough quotable material to enable the Bartholomews of this world to keep their flocks in order. If not, you could always show persistent offenders the door. Now what scripture could I possibly get my most troublesome students to read out aloud to the rest as a suitable act of penance and contrition? The complete provisions of the *1944 Education Act*, say? Hmm. Make it the *College Prospectus*, especially the bit about the duties of both parties (I'm talking students on the one hand and staff on the other) to act in accordance with the fulfilment of their contract to one another. I like to think I could have worded that section myself.

I won't weary you with more quotations from various apostles and epistles. Or with what I found, in the course of reading more pages of the journal. Suffice it to say that by the time I put the thing away, the pages I'd finished reading lay at my feet in a growing pile, ready for gathering up for safekeeping in a separate folder. No point putting them back among the rest, now was there? Come on, there is some method to GMan's filing system, don't deny him that.

*

I was woken out of my sleep that night by a phone call. My bedside clock said three thirty. Nobody rings me at that hour. I had to be dreaming. And since I clearly wasn't, it had to be a prank. Or an emergency. You-need-to take-this-call-right-away sort of emergency. Someone has died; there's been a fire; a plane has crashed onto your sister's farmhouse; why are you still lying there?

It was Adrian. Calling from Bangkok Airport. Or so he said. To judge by the high level of static on the line the monsoon rains had arrived. In fact, he assured me, it wasn't raining there, and no, he hadn't realised that if you call England from Bangkok at ten thirty in the morning local time you are going to wake your dad out of his sleep because he is at least seven hours behind you as the globe turns. So, what did he want? Was something wrong? Had they arrested him and Eve for trying to smuggle dope in or out of the country?

On reflection, I should have shown more interest and asked him if they were having a lovely time out there, what the food was like, and the accommodation. Personally, I couldn't picture Bangkok without seeing endless rickshaws and street corners littered with beggars and drug users, police with firearms, girlie boys touting for business, a single unflushed loo shared between a dozen or more impoverished locals. Okay, I've never been there so my view of the place may have been influenced by those lurid tales of what can befall young western backpackers who stray off the beaten track and accept lifts from psychos.

So, what did my son want?

I should have known. Their pockets had been picked. Somewhere between one hostel and the next. Not a hope someone would find their cash and hand it in. Be serious, Dad. They were pursuing the matter with the travel insurance people to see how much they could recover, and how soon. In the meantime, they were borrowing off friends and would I help out by transferring a modest sum into my son's account so they could draw on it? When I explained that whilst the banks might be open right now in Bangkok, they didn't open their doors over here for several more hours, he said he could live with that little problem so long as he knew the funds would be made available fairly soon.

'So tell me,' I asked him, having done the decent thing and agreed to a bail-out, 'before you put the phone down, didn't you once tell me Eve had a friend who—'

'Sorry, Dad. Can't hear you. Have to go.'

Charming. The line went dead. No more coins left for small talk, evidently. So why, you may wonder, was I asking after Eve's friend at that hour of the night? Well, Adrian had woken me from a dream, as it happened. A particularly vivid one, let me tell you, in which Eve invites me to meet a friend of hers. Don't ask me if it's a girlie friend or a bloke; that bit doesn't seem to have been vivid enough to matter.

So okay, to meet this friend we have to board a train, Eve and me. And the train is packed, and we have to stand together, face to face, hanging onto those ceiling straps. Only in the crush Eve (who's quite a bit shorter than me) loses her grip and I can't stop her sliding down against me till she's down somewhere between my legs, tugging at my trousers which I just know are going to start sliding southwards too, and – okay, I guess you get the picture, you don't need me to go on, but bear with me, this story does improve, I assure you – the train lurches to a stop and we are all flung forward. Eve, I find as I regain my feet, isn't there anymore. Not on the floor. Not in the carriage. No sign of her. Instead, I'm sitting alongside Adrian, aware my trousers are not where they should be, but that's all right, he takes no notice. He's looking at his watch. He doesn't seem at all concerned where Eve might be. An alarm bell rings, and nobody takes a blind bit of notice except me. I sit bolt upright, wondering what it signifies, and that's when I find it's the phone ringing downstairs, don't I? And it's three thirty in the morning. British Summer Time. It will soon be getting light.

When eventually I climbed back into bed, I lay awake for a while, thinking. About what Eve and Adrian might be up to, mostly. And how lucky Adrian was to have a girl like Eve on holiday with him, thousands of miles from his dad's gaze, doing whatever young people do together on their globe-trotting travels these days. I couldn't recall having Julie at my side in such an exotic far-away place. At least not before I'd vowed to make an honest woman of her and promised to share all my worldly goods.

So, this matter of Eve's friend I'd tried raising with Adrian, what was that about? Well, I'm pretty certain Adrian had mentioned to me, soon after the story broke about Gordon Verity's death, that a friend of Eve's had known the guy. Gone out with him or something. Another possible source of information you see, about GV's state of mind in his last few days.

I paid the promised visit to my bank next morning. And while there I did wonder if Julie might be giving me a ring next with tales of a cash flow problem of her own. How many hours ahead of us are the Greek Islands? A shameful thought, I know. And not Julie's style, to be honest. She had the Bank of Widowed Mother to draw on if the need arose. So, was I being unreasonably tight with my money? As I believe I've said on more than one occasion to my students, it's not how you perceive yourself that matters, or even how others perceive you, but how soon others give up on getting you to see yourself as they see you. Are you still with me?

Well, later in the day I did, as it happened, receive another phone call. Not from Julie, though. My niece wanted a word. Sam had tried several times to phone me, apparently, and got no answer. I wasn't an easy person to get hold of, as she put it. She sounded annoyed.

I tried soothing her by injecting a generous measure of charm into my voice. 'Nice to hear from you too, Sam. A lovely day, isn't it? So, what can I do for you?'

Well, at least she wasn't asking for money. I would have happily obliged if she had been, I'm sure, bearing in mind she couldn't have been earning much at the pie shop. No, Sam had something else on her mind. She'd found out the farm was going to be put up for sale, and she wasn't best pleased about it. Moreover, she demanded to know why I was involved. Why I was, as she so pointedly put it, poking my nose into matters that did not concern me and pressuring her mother into putting the farm on the market.

'Hang on a minute, young lady,' I protested. 'What makes you think I have any influence over what your mother decides to do? The decision to have the farm valued wasn't mine.'

'You took her to see the estate agent.'

Took her? Forcibly? At gunpoint? 'I went with her, if that's what you mean. She asked me to go along. She asked me to meet her in town.'

Either a For Sale board had gone up already at the farm, or the Kendrick woman had opened her big mouth. It dawned on me that Mrs K's charity shop and Fletcher's pie shop weren't exactly miles apart.

'Whatever.' Sam sounded distinctly unconvinced. 'Why did she want you along anyway? You could have talked her out of it. She listens to you.' As if! My niece clearly misunderstood my relationship with her mother. 'I bet you never considered my views about it, did you? I am family as well, you know.'

What was it about family that was beginning to lose its appeal? 'I thought you didn't want me interfering. It sounds like you want me on your side.'

'Listen, Uncle Adam, we've got plans for the farm, me and Luke. It wouldn't be right for Mother to sell it without consulting us first. She's had her go at farming the place. It's our turn. Ask Adrian. Or Charlotte. How would they feel in my shoes?'

Like that, was it? Get out of the way, you old folks, we young ones know what's fair and what isn't. Oh yeah? Since when did our kids enjoy that kind of monopoly? Give me a break. 'Have you actually sat down and discussed any of this with your mother?' I heard myself ask. 'I mean, have you really put it to her how much the farm means to you and Lou?'

'It's Luke. With a 'k'.' Isn't that what I said? Evidently not. 'She won't listen. One minute she's fine with us, the next she's saying we'll have to leave. But where would we go? The place has a lot going for it, anybody can see that, and Luke has given up his job and spent a lot of his time doing up the buildings for her.

He'll lose all that if it's sold. That can't be right, can it?'

I was being put on the spot here, in case you hadn't noticed. By a niece who actually could once have relied on her looks and youthful charm to win her uncle over but now chose to hector him instead. If we'd been having this conversation face to face in Fletcher's pie shop, I dare say a pastry or two might have been lined up as ammunition by now. Sam always did have a volatile side to her.

'Did your mother actually ask Luke to work on the buildings?' This wasn't the pie shop so no harm, I thought, in a spot of fact-finding.

'She didn't tell him to stop when he offered.' A no, in that case. 'He wouldn't have offered if he thought Mother was going to put the place up for sale, now, would he? It stands to reason when you think about it. Anybody can see that. Luke's not a fool, you know.'

Hmm. Not having met the guy yet, I felt I wasn't best qualified to say one way or the other. Sam's record with previous boyfriends didn't exactly inspire confidence. And I've already mentioned my niece's innate distaste for anything to do with animal husbandry. Still, I didn't want her feeling her favourite uncle might be biased one way or the other, did I?

'I'm sure Luke is no fool,' I assured her. 'But does he get on all right with your mother? I think she finds him a bit...' A bit of a thug? 'Well, difficult to talk to. A bit intimidating, if you know what I mean.' On top of which, come on now, doing things such as intercepting her mail and fitting new locks everywhere isn't the best way for him to win her over, now is it? Be honest.

'I see. Mother's been telling you all about him, has she? Listing all the bad things, eh? Making out he's no good, and hasn't any manners, and won't take any notice of her when she speaks to him. Typical.'

You can tell, can you, that Sam sort of expected the Goodmans to stick together on issues like this? In the face of this kind of solidarity she felt compelled to point out that Luke had a better side to him that I just might care to hear about rather than taking my sister's word for what a delinquent he was.

'Steady on,' I protested. 'I'm sure when I meet Luke, I'll find he's a regular nice guy and we'll get on just fine. Maybe your mother has judged him a bit harshly. I don't know him, do I?'

Sam saved me the effort of asking her to list Luke's good points for me. 'I know what you're trying to say,' she declared. 'Let me say it for you. My mother thinks he's a bad influence on me. Because he believes in things that she stopped believing in years ago. Because he does a lot for our church, and she finds that odd. Because it isn't the same church she went to once upon a time, donkey's years ago. I bet she hasn't been inside a church, any church, since Dad's funeral. And she thinks our church is rubbish and up to no good. I bet she's told you that much, hasn't she?'

Well, yes, now Sam mentioned it, Hilary did think Luke was a disappointment. And no, she hadn't been inside a church for a while. And she did have reservations about the activities and intentions of a church that didn't resemble the sort of church she'd got married in. If it had been a Methodist Chapel, mind, she might have felt differently, knowing as she did that the village hall was a former non-conformist meeting place. But this latest lot, the Sahara Street Mission or whatever they called themselves, that was asking too much. Who were they? I thought of asking Sam to invite me along to one of their meetings and maybe I'd persuade Hilary to come along too. Don't make me laugh, she'd reply, we're a church, not an old people's day care centre. So, I asked her instead, being genuinely curious, to tell me how her church came by its name. I mean, Sahara Street does sound a bit unusual, don't you think?

'Does it? And what's that got to do with anything? Why is St Michael's called St Michael's?'

Search me. Ask a question like mine and you get an answer like hers, I suppose, so why on earth follow it with another pointless query? 'Why should your mother think your church is up to no good?'

'Ask her!'

'Enlighten me. I've led a sheltered life.'

Sam was having none of it. 'Come off it! You may be a teacher but you're not totally dumb.' Hmm. Interesting to see where she might be going with this one. 'Remember that student at your college, the one that topped himself? Well, people have never stopped talking about him, have they? And blaming Sahara Street for what he did. If he'd attended St Michael's, would they have blamed the C of E for it? I don't think so.'

Okay, point taken. 'So why do they blame Sahara Street?'

'Because that's the way people are. Because it's different. Why do you think? Anyway, I must go. I've got things to do. I'm a busy girl these days. I can't take time off, like you teachers. I'll leave you to ask my mother to think again about selling the farm. It's wrong and unfair of her. Even Grandma says so. Think about that. Bye.'

'You could get her to sell it to—'

To you and Luke. Too late. Sam had hung up. Point made as far as she was concerned. She'd rebuked me for taking her mother's side and done her best to point out where my loyalties should lie, me being a teacher and all that pillar-of-the-community stuff, not to mention a parent who should be more in tune with his offspring and their innate sense of fairness.

Only later did I wonder if she'd been told that her uncle would be taking over at Foolsmeadow while her mother was on holiday. Likewise, it slipped my mind to ask her if she'd got to know Gordon Verity at all at her Sahara Street meetings. Or whether there was any truth in the rumour that Sahara Street were looking for a likely spot for a seminary.

Even Grandma says so! Sam had to be pulling my chain. My

mother was surely the last person to be drawn into an argument about the future of the farm. On the other hand, she was family, and that seemed to have become an increasingly important factor lately in deciding who demanded loyalty from whom.

It so happened I was due to pay Mater a visit. I'd already told her I had no holiday plans to keep me from her door. So, what was I waiting for?

*

My mother (our mother, I should say, Hilary's and mine) lived alone in a house several sizes too big for her on the other side of town. An austere Victorian terrace affair. If anyone should have been contemplating a move to smaller premises, Mater should. But you know what they're like, she'd left it late and now, to be blunt about it, she faced the choice of either ending her days there or moving into a care home. Mind you, they'd yet to build a home designed with her in mind, she'd say. Another way of admitting she wasn't ready to move, she enjoyed her independence, you know how it is. That didn't stop her moaning to anyone who'd listen about how lonely life had become for her, and how she'd no one to talk to now Dad had gone and her children had deserted her. Not true about her children, let me say. Not in the sense she meant. She received regular visits from Hilary, and my own visits were not exactly rare occurrences. She made friends all over town. She belonged to the WI and the local bridge club, and that fact alone ensured some old dear was always dropping in to see her, or else she was out partnering one of them – Margaret usually, though I'd yet to meet the woman – for bingo or a game of cards.

That evening, having taken my usual precaution of phoning ahead to check she'd be in and on her own, I found her buried in her worn-out easy chair in front of the telly watching an episode of one of those awful soaps that Julie watches.

'Why did you tap on the window like that?' she wanted to know. 'You frightened the life out of me.'

'Sorry. Didn't you hear the doorbell?'

'Did you ring it?'

'I always ring it. It's you. You have your telly on too loud.'

She had long ago agreed to get her ears tested but hadn't made an appointment yet, as there were others in far greater need than she was, and she'd get round to it by and by. If she could still make out what Bet Lynch was saying, her hearing wasn't so terrible, surely.

'Put the kettle on now you're here,' she urged me, and added, 'I bet you're feeling left out of things now you're on your own. I can tell, you know. What with your family away and all.'

I guess I looked a predictably miserable specimen. I stood and eyed myself in the living room mirror. That particular mirror had never been one to flatter me, not at any stage of my upbringing in that house. Something to do with the way the light fell on it. Hilary had felt the same. Day or night seemed to make no difference. Mater had always insisted it didn't lie.

'You looking for grey hairs again?'

'Just looking at what a handsome son you have.'

And from the kitchen I added, 'I don't mind my own company. It's quite peaceful really, with nobody in the house to contradict me.' I could have been talking to myself, I realised, as no way was Mater going to hear what I said over the combined noise of the telly and her ancient kettle. From the look of them, the kitchen walls hadn't seen fresh paint in a decade or more, and the cooker was a brand no longer listed in any of the brochures. Whose fault was that?

For no good reason at all I found myself imagining a scenario in which Hilary moved back in here with Mater after selling the farm. A new broom around the place, you might say. Knowing Hilary, she would have these walls stripped and repainted in no time, and new furniture moved in. On the other hand, knowing

Hilary, I decided she'd rather emigrate than move in with her mother.

'Did you speak?'

What did I say about a hearing test? Mater had no problem hearing the things she expected you to say and was deaf to the rest. Some people said her hearing came and went to suit her mood. I put two teas down on the table between us. 'I was saying—'

'You don't mind your own company. I heard you.' You see! That's what I hear from your sister, too. Thinks she can be happier if she goes and lives on her own somewhere. Away from the farm and everybody. I don't think she knows what she wants any more. Not since Philip passed away, and that dog of hers went and died.'

Marley. The border collie. I'd forgotten about him and the way he used to come out to greet me whenever I turned up at Foolsmeadow. I can't say I'd noticed his passing make much difference to Hilary, though.

'She reckons the dog was poisoned, you know.'

Don't tell me. Sam's new boyfriend did it. Except the dog died long before Luke appeared on the scene, if memory served. 'I thought it was old age,' I heard myself remark. Mater didn't appear to hear me.

Over tea and a scone of Mater's, I got round to the subject I wanted to raise. 'Seen anything of Samantha lately?' Definitely not Sam where Mater was concerned. That wasn't the name on her granddaughter's birth certificate, she'd have you know. It wasn't the name she'd suggested to Philip and Hilary either, when they'd run short of ideas of their own.

'What's she been up to?'

'I thought you might be able to tell me. Somebody said she's got involved with one of those weird religious groups. Sahara Street. Know anything about it?'

'Your sister did say something to me, now you mention it.

Mind you, your sister has been telling me lots of things lately. Don't know about religion though. But she did mention a new fancy man she's been seeing. A teacher at your place, I believe she said. Can't recall his name. Stephen, is it?'

'Did Hilary tell you about Samantha's new boyfriend? About Luke, by any chance?'

'Luke, did you say? I thought it was Stephen.'

'Never mind. Has she told you about Sahara Street?'

'Sahara Street? Isn't that where your sister's going to live after she's sold the farm?'

At least I could take it Mater knew Hilary was thinking of putting the farm on the market. Her knowledge of Sahara Street was something else. Try a different tack. 'I don't think Samantha likes the idea of the farm being sold. She's probably told you so herself. She's got plans for the place, she and Luke. To carry on farming, I mean. Or did you already know about that?'

'Whatever your sister decides to do with the farm is up to her. I don't agree with it myself, mind.'

'Well, Samantha definitely doesn't agree with it.'

'She's been moaning to you about it, has she?'

'I wouldn't call it moaning exactly. She tells me she's been talking to you about the farm. And about that church she goes to, Sahara Street. She says you know all about Sahara Street.'

Mater looked blank. 'Is that what she says?'

We'd been down roads like this a number of times recently, Mater and me, as you can probably guess. I ask her a question, and she answers with one of her own, uncertain of the line between what she remembers and what she's expected to remember. I'd stopped short of asking her to name the current PM. Doesn't mean a thing, I find. Don't always know the answer myself. Interestingly, Dad had failed that test some years earlier before progressing to the stage where you couldn't ask him anything at all without hearing him repeat the question. Then he stopped talking altogether, and one day he just opened his mouth as if he had something he wanted to say, and that was it. His mouth stayed open. The end. A last gurgle by way of farewell.

'Didn't you hear me?'

That's right, Mater had caught me not listening for once! She was wondering if I'd put sugar in her tea by mistake. In fact, I'd given her the wrong cup. 'Sorry. Yes, I heard you. Anyway, what was I saying? Oh yes, Samantha says you're on her side. You don't want Hilary to sell the farm.'

'I'm not on anybody's side. It's not my place to get involved, is it? Anyway, what's that you said about her getting mixed up with some religious crowd? Doesn't sound like Samantha to me. She's a sensible girl.'

My feelings too, once upon a time. 'They call themselves the Sahara Street Mission Church. Have you heard of them?' I asked. 'Sam – Samantha – says you know all about them. About who they are, and what they get up to.' I'm flogging a dead mare here, I can see by the blank expression on Mater's face as she slurps her tea from the saucer – the first time I'd seen or heard her do that sort of thing, as I recalled. I pursued my point. 'Samantha reckons if anybody knows about Sahara Street, you do.' A bit of a fib, I know, but in a good cause.

'Samantha says so, does she? Well now, unless I'm very much mistaken, Sahara Street is where the barracks used to be. What we called the drill hall. I don't think it's there anymore, though. I think they pulled it down.'

Hmm. 'And what did they put in its place?'

'Oh, it's no good asking me questions like that.' No good at all by the sound of it. 'You could always go and look for yourself. What does the drill hall have to do with Samantha, anyway?'

I changed the subject at that point and asked how long since Mater had baked the scones.

'Would you like another one?' she asked. 'There's plenty more. I baked them yesterday.' Last month, more like. There was a time when I couldn't eat enough of Mater's scones, especially while they were still warm and fresh from the oven. The ones on offer now should have come with a warning. 'Not like you to refuse another scone,' I was told. 'Are you off your food? Waiting for Julie to get back, eh, and do your baking for you, is that it?'

'I told you, I'm enjoying my own company for a change. The peace and quiet. I'd forgotten how peaceful life can be.' How lonely too, actually.

'Where is it you said Adrian's gone to? Japan?'

'Thailand. At least he rang me from there. In the middle of the night, before it got light. He'd forgotten about the time difference.'

'Is he still with that girl? What's her name again?'

'Eve. Yes, they're still together.' My future daughter-in-law, the way things were shaping up. No complaints from me, as you can imagine. But not the time or place to be dwelling on Eve and the way she was shaping up. Mater, I learned, had also received a call from Bangkok but, unlike me, had taken the call at midday.

'Don't tell me! He asked you for money as well?' I should have guessed.

Nothing like hedging your bets. Why stick at Bank of Dad when Granny's Vaults are there to be plundered? And if both oblige, well, there's enough in the kitty for a treat or two. A trip to the opium den, perhaps. Or a seat at one of Bangkok's gaming tables.

Mater shrugged. 'I don't mind helping them out. You're only young once, you know.'

Very noble. I knew for a fact she'd given Adrian a generous wad of cash before he and Eve departed. Mater invariably dealt in cash – anything else, by definition wasn't acceptable tender. Now Adrian was on the other side of the globe, however, giving him more cash presented her with a problem. Not one that Adrian couldn't solve, mind. He'd suggested, bless him, using my account to launder Mater's further donation. Me, that is, to do a second bank transfer to Bangkok in return for a cash reimbursement from Mater's savings. I told Mater to forget it, but she insisted, and went and fetched another wad of cash from somewhere to cover it. One hundred pounds. The amount I'd already taken it upon myself to transfer that morning. You're only young once, eh? More or less the words Julie would have used if I mentioned any of this to her.

'Half this amount would be plenty,' I argued. I could only guess at how much cash Mater kept stashed away in the house for occasions like this. Burglars had been known to operate in her neighbourhood, I reminded her. 'They always know where to find your cash. You should let me open a bank account for you.'

'What for? So all those people at the bank know what savings I've got? Don't be silly. Anyway, I don't mind parting with some of it if it's going to a good cause. At least Adrian isn't going to smoke it away, is he?'

I'd reached for my cigarettes, hadn't I? In full view, in the living room, without thinking. I put the packet away again. 'Not sure what he's going to do with it,' I admitted. At least I had no problem lighting up under Hilary's roof. 'Has Hilary told you?' I asked. 'She wants me to look after the farm while she goes on holiday?'

'Can't Samantha do that? She's not a child anymore.'

'Hilary wants me to be in charge, apparently.'

Mater shook her head. 'And whose fault is that? They've never got on, those two. And I don't know why not. Samantha was such a lovely child.'

'I guess you can't always get on with your children.'

'Going on holiday, you say? Going away with that new fancy man of hers, is she?'

Fancy man. That's twice she'd used the term. 'Yes, she's going with Steve. I don't think you've met Steve yet, have you?'

She knew he taught at the college, and as a colleague of mine, had to be somebody in the world.

'She could do worse for herself, I suppose.' You see. She approved. 'Where are they going?'

'Scotland, so I'm told.'

'Miserable place, if you ask me. Always raining. Whose idea was that?'

'Dunno. But looking after the farm while they're away, that looks like being my holiday for this year.' Unless, okay, Hilary changed her mind again and dropped the idea.

Mater gave me a long hard look. 'Daft time to be offering the place for sale, if you ask me. Unless your sister expects you to sell the farm for her while she's gone. That'll be the reason she wants you there. Mark my words. That's Hilary for you. She's not daft.'

Trust Mater to name an ulterior motive when she saw one. Was I to be the caretaker showing prospective buyers round the place while the owner took off? Sam certainly wouldn't qualify for the job; moreover, Sam, I reckoned, would not be happy to see her uncle in the role either.

I tried making light of it. 'Do you think I should ask Hilary to pay me commission? Along with a retainer for standing in as caretaker while she's away?'

Mater shrugged. 'No good asking me about it, it's got nothing to do with me. I just hope Samantha isn't going to be the one to get hurt in all this business of selling the place.' She waved an arm in the air to signify that was as far as it went. 'I've said enough,' she concluded. 'I'm keeping my mouth shut.' She pointed to the scones. 'If you're not going to eat any more, put them away again for me, would you? So they stay fresh.' Yeah, we don't want them going stale, now, do we?

When I got back from the kitchen Mater wanted to know if I'd ever stopped overnight at the farm. I knew what was coming. I'd heard it before, more than once, Mater never missed an opportunity to tell the tale of the haunted upstairs room. The room she'd slept in on some distant occasion in the past. In the attic, as it was then called, long before Sam had the top floor turned into a flat for her own use.

'You know very well that me and Julie have stayed there on occasions. Up in the attic. And no, before you tell me about it for the umpteenth time, neither of us have ever seen or heard anything spooky up there. Or anywhere else in the house, for that matter. We've obviously not got your sixth sense for these things. If I didn't know you better, I'd say you've been talking to Hilary's new friend, Pauline, putting ideas in her head. Hilary thinks she's psychic.'

Mater didn't know who I meant. Pauline was a new one on her. 'All I'm saying is it's an old place,' she insisted. 'And old places have a way of telling you things whether you want to hear about them or not. They talk, you know, don't just take my word for it.'

'I've not heard Samantha complain about anything yet,' I pointed out. 'She's been living up in the attic for a while now.' Not that she was likely to have taken her uncle into her confidence about it, mind.

'I'm just telling you, that's all,' Mater insisted. 'I've never mentioned it to Samantha. I wouldn't tell her anyway. She doesn't want to hear her gran telling her stories like that.' It didn't stop her from asking me which part of the house I'd be sleeping in. As if I already knew!

'All I know is I won't be sleeping with Sam in the attic, will I?' Not unless she invited me, of course.

I found one of Mater's bosom pals on the doorstep as I took my leave. Margaret, I presumed. A tall angular specimen with a handbag and a hairy chin. 'You must be Adam,' she beamed. 'I'm not intruding, am I? Is Alice at home?'

Alice? For a moment there I had to remind myself that Mater led a whole separate life of her own, one I knew precious little about, under a name I didn't use, a name I seldom heard. 'It's someone asking for Alice,' I shouted into the house.

On this occasion I didn't doubt Alice would hear me perfectly.

PART **2**

FOUR

MRS VERITY

Two trips into town with Hilary in the same week, it had to be a record. That's what I told myself as I put the phone down. And to think we'd been leading such totally separate lives, the two of us. What on earth was going on?

She'd called to tell me the estate agent had been in touch. They couldn't proceed with the sale of the farm, apparently. Not until the contents of a letter they'd received had been discussed. What letter was that? They wouldn't discuss it with her over the phone. They wanted her to drop into the office. And Hilary wanted *me* to go along with her again. And since we were family, and since I had nothing else planned for the day, I felt I didn't have much choice.

Hilary had had her car looked at and put right. Now here she was on my doorstep, hair up and dressed in the same outfit as before, ready to give me a lift. If I'd been asked for my honest opinion back at Lily's place, I would, as you know, have advised caution before instructing an agent to sell. But, hey, Hilary being

Hilary, she'd gone ahead and put it on the market, regardless. Without considering there could be setbacks. Without thinking of a possible legal challenge, say. Or a letter from an aggrieved party. Ted Shimwell up in arms, for example.

Hilary thought it unlikely to be anything to do with Ted.

I wasn't so sure. 'Hasn't Ted a right to be worried about how he'll go on with grazing his animals?'

Hilary doubted Ted would want to make a fuss about it, not in a letter at any rate. From what she knew of him, he was the sort of guy who preferred to speak his mind to your face. His missus, on the other hand, might be something else entirely. She could have advised him to hire a lawyer. 'Do you know, Adam, it's got me all worked up has this business with the farm. That's why I asked you along.' I helped keep her calm, apparently, in the face of life's slings and arrows.

'Watch this guy on the bike!'

I can be a nervous front seat passenger at the best of times. Driving in traffic wasn't normally a problem with Hilary, let me say, but she did have a habit of taking her eyes off the road and looking my way whenever she wanted my agreement or my attention.

We were greeted by Mr Sharp himself, partner and smart older man in a suit who led us over to a desk and comfortable seats for us all in a corner of the open-plan area where details of a range of properties were on display. Once seated, he informed us there was this small matter of a letter he had received by fax first thing that morning and which he proceeded to take from his desk and pass to Hilary to read. In no time at all she'd passed it on to me and sat waiting for me to digest its contents and pronounce on their significance.

Actually, the letter was quite brief. From Messrs Brownlow, Bush and Pugh, a firm of solicitors with an address in the city, who pointed out that the house, adjacent buildings, and the not inconsiderable acreage of land attached to it and known in its entirety as Foolsmeadow Grange could not be sold with vacant possession as their clients, Ms Samantha Pope and partner Mr Luke Beresford, enjoyed a right of tenancy thereto and would assert their right in a court of law if necessary.

Well, as you can imagine, Hilary put a very concerned look on her face with which to browbeat the aforementioned Mr Sharp. 'A tenancy?' she queried. 'What are they on about? I've never signed any tenancy agreement, have I, Adam?'

Well, not according to what she'd told Ernest Bower, as I recalled. I knew he had made the point to her that, in the event of a tenancy agreement having been signed, she could not expect to go ahead and sell, at least not with vacant possession. Hilary had insisted then that she'd signed no such document. So, she now put it to both Mr Sharp and me, shouldn't the person claiming there *was* a tenancy agreement be expected to show some proof of its existence? Produce a signed copy or something? Had such a copy come to light, I enquired of the man in the suit? As if I was the half of this vending duo who knew precisely what was kosher and what wasn't.

Mr Sharp looked at me for a moment before turning his head in Hilary's direction. 'I'm afraid, Mrs Pope,' he declared, 'that because of the uncertainty of the situation in this particular case, I have to decline your instruction to put the farm on the market. At least for the time being. I simply cannot ignore the letter, as I'm sure you understand.'

It seemed it was Mrs Pope's word against the word of her daughter. I put my question again to the man behind the desk, only for Hilary to intervene before he could begin to answer. 'What my brother is trying to tell you is that it takes two to make an agreement. Or at least it always has done in my experience. Anyone can pretend they have a tenancy but producing evidence for it is something else.'

Mr Sharp's upper lip stiffened as he nodded towards the letter now back on his desk. 'No solicitor is going to threaten court action without having sufficient and genuine grounds to proceed,' he pointed out.

I sat up tall in my chair at that and adopted a suitably authoritative tone. 'Are you saying my sister must have signed an agreement, whether she remembers or not?' My *sister*, notice. We siblings stick together, sort of thing.

'I'm not suggesting anything of the kind, Mister…'

'Goodman,' I obliged. And added, 'It sounds very much to me as if that's precisely what you are suggesting, Mister Sharp.' I'd not forgotten *his* name, you see. 'And I'm disappointed, to say the least, with the manner in which you are as good as telling Mrs Pope she is not being straight with you.' Lying, in other words. I caught Hilary's nod of approval at my side.

'Mr Goodman, sir.' The man switched his gaze back from me to Hilary. 'And Mrs Pope. It's not a case, I assure you both, of doubting your word. This firm acts in absolute good faith in taking instructions from clients regarding the sale of their property. Without the letter and its reference to a tenancy agreement, there would be no problem whatsoever in offering the farm for sale with vacant possession. However, as I've already made clear, I cannot simply ignore the claim, coming as it does from a firm of solicitors for whom I have the highest regard. That would be irresponsible of me. Negligent even.'

Hilary looked dumbfounded. I'd not seen her look like that since the day Sam rushed indoors and told her one of the cows had pissed all over her foot – the first time she'd heard Sam use that word, she told me afterwards. You had to hand it to this guy. However obnoxious, he stood his ground on what for him clearly represented a point of principle.

I cleared my throat and dropped my voice to a level consistent with the need to ask this guy a small favour. 'Given the circumstances,' I put it to him, 'and the position you say the letter leaves you in, what, may I ask, would be your advice to Mrs Pope?'

No need for him to have to think about this one. 'I'd see a solicitor. Put it in his hands. And get the matter cleared up. The sooner the better.'

*

Outside in the street I reminded Hilary she was under no obligation to take the man's advice. Then kind of implied the advice did make a lot of sense. Okay, I conceded, a fee would be involved, whichever firm of solicitors she chose to consult. Perhaps best, I suggested, if she gave herself time to think this whole thing through and put the sale on hold meanwhile. Till after she got back from Scotland, certainly. Better still, till after my new term started. By then, perhaps, she might learn the tenancy was all a hoax or something, and the sale, if she still insisted, could go ahead. By then, too, my family would be back in harness, and I could make out I was simply too busy with my own affairs to be of further assistance. Julie would see to that, anyway.

'I hear what you say, Adam, but that's not my way. Let's try Barker's instead.'

Why did I bother? Barker's – or Barker Liddell, as they were now known – had a branch a couple of streets away, and we took off in that direction. On the way I did what I could to highlight the strong likelihood that they, too, in their turn, would receive an identical letter the minute they put the farm up for sale. Sure as flies settle on cow pats, I pointed out.

Hilary wasn't listening. If ever an occasion required divine intervention, a blinding light on the Damascus road, an epiphany of some sort, this had to be it, I reckoned. This is where I must have come close to shutting my eyes and, if I'm honest, close to praying we wouldn't make it to BL's door. I guess somebody up there heard me, for ahead of me next minute I saw Hilary stumble. Her heel gave way, got caught in a crack in the pavement, or something. She wobbled for a moment, struggling to keep her balance, then fell over with a clatter and a groan, in full view of dozens of shoppers and probably not a few CCTV cameras covering that part of the street.

Unbelievable. One minute she was on her feet, in full stride, the next a couple of passers-by were hoisting her upright again and demanding to know if she was all right when even *I* could see she wasn't in control of her legs and kept buckling at the knees. Short of telling everyone I was a doctor, I hastened to assume command. She'd gone over on one ankle and looked quite shaken. I suggested – and Hilary agreed – that we needed to sit her down, catch our breath, and assess the situation, and the best place on hand to do that was the nearest shop which happened to be Vee's Footwear. Inside, as you'd expect of a shoe shop, they had chairs and footrests, not a single one in use, as it happened, so not a problem for Hilary to park herself in reasonable comfort with the offending foot off the ground.

The young female assistant soon realised we weren't there to try on shoes. This was an emergency, she could see. A case of a woman with a now painfully swelling ankle who wouldn't say no to a glass of water, or even a cup of tea. Meanwhile, I bent to examine the joint in question for a sign of anything broken.

I won't deny I felt relieved to find none. Doubly relieved, if I'm honest, that we hadn't made it as far as Barker Liddell's office. But somewhat chastened, as you can imagine, by the promptness with which my supplication had been answered. Be careful what you wish for, don't they say?

It appears we weren't done yet with the hand of fate that morning. Hard on the heels (if you'll forgive the pun) of Hilary's stumble, came one of those coincidences that only happen in real life, never in fiction, you'll have noticed. A woman walked into the shop and introduced herself to us, after a brief word with our young assistant, as Mrs Verity, the manageress. That's right, *Mrs Verity*. Definitely the name she gave. I didn't mishear her. 'I'm the person in charge. Mrs Gertrude Verity,' she announced. 'Everyone calls me Trudi. Is there anything I can do to help? Call you an ambulance perhaps? Or a taxi?'

It was pretty obvious the woman was in charge. The way she spoke, the brisk manner, the head held high on a slender neck, the merest glance in our direction, her young assistant's readiness to defer – what else could she have been? She brought authority with her the minute she walked in. She could have been a fellow teacher as far as I was concerned, calmly greeting her class. She certainly had *my* attention.

Only *who* was she exactly? With a name like that, was I gazing at GV's mother? And if she wasn't his mother, was she related in some way? Curiously (you must have noticed it too), she had the same initials, GV, as my erstwhile student. And she had the looks that Mo had found so strikingly attractive in the woman called Marti, you'll recall. A young man of sound observation, Mo, I thought. I wondered how plausible it was for a town the size of Willsborough to house several different families with the name Verity. The phone book would settle it, one way or the other. Maybe they were all from the same good-looking extended family, the lot of them.

'You'll have to excuse my brother,' I heard Hilary tell the woman. 'He doesn't usually stare at people like that. Not in my company anyway. He probably feels he's seen you somewhere before. Take no notice.'

'I was about to say how sorry we are, actually,' I explained, 'for putting you both – you and your assistant, that is – to so much trouble. We'll be on our way shortly. I hope you don't mind.' I wasn't usually this apologetic, but never mind, the woman was giving me a reassuring smile.

'It's no trouble, I assure you,' she told me. 'I've nearly fallen over in the street myself a time or two, so I know what it's like, how much it can shake you up.'

Really? I couldn't picture this woman falling over, she had such poise, such presence. Well, maybe I could if I tried. Women like her kept their cool and their balance in my experience. Yet if she *was* GV's mother, she must have experienced her share of serious grief and upset recently and, to judge by appearances, had managed to come through it looking remarkably unscathed. With the help of a supportive *Mister* Verity, presumably. And what did *he* look like, I wondered.

The woman leaned forward to take a look for herself at Hilary's ankle. 'Would you like me to call you an ambulance?' she suggested. 'It does look awfully painful. It could be broken, you know.'

Hilary flapped an arm in protest. 'It's nothing serious,' she insisted. 'I'm pretty sure it's not broken. I've suffered worse falling out of bed. I've sprained it, that's all. We'll be moving on very soon, if that's all right.' Just as soon as my brother here can take his eyes off you and sort out some transport for me, she meant.

'Some ice would be useful,' I suggested. 'I don't suppose you'd have any, by any chance?'

Like shoe shops made a point of stocking ice these days. The woman still hadn't straightened up and I had a close view of her beautifully arched torso, noting she was not exactly on her knees but had her head down, her hair done up and held in place by an oversize comb or grip, you know the sort of device some women use. It exposed the nape of her neck, and the olive hue of the skin there. When she eventually stood up straight, we came face to face for a moment before she turned to speak to her assistant. 'Lucy, would you nip across and see if Mr Marchant has any?'

'Ice, do you mean?'

Lucy took the absence of a reply to mean yes and disappeared into the street. Mrs Verity meanwhile headed towards the back of the shop. 'I'll see what we have in the First Aid cupboard. We should have a roll of bandage to bind that ankle up for you. And I'll put the kettle on. A cup of tea would be welcome, don't you think?'

'I'm putting you to an awful lot of trouble,' Hilary protested.

My thoughts, too, but meanwhile I was struggling to spot a trace of GV's face in those features of hers and not having much success, frankly. No sign in her eyes, either, to indicate she might know me from college, for instance. From one of our Open Days, perhaps, where she might have accompanied GV on a tour of the place and spotted me hanging about. I imagined I would remember if I'd spotted *her*.

By the time Lucy returned with a bag of ice cubes, the resourceful Mrs V had not only bandaged Hilary's ankle but brought us both a mug of tea. Lucy wasn't alone coming through the door, as it happened; close behind her came the last person I wanted to see joining us at the shop. She seemed to be turning up everywhere lately. No prizes for guessing it was the ubiquitous Mrs K. It seemed you couldn't fall over in town these days without the Kendrick woman knowing about it. And if it was my sister doing the falling, well, I mean, her new friend *was* reputed to be psychic after all, wasn't she?

'Hil! Good grief, Hil! What on earth have you done to yourself?'

She'd been in Marchant's, apparently, when Lucy dropped in to ask for ice. She'd come straight over. I'd say Marchant was the local fishmonger, judging by the smell from the bag Mrs K brought in with her, though I could have been doing the guy a disservice, I guess, and picking up Mrs K's very own eau-de-Pauline.

Something else to ponder: Mrs K and Mrs V appeared to be on cosy first name terms, like they knew each other from way back. Consider Mrs Verity's greeting. 'Oh, thank you ever so much, Pauline, for dropping in. You know this lady, don't you? She's given her ankle a nasty sprain. Fell over on the pavement outside. I've just finished binding it up for her and was about to suggest ringing for a taxi to take her home.'

Lucy, I noticed, still had the bag of ice cubes in her hand, in two minds what to do with it till her boss reached out and took it from her.

Mrs K's turn to take a closer look at Hilary's ankle. 'My, you've done a good job there, Trude, binding it up like that. Can't fault you there, luv.' She straightened up. 'This is Hilary Pope, Trude, from the farm. She works with me at the shop. Surely you two must have met. And this is her brother, Adam. He's one of the good guys.'

I acknowledged the compliment with a nod, thinking, *please God, why oh why couldn't my sister have taken up with someone like Mrs V, someone with class, instead of this overweight clown? Surely you two must have met, Mrs K had said. If only!*

I heard Mrs K go on to list more of my virtues. 'He teaches at the local college. And he's a useful man to have around,' she added. 'I have him to thank for rescuing me the other night when I crashed my car. Not only that,' she went on. 'Adam was Gordon's tutor, you know. Yes, it's true. He looked after your Gordon's welfare. Couldn't have been in better hands, though I say it myself.'

I saw Mrs V's eyebrows go up, and her lips part slightly, in what I took to be mild surprise. So here stood the man, I could have told her, who mislaid your son's written work, that journal of his you wanted returned and which I still have at home, believe it or not, and would be only too pleased to hand over to you, just say the word. She smiled, as if at the thought, and declared herself pleased to make my acquaintance. But that was as far as it went. She had a taxi to order. If Mrs Pope could manage to stand.

Mrs K had a proposition of her own. 'No need for a taxi, Trude. I'll run these two home myself.'

The merry gang of three together again. How cosy! To her credit Hilary protested. 'Adam here will run me home. He's perfectly capable of driving my car. Aren't you, Adam?'

Her friend wasn't having it. 'Nonsense, Hil!' She shook her

head, and I had the impression a few other parts of her joined in. 'My car is parked close by. Practically on the doorstep.'

The doorbell tinkled at that point and a white-haired man walked in, followed by a white-haired woman, each feeling their way with a stick. They stopped in their tracks by the door, looking as if they'd stumbled into a hospital ward or something. Customers at last. Lucy dutifully went to their assistance. That's when between us, Mrs K on one side, me steadying her on the other, we managed, after two attempts, to raise Hilary to her feet and keep her there.

Meanwhile Mrs V disappeared into the rear of the shop and emerged with a stick of her own. For Hilary's use, she insisted. To be returned at Hilary's convenience.

On her way out, Hilary hinted she might drop in and buy a pair of shoes for herself next time she was in town. To repay her debt, right? And return the stick, she promised. I wanted to suggest doing the same thing myself but didn't know if I'd go so far as to buy any shoes. There was the other matter to raise, now I knew this woman was GV's mother. Far more important, if you ask me.

*

Practically on the doorstep, did she say? By my calculation Mrs K's Mini was parked much further away than the multi-storey where Hilary had left the Ford.

It fell to me, having seen Hilary safely to a front seat in the Mini, to collect her car and drive it back to Foolsmeadow for her. That gave me plenty of time to reflect on the morning's events. On the role providence had played, for instance, in bringing us face to face with Mrs V. Such an attractive woman, too. In my experience there weren't that many good-looking women in and around Willsborough, and it was just possible, I dare say, they all belonged to the same family. Only one answered to the name

Gertrude, though, I felt certain. Not a common name at the time.

Not surprisingly, I got to wondering how valuable GV's journal actually was to this woman. Soon I was asking myself to what lengths she might be prepared to go in order to recover it. Innocent enough, surely? For all I knew, she could have given up on ever getting it back since I'd told JR I didn't have it. Should I give her a clue? Let her know I'd found it? Offer to hand it over? The idea set me thinking. About my options, I mean:

As already suggested, I could return to the shop. On my own. While everyone, including Hilary, was away. Ostensibly, to try on some shoes, I didn't have to buy any. We'd get chatting, the two of us, reminiscing about GV, and I'd ask her if she'd ever answered to the name of Marti. Explain my sources. Move on to the subject of the journal. Quote bits from it. Whet her appetite for more, sort of thing. Any good? Hmm, not certain. Maybe not the ideal surroundings, a shoe shop, eh?

I could ask Mrs K to let the woman know I'd located her son's missing written work, and did she want me to drop by and hand it over, preferably just before closing time. Fine, except I could see Mrs K offering to hand the work over for me. Not really what I wanted. Forget it.

I could make enquiries about worshipping at the Sahara Street church (assuming the woman did actually attend meetings there). Ask my niece to put my name forward for trial membership, claiming I needed to mend my ways, make better friends, that sort of thing. Sam would think I was having a laugh, and who could blame her? A non-starter then? I think so.

No Option 4 as yet. But I'd keep working on it. I had plenty of time. Where there's a Verity, there's a way, if you like. And as Trudi was such an attractive woman, odds were likely a *Mister* V lurked not far away. At what point, I wondered, would I come face to face with *him*.

*

I arrived at Foolsmeadow to find my way into the yard obstructed by the entrance gate, which stood partially closed. On either side of it, facing each other, stood two figures who appeared to be engaged in some sort of argument. I let the window down and found I'd interrupted a heated exchange between Steve on the one hand and Sam's boyfriend on the other. I took it Steve had come to see Hilary, though whether she'd arrived back yet wasn't clear. He beckoned me to join him. 'Adam, I'm glad you're here, mate. Just come and take a look at this, will you?'

Since neither of them seemed keen to push the gate open wide enough for a vehicle to pass, I got out of the car, expecting I was about to be drawn into Steve's side of this argument. He certainly looked redder in the face than usual. Something had got him wound up and I dare say the look he was getting from Luke didn't help. Luke was larger and heavier than I'd realised. I'd only seen him up a ladder, remember, and not up close. You wouldn't call Steve's build slight, but next to the younger guy he looked – what shall I say? – somewhat out of shape, and definitely out of his class. Luke had the build of a guy I for one would not choose to pick a fight with. I fancied I was about to be cast in the role of accessory, manager, chief supporter, or similar, as both men stood eying each other, Steve with a screwdriver in his hand, Luke with a toolbox at his feet.

Steve pointed to a metal postbox, newly bolted to the bars of the gate. 'He's just fixed that on there. On the gate. Today. While Hilary was out. What do you make of *that*?'

Personally, I thought it would save the postman a walk to the door. I could see the box was lockable but for reasons of clarification I asked if it locked.

'That's the whole idea!' Steve explained. Rather sharply, I thought. Like he thought I might be missing the point. 'Hilary doesn't have a key to it. She won't be able to get at her mail.'

I turned to Luke. 'You've got a spare key for Mrs Pope's use, haven't you?' My classroom technique in action, for your information – you look your student in the eye when you talk to him and always have something pertinent and polite to say, however ugly the situation. 'She's obviously going to need one, isn't she?'

Luke looked back at me as if it might be a trick question before eventually nodding.

'That's not all, Adam. What about this?' Steve pointed to an intercom panel newly fixed to one of the gate posts.

'Is that what I think it is?' I queried. I confess I hadn't noticed it before.

Steve confirmed it was indeed an intercom. But one that didn't connect to Hilary's part of the house, he explained to me. 'When it's all connected up, mate, it will operate a lock, see, so the gate can be opened. Except Hilary won't be able to open it. How fucking clever is that!'

Luke intervened. 'It isn't wired up,' he pointed out.

'That's because I didn't give you the chance to finish the fucking job,' Steve barked at him.

I did my best to defuse the situation.by asking if we could get the gate opened up fully meanwhile, so I could park Hilary's car in the yard. Whereupon Luke decided that was Steve's responsibility and began walking back into the yard, taking his toolbox with him.

'Don't forget what I told you,' Steve called out after him. 'If these fucking things aren't gone next time I'm here, I'll be removing them myself. You'd better believe it, sonny.'

Luke's reply didn't sound polite, if I'm honest. Steve must have heard it and, before I could advise against it, ran after him. And stopped. Abruptly. Struck squarely amidships, I saw, by the toolbox which Luke swung by its handle like a ball and chain so that it dealt Steve a visibly low blow, one which, from where I was standing, looked like it could disable a man for days.

I believe I might have remained rooted to the spot in some shock myself but for the timely arrival on the scene, waddling from the direction of Hilary's kitchen, of that woman again. An indication, obviously, that she and Hilary *were* back before me, the pair of them. And now the lollipop lady was intent on sorting out the men from the boys. I heard Steve give a gasp and shout, 'You brainless fucker!' as Luke stood his ground. Before further insults or blows could be traded, Mrs K stepped firmly between them. 'What the hell is it with you two?' she demanded to know.

Steve, it turned out, had not just run after Luke. He'd thrown something at him. The screwdriver, apparently, which now lay in the dirt at Mrs K's feet.

I believe I did what most men would do in the circumstances. I winced in sympathy as I asked Steve if he was okay. In fact, the blow from the toolbox didn't appear to have made the intended contact. He'd fended it off with his arm, he told us, and made a point of demonstrating to us that the arm still functioned as it should, and it would take more than a blow from a toolbox to put him out of action.

Luke meanwhile had picked up the screwdriver and, still holding the toolbox by his side, walked off without a word.

'I was just showing Adam here what our friend has been up to with his fancy DIY skills,' Steve explained. 'He didn't take kindly to me telling him to remove them. Got physical about it. Picked on the wrong guy, though.'

'So I see.'

Did I imagine it or did Mrs K give me a surreptitious wink before she waddled off back to the kitchen? As I climbed into the Ford, Steve turned to me with a rebuke. 'I hear you've been trying to sabotage my holiday plans,' he said. 'Pushing your sister over in the street like that. I've heard all about it. Lucky for you, mate, she's not broken any bones. That's set us up for a fine start, I must say.'

I don't recollect I had an answer. They'd either go to Scotland, or they wouldn't, simple as that. Their call.

THE HORSE'S MOUTH

Hilary's kitchen didn't hold many people at the best of times. Today it seemed positively full, with four of us inside it, and on this occasion only three available chairs. Seeing my plight as the last person in, Hilary freed up the chair on which she'd rested her ankle and got Mrs K to find me a mug and pour me some tea.

'Mine's cold,' said Steve. 'Can I have another one, Pauline? It's thirsty work out there, you know, keeping the villains at bay.'

'How's your old man?' I asked him. Well, it was the first time I'd had occasion to enquire since our session in the Carpenter's Arms. He was fine, apparently; fit as a fiddle once again. Would outlast me if I wasn't careful. When I asked Hilary, having dropped her car keys into her hand, how her ankle was, she pursed her lips and shook her head. 'That bad, is it?' I commented. 'You'll not be off to Scotland in a hurry then?'

'And it's all your fault,' said Steve. 'She would have been fine if she'd been with me. Some of us know how to look after a woman when we take her out.'

'It won't stop me from sitting in the passenger seat,' Hilary pointed out. 'You don't need two good ankles for that. I was okay in Pauline's car. Wasn't I, Pauline?'

Mrs K nodded from where she stood over the kettle.

Steve nodded as well. 'I'm sure you're right, Hilary. Just say the word and I'll bring the Landy to the door. Fitted with a stairlift, if that's what it takes. You know me.'

Mrs K started pouring tea and suggested, as she did so, that a tour of Scotland would not be complete without a visit to Edinburgh Castle. She and Boyd had visited the place one year. A long time ago, mind. Before Boyd fell ill.

'That can be arranged,' said Steve. 'If that's what we fancy doing. That's right, Hilary, isn't it?'

When I asked him if he fancied giving me a lift home, he told me Pauline had volunteered for that job. 'I offered to do it, mate, honest. But Pauline wouldn't hear of it. She insisted. She's like that, you know. Once she's got her mind set on something, there's no changing it. I'd go along with it if I were you. It sounds a generous offer to me.'

Did I have a choice? I took a sip of Mrs K's tea and resigned myself to the prospect of a lift in the Mini with a woman twice my size at the wheel. I'd started to wonder how I'd cope when a fresh sighting of Luke took our combined attention. Hilary pointed him out. 'There he goes, look. What's he up to now?'

We watched as he carried his ladder from one outbuilding to the door of another.

'Did you see the way the bugger glowered at me, Adam?' Steve wanted my opinion, clearly, as the leading eyewitness to their encounter. 'He wasn't prepared to take no for an answer, was he?'

'You weren't exactly extending the arm of friendship to him, now, were you? Not that I saw very much, mind. It was practically over by the time I arrived.'

Okay, Steve expected more of me than that. 'Seriously, Adam, don't you think he should at least have had enough about him to ask your sister's permission before fixing those things to the gate? A bit of common courtesy, I mean. Who does he think he is?'

Hilary wasn't sure, when I put to her, if she'd been consulted beforehand or not. She believed Sam could have mentioned it to her. But she'd had a lot going through her head lately, and if Sam *had* mentioned it, she'd taken it to be a *suggestion* and nothing more. Something to be discussed in more detail at a later date and not something she expected to come home to find had been done behind her back.

'Sly, that, Adam, don't you think?' said Steve.

That's when Mrs K gave me another knowing look over Steve's head, like I needed reminding how Steve had sorted it out all by himself.

After I'd finished my tea, I stepped outside for a smoke and a breath of air. To be honest, I expected Mrs K to take the hint and announce that she, too, had to be moving and she'd drop me off on the way back to town. But she evidently preferred to hang on in the kitchen, and didn't even seem to need a cigarette herself, either.

Once outside I got to thinking Luke might reappear and give me an opportunity to talk to him. As his girlfriend's uncle, let's say. I could ask him about Sahara Street, where they held their meetings, and how often. I could show some interest in the work he was doing to improve the place. I could even mention that I'd be moving in soon to look after the farm while Mrs Pope was away. Nothing confrontational, just a friendly chat between sensible grown-ups.

I wondered if he smoked or took drugs, and decided no, he didn't, Sahara Street would have seen to that. Mister Bartholomew would not have approved. Nor would Sam, come to think of it.

The yard remained deserted. I assumed Luke had to be in one of the outbuildings, putting his ladder or his toolbox away or something. Watching me, even, as I picked my way across the yard, making for the gap that divided the buildings, an archway that gave access to open fields beyond. Quite a time since I'd walked through here, if my memory served. At one time Philip used to park his tractor under the arch. It had also once been a regular thoroughfare for Philip's cows to tread their way to and from the milking parlour. Cowshit alley, as Sam had once been heard to call it. When she was still young enough to be reprimanded.

It was clear no cows had walked this route lately. The ground was hard and dusty. When I emerged at the other end of the arch and looked to left and right, I found myself looking down the length of a building that hadn't changed a bit over the years. No change I could see, anyway. Whatever repair work Luke had done, clearly, he hadn't done it here. No pointing, no replacement of window frames, no realignment of the guttering. If I'm sounding pretty technical here, that's because my neighbour had recently been doing precisely this sort of work on his property and had spoken of it to me over the garden fence, the way neighbours do, at considerable length in his case.

So, where was Luke when he wasn't up a ladder or bolting a letterbox to the gate? Maybe he was taking a break himself, up there, on his own, in Sam's flat. Instinctively, as I turned to retrace my steps through the archway and finish the last of my cigarette, I glanced up at Sam's attic window. It was the only window of hers that looked out over the yard. Quite a viewpoint, as I recalled.

Anyway, that's where I was looking when I saw someone looking back at me. It had to be Luke's face at the window. Except it wasn't Luke, I'd seen his face from close quarters, remember, at the gate, only a short time earlier. This was a woman's face. But it wasn't Sam. I'd recognise my niece behind glass, believe me. And Sam wasn't due back from work for a few more hours, and to confirm the point, I could see that her little Fiat wasn't among the cars parked in the yard.

So, who could it be? Well, three possibilities came to mind. (1) Luke had a friend up there with him. A woman friend. One who visited him when Sam was at work. Not a noble thought, I know, and one I promptly dismissed as unworthy of me. I'd not yet had a chance to get to know my niece's boyfriend properly. (2) Sam and Luke between them had a house guest I'd not been told about. A perfectly innocent party simply admiring the view or curious to know who I was. Or (3) I was looking at the face of the presence that Mater believed haunted the attic.

Well, whoever it belonged to, the face soon got sick of looking at me and turned away before vanishing from sight. Not a ghost after all then, as don't they simply fade into the stonework? Someone, I decided, was up there, and that person was real enough as far as I was concerned. So, what now? So nothing, I decided, and continued making my way back to the kitchen door. I could have been imagining things and decided I probably hadn't seen a face at the window at all, merely a reflection on the glass. Not likely to be of much interest then to the trio in the kitchen.

I considered it best not to say a word. Maybe I'd get the chance to put it to Sam later. Maybe, like I said, she had someone else from Sahara Street sharing the flat with her. Luke's mother, perhaps? Luke's sister? There was bound to be a simple explanation. That's what rational people maintain, isn't it? Regardless of what their mothers or their sister's psychic friends have to say on the subject.

*

What can I tell you about the lift home? You can imagine it, can't you, me and Mrs K squeezed side by side into that tiny Mini of hers? You couldn't have found a tighter space for two adults to be together without people talking. It made my Astra seem downright roomy, and positively respectable. A Mini, I've always maintained, is not a proper car for two grown-ups to travel in. Not side by side. I should have sat in the back. Or walked.

For a time, we travelled in silence. Enough time, let's say, for it to become obvious to me that my right leg got in the way of this woman's left arm every time she reached for the gear stick. Another thing: I hardly dared look her way (in the line of polite conversation, I mean) without becoming aware of significantly more cleavage on display than had been the case in Hilary's kitchen. We're talking about a big woman here, remember. She must have discarded whatever top she'd been wearing, as I'm positive the goods weren't nearly so visible across Hilary's table. In addition, as the car's interior warmed up and the air inside circulated, the mix of aromas began to become more noticeably toxic, and I found myself trying to breathe more slowly, or not breathe at all.

'You all right there, are you?' she wanted to know after a while.

I heard myself pretend everything was fine. Short of telling her to stop and let me out, there was nothing I could do, come on. When she fished a cigarette packet from somewhere and started flicking the top open, however, I did start to cough rather loudly. She got the message. 'Just checking I've still got some left,' she told me. 'I should have joined you in the yard, shouldn't I?' Now she tells me! She put the packet away again. 'Filthy habit. I keep promising Boyd that I'll give it up. One of these days. You know how it is. We smokers, eh? No willpower to speak of, any of us, have we? Could save ourselves a bleeding fortune if we put our minds to it.'

The Mini's ash tray, I saw, was crammed full of cigarette butts. All hers, presumably, unless Boyd used lipstick too. Hilary, I must have mentioned, didn't smoke at all, so couldn't have contributed to the state of the ash tray, and *I* most certainly wasn't inclined to add to the mess, no smoking in the car being my rule, as you know. The secret of safe and sane car travel with this woman, I felt, was to refrain from bad habits (like smoking) while keeping my eyes *off* the road and my nostrils as inactive as possible. Pretend you're elsewhere. Make out you're asleep.

The woman must have read my thoughts because she started talking about how Hil did the exact same thing when sitting beside her in the car. 'Don't you find some people are just nervous passengers, no matter who's driving?' she put it to me. 'Not surprising, though, is it, considering the number of mad drivers you come across on the roads these days. Lucy took her test the other week and a bleedin' truck ran into her. What a thing to happen to you on the day of your driving test, eh?'

Lucy? For a minute or two I had to think hard about who she meant. She saw my problem. 'You know, Trude's assistant, the girl who works for her in the shoe shop. Get with it, Adam! You saw her this morning, for Christ's sake. Lucy Hadley.'

Oh, *that* Lucy. Mrs Verity's Lucy. I perked up, not surprisingly, at that juncture, at the prospect of learning more. 'It didn't happen to Trude then?' I suggested, in a rather obviously facetious aside. Part of my roundabout way, I should make it clear, of raising the real issue that was on my mind. 'You and she are good friends, I noticed. Known her long, have you?'

It turned out they'd gone to school together. The shoe shop had been her father's, and Mrs V had taken it over after the old man died. He'd left her quite a bit of money too, she and her brother Lance being joint beneficiaries.

Naturally, I was curious to know if Trudi had got married, and if so, how come her married name was still Verity. Don't tell me the Verity family only married their own! I was poised to raise this point when my driver suddenly got distracted. 'What's that wanker behind us up to? Excuse my French, only I'm a bit choosy about the sort of bloke I want pushing me hard up my arse end.'

Now I don't know about you, but in the circumstances (tiny car, respectable male company, civilised line of conversation) this kind of outburst seemed out of place and uncalled for. I mean, did Mrs K make a habit of sounding off like this when she had Hilary in the car with her? I do realise that some women, when they are together, can get carried away, especially when referring to the menfolk they come across and their quirky habits. I make no claim to know how my sister behaves when I'm not with her, but did wonder if, in my place, she would have been shocked. I shot a sidelong glance for signs of realisation on Mrs K's part that she'd overstepped a line. But apart from a series of impatient sighs, grunts and hisses till the tailgating driver turned off down a side road, she seemed unaware of my concern.

'That business with that student of yours,' she resumed.

'Trude took that pretty badly, losing a member of the family like that. You'll know all about what happened, of course, with you being a teacher and all at the college. Christ, it shocked everybody, that little episode. Well, it would do, wouldn't it?'

Including *Mister* Verity? Did it shock *him*? I was convinced that any minute there'd be a mention of GV's father; I merely had to hang on in there and keep ignoring the road meanwhile.

'Mind you,' Mrs K continued, 'he was never the same – Gordon I'm talking about – after his mother was put away, you know.'

Okay, stop there a minute. *His mother was put away.* Were we still talking about Trudi? Had she, at some time or other, been detained somewhere, for her own safety? Was there more, in other words, to GV's mother than the glamorous image and money in the bank? Was she a crazy woman? A fruitcake? Likely to whip off one of her stilettos and slash you across the face with it if you got the wrong side of her, said something out of turn? Was she safe to be running a shoe shop in town?

Mrs K must have sensed the questions lining up in my head. 'You wouldn't know about *that*, of course you wouldn't. Yes, little Felix got very sick and died, and then her marriage went down the pan and she couldn't cope after that. That's when Trude, bless her, stepped in, or Gordon would have been taken into care. You're looking as if you've lost a tenner and found a tanner, Adam, if I can put it that way. Are you having a problem keeping up? Can't say as I blame you. It's a right arse-over-tit story.'

I believe I made clear that some clarification would not come amiss. Those Marti and Marcie characters came to mind as maybe having a certain relevance here, being rather more than a confused reference to the same mother figure. As for Felix, I'd not come across any mention of him yet in the journal, or else I had and not realised it.

Seeing my puzzlement, Mrs K sort of chuckled (gave an

asthmatic wheeze, more like, that set more than her cheeks wobbling, let me tell you). It evidently amused her that a man like me could be having a problem with the Verity line-up. 'You thought Trude was Gordon's mother, didn't you? No, that was Claire. Trude is Gordon's aunt. She took over, like I said, after Claire had a breakdown. Dreadful shitty business, but there you go, some of us crack up under the strain. Life can be a bummer, eh?'

Something like that. Of these two Verity women then, Claire and Trudi, I assumed Trudi was the one asking after GV's journal. Only I didn't say anything. I didn't want Mrs K to know about the journal. Not yet, at any rate, as I hadn't figured out what to do about it. I had to consider the possibility Trudi had lost interest in GV's work by now. I'd find out in due course, in my own way.

'At school,' Mrs K went on, 'Trude was always the bright one. I was crap, I really was. She was popular with the boys, too. Knew how to dress, what clothes to wear, what shoes. She put me in the shade, I can tell you.'

I think I'd worked that bit out for myself. Curiously enough, my mind was on Mrs V's choice of footwear when Mrs K started on about the age of the shoes on her feet. She'd read my mind again, evidently. 'Just look at them,' she said. Well, I couldn't, could I, not without leaning into the woman's lap for a better view, and that simply wasn't going to happen. 'What about them?' I asked.

'They're bloody awful, that's what! Fit for throwing. Boyd reckons I should put them on display at the shop and offer them for sale. Some poor bastard will buy them, he says.'

I so wanted to hear Boyd's views on his missus's footwear! I considered that if I suggested Mrs K made a deal with her friend Trude for some new shoes, we'd soon be back to talking about Mrs V. So I asked her. I said, 'Won't Trudi let you have some new shoes to replace the ones you're wearing?'

Heavens, no! The two of them never interfered in each

other's business, apparently. Never asked favours of each other. In any case, people were always donating their unwanted shoes to the charity shops these days, there were always plenty there to choose from. Now, if I cared to drop into the Cancer Research shop next time I was in town, Mrs K would be happy to sort me out a pair of nearly new size eights at a bargain price.

'You do take an eight, I'm guessing. You have quite small feet, don't you? I like men with small feet.'

Oh yeah. I refrained from telling her I like my women to be small in all departments, never mind their feet.

'You tosser!'

With a screech we'd pulled up at a crossing to let an elderly gent, an ex-military type in a blazer, wave his stick at us for not quite knocking him over.

'Did you see that? Not a clue which way to look. He's lucky I managed to stop in time. Could have been Lance's double, that one, mind. Looked just like him.'

Lance, I needed reminding, was Trude's brother. He'd married Claire, then abandoned her after their youngest child (Felix, she confirmed) took ill and died. He'd gone to Australia to make a new life for himself and hadn't been seen since. Wasn't Trudi married, I asked finally. Well, no, now I mentioned it, she wasn't. Trude had had an affair, many years ago. A brief fling, to use the jargon, and had a son to show for it. I was treated to the spectacle of Mrs K wagging a finger at me, like I'd asked her if I could put my hand on her knee.

'Trude,' she explained, 'is a very – how can I put this – she's a very private woman, always has been. Religious with it, too. You know what I mean? Doesn't like people knowing about her past, about her guilty secrets. There *was* this bloke, a long time ago. She doesn't like talking about it, not even to me. She never did marry, and I can't say I blame her. Not what it's cracked up to be, marriage, is it?'

I wasn't getting drawn into *that* argument. A bloke, eh? I

tried to picture the sort she would have found attractive but couldn't decide between a gamekeeper and a member of the local Liberal Party, being rubbish at this game, I confess. And meanwhile, I was missing more revelations about Lance and had to pretend the sound of the traffic had drowned out what was being said.

'I was just saying how Lance expected some sort of miracle cure for little Felix, and when it didn't happen that was the last straw for him. Faith healing, don't they call it? Not my scene, if I'm honest, or I'd have asked them to do something about my other half, wouldn't I? Know what I mean? If I'd been the religious type myself, I mean. *You're* not religious, are you?' She decided I wasn't and shook her head. 'I thought not. You're not the type. You're like me. Not into religion or any of that crap. Both feet on the ground. Boyd's the same. You'd enjoy meeting him.'

I didn't get the chance to reply. My stop, I realised, as the Mini pulled up at my gate. How about that? And I'd not even given the driver my home address. The woman was psychic, of course. Or she'd got my address off Hilary. At any rate, I was still in one piece! Albeit a stiff-jointed creaking piece as I struggled to extricate myself and stand upright on the pavement once again.

'I won't come in. Got to get back to the shop, you understand. No rest for the wicked, eh? See you soon,' was the woman's parting shot.

*

Had Mrs K, when all's said and done, given me any evidence to conclude that GV had good reason to do what he did? Being abandoned by *my* dad and seeing *my* mother lose her mind could have been enough to push *me* over the edge at that age, I dare say. On the other hand, I think having an Aunt Gertrude take over in Mater's place would have convinced *me* life was worth a few more rolls of the dice. Unless Aunt G turned out to be as much of a fruitcake as her sister-in-law, of course. One more victim of the Verity family curse, as you might say, a result of all that inbreeding. Would I find evidence in the journal that she'd made GV's life a misery, behaving more like the wicked stepmother than a glamorous aunt? I'm sceptical, to be honest. Whatever drove GV to the brink, I refused to believe it could be *her*. I remembered the walking stick she'd fetched out of the closet for Hilary to use and thought that was hardly the act of a mad bad crazy woman. Whatever else she was, Trudi Verity was not heartless. I was prepared to bet money on it.

How reliable was Mrs K's word about the Veritys, anyway? Put me on a witness stand and I'd feel bound to describe my source as *not necessarily* a trustworthy one. Okay, she'd known Mrs V from the time they were at school together, so she said. One way to find out how accurate her information was would be to cross-check some of it with the journal. Easier said than done, of course, when you factored in those unnumbered pages, along with GV's habit of encrypting people's names. Give me a tough crossword any day.

I kept wondering what age GV could have been when he first picked up his pen. He'd written about his mother Claire, so perhaps he'd written about Lance too. And Felix. And maybe a bit about Aunt G's bloke and whether he was a teacher or not. Because this stuff was new to me and hot off Mrs K's lips, so to speak, I felt I should at least do something to check its accuracy. It wasn't as if I had much else to occupy me for the rest of the day. I feared I'd soon forget what she'd told me if I did nothing.

Inevitably, out it came again, the folder and the bundle of loose pages I'd still to read. Okay, so Claire, aka Marcie, had already had a mention. She was (let me run with this for a minute) Ma C (for Claire) and Marti had to be Ma T (for Trudi). Get it? Working on the same principle, Lance had to be in there somewhere. Under D for dad, was it? Or F for father?

Or L for Lance? I felt I was, at last, beginning to get inside GV's head and imagined maybe that's what he'd always intended and that's why the journal had ended up in *my* hands. If anyone could decipher GV's shorthand, GMan could. With a new spirit of optimism and anticipation, I pulled a sheet at random from inside the pile. Rather like picking a card. Here's what I found:

> 'Boys should try and be nice to their mother, she used to say. Things were getting her down and she didn't want to hear about anyone else's problems. I can tell by the way she changes the subject. She's more interested in what we're having for tea. I wonder if she had problems when she was at school. I know she cries a lot when she thinks we're not looking, and even when we are, but she won't say what it's about. Says it's nothing. She phones people all the time and I hear her say It's only me a lot and Sorry to bother you and Not sure I can carry on.'

Sounds a lot like he could be referring to Marcie there, wouldn't you say? About the time she was starting to lose her marbles. But no clue as to how old GV might have been then, or how long he'd been putting pen to paper. No mention either of what Lance could have been up to. Perhaps he'd already packed and gone. Perhaps he wasn't going to get a mention at all, being a total turd in his son's eyes.

Somewhere else on the same page I spotted this:

> 'Winifred's been to see us again. She asks how things are. One time I overheard her telling Marcie how much they'd collected. That was after the funeral was over and everybody was being very kind. I remember wanting to ask her, why do some people die so young before they've hardly started out in life. I asked Marcie but she choked up and just wanted a hug. People said Winifred had been

> *healed of some illness she had when she joined SS, but they can't heal everything and everybody or the world would get too full of people. Disease is God's way of making sure there aren't too many of us living in the world and that seems pretty sensible to me only it's not much of a comfort for Marcie. If anybody needs healing, she does.'*

I'd say the funeral had to be Felix's. No idea who Winifred could be, but no prizes for guessing the meaning of SS. Still no mention of Lance. But wait a minute, this had to be him surely, lower down on the same page, a guy called *Pal*, what else? Pa L (for Lance), this is getting too easy, wouldn't you say?

> *'The call had to be from Pal, because Marcie went very white and shaky and nearly dropped the phone, she shook so much. PLEASE STOP CALLING HER. YOU'RE MAKING HER WORSE. CAN'T YOU SEE? He can't hear me say anything because I don't say it out loud, but anyone can see the way he upsets her. Whatever it is he's calling about Marcie doesn't say, but she comes off the phone in tears again and runs upstairs where we can't see her. But we can hear her, talking to herself like she does. I don't think Pal calls her intending to upset her. I just wish he'd come back, F as well. We all had such fun times together. It's like they BOTH OF THEM died and left the house feeling a lot emptier. It would be nice to have them come back so we could be a proper family again. Pal did say, "See you again soon" when he got in his car and drove off. I heard him.'*

Pal, eh? Was that also a comment on how close GV had been to his dad? If you ask me, GV had a sly sense of irony that for some reason hadn't manifested itself in my tutorials. Not within earshot, at any rate. Yet here it was, alive and well in these pages.

Hardly the observations of a would-be suicide, I thought. But then I was no psychologist, trained in spotting these things.

I searched through more pages after that in the hope of coming across the time when Marti took over from Marcie. No luck. I fell asleep in the end, and dreamt I was sifting through endless boxes of shoes. Not opening them, mind. Just checking the labels for size eights, and not finding any. Couldn't say whereabouts I was in this dream, but I do recollect all the labels bore the words Venus Footwear. I guess that answers the question.

FIVE

MOVING IN

A weekend went by before Hilary rang and told me she was going ahead with the holiday. The ankle wasn't going to stop her. She and Steve would be departing for Scotland the day after tomorrow, so would I move in, assuming I hadn't changed my mind, sometime during that afternoon or evenin g? I could pick up the key at Mater's. She would label it so as not to confuse Mater into handing me the wrong one when I called. Like Mater kept dozens of keys on rings about the house and, if they weren't labelled, got confused as to whose locks they fitted.

Mater's concern when I arrived was her washing machine. She couldn't get it to start. No good asking me to fix it, I told her, but I made a cursory check all the same to see if she'd plugged it in and switched it on, as she had been known to overlook this elementary step in the past. Sure enough, she'd switched on but not pushed the plug far enough into the wall socket. Couldn't reach it properly, she said. Too many things in the way.

'I suppose you've come for Hilary's keys. Now where did I put them?'

Them, mind. Like there was an entire set. She hobbled off to find them and I thought, seeing her fumble with several sets over by the corner cupboard, that maybe Hilary had a point in insisting on labelling hers. Dozens of people obviously left their keys here for safekeeping and collection.

As I've said before, we'd grown up together in this house, Hilary and me. We'd kept some of our toys in that same corner cupboard and accused each other many times of taking up too much space on the shelf we shared. As the older sibling I was expected to refrain from pushing my kid sister around. She was a girl, and boys don't behave like that towards girls. If this house had ghosts, they had to include me and Hilary running the length of its corridors, climbing in and out of its big-windowed rooms (the ground floor ones, obviously), huddling together in front of the living room fire on cold winter evenings, and talking to each other after lights out.

The toys had long since gone of course, but quite a few of our teenage possessions, I'd been reminded on occasions, lay unclaimed in some of the upstairs rooms. You know the sort of thing – school exercise books, artwork portfolios, collections of ancient vinyl singles and LPs, stuff nobody played any more – all the clutter of adolescence left behind in the flight from the nest. Downstairs a few framed photos of each of us, both looking impossibly young, still adorned the shelves and walls.

'There you are. She's labelled them for you. And left you a note.'

So she had. I warmed towards Mater. 'Do you want me to bring you some eggs while Hilary's away? There'll be plenty to spare.' Always generous with my sister's stuff, you'll notice.

'She's asked you to look after the hens, has she? It must be serious then, this holiday she's having with… what did you call him? How long will they be gone for? Has she said?'

'Steve. Nope, she hasn't. I don't think she knows herself.'

'Like that, is it?'

How long they'd be gone would depend on a number of things, I'd say. The weather for a start. Then there was that ankle. Oh, and how long before my sister started to miss her psychic friend's company. Plus, how long before the novelty wore off. The critical factor, this one. I gave the pair of them a week; ten days at most. In the meantime, according to the note, I was to consider myself at home in Hilary's part of the house, i.e. on floors one and two. Help myself to what food I could find and that included the eggs I collected. There was the TV to watch, the radio to listen to, the hi-fi to play. No reason at all for me to get bored.

I could entertain guests, too, if I wanted. With Sam and Luke free to come and go as they pleased I took it they'd likewise leave me to my own devices. Live and let live, sort of thing. Otherwise, there were no neighbours close enough to bother me, and in that respect Foolsmeadow represented the perfect hideaway. I could go into town at my leisure, pop into college if I wanted, browse in the library, do all the things I could do from home, more or less, including go out and buy myself a new pair of shoes if the inclination so took me.

I'd already decided to take the journal with me, expecting there'd be plenty of time to finish reading its pages. Plenty of time, too, to consider how best to sound out Mrs V's interest in its contents. Time, too, to consider whether my interest in Sahara Street extended to accompanying Sam and Luke to one of their meetings. Stranger things have happened, and in my experience these backstreet churches don't turn away new recruits. Okay, Sam might raise an eyebrow, but I could cope with that.

'You look lost,' Mater commented. 'What will you do with yourself all day out there? You're not exactly any good at farming, are you? It's a long way out of town, you know.'

'Don't worry about me,' I assured her. 'I can always do some research into the history of the place. Go look round the local church. Visit Philip's grave.' Stretching credulity somewhat, but you never know. 'Pass the time of day with the locals. Meet up with Ted Shimwell again. Trust me, I'll be spoilt for choice.' Not very convincing perhaps, but never mind.

'Don't forget you'll have those hens to look after. You don't want your sister coming home to find the fox has had the lot.' As if! Then out she came with the inevitable sooner-you-than-me routine. 'Hilary doesn't expect you to sleep in that house on your own, does she?'

'Well, she hasn't provided me with a sleeping partner, as far as I'm aware. And anyway, if Hilary can sleep there on her own, I'm sure I can do the same. I sleep on my own at home. What's the difference?'

I know, my house didn't harbour a presence in the attic, that was the difference. Mater gave me the eye. 'Don't come the innocent with me. You know what I'm talking about. You be careful, mind, don't go setting the place alight. With your cigarettes, I mean.'

'Isn't it time you got smoke alarms fitted in here?' Two could play this game.

'I don't smoke, do I?'

True, but she had been known to leave pans to burn dry and burst into flames on the cooker top while she put the washing out. At the farm ashtrays were provided. And smoke alarms were fitted – originally, at Philip's insistence.

'At least Samantha doesn't smoke. A sensible girl she is. What does *she* have to say about your being in charge of the place?'

'She's not voiced an opinion, but I wouldn't imagine she's bothered one way or the other, to tell you the truth. I'm just another grown-up to her, aren't I?'

'What's that supposed to mean? Sometimes you talk in riddles, do you know that? Like your sister. I always said there isn't much to choose between the two of you.'

Not what I meant at all. And I was nothing like Hilary, as I'd pointed out to Mater many times. To start with, I wouldn't have married a farmer. And if I had, I wouldn't have asked my sibling to look after the place in my absence, I felt certain.

I'd expected Hilary's note to contain more details of where to find things. Important things like where the chicken feed was kept, how much to give them and how often. Which room and which bed to make myself at home in. Likewise, which wardrobe and which drawers to use. Details, too, of how to ensure the shower didn't run cold, how the TV remote worked, when and where to put out the refuse bin.

I presumed I'd have the use of Hilary's phone. We're talking land lines here, remember. The old, shared line was supposed to have been replaced recently by a new line to the upstairs rooms and another to Hilary's kitchen, each with their separate number. An arrangement Hilary suspected wasn't working as it should, judging by the size of her bills.

'Is your sister still expecting you to sell the farm for her while she's away?' Mater wanted to know. 'She hasn't said a word to me about it.'

Hmm. 'It's a long story. Let's just say a complication has arisen, and the sale is on hold for the moment.'

'Thank heaven for that.'

Thank the guys from the old drill hall, I had an urge to tell her.

*

As I drove out of town, I couldn't help thinking Mater looked tired these days. She looked her age actually, if I'm honest. I tried picturing myself at her sort of age – the children with families of their own paying me the occasional visit; Julie long since expired and residing in an urn on the mantelpiece; me reduced to rambling nostalgically about how the world used to be a better place; boring everyone with my memories; dribbling in my pants too if I didn't remember to take myself off to the loo more regularly. Worst of all, being reminded by Adrian (or would it be Charlotte?) of the importance of changing my underwear more often. And eating properly. And cutting out the cigarettes.

Would I be waiting most evenings, like Mater, for my bridge partner to knock at the door? My very own Margaret? I doubted we'd be playing bridge together, frankly. The Margaret I'd want at my door would be one with a penchant for teaching tricks of a very different kind, nothing to do with cards if you must know.

I'd turned onto the lane and was approaching the gate to the farm when I saw that a For Sale board had been put up by the gate post. My first and obvious thought: Hilary's been and got her skates on, ankle or no ankle, and played me for a sucker. My second thought: Messrs Barker Liddell had either not received a copy of the solicitor's letter, or they had chosen to ignore it.

Just like Hilary to push off and leave me to hold the ring. Mater had read the signs correctly, it seemed. I could refuse, of course, and ask Barker Liddell to kindly take down their For Sale board till the owner returned. That way I wouldn't have to put up with prospective buyers looking round the place on my watch. 'Viewing strictly by appointment', the sign read. If I interpreted that correctly, I could delay visits anyway until after Hilary returned. Problem solved.

In the kitchen I came across the second of Hilary's notes – basically, the one that filled the gaps she'd left in the first. I was to help myself to whatever food I could find; remember to switch on the TV at the wall first; find feed for the hens in a bag in one of the kitchen cupboards; throw them any scraps from my table (what scraps?); be careful using the phone, in case one of *them* was listening in (the shared line had been replaced by now, surely); if I wanted a wash or a shower, the water heater required switching on half an hour or so beforehand; there were towels to be found in the airing cupboard; instructions on the use of the washing machine were in the top left-hand kitchen drawer. Finally (get this!) would I check that Barker Liddle's man (her spelling) wasn't prevented from putting his board up by you know who (too late, Hil, the board's gone up) And –wait for it – would I be kind enough to show any interested parties round who might turn up to view the place before she got back?

Round where exactly? The top floor was best described as off limits. I didn't have keys for there or the outbuildings. In any event, I'd decided on Plan B, hadn't I? Defer any and all viewings till the owner got back. The problem, in other words, didn't apply.

Had a For Sale board gone up at the *end* of the lane, I wondered. That would be the sensible place to put a board, where most of the passing traffic would see it. I hadn't noticed one on my way in. But then, I hadn't noticed either if Luke's handiwork had been removed from the gate, had I?

Talking of Luke, where was I likely to find the guy? It had started raining so I dropped the idea of going outside to look for him. In any case, I had to decide what it was exactly that I wanted with him? He already had his jobs to do, but where he went when it rained would be a start. Probably upstairs, if he'd any sense. To join that girl up there, would that be? Once and for all, I put the thought out of my head, and decided it would be best to wait for Sam to return from work and get her to introduce us properly. *This is the guy I'm living with, Uncle Adam. He doesn't talk much, as you must have noticed, but if you're lucky you might get him to give you a smile, but as for anything resembling a conversation, forget it. He leaves the talking to me.*

That last bit I could understand. Sam had more than enough mouth for the pair of them. For now, I felt I could relax and take time out to explore my part of the house. The front door, I knew, led to the two flights of stairs up to Sam's flat. I imagined one of my keys would fit it and another might also open the connecting door to the stairs from Hilary's living room. My emergency exit, this route, in the event my chip pan caught fire in the kitchen. That left a ground floor room on the other side of the staircase, which was mostly used, I knew, as a storeroom. A rear staircase (the one the servants once used, I guess) led to Hilary's first floor rooms. These included her bathroom and shower which lay immediately below the one more recently installed in the flat above. You could be in here, according to Hilary, and not only hear movements above (I pun, in case you're wondering) but actually feel the vibration caused whenever someone flushed the loo over your head. Plainly a moving experience (sorry, I couldn't help myself). My room for the next few days was next door. What you could hear taking place above your head in there was anyone's guess. The room boasted an empty wardrobe and drawers for my clothes along with a bedside table complete with bedside lamp. If pressed on the matter at such an early stage, I'd award the accommodation three stars.

Judging by the number of rooms and their size, I'd say Foolsmeadow had to qualify in anyone's book as a substantial farmhouse. It was a listed pile, too. A one-time monastic "grange", Philip once told me. A fine example, apparently, where you could imagine monks spending their days in pious thoughts between bouts of wine making, goat herding, and brewing ale. They would have had a library, and most certainly a chapel. Monks did a lot of praying and scourging of themselves in acts of penance, so I'm told. Particularly after a night on the elderberry wine or round at the nearby nunnery. If only these walls could speak, as they say.

One thing I'd noticed on my very first visit here was the way the add-on kitchen didn't match the style of the rest. It had been put up later by someone who obviously had no sense of architectural integrity. Not Philip, I should add. I checked with a copy of Pevsner taken from one of the bookshelves in the front sitting room (originally Philip's library) and found it didn't list the house as being worthy of his attention. So there you go, one man's architectural gem is another's heap of old stones.

The choice of dark-wood furniture throughout had always seemed to me to make the place look and feel cold, rather like a museum. As for the few ornately framed landscape paintings hung on the walls, well, they could have been priceless for all I knew but they weren't pieces I would have wanted on *my* wall, to be honest. Photographs of Philip adorned the mantelpiece. I knew these from previous visits. One of him in his younger days hugging a newly bought tractor; another holding his prize bull by the nose; one of him holding Hilary, but by the waist; another with Sam in his arms, a chubby-faced infant then of only a few months, as I recall.

As for the larder, what can I say? A couple of stone steps descended into it, a reminder that this had once been the entrance to a cellar which had long since been filled in. Who uses a larder these days, let alone a cellar? Well, Hilary did. This was where she kept her stock of tinned foods by the look of it. Mine for the taking, if I fancied vintage soft herring roes, or five-year-old sliced peaches in syrup. A window fed air and borrowed light from a grate outside. A mouse had tumbled in, and expired behind the glass, I couldn't help noticing. Within sight of all that food, too.

Back in the room set aside for my use I began unpacking the few personal belongings I'd considered I couldn't manage without. The window looked out onto the farmyard and the archway where Philip's new tractor had once stood and that prize bull of his might have been tethered. Now an older rustier machine stood there with, look, somebody climbing aboard and starting it up in a cloud of blue smoke. And blow me, if it wasn't the elusive farmhand himself at the wheel as it chugged off and out of my view. Farming did still go on here, evidently. And why not? If I took the trouble to walk across the fields, I dare say I'd come across beasts grazing and a crop being harvested. And maybe I'd run into Ted Shimwell and see if he'd grown any older and wiser since the last time we met.

The rain had stopped by the time I stepped outside for a smoke. I took my familiar route across to the archway and from there looked for signs the tractor might still be in view, along with the driver. I'd settled on feigning an interest in old farm machines like his as a way into conversation with the guy. Except he'd disappeared again, without trace. Thinking he might have gone back indoors, I steeled myself and took another look up at Sam's window. A long hard stare this time. Just in case, you know, he or she (whoever *she* was) might think to gaze out again over the yard. No luck there either.

It seemed I had the house to myself. For the time being, at any rate.

*

I'd made a meal, eaten it, and settled down with a cigarette by the time Sam's Fiat drove into the yard. If I expected to hear my niece tap at her uncle's door and greet him, I was in for a disappointment. My car stood large as life next to where she parked hers but okay, never mind, she ignored it and walked straight past my window with her head in the air. I guess she'd seen the For Sale board too, and wasn't feeling too pleased about it, having probably linked my arrival with the erection of the board and concluded I'd stuck my nose into her mother's affairs again, in spite of our earlier phone conversation.

I heard her footsteps clatter up the stairs and a door slam. What now, I wondered. Phone her? You'd think there'd be a hotline enabling mother and daughter to bypass dialling their respective six-digit numbers. I didn't see one. Dial 1, maybe? Or 9. Would that do the trick? And if Sam answered? In that case I'd invite her to join me in the kitchen for a drink and insist Luke join us. You couldn't say fairer than that.

Before I could get to my feet to make the call, I heard a crash from overhead. Sam had knocked something over, presumably; or had fallen and injured herself. If the latter, then my guess was she would ring me for help, knowing as she did that her uncle was now very much in residence. So I waited. When nothing happened, I got up and went over to the phone and dialled 1.

'Hello. Anybody there?'

Dead. I tried 9 and met with the same response. So I tried Directory Enquiries. Yes, there was a number for Ms Samantha Pope at Foolsmeadow Grange Farm (and no, it wasn't the same as Hilary's number). Did I want to be connected? Why not? Nobody answered. Instead, a woman's voice that could have been Sam's asked me ever so politely to leave a message after the tone. I declined just as politely and put the receiver down. Immediately the phone rang.

'Was that *you* just now, Uncle Adam? Calling me?'

'Yes, it was, as a matter of fact. I was—'

'Is it important? My shower's running and I'm late.' So if it's all the same to you, Uncle Adam, can we do this another time, when I'm not in a hurry and not standing here starkers?'

The line went dead. Whatever the crash was about, clearly it hadn't improved Sam's disposition or made her more receptive to my overtures. Late for what, I wondered. Not a Sahara Street meeting, surely. It was Wednesday evening. Where else might she be going? And would Luke be going with her? I assumed he was up there with her, changing and showering too. In his shoes that's where I would be. And I imagined that soon the pair of them would come clattering down the stairs, get in the car, and drive off, leaving the house empty once again.

I decided it was not the right occasion to ask to go along for an SS taster session. Instead, I stood at the kitchen window with my hands in the sink and my eyes on the Fiat, wondering, as you do while washing up, about who else might be getting ready for a midweek prayer meeting and whether *she*, perhaps, might be putting away shoe boxes and eying herself in the mirror, sort of thing, prior to joining the rest of the worshippers. Lost in my reverie, I let a plate slip from my grasp, one of Hilary's prized collection. It shattered at my feet, making a noise that must have been heard all round the farm.

They must have heard it upstairs, but the phone didn't ring. Too busy showering and changing to pay it any attention, obviously. I could have cut myself picking up fragments and been lying there, bleeding. Never mind the fact only a couple of flights of stairs separated us, we could have been literally worlds apart, not to put too fine a point on it. Sorry, but there you go, I was used to being noticed and made welcome. This wasn't my idea of housewarming at all.

I think I switched the telly on after that. I must have been dozing when I became aware of voices outside. It was still light, and I saw that a car had pulled into the yard. Quite a large car; the sort a chauffeur might drive. Or a funeral director. Sam and Luke were out there, with things to say to each other and to the driver before opening doors and climbing aboard. Dressed up to the nines, the pair of them as well. Luke in a suit, would you believe, that fitted him better than mine fitted me. Sam, too, I must admit, looked elegant as ever in a royal blue outfit. What on earth was going on? People don't go to prayer meetings in glam rags and a chauffeur-driven limousine these days, do they?

If either of them spotted my face at the kitchen window, they did a good job of hiding it. What a miserable sight my face must have been, it struck me. I won't go so far as to say I would have given my month's salary to join them out there, but I did get a sense of how Cinders must have felt on being left behind. I may even have waved feebly as the carriage departed.

As it was far too early for bed, I decided to console myself with another dip into GV's journal and congratulated myself on having packed it. Hopefully, this time I'd find something on his Aunt Gertrude. Something elevating, for a change. Something to lift my spirits, cheer me up.

*

Find Marti, okay? Read about her takeover from Marcie. Only where exactly do you look to find it? Well, working on the principle that it had to be in there somewhere, I picked up page after page before eventually being rewarded by coming across the pair of them, M and M, not only on the same page but, blimey, in the same paragraph. Changing shifts, as it were, just as I'd been told they did. Clearly, Mrs K hadn't sold me a pup, or led me up a garden path. Whatever her failings (I may have mentioned a few), I had to admit the woman did know her Veritys and hadn't held back on the detail. Take a look for yourself:

> 'God will provide, Marcie kept saying before she left, and I know she and Marti had arranged it between them and God made it possible through the power of everybody's prayers. Angels are people really. They step in when you need them, to guide us when life gets hard. Marcie did her best, but things got too much for her and she spent a lot of time sitting at the table with her head in her hands, asking what was the matter with her and saying she was sorry for what was happening.
>
> 'It was Marti did the talking for her in the end which was as well because Marcie didn't talk a lot of sense if you asked her questions about things. She wouldn't be long at the doctor's was what she said. Only everybody knew she wasn't going to the doctor's and wouldn't be coming back. You don't take a suitcase with you to the doctor's. God would provide for us all, she told us. She meant Marti

would be running things at home for her. Marti had as good as moved in with us a while back, to help out with things like washing and shopping and keeping the house clean. For a time I thought Pal might come back and patch things up and Marcie would come back too, but it didn't happen that way. Marcie told me before she left that I had to behave and not give Marti a hard time. I'd understand one day, she said, when I had children of my own, why that was important.'

Nothing so far to indicate how well Aunt Gertrude took to the role of mothering her nephew, but what's this? More relations coming into view? Mrs K hadn't told me about these:

'Old Mr and Mrs B lived in the house Marti once lived in, she told me, and she wanted me to go inside with her and meet them because they were church folk like us, she said. I don't recall ever seeing them before and I usually remember old people's names and faces. Marti said she liked to think I'd remember them in my prayers because they wouldn't always be there to greet us.'

Marti's parents, were we talking about? Now if I'd got this right, they'd be Lance's parents as well, and in that case, they would be old Mr and Mrs V, surely, and not Mr and Mrs B. No, these were newcomers on the scene. Bear with me while I speculate on the possibility that they had something to do with the *other* side of the family, with the mysterious Mister One-Night-Bloody-Stand and *his* forbears. I bet Mrs K would know. Where was the woman when I needed her? I went through a few more pages, in an attempt to find the guy, then gave up and switched on the telly. I was on holiday after all. Beholden to no one, and perfectly entitled to relax when I felt like it.

By the time I headed for the stairs and my new bed I was

still, so far as I knew, the only living soul in the house. By the time I'd finished in the bathroom and got under the duvet, my fellow residents had returned. And not just two of them, by the sound of it. I reckon they'd invited the chauffeur to join them. Stamping up the stairs like they had the house to themselves and there was no one else for miles. Never mind whose Astra they'd parked alongside in the yard, or whose bedroom light had just gone out. Did prayer meetings always finish so late? And was this a taste of the regular nightly disturbances Hilary had complained of? Okay, the worst seemed over for now, all I could hear from above as I settled down were muffled voices. Too muffled to hear what anyone was actually saying. As time went by, either their voices got more distant or my nightcap took effect and I drifted off, promising myself I would make a really serious attempt to engage with my two housemates next day.

*

The dream I had that night, as I recall, started in a burger bar (or it could have been a hot dog stand, not that it matters, I suppose) where I was the guy in the apron and hat slaving over a hotplate and serving a succession of customers, all of them young people, and some of them not too happy with the food by all accounts. One complained of stale bread; another moaned I'd been mean with the ketchup (or was it the mayonnaise?). Just when it was all starting to get out of hand and a revolt looked imminent, the scene dissolved, and I found myself alone inside a shop. Definitely a shop, only this time it was far from clear whether I was there as a customer or was serving behind the counter. It didn't seem to matter, as the place was bare anyway, with not a thing on display. Upstairs, however, somebody was stamping on the floorboards urging me to get on with it and *do* something, rather than just stand there.

Then a woman in a hat entered the shop and sat down on a chair placed there for her. I didn't recognise her, but she seemed to know *me* and went on about how glad she was to meet me. Except she couldn't get the words out right and they sounded more like how *rude* she was to *barge in on me*? Then she changed it again to *extremely rude of me to crash into your acquaintance like this*, some nonsense at any rate, till all at once – you know how it is with dreams – the pair of us were no longer in a shop but out in the open somewhere, struggling under a blazing sun to get to the top of a shifting sand dune but not really getting anywhere. By this time the woman had lost her shoes, along with the hat, and was having difficulty staying on her feet. She would have collapsed into my arms (well, it *was* a dream!) if I hadn't heard a clap of thunder overhead and stopped in my tracks to look up.

I was awake, I realised. Sitting upright in the darkness, trying to figure out if it was a noise I'd heard in my sleep or for real. Had someone above me fallen out of bed? The fingers of my glow-in-the-dark wristwatch pointed to three in the morning. Now I heard voices. Perhaps I wasn't the only one whose sleep had been disturbed. Then I heard a bed creak, and creak again, several times. Then a whole series of creaks, more regular and rhythmic this time, and really insistent, as if two consenting adults had begun engaging in serious sexual congress over my head. Not an easy activity to ignore, I found, especially when it's taking place directly above your head and the light fitting is starting to sway. I appeared to be a witness to how devotedly my niece's boyfriend took his duties.

Notwithstanding the distraction, my eyes must have closed again, and my dream resumed. But not from the point where it left off. This time I was on a hillside gazing round aimlessly till I caught sight of Steve – definitely him, and halfway up the ladder to the roof of his Land Rover, roped up and feeling his way towards the top rung, curiously enough, like a rock climber. Demonstrating to me, as the dream would have it, how an expert might perform a manoeuvre of this kind for the benefit of an amateur like me. But I lost interest. The woman from the sand dune reappeared, now fully hatted and shod, and still I couldn't put a name or face to her. Steve saw her too, and in no time at all had climbed down to join us. Next thing we were all three standing at the bar in a pub somewhere. Only the woman was now in uniform beside us and shaking one of those Sally Army tins under our noses, which didn't go down at all well with Steve. He started arguing with her, till in the end the barman told us to leave. I recall shivering as we stepped out into the night air. Except it wasn't night-time at all. It was daylight and the sun was streaming in through the bedroom curtains and the duvet had fallen onto the floor.

Well, what did *that* all mean? I don't need to point out (or do I) that the nameless, faceless woman had to be Mrs V and the shop belonged to her. And aren't sand dunes a feature of the Sahara? And Sally Army uniforms a manifestation of a serious religious inclination? As for the collecting tin, I've already described Steve as one of the most tight-fisted guys you could shake a tin at. And yes, he did have a luggage rack fitted to the roof of his Land Rover.

But the burger bar stroke hot dog stand and its disgruntled customers, what was *that* about, eh? A comment on my performance in the classroom? In the hot dog business, I dare say you get fired for not having sold enough of the product by the end of the day. Not quite like that in the tutoring game, though, is it? You've had a rough old year, Goodman old chap, what with one thing and another. Put your feet up this summer and take a well-earned rest. Go recharge your batteries. Take it easy. Hence the aimless way I appeared to stand around in my dream – in the shop, on the hillside, in the bar. I was reminding myself in my sleep, you might say, of the need to heed the boss's advice.

As I headed for the bathroom, I decided I must make the most of my first full day on the farm. Soon I'd be cooking my first farmhouse breakfast, then having a word with the people upstairs before they disappeared in the direction of work. Oh, and I had to remember to let the hens out and give them a feed before they, too, complained I was mean with the helpings. That, of course, was the moment I realised I hadn't remembered to lock the hens away before bed. Too many other things on my mind. Too many distractions.

Not the most auspicious start, eh?

DAY ONE

By nine o'clock, my plan to make contact with the other two occupants of the house had come well and truly unstuck. I'd overlooked two very obvious points: firstly, it was midweek and Sam had to leave early for work; secondly, I'd clean forgotten how early a working day starts on a farm. Over breakfast I heard my niece clatter down the stairs and across the yard, slam her car door and drive off. As for Luke, not a sign or sound of him. He could have got up, as farmhands do, at the crack of dawn and gone to work in the fields, the milking parlour, the hay meadow, who knows? For all I knew he could have been up for hours, done half a day's work, and gone back to bed while I slept. Maybe he was still up there, catching up on the sleep he lost last night and dreaming of what he might get up to with Sam tonight.

My first job before even thinking about breakfast was to attend to the hens – if there were any left alive, that is. And blow me, I discovered they'd been shut away safely after all and were shouting to be let out. Had I done it myself and forgotten I had? Don't make me laugh. More like I had Sam or Luke to thank for doing the charitable thing and going out of their way after evening prayers to show me they weren't bad people really, when all's said and done. I made a resolution on the spot: find Luke, talk to him nicely, and thank him. That had to be my morning's mission after I'd fed the hens and fed myself.

As it wasn't a bad morning, I opted for a stroll round the farm as the likeliest way to come across the guy doing whatever he did. After drawing a blank in the yard and the outbuildings, I moved onto one of the fields in the hope of spotting him at the wheel of the tractor somewhere.

It occurred to me there had to be a shop in the neighbourhood that sold cigarettes and newspapers, and cartons of milk. No mention of a shop in Hilary's note, presumably because she'd expected me to bring my own little luxuries with me. Have you ever given a thought to how isolated a place a hill farm can be for a townie? If I'd passed a shop on my way to Foolsmeadow, its whereabouts escaped me. But there had to be one, surely, and maybe Luke would be able to tell me where to find it.

I went back for a coat, grabbed my wallet and cigarettes, locked up and set off in earnest this time. After checking a couple of things first, mind. Like the For Sale board, to see it hadn't been removed or defaced (it hadn't); and the Astra, to check it hadn't been interfered with (it hadn't, but this was a neighbourhood new to me, remember). After that, well, I just had to take another look at the attic window from the yard, didn't I? In case I caught sight of Luke up there (I didn't, so I pressed on). I opened the gate to the second field which I knew, from having walked it on previous occasions, led to a brow with a view of the town below. Quite a panoramic viewpoint. On most days you could see the high ground on the far side of town, twenty miles or more away. Today was no exception.

Below me, in the next field, I saw cattle grazing. Some were on the move, heading towards an unmistakably two-legged figure who appeared to be leaning against a wall. Even at that distance it looked nothing like Luke. But it did resemble the figure of Ted Shimwell. I'd say it was the flat cap that gave him away, specifically the way he took it off more than once to scratch at what remained of his white hair. By the time I'd drawn near enough to speak without shouting, he'd resumed work on rebuilding part of a wall that had collapsed, and the cattle that had gathered to watch him shied away at my approach.

'Hello, Mister Shimwell,' I greeted him. Important to be polite, I thought, seeing as it was my first day. 'You look very busy, I must say.'

He straightened up, shielding his eyes against the sunlight. 'You, is it? Not seen you round these parts in a while.' He could place my face but not my name, apparently. 'You're keepin' well, I see.'

'That's right. You recognise me, don't you? Adam Goodman. Mrs Pope's brother.'

He didn't say. His gaze turned to the stone he'd been trying to fit into place in the wall. I'd have worn gloves myself. Too late for Ted's hands. His fingers looked like they'd rip gloves to shreds, assuming he could find a size big enough.

'Nice job you've got here. Out in the sun,' I commented. 'Even the animals look envious.' Presumably they *were* Ted's cattle and presumably they'd knocked the wall down in the first place, so they could watch him build it back up.

'Somebody's got to do it, 'aven't they? Walls don't mend themselves. I can't see Missus Pope goin' round mendin' them, can you? Not these days at any rate.'

Point taken. Hilary was the last person I could imagine spending her time in the fields rebuilding walls. Rebuilding anything these days around the farm. Hadn't she handed those jobs over to Luke? Precisely my question to Ted, except he acted as though he'd not heard me and came up with a question of his own. 'Is Missus Pope at 'ome today?'

'She's away at the moment.'

'On 'oliday, you mean?'

'Yes. She's gone touring, with a friend. Gone to Scotland, so I believe.'

'With that new friend of 'ers, you mean?'

Steve, would that be? Or did he mean Mrs K? Did it matter? 'Yes, she's gone with a friend. She's left me to look after the place for her. Smoke?'

Ted had taken his cap off to have another scratch. He didn't care for my brand of cigarette. Preferred to roll his own and, having lifted another stone into place on the wall from the pile of rubble at his feet, proceeded to demonstrate how it was done. Complete with muttered commentary. Not that I heard much of what he said. A low-flying jet roared over us and off towards the town, and the cattle galloped away to the far end of the field, prompting me to ask, once the noise had passed, if the animals were his.

'Not for long they're not. They'll be off to market soon. Tourin', you say? I see she's sellin' the place. Too much for 'er, eh, these days? Can't be much fun, mind, not for a widow on 'er own.'

'I thought she had someone doing jobs round the place for her. Her daughter's boyfriend, Luke.' If at first you don't succeed, ask, ask again. 'You must have seen him around.'

Ted blinked. And flicked one ear where a fly kept trying to land. He finished rolling his cigarette and accepted my offer of a light.

'Is that 'is name?' He looked at me, then turned to look at the view while he took a few drags on his cigarette. Then, without turning back to me, he muttered something I didn't catch that sounded, if I'm honest, very much like an uncomplimentary comment about Luke's parentage.

'Not seen him this morning, have you?' I asked, resisting the urge to ask him for clarification.

Ted gave what I took to be a shake of his head as he lifted another likely stone from the rubble pile. Having found a place for it in the wall, he stood and reflected before asking me if I remembered his dog. I nodded, though I couldn't honestly bring the creature to mind. 'What about him?'

'Her. She'd been with me for years. It was 'im as killed 'er. It was 'im killed my Spot.'

'Spot?'

'Can't prove it, like, but I know it was 'im. Ran over 'er, ee did, with that bike of 'is. Denied it, o' course.'

'An accident, you mean?'

'That's wot ee reckoned. But I know ee did it on purpose. Only I didn't see it 'appen, see, so I can't prove it, can I?'

'Why would he do it on purpose?'

For a moment Ted eyed me closely, as though suspecting I'd heard Luke's version of the story and Luke being family (as good as, after last night's performance, let's face it) there was no point hearing anyone else's account. 'You tell me,' he said at last, giving his head another shake as he spoke, presumably to denote it wouldn't surprise him to learn I was party to a conspiracy of denial.

'I didn't know Luke had a bike,' I confessed. 'A motorbike, do you mean?'

That look again, like I *knew* all right, so why was I pretending I didn't? I shrugged and raised my eyebrows as high as they'd go – my way, you understand, of conveying my ignorance in the matter, along with my innocence of anything remotely conspiratorial.

How was I expected to know Luke kept a motorbike on the farm? According to Ted, he rode it round the lanes frequently. For fun. With no regard for the safety of others. Spot had chased him on more than one occasion, as dogs do. No reason for Luke to deliberately run the dog over, but that's what he'd done. A wild youth with a grudge against the world, and with a history, too, or didn't I know about that? He'd been in trouble before, according to Ted.

'You've got some catchin' up to do,' he muttered. And added, with a hand cupped to his mouth to prevent the cows overhearing any of it, 'I've 'eard it said as ee's been inside. Only don't ask me wot for. Ask *'im*, more like.'

It crossed my mind to wonder if Sam knew about this. It seemed likely she did and putting the youth to work on the farm was maybe her part in his rehabilitation programme. It made sense of Sahara Street's involvement, too, if you looked at it that way. 'Luke *is* a bit of a character,' I heard myself explain. 'And not an easy person to get hold of when you want a word with him. I was rather hoping you'd know where to find him.'

Ted fetched a lighter out of his pocket and relit the bent end of his cigarette. 'You could try the Barn,' he suggested. 'Lord's Barn, as they call it. Ee's been spending a lot of 'is time over there lately. Been doin' work on it. Reckon as Missus Pope's got a mind to turn it into some kind of 'oliday cottage. Though maybe she's changed 'er mind and wants to live there 'erself, now she's set on sellin' the farm.'

Lord's Barn? I didn't recollect ever hearing it mentioned, either by Hilary or Philip. I knew there were a number of stone barns scattered across the farm, most of them roofless and derelict by now, but I didn't realise they had names. Where would I find this one? Ted did his best to explain a route for me to take, but he couldn't guarantee I'd find anyone there and didn't want to send me on a wild goose chase. He offered to share some of his coffee with me, while I made up my mind about following his directions and took a flask from his haversack.

Ted's coffee had brandy in it – enough of it, let's say, to make the beverage palatable. A couple of sips of it, at any rate. 'Go on,' he urged me when I held the cup out for him to take back. 'Finish it. There's plenty left for me. There, you see. Does wonders for the hair on your chest, as they say. And on your legs. I'm sure you'll make it to the Barn in no time at all. A young fella like you.'

He took the empty cup off me before going on to ask me something I wasn't expecting. ''Ave you met the lad's mother yet?'

'His mother?'

Should I have met her? Did he have one? Sorry, I mean did she live in the neighbourhood, and take an interest in what her son got up to? My uncertainty must have been visible because Ted went on to enlighten me. 'Odd one, she is. Acts like she's in charge of the place. Asked me where I'd go if I didn't graze my beasts on these fields, like. Wot do you make of that?'

'Was she suggesting you find somewhere else?'

'Not sure wot she was suggestin'. That's wot I wanted to 'ave a word with Missus Pope about. She's still the gaffer as I reckon. Till she's sold the farm, she is. And now you say as she's gone away. Did she say when she'd be comin' back?'

My estimate of a week or so got Ted scratching his head again. He wanted to know if I thought Luke's mother had her eye on buying the farm. Christ, how did I know the answer to that one? I told him I might get some answers out of Luke once I'd located the guy. And maybe I'd get a chance to meet his mother too, before Hilary returned. 'Let's see what *I* make of her,' I promised. 'Maybe she'll want to know what business I have wandering round the place like I own it.'

Ted stood with his coffee cup in hand chewing over my reply before eventually putting his flask away. He tossed his cigarette end over the wall and muttered, 'I'll just 'ave to leave it till the gaffer gets back then, won't I?'

*

Ted wasn't wrong about Lord's Barn. It *was* where he'd directed me, and *was* being converted into some kind of dwelling; and his fear of sending me on a wild goose chase *was* spot on, i.e. Luke didn't appear to be there. The place came into view as I gained the summit of a long rise of land in what must have been the most distant corner of the farm. Did I remember this corner from previous visits? Frankly no, though I did recall driving up (or it may have been down) Briar Lane which formed the boundary of Hilary's land on this side of the farm. An open gateway connected the Barn to the lane. Easier to get there by car than on foot, I concluded, now I knew where it was.

As I say, Luke didn't appear to be there. From my vantage point I had a bird's-eye view of the place and it looked deserted. Plenty of evidence of work in progress, though – heaps of sand, some scaffolding, a cement mixer, a bucket or two and a shovel, a hosepipe attached to an outside tap, a ladder on the ground. But none of those familiar DIY sounds – hammering, drilling, mixer on the go. Nothing to tell me that today, right now, a handyman was at work on or inside the place, renovating it, even if not actually in view. There was no vehicle parked outside, not even a tractor. Or a motorbike, for that matter. But there was a small outbuilding I couldn't see into where a bike could presumably be stored.

The Barn had a new slate roof that included a modern skylight window. A chimney too. It stood in a clump of trees which sheltered it on all sides except mine. The brow I stood on completed the job of making the place private and secluded – a proper hideaway you might say, if that was your thing.

My presence on the skyline, I thought, just might be prominent enough to catch the attention of someone working below. But no one seemed inclined to show themselves. And I wasn't of a mind to wave my arms over my head or shout Luke's name. The one thing I certainly didn't want to do was walk all the way down there only to have to retrace my steps on finding the place as deserted as it looked. I resolved to try a visit another time, preferably in the car. As it was not far short of lunchtime, I presumed Luke had taken a break. Maybe I'd even come across him in the fields somewhere on my walk back.

*

Well, I made it back to my kitchen without seeing another soul. And on the way had ample time to reflect on Ted's remarks. I didn't recall anyone mentioning Luke's mother before, let alone hinting she had an interest in the farm. How about his father? Or his brothers and sisters? Did *they* have designs on the farm, too? Were the family going to make for my door with offers to buy the place while Hilary was away?

Hard as I tried, I couldn't imagine myself in Ted's shoes. According to Hilary, he had a bit of a reputation for chatting up the ladies. After Philip's death, he'd tried his luck with Hilary too, apparently, but not had any success, I was told. So now, what, you may wonder, was stopping him from exercising his charms on the woman he suspected might be likely to take over the farm in Hilary's place? Well, she might have a partner for a start. A big jealous sort of guy. Or Ted could have made a move already and been soundly put back in his box, who knows? Maybe that's why Ted was so sour about her.

Back at the farm I still saw no sign of Luke. Not even after I'd grabbed a sandwich and a drink and taken a seat on the kitchen doorstep for a quiet smoke in the sun. In which of the buildings, I wondered, did he keep his motorbike if it wasn't over at the Barn? Perhaps he'd taken it for a spin. That's when I noticed the tractor was back in the yard and had a trailer attached to it which was loaded high with bales of hay. More evidence, if I needed it, that Luke took his farming more seriously than I'd given him credit for. I assumed he'd been busy making hay whilst I walked the length and breadth of the farm looking for him. Clearly, as Ted had reminded me, I had some catching up to do.

But, hang on a minute, whose car was this? A silver Toyota pulled into the yard. A friend of Luke's, was it? Come to lend him a hand with the hay? A bearded man in his forties, a smart professional-looking type, hardly a farmhand, stepped out and looked round, weighing up the place while his passenger stayed where he was. Of course, I realised, here was someone interested in viewing the farm. The estate agent had probably rung in my absence to tell me these two were on their way. Any minute they were going to ask for a word with Mrs Pope. Maybe even take me to be her partner.

'Is this Meadow Grange?' the bearded guy asked me.

I'd already got to my feet. 'Yes.' Near enough, at any rate. No point splitting hairs. 'What can I do for you? Have you come to look round the place?'

'Sort of. Are *you* in charge?' Was I Mrs Pope's better half, in other words? I told you so.

'Yes, for the time being. Mrs Pope's away. She's the owner. Can I show you round? I take it that's why you're here.' *Sort of*. What did he mean? Either they'd come to view the place, or they hadn't. Was English not this guy's first language? He spoke without an accent, but you can't be sure these days, can you?

'We'd certainly like to see what's on offer. All tastes catered for and all that.'

Was I mistaken or did the guy accompany his last remark with a wink? It seemed to be a habit round here. *All tastes catered for and all that*. What was he talking about? I suspected a trick, a hoax of some kind. A stunt, the sort students pull on unsuspecting members of staff. At the very least we seemed to be talking at cross purposes. I looked across at the car, half expecting the guy's passenger to be filming our little scene, for inclusion in one of those awful TV programmes, you know the type. So I confronted the guy. 'Can I ask you exactly what it is you *are* here for?' And added, just to be sure, 'Did the estate agent send you?'

'We've come about the ad. The one in the *Gazette*.'

Not possible, surely, for Barker Liddell to have advertised the farm in the local paper so soon, was it? The *Gazette* was a weekly rag, published on a Thursday. Today, in fact. Just possible then that it could have made this week's issue, the one I'd still to go out and buy.

'Can I see it? The ad you're talking about, I mean,' I asked.

For a minute the guy looked at me as if I'd asked him to turn out his pockets. Or show me his passport. 'Sure,' he said at length. He walked back to the Toyota's open door, leaned in and took hold of a newspaper obligingly handed to him by his passenger before coming back with it and telling me it was all in there. By then I'd established the passenger wasn't filming us but merely keeping his distance and leaving the talking to his companion.

The advert was not in the property pages at all but under Personal Services where it had been circled in red. A Small Ad in effect, and hardly my column of choice, Personal Services, let me make clear. Normally I wouldn't have given it the time of day. But it did catch my eye, I had to admit:

Professional massage at Meadow Grange, 4 miles out of town, at end of lane, easy to find. New staff. All tastes catered for. Discretion guaranteed. Discount with this advert.

I imagine the look on my face (along with the way I shook my head and handed the newspaper back) must have convinced my visitors they'd made a mistake, taken a wrong turn, and come to the totally wrong address. When I suggested there appeared to be a practical joker at large, as this was certainly not the Meadow Grange advertised, they drove away without another word. Well, not another word to *me* at any rate.

*

So much for my first visitors.

I wondered if Luke had watched any of it. Eavesdropped maybe from close by. Had placed the advert himself even, as a practical joke, a means, you know, of embarrassing the new occupant and suggesting he wasn't welcome. Then I remembered what I knew of Luke's vocabulary – not a lot, admittedly, but it hardly equipped him to word an ad so succinctly. Somebody, his mother maybe, had to have helped him. Or else Sam had been behind it, though I doubted it was her kind of joke, to be honest. I'm sorry, but, as you can see, my imagination had got to work and got me fingering all sorts of likely contenders. The only person I hadn't implicated yet was Mrs K, and that was because I couldn't see a motive. But I'd work on it.

Back indoors I located Hilary's phone book and looked up the number for the *Gazette*'s advertising desk. Have you ever tried asking after the identity of the person responsible for placing an ad in the Personal Services column?

'I'm sorry, sir, I don't believe I have that information. You could try the phone number.'

The phone number? What phone number? 'I happen to be the owner of Meadow Grange.' Well, near enough, for the purposes of this conversation. 'And your advertiser is libelling the good name of my property. There are laws against libel, as I'm sure you must be aware.'

'Yes, I understand that, sir, but you would have to take your complaint up with the person responsible for placing the advert.'

I thought that's what I was attempting to do. 'That's why I'm asking you for that person's name and contact details. I'm calling from the Grange right now. This is not a hoax call.' Pay attention, you moron.

'Can I have your name again, sir?'

Christ, is this guy for real? 'Look, is it possible to pop in this afternoon and have a word with whoever's in charge?' This matter is too important, in other words, to discuss over the phone with a smart-arsed junior.

'That would be Mr Carling, the advertising editor. What name is it again, sir? Thank you, sir. I'll let Mr Carling know you'll be calling in to see him. Yes, this afternoon will be fine. Will that be all, sir?'

You won't have heard of Nigel Cartwright, a former teaching colleague of mine. Or of Dan Smithers, a onetime student in my tutorial group. Dan had come to me one lunchtime with a problem, and in order to find a quiet place to discuss it with him I let us both into one of the vacant lecture rooms. At least I assumed it was vacant. In fact, Nigel was already in there, seated by himself over by the window, with his back to us, oblivious to our presence, it seemed, till I coughed to let him know. By then Dan and I had overheard him unleash a tirade of colourful epithets, all of them directed at an unseen third person. Today you would take it he was speaking into his mobile phone rather than talking to himself. When eventually he turned round and saw us, he was mortified, naturally. He later approached me to say I'd caught him while he was smarting after a particularly bruising encounter with JR.

Is there a point to this tale? Well, on a number of occasions since then, I'd found myself doing a Nigel-style tirade. In a room. On my own. This was the latest such occasion, and I had the entire house (well, my part of it) to myself. If Luke had put his head round the door to see what the outburst was about, I dare say I would have been barely able to stop myself from asking him what the fuck he wanted. Mad as that! But he didn't, and I may have been still mouthing vitriol by the time I drove out of the yard. Destination: the offices of the *Willsborough Gazette*. Where else?

On the way I stopped at the first likely shop I spotted. A tobacconist's which doubled as a store where you could buy numerous other things, including a copy of the latest *Gazette*.

Here it was again, the box advertising a discreet, newly staffed, out-of-town massage parlour that catered for all tastes. And yes, there *was* a phone number. I'd missed it earlier. It certainly wasn't Hilary's number, but it could have been Sam's, her number had simply gone walkabout in my head. The possibility Luke might answer if I rang it struck me as unlikely. I'd give it a go later.

The priority, as I saw it, was to convince the guy at the *Gazette* that the ad was a practical joke and to persuade him to exclude the ad from future editions. As far as I was concerned, two punters had already turned up on the doorstep expecting a massage. There was every reason to expect more would follow. And no reason to assume they would all be as polite and understanding as the first. I would insist on prompt action. On pain, let's say, of a solicitor's letter to back me up.

Speaking of solicitors' letters, having found a spot in town to park the car, I happened to pass Barker Liddell's place on my way to the newspaper office. Foolsmeadow Grange, I noticed, was not among the properties advertised in their window. Nor did I find any sign of it among the display boards inside. Surprise, surprise, on making an enquiry I learned it had been taken off the market pending clarification of a small legal matter. But if I wished to leave my name, address and telephone number, someone would get back to me as soon as the matter was resolved. When I enquired about the asking price (sorry, my curiosity got the better of me), I was told I'd have to speak to Mr Barker personally if I wanted that kind of detail.

Bring him on, I thought, only Mr Barker wasn't nearly so welcoming as his young female assistant. He perspired too much for one thing, and he looked me up and down like he thought I might be a timewaster. He softened somewhat, when I led him to think I was Mrs Pope's other half, and invited me into the privacy of his glass office.

'We've had to take the property off the market,' he informed me. Oh yeah, received a letter from Messrs Brownlow, Bush and Pugh, had he? Making out the farm couldn't be sold while the tenants insisted on its use as a brothel? 'I'm afraid we need assurances from Mrs Pope,' he continued, and proceeded to run off a copy of the letter (the same one, yes, about that tenancy) which he expected me to forward to the lady in question, presumably for her to hand on to her solicitor. 'She's on holiday at the moment, you say? No doubt she'll drop in and give us the assurance we need as soon as she gets back.'

Yes, something like that. The For Sale boards meanwhile (two of them, see, I'd missed the one at the end of the lane), they would be removed, he assured me, till they heard further from Mrs Pope. I believe I actually shook the man's hand on that point as I stood up to leave, thinking at least two people I knew would be happy to see those boards come down.

*

The *Gazette* staff, I'd read somewhere, were due to relocate shortly to newer premises on the edge of town. Today their office on Palmerston Street had an already abandoned air about it. Pictures and post-it notes had gone from the walls; furniture was in short supply; and types like me wandering in off the street were plainly not welcome. I had to ring the bell on the counter a number of times before a long-haired youth put down a box he was carrying and came over to see what I kept ringing it for. He could find no record of my earlier telephone conversation on his notepad, having assured me the pad would contain all the relevant details. I had to be mistaken. As for Mister Carling, there *was* such a person, yes, but he was not in the building. Instead – take a guess – he was most probably to be found over in the new premises where nobody could get hold of him because the place was currently a shambles (his words).

Marvellous, eh? I thought of scribbling a note for the attention of the advertising editor but ended up jotting down the address of his new office. Intending, as you do, to put my concerns in writing to the man himself and requesting, ever so politely, that he divulge the contact details of his advertiser and refrain from running the ad in future editions because if he didn't… Well, let's just say Brownlow, Bush and Pugh would be on his tail. They seemed to do an excellent job of putting the wind up people.

Where next, I debated with myself, seeing as I was in town? How about a new pair of shoes? Really? Seriously? So soon? On reflection, a call at Vee's Footwear didn't seem unreasonably premature, bearing in mind I'd promised myself a return visit sooner rather than later. No need to actually *buy* anything. They'd be glad to see me, surely. Anyhow, here it was, right in front of me, it seemed a shame not to drop in.

Inside, standing beneath the shop's noisy doorbell, I saw no sign of Mrs V. But Lucy, I could see by her face, thought she recognised me from somewhere. When I enlightened her, she asked, clever girl, if it was Mrs Verity I wanted to see, and told me the woman had popped out for a minute. So I feigned interest in a pair of black brogues which, as it happened, were available in my size. A good choice, Lucy complimented me, as I sat and tried them on. Quite the young saleslady, it struck me. Coached, I didn't doubt, by her boss, and told to be at her best in both manner and appearance. By the time Mrs V herself came through the door, I'd put my old shoes back on and was debating whether or not to actually buy the brogues. Mrs V's appearance clinched it for me. 'I'll take these,' I said with a smile in the boss lady's direction.

Mrs V had grown several inches, I swear. And looked even more glamorous than before. She was wearing one of those power suits (isn't that what they call them these days?), with exactly the right length and girth of skirt. She recognised me the minute she came through the door (I can tell, you know), but gave me the sort of greeting and smile that I dare say she gave all her customers. Nothing special about me, then.

'This gentleman would like a word with you,' said Lucy, and off she went into a corner to give the pair of us the space she imagined we wanted while she wrapped up my purchase and sorted out a receipt.

'What can I do for you, Mister…?' She'd forgotten my name! But only for a moment. 'Goodman, isn't it? That's right. Mister Goodman. I remember you now.'

I was the gentleman whose sister fell over and hurt her ankle and who brought her into the shop to recover. Not the guy, then, who'd been tutor to GV, the one who'd made off with his journal? She spoke rather crisply, more so than I recollected, and with a faint twitch of impatience on her face, as if I might be keeping her from attending to matters far more pressing. What was it Mrs K had told me about this woman having no time in her life for men?

'Well,' I said, feeling just a tad uncomfortable, as though I'd made a pointless journey, 'I had intended to return the walking stick you lent my sister, but I clean forgot it, to tell you the truth. She's away at the moment, on holiday in Scotland, as a matter of fact.'

I was going to mention how quickly Hilary had got back on her feet, but the woman cut me off. Rather curtly, I thought. 'There really is no hurry, Mr Goodman. But thank you for reminding me you still have it.' And with that she strode past me to the till where Lucy stood with the drawer open, and from two bags of change she proceeded to empty coins into the drawer's compartments.

Was that it then? Audience over?

Lucy seemed to sense that was indeed the case and came forward to hand me my box of brogues and my receipt. Maybe the sight of the shoe box changing hands did it. Swung my luck. Caused the woman to remember I was not just another customer. Drove her to open her mouth and, with her weight shifted onto one leg while she rested the other, impelled her to indulge me a little longer. 'How did you say your sister is, Mr Goodman?' she asked. 'On holiday in Scotland, is she? I hope she's taking care of that ankle.'

'She's on the mend,' I replied. And added, 'I'm looking

after the house for her while she's away,' in case that piece of information should be of interest. I had it in mind to make out what a lonely place it was too, but then got asked whereabouts in Scotland my sister had gone. When I said she'd not left me any clues about it, the woman did something rather unexpected. She broke into a laugh. As though I'd said something highly amusing.

It was actually quite a genuine laugh. More melodic than I was accustomed to hearing from Julie's lips, if that tells you anything. Not surprising then that it made me want to laugh along with her, deliver a few more amusing remarks, only all I could find to add was, 'We don't always talk to each other as much as we should, my sister and me.'

'I take it she's not another teacher then, your sister.'

I'm not sure how my face reacted to the way Mrs V so neatly brought the small talk round to the subject of what I did for a living. Okay, she already knew I'd been GV's tutor. She could guess I'd marked written work of his. But did she know I had his journal? More to the point, did she give a monkey's?

'No, she's not,' I conceded. A teacher, that is. Imagine Hilary taking a class at the local primary school, say. Well, why not? I could think of worse examples. 'She thinks teachers have an easy time of it,' I quipped. 'Like a lot of other people, I suppose.' Her friend Mrs K being among them, for one.

But not Mrs V, eh? Apparently not. I was given a long, rather beguiling look. Like the two of us, in our separate jobs, shared a thing or two. Memories, notably. Of the way GV had worked at his studies; as if the two of us had shared a personal investment in the youth's future, only to see it squandered in that brutal last act of his. As though, basically, she recognised teachers as the good guys in the story of her family's loss. When she finally spoke, it was to tell me that teaching was not a job she would want. 'Not if they paid me several times what you're paid,' she concluded.

I wasn't tempted to compare salaries, don't get me wrong, but I did start to say what a difficult year it had been for all concerned, how it had affected me personally and put me behind with the marking of students' work. So much so that any one of my students could rightly claim I still had work of theirs to hand back. You can see where I was going with this, can't you? I dare say I would have arrived at the subject of GV's journal if I hadn't been interrupted by the bell. The tinkle of the shop's doorbell, heralding the entry of a customer who announced herself as Mrs Porter.

She was expected, it turned out, and had called to collect a parcel which Lucy was instructed to fetch from the back room. Meanwhile, Mrs V shut the till drawer and stood up straight, her weight on both legs now, her gaze no longer directed my way. You can always tell when a woman has switched off, I find. It's in their eyes. The light goes out. The face stiffens. That will be all for now, Mister Goodman, but thank you for your custom.

That wasn't quite all, in fact. As I pulled open the door to the street, the woman did call me back. 'Your shoes,' she reminded me. And then apologised for having distracted me from picking them up. 'Good day to you,' she said finally.

As I headed for the car park, I must say I did not feel I'd been talking to a woman intent on retrieving her late son's diary. I considered I'd given her adequate opportunity to raise the subject with me. I might have concluded she was the type who preferred cosier surroundings in which to discuss confidential matters, except that she hadn't given me grounds to conclude that much either. Instead, I concluded she wanted to keep me guessing. On all fronts.

Okay, if that was her game, I'd say nothing and hang onto it until a more auspicious occasion presented itself. Whenever that might be. Meanwhile, I promised myself, I'd keep dipping into GV's pages. Purely to rule out if it contained bits that Aunt Trudi might prefer I didn't read, for whatever reason.

STILL DAY ONE

My final call before heading back to base was Fletcher's pie shop. Sam worked there, remember, and I thought I might catch her in her apron, so to speak, and have a quick word, seeing as I'd had no success talking to her at the farm. Only it turned out she'd left early, and I'd missed her. By ten minutes or so. She'd left to go to a meeting. Another one? Definitely something to do with her church, now I asked about it.

So much for my good intentions. Our evening together would have to wait. Along with the opportunity to hear views from the pair of them on how they saw their future at the farm. Serious stuff, in other words. Especially now the sale was on hold. And besides, I wanted us to get to know one another better. I wanted to look my prospective nephew-in-law in the eye and ask him, you know, if his designs were honourable ones, as they say.

Now it was beginning to look as if I'd fare better by joining the Sahara Street ranks after all. Doubtless that's where I'd find everybody under one roof, Aunt Gertrude included, now I thought about it. It struck me the woman was possibly on her way out of the door this minute, leaving Lucy in charge of the footwear sales. If you ask me, these people took their prayers pretty seriously, if that's what they were intent on.

Nothing for it, I concluded, but to head back to the farm for another quiet evening in. This time I drove via Briar Lane. I wanted to take another look at Lord's Barn, see it from the road, park up and make a closer inspection. I calculated that since Sam had left early, Luke, too, must have knocked off by now and joined her, and I wouldn't be disturbed. It was a surprise, therefore, as I pulled onto the hardcore parking area, to see the tractor already there. Not only that. At the far side of it stood a hatchback. A VW Scirocco, if I wasn't mistaken. In silver and black. Rather smart. Whose could that be? Curious, I parked up and went over to have a look.

Hardly the car a farmhand would drive, I thought. The registration plate was too recent, for one thing. And the bodywork was just too clean. No dust on it, no mud. Another city type looking for a massage, perhaps? Well, whoever it was, they had to be around here somewhere, as did Luke, though from the outside the place looked as deserted as it had done on my earlier trip.

I went to the only door I could see and knocked. Several times. Then tried the door handle. It turned and the door swung open into a room too dark to see who or what it contained. Why so dark inside, I wondered. Well, for one thing the blinds at the windows were pulled down. Something to hide here, was there?

'Anyone at home?' I called out. As you do in those situations, when you've no wish to cause embarrassment or interrupt a private function.

Eventually, as my eyes adjusted, I could make out the room was empty, at least of people, and that blinds at all the windows had been lowered. I reached instinctively for a light switch. And found one. After all, this wasn't a run-down barn anymore, was it? It had mains services, including electricity, and look, the light switch worked, and a light came on in the middle of the ceiling. And now I became aware of a familiar noise. The sound of a shower being run. In an adjacent room. No need to wonder if water had been laid on as well. Maybe the place was already functioning as a holiday let and new occupants had moved in. Or else *this* was the iniquitous Meadow Grange massage parlour I'd walked into.

From the doorstep, looking in, I was impressed. Someone – presumably Luke – had gone to considerable trouble furnishing the place, if this room was anything to go by. A very comfortable lounge by the look of it. Rugs on the floor. Pictures on the walls. Cushions on the sofa. A low table with, look, used cups left on it by somebody. A cosy hideaway indeed. With more than a bit of the Marie Celeste about it, if you ask me. Where, in other words, *was* everybody?

'Anybody there?'

I took a step, and then another one, over the threshold. And that's when it happened. I tripped. Stumbled. Lost my footing in some way and fell forward. Pitched headlong into the coffee table, sending cups flying. Rows of green frogs against a white background – I couldn't help noticing the pattern on them as they scattered. Then I was struggling to get to my knees, aware the door to the shower room was opening in front of me and I was gazing in no time at a bare wet foot that emerged and dripped water onto the rug under my nose. Before I could make it to my knees or lift my gaze to check if legs and torso were also bare, the foot was withdrawn, and the shower room door slammed shut again in my face. But not before I'd noted that the leg – at least what I'd seen of it – was smooth and hairless, and the foot had painted toenails And not before I'd heard a tongue click in a fit of exasperation.

Had I tripped? Stumbled? Done a Hilary, as you might say, and gone over on my ankle? As I struggled to regain my feet, I remember asking myself if I knew that click but then a man's voice took my attention. Luke's, I realised, as I turned round. He stood where a moment ago I had stood, in the doorway. He must have stepped into the room behind me. No toolbox in his grasp this time, thankfully, merely a raised hand that he dropped to his side as he saw who I was.

'Thought you'd broken in,' he muttered. 'Didn't see it was you.'

He'd *hit* me! Raised a hand and thumped me in the back with it and sent me sprawling. Mistaken me for an intruder, or something. He knew my car by now, come off it. Knew *me*. Knew who I was. Knew what my back and shoulders looked like, the kinds of clothes I wore. Knew I looked nothing like Steve Forrester from the back. In spite of which he'd gone ahead and attacked me. Treated me like I shouldn't be there. Like I really had, as he said, broken into the place. Or at least walked in uninvited. Which I guess I had.

So what now? A line had been crossed, surely. A mark overstepped. Shouldn't he offer me some kind of apology? The mistake, after all, had been *his*, not mine. And there'd been no call for violence, no provocation you could point to. Not from where I stood. 'There was no need for that,' I told him, at the same time flexing my arms and shoulders, as much to reassure myself no bones were broken as to make clear I'd suffered an unprovoked assault at his hands.

Luke stood his ground. 'Didn't see who it was, did I? Thought you'd broken in.'

So he'd said. I must have given him my quizzical look, the one I gave students who owed me a better explanation for their behaviour. It didn't work, so I thought it wiser to attempt to move things on. 'Whose is the car?' I asked. My way of enquiring, you'll gather, after the identity of the person in the shower. The one with the painted toenails who didn't seem awfully keen to show herself at this stage of the proceedings. Not surprising, I suppose, though the shower had by then been turned off and she, whoever she was, must have been able to hear our every word.

'Just somebody I know. A friend of mine. Not doing any harm.'

A *friend*, eh? A masseuse by any chance? I resisted the urge to ask him. Instead, I asked if Sam was about. For I'd come to the conclusion that, whoever the woman in the shower might be, she most definitely wasn't my niece. It crossed my mind that I'd already made too many assumptions as to what my niece and her boyfriend were up to at this end of the day. When Luke shook his head, I began to wonder if Sam even knew where the boyfriend was to be found. If she had any idea what he could be doing on this side of the farm while she was at work. The expression "making hay" came to mind.

'Any idea where I could find her?' I asked.

His eyes narrowed, like he was casting round for an answer to a trick question. Did he *know*? More to the point, did he know as much as *I* knew? About Sam leaving work early, I mean. He still blocked my way to the door, and I really did not want to provoke this guy into believing I posed any kind of threat to him. Further questions about the identity of the friend in the shower were best postponed for another occasion, I decided, much as I would have liked to learn more. As for Sam's whereabouts, I felt I had to help this guy out somehow with suggestions, for my own benefit if nothing else.

'Could she have gone to a church meeting, for example?' I put it to him. 'Or be on her way to one?'

He shrugged. Whether she'd gone to a meeting or not, the matter did not seem to concern him, and I found myself dropping the notion that wherever Sam went, Luke went too. Another assumption of mine. Plainly, theirs was a relationship I'd much to learn about. And one I wasn't keen to start asking questions about right now.

'I'd better see if I can find her at the farm,' I said, and took a step towards the door.

If the guy was going to stop me, now was the time for him to go ahead and do it. That's when I'm sure I heard the door to the shower room open again behind me. I even saw Luke's eyes register the fact. And maybe the presence behind me of the third party, whoever she was, influenced the outcome in my favour, for he stood to one side, leaving my exit route clear. I could have turned round, yes, and taken a look for myself. Come to a decision as to what sort of friend she was exactly. Made up my mind about the massage parlour business, whether I'd stumbled upon its centre of operations or was making more assumptions about other people's behaviour. Truth is I'd no wish to turn my back on the guy a second time, even for a minute.

Only after I resumed my journey along the lane did it occur

to me that I'd overlooked to mention the hens and to tell him how grateful I was for going to the trouble of locking them away for me.

*

That evening Sam didn't arrive home till dusk. Long after Luke had returned the tractor to the yard and clomped up the stairs. On his own, I should add. No recently showered companion at his side. And long after I'd made a telephone call to Chris Lambertson. Not to ask Chris if he remembered playing rugby with Ernest Bower, though that did get a mention in passing, I'll admit. It was the benefit of Chris's advice I sought. On two points of law – namely, agricultural tenancies for one; libellous newspaper adverts the other. A colleague like Chris can come in very handy, let me tell you, to help get to grips with tricky issues like these.

I'd begun drafting my letter to the *Gazette*'s advertising editor and in the process had this idea that a word with Chris might help. Contract law, I knew, was his area of expertise, and yes, he assured me, he would do his best to address my concerns on both points as long as I didn't treat his opinion as the equivalent of professional advice from a practising solicitor. Scout's honour, I promised him. We agreed on a lunchtime drink the next day. He suggested The Dog and Duck, the pub on the Drovers Road, you'll recall. Why not? I was a free man.

As I say, Sam didn't return till dusk. I thought about going outside for a word with her on hearing her car in the yard. But you know how it is – it was late, and she was most likely exhausted at the end of a long day. And what sort of word exactly had I in mind? The ad in the *Gazette*? Ted Shimwell's concerns about Luke's mother? My experience at Lord's Barn? Did I even *want* to raise with Sam the question of what might be going on there? Or quiz her about other women in Luke's life? For all

I knew, Miss Painted Toenails could be a perfectly legitimate friend of his, taking a well-earned shower after helping him mix concrete, say, or plumb in a new bathroom suite. What did *I* know about these matters? Okay, she did drive an expensive car (which she'd possibly borrowed from her wealthy parents). And she did make a point of keeping out of my way, doubtless because (1) she had no idea who I was and (2) she had no clothes on.

With hindsight, I didn't see how I could have handled things differently with Luke. The encounter had taken me by surprise, him too, and now he'd be on the defensive, you could bet. Tackling Sam about it could make matters worse. So when the Fiat rolled into the yard, I left her to it and picked up GV's journal again, intending to read a few more pages before bed. Unfortunately, I dozed off in the attempt – not for the first time, eh?

I woke to hear someone knocking at my door. More punters after a massage, was it? A bit late, I thought. It had gone dark and there were no car lights on out there, but the yard *was* lit up. Someone had triggered the PIR lantern over the kitchen door. Luke with an apology perhaps? A reminder to put the hens to bed? Unlikely on both counts, and in any case, I'd already seen to the hens.

No, it was Sam at the door, interestingly enough. On her own. Asking if she could come in for a word, presumably a word about my encounter with Luke. In a state of anticipation then, I let her in, then took my time, going methodically through the formalities, as you do – sitting her down on one of her mum's chairs, switching on an extra lamp, checking she'd eaten (she had, thank you), offering her a drink of one sort or another (she declined), praising her hairdo (she shrugged) – before getting round to querying the purpose of her visit.

I was right. She wanted to talk about Luke. About me and Luke, and specifically our encounter today. He'd complained to her, apparently, about how rude I'd been to him while he was working at the Barn.

I must have looked at Sam over my glasses, made a face or something, for she accused me of not taking the matter seriously. 'You're right,' I told her. 'It is a serious business. I came across Luke at Lord's Barn, yes. But I wasn't there five minutes. I think maybe I interrupted something.'

'So you were spying on him?'

You can see this wasn't going to be easy, can't you? 'I wasn't spying at all. This morning I went for a walk round the farm and met Ted Shimwell repairing one of the walls. He told me I'd probably find Luke at the Barn. Even told me how to get there.'

Sam looked unimpressed. 'A walk, eh? You turned up in your car, Luke says. So what did you want to see him for?'

Okay, I know, for brevity's sake I'd compressed two visits to the Barn into one. Did that make me a total jerk who couldn't sound convincing if he tried? 'I wanted to thank him, actually,' I explained, 'for putting the hens away last night. Or was that *you*? Both of you, I guess? I've hardly had a chance to meet the guy, remember.'

'A funny way to thank him. He says you asked him what business he had at the Barn and more or less told him he needed your permission to be there.'

Excuse me? I don't know about you but my way of dealing with this kind of counter-allegation is to stay calm and challenge it. Sam, as you can see, had her moments, and clearly, in her eyes I was the person in the wrong here. I guess I shouldn't have been surprised to hear she believed the boyfriend she slept with over the uncle she shared a house with, but there you go. She hadn't heard her uncle's version of the story yet.

'That's not how it was,' I began. And thought how can I give my niece a straightforward account of what happened and avoid her reaching the same conclusion I'd reached, I hadn't actually caught Luke doing anything blatantly amiss, if you think about it. Nothing you could cite as irrefutable proof of infidelity. The fact the other party had no clothes on was neither here nor there. She was taking a shower. All by herself. While Luke had been outside, fully clothed.

'Are you saying Luke isn't telling the truth?'

How to word this? If I dismissed the boyfriend's accusation, I as good as called him a liar. If I compromised, I came across as a mealy-mouthed creep. A no-brainer, then. 'If you must know,' I told her, 'I tripped and fell over the doorstep the minute I got there and yes, I may have let fly with some questionable language, but it wasn't meant for *him*. I'm sorry if he thought it was.' There, I'd managed to explain my bruises, such as they were, without incriminating the guy responsible for inflicting them.

'It's Luke you should be apologising to. He's very cut up about it.'

I bet he was. Doubtless the guy was experiencing problems getting over the way I'd turned up like that, out of the blue, unannounced. A few minutes either way and who knows what sort of scene I might have been witness to? (Sorry, I'm doing it again, aren't I? Pre-judging the guy. I really must get a grip). 'I'll have a word with him next time I see him,' I promised. 'I'll see him right.' Whenever that might be.

Meanwhile, had she seen the latest *Gazette* by any chance? I put my copy down in front of her, open at the advert which I'd ringed in red 'What do you make of that?' I asked her.

Not a lot, it seemed. Sam shrugged. Like she knew all about it and didn't see it as a talking point at all. 'It's not *this* place,' she informed me. 'It's a big house on the New Road. Far Meadow Grange. We do get people turning up here by mistake from time to time.' And that was all the attention she seemed to feel it deserved. If people mistook Foolsmeadow Grange Farm for Far Meadow Grange House, so be it. People got addresses wrong all the time. Even the postman got them wrong. You learned to live with it out here, it seemed.

She asked if the farm was advertised yet in the paper. She had her legs together and both knees pointing at me as she spoke, and I was reminded of what a fine-looking young woman she'd grown into. Far more striking than Hilary had been at that age, I thought. With far shapelier legs. My attention must have wandered because next minute, obviously convinced I wasn't going to reply, she'd opened the paper and taken a look for herself. And not found it, of course. And drawn her own conclusions.

She put the paper down and asked after Ted. For something to say, I think, as an alternative to asking me to confirm that the farm had been taken off the market.

'Ted told me he's been given notice to quit,' I told her. 'More or less amounts to that, at any rate.' Was I over-egging the pudding somewhat?

'Who's told him that?'

The knees parted and one leg was lifted across the other. 'Who's told him that?' I repeated, reminding myself this was my niece I was addressing and not some leggy student I was interviewing for a place in my tutorial group. 'He said he's had notice to quit from Luke's mother, so he reckons,' I went on. 'Sounds odd to me. I told him to hang on till your mum gets back and she'd sort it out.'

Sam kept her legs where they were. 'Luke's mother? Is he *serious*?'

'What do you mean?'

'Luke's mother isn't exactly a common sight round here. Can't imagine her having words with Ted Shimwell, let alone giving him his marching orders. He's pulling your leg.'

'I see.' In that case, I ventured to ask, was the guy pulling my leg about Luke's involvement in the death of his dog, too?

Sam sniffed at the suggestion. 'That was an accident.'

She confirmed Luke owned a motorbike and rode it up and down the lanes. But she called the dog a menace that chased after anything and everything that moved. Then she added, 'There's something else I came down to tell you. Something you should know. About this weekend.'

Oh yes? Were there going to be more high jinks at the Barn? A Saturday night rave perhaps? More of those rustic carry-ons that Hilary really should have warned me about before disappearing up north?

'On Sunday it's our annual church convention,' she explained. What did I tell you? 'On Saturday,' she continued, 'Luke will be helping with the preparations. Me too. There's a marquee to put up in the ten-acre field, and seating to arrange. There'll be a car park roped off as well. Cars will be coming through the yard on both days. I'm guessing Mother didn't mention it.'

The look on my face gave that much away, clearly. I leaned back, hands behind my head, trying to decide if now was the time to offer some help of my own, as part of that new desire of mine to ingratiate myself with the Sahara Street crowd, not to mention my wish to get to know Sam and Luke better. Wasn't this the perfect opportunity? What did I have to lose? An auspicious event like this was bound to attract the presence of you-know-who. No need to go to the mountain, it looked like the entire range was on the move and heading to a field near me. Just one point to clear up.

'Does Ted know about it?' Now why on earth, I wondered afterwards, bring *him* into it.

'The ten-acre isn't one of his fields.'

In other words, he hadn't been told. Sam got to her feet, signalling mission accomplished as far as she was concerned, she wasn't going to hang about for more of my pointless questions. As she moved towards the door, I felt I still needed to offer to get involved in some way, so I asked her, 'Can anyone turn up and take part in this… this convention, as you call it? It's on my doorstep when all's said and done. I'm sure I could be of some use.'

Not quite at my most fluent, perhaps, but there you go. Sam gave me an understandably lofty look, like what possible use could I be, I didn't even know how to be civil to her boyfriend. What's more, would I stop being such an obvious perv where her legs were concerned. She was a grown-up now, a big girl with no time for sad cases that pretend they're something they're not, teacher or no teacher!

I reached for my cigarettes, thinking right, young lady, have it your way, but we both know there's more than one road to celestial pastures. 'The offer stands,' I told her, and looked round for the ashtray. The one I'd used earlier. The glass one.

Sam nodded towards where it lay on the worktop as I lit up. 'It's one of our rules,' she told me. 'It goes for all members and their guests, without exception. No smoking. And no alcohol.'

I didn't ask about fornication.

PART 3

SIX

DAY TWO

A clergyman turned up at my door next morning. On a bicycle. With a fancy name and title. The Reverend Langley-Carter, hyphenated, rector of St Michael's Parish Church, looking to have a word with Mrs Pope. When I told him who I was, he looked at me hard (for signs of a family resemblance, I guess) before inviting me to call him Bernard and asking if he could come inside for a few minutes of my time. 'I don't believe I've heard Mrs Pope mention she has an older brother,' he told me. 'But I confess my memory's not what it was. You teach, do you? At the college, eh? Awful business, so I heard.'

News got around, clearly: bad news especially. 'Young people these days, eh?' He sighed and turned his eyes up towards the kitchen ceiling. 'Terribly sad business all round. I feel for his parents, I really do.'

Yes indeed, I echoed, and just happened to mention that GV had been a keen churchgoer, too. But not C of E, or perhaps the rector already knew that.

'*No!* he exclaimed. 'Sahara Street, you say? *How interesting*! That's your niece's church, too, if I'm not mistaken. Does she still attend?' As though she might by now have seen the light and expressed a wish to be taken back into the fold.

'Yes. Very keen she is, too. She and her boyfriend. A bit of a surprise to me, but there you go.'

'Do I gather they've not managed to convert *you*?' Voiced as if there was hope for me yet, even if he'd given up on Hilary long ago. 'I'll give that church of theirs due credit,' he conceded. 'They do seem to have a winning formula for putting bums on seats. A trick our lot could learn from, if you ask me.'

He'd brought a copy of the parish magazine with him, expressly for Mrs Pope to look at, but thought I might like to take a look at it myself, as a bit of light reading. I could learn who would be doing the flower arrangements this month, for example, or which of his parishioners had been committed to the ground. The churchyard, he informed me, had room for only one more burial, with standing room only after that, he chortled. At least till some kind soul with land to spare donated some of it for use as an annexe. He gave me a nod and a wink, as though I might care to persuade Hilary to give the matter some serious consideration. Then chortled to himself again, as if the idea she would agree struck him as downright delusional.

That's when I found myself wondering what the Sahara Street lot did with *their* dead. Perhaps that's why they wanted the farm, and perhaps a few of theirs were due to be buried under the ten-acre on Sunday or burned on a communal pyre. I must have pulled a face or something at the prospect, for the rector offered me a penny for my thoughts.

'Nothing really,' I told him. 'Just thinking about graveyards and funerals. A big part of your job, I suppose, ushering people into the next life. And convincing the ones left behind that it's a great place to go to when the time comes.'

'I don't know about that,' he said. 'We're all mortal. And

it's natural, as we get older, to start thinking about what comes next. My job is to help people by giving them guidance and comfort. As best I can, of course.'

'Mine too. The guidance bit, I mean. Our jobs aren't so very different, really, when you think about it.'

He hadn't thought about it. But now he did, he soon came to the conclusion that teachers fell somewhat short of the mark these days. 'Take the curriculum,' he suggested. 'It doesn't seem to include teaching young people respect any more. Certainly not for their environment. We have an awful problem at the church with litter. Youngsters gathering outside the south door in the evenings and dropping drink cans and food trays. Spraying graffiti on the gravestones. Leaving used condoms lying around. It's not a pretty sight, I can tell you.'

He picked up the parish magazine he'd left on the table for me and found me the page where he'd written about the problem in this month's edition – the follow-up to a recent sermon he'd given on the subject, he told me. 'You should see the mess the graveyard's in,' he continued. 'That's one of the things I wanted to raise with Mrs Pope: the state of her late husband's grave. It's in dire need of some TLC, if I can put it that way. Along with several other graves I could mention.'

He could put it any way he liked, I could hardly guarantee that Hilary would take steps to make Philip's grave any tidier, even if I mentioned it to her. Which I would do, of course, willingly. As soon as she got back, I promised.

'Good man,' he said. And then chortled to himself about the way he'd inadvertently taken my surname in vain. 'Now unless you have a cup of coffee going spare, I suppose I ought to be on my way as I've a few other calls to make before lunch.'

What's that saying about God helps those that hint the loudest? I put the kettle on, telling myself I couldn't send him on his way thinking I shared my sister's woeful sense of hospitality.

He continued to chortle merrily between sips of the coffee

I made him (strong, no sugar, just a sniff of milk), regaling me with tales of the mixed hospitality he'd received over the years at the hands of some of his far-flung parishioners, older ladies mostly. Then told me, leaning in to my ear, in a somewhat louder voice, 'I think that's someone at your door.' As if I'd switched off the old hearing aid and left him to gabble on.

It was Luke, of all people. Holding out Friday's mail (a couple of letters) for me to take from him, and not quite meeting my gaze as he did so. I assumed he'd taken them from the postman at the gate. 'For Missus Pope,' he muttered, and looked past me as he spoke, presumably for a glimpse of the guest I was entertaining. And why not? I'd caught *him* with a girl in the shower, now it was his turn to catch *me* entertaining the rector. My fully clothed, chortling rector for his thoroughly naked Ms Painted Toenails. One telling exposure for another, as you might say.

Sorry, there I go again. I managed to put a smile on my face. 'I'm with the rector right now,' I explained. 'We're having coffee. Do come in and join us. The kettle has just boiled.'

Step inside and see for yourself, in other words, what a clean God-fearing ship I run here. And while you're at it, why not relax and give your uncle-to-be the benefit of your company so he can get to know you better?

No such luck. Luke had things to do, jobs to get on with. Like a shower to fix (sorry, can't help it, can I?). Difficult to tell what was going through his head as he backed away, having handed over the mail, before turning and disappearing in the direction of his own front door. So much for the opportunity to get better acquainted.

'Bills,' I told the Reverend as I put the letters down on the mantelpiece. 'They never fail to arrive. Thankfully, none of them for me.'

'Your niece's boyfriend, I take it?'

Didn't miss a trick, did he? 'Yes. Not exactly the talkative type, you'll have noticed.'

'Last time I was here Mrs Pope gave me to understand he does jobs on the farm for her. Quite a useful young man to have around the place, now the man of the house is no longer with us to do them.'

'Quite the handyman, yes, so I understand,' I conceded.

The Reverend nodded towards the window. 'I couldn't help seeing the For Sale board on my way in. I'd heard rumours Mrs Pope was thinking of selling, so it doesn't come as a surprise to learn she's made up her mind about it. Where will she go?'

'Your guess is as good as mine. She hasn't discussed it with me. I'll probably be the last person to know.'

'You've met Ted Shimwell, have you?'

'I was talking to him yesterday. He rents some of the fields.'

'That's him. I get on well with Ted. He's one of my regulars, a staunch churchgoer, if ever I met one. He thinks Mrs Pope will change her mind about selling and go and live in one of the cottages she's having renovated on Briar Lane. She'll leave the youngsters to do the farming, he reckons.'

Not quite the version I'd heard from him, shall we say. 'Did Ted tell you that?'

Apparently so. I mentioned Sunday's forthcoming event in the ten-acre field and this time received a blank look. I suggested Ted must have heard about it.

'Can't say I've heard him mention it,' was the Reverend's response. Well, well, a hiccup on the grapevine. He confessed he'd no idea which was the ten-acre field, and on that point I felt unable to enlighten him.

'Will you be attending?' he asked.

I told him I'd still to make up my mind. The truth, in other words. Well, I didn't want to dash the guy's hopes so soon that I might turn up for his service on Sunday morning, did I? On the other hand, as the person left in charge during my sister's absence, I pointed out that I did have a responsibility to keep an eye on things round the farm over the weekend. Liabilities, eh?

'Your niece will be on hand over the weekend, surely…' Seeing the doubt on my face about that, he contented himself with making his offer. 'Feel free at any rate to come along to St Michael's on Sunday. Take the opportunity to meet some of the locals, you'll find them very friendly, very genuine people, though I say so myself.'

I told him I'd give his invitation some serious thought.

*

Chris Lambertson's car was already in the car park at The Dog and Duck. And inside, by the window, there he was, a pint already half consumed in front of him. He'd sat, curiously enough, in the same seat Mrs K had occupied, where he could see more clearly what he was drinking.

I bought my own drink at the bar before going across to join him. He'd brought a folder with him, and I put my copy of the *Willsborough Gazette* down next to it, open at the offending ad. Our respective notes for reference and easy access, you might say.

'First time I've been in this place,' Chris informed me. 'Passed it a number of times, but never felt the urge to stop and come inside. Looks like I didn't miss much.'

'Make the most of it,' I suggested. 'It may not be here for much longer if business remains as brisk as this.'

Chris took a good long sup of his brew and nodded appreciatively as I looked on. 'Not bad ale, though, if I'm honest. Is this your regular watering hole then?'

'Good Lord, no! It just happens to be close to my sister's farm, that's all. I'm residing there, remember, while she takes a holiday with Steve. I'm the guy she's left in charge. The caretaker.'

'How is Steve's dad, by the way?'

'Fine, as far as I know. Improved, at any rate, or Steve wouldn't have taken off for Scotland.'

'And this farm of your sister's, that's the farm she's trying to sell, right?'

'Correct. And she's being told it's subject to a tenancy agreement, which she denies, like I said over the phone.'

Chris reached for his folder. 'I've brought you some light reading.' He took out a wad of papers. 'It's in here, a copy of the *Agricultural Holdings Act*. You won't need to read all of it, you'll be pleased to hear. I've highlighted the sections which I think you'll find relevant.'

True enough, on the sheets he handed me he'd underlined words, circled paragraphs, made notes in the margins, inserted exclamation marks here and there, all in red ink, for my benefit. He handed them over like he was returning a sample of my homework.

'What's your verdict, then? The bottom line?' I enquired. 'I can read all this small print later, at home, can't I? On the loo. Come on, you're the lawyer.'

Chris looked at me from under his hairy eyebrows. 'I thought *that's* what you wanted, the detail. Chapter and verse, you said. Well, there it is. If you want me to summarise, okay. It goes something like this: if your sister consented to her daughter and boyfriend living together on the premises, paying her rent and doing jobs for her round the farm, then those are grounds, under the Act, for them to claim that a tenancy agreement exists. Simple as that, I'm afraid.'

'No need for anything in writing, you mean?'

'Afraid not.'

'No way out for my sister, then? No means of terminating the agreement from *her* side, cancelling it, making it null and void?'

'Not unless the daughter and boyfriend fall into rent arrears. Or are shown to be in serious breach of the agreement themselves. The spirit of it, that is, since none of it is in writing, obviously. Even then, your sister would have to prove the tenancy was causing *her* greater hardship than its annulment would be likely to cause her tenants. A bit of a bind, I'm afraid, but there it is.'

One way of looking at it. Certainly not the sort of news Hilary would want to hear. Like me, she'd probably wonder how Sam came by *her* knowledge of the Act in the first place. Sam was no trainee lawyer. She worked in a pie shop, for Christ's sake. And forget about Luke. As for Sahara Street, now that was a whole different ball game. Their elders, or a slick city agent acting for them, had to be behind the letters fired off by a solicitor to intimidate provincial estate agents. As I'd told Hilary, solicitors don't come cheap, and certainly not those with an office in the city.

Reading my thoughts on the subject, Chris offered to give me the name of a bargain firm of solicitors, if that would be any help. I promised to bear it in mind, but frankly, when all's said and done, it wasn't *my* fight, now was it? Hilary, as usual, would go her own sweet way, notwithstanding any advice from me. I certainly couldn't see her accepting the idea that if Sahara Street were so keen to get their hands on the farm, then she should offer it to them. At a suitable asking price, naturally. On the assumption they weren't short of the means to buy it. Minus the Lord's Barn and its plot, if that's where Hilary wished to move to. A happy outcome for all concerned, wouldn't you say?

Chris wanted to move on, now he'd sorted out the tenancy legalities. Hadn't I a question for him on slander? Or was it libel?

No Act of Parliament to show me this time, merely a couple of questions for me once I'd drawn the newspaper ad to his attention. Sam, you'll recall, had told me about the existence of *Far* Meadow Grange, so yes, I told Chris, there *was* a place nearby with a similar name that appeared to be misleading would-be punters. As for who had placed the ad, the obvious answer had to be the person or persons living at the other place whose name I didn't know yet. Only that was to miss the point, the point being, as I saw it, the confusion sown in punters' minds because of the ambiguous way the ad was worded. That, surely, had to be the responsibility of whoever accepted the advert on behalf of the *Gazette*. Didn't it?

Strictly speaking, no, Chris maintained. Newspapers as a rule denied liability arising from printing pages of small adverts. And since this ad contained no inaccuracies, merely an oversight or omission (a *Far* Meadow Grange House, with or without the Far, did exist as and where stated), and contained nothing in the way of offensive or libellous language (I wasn't so sure about that), there was nothing *legally speaking* that could be objected to. Nobody, in other words, had set out deliberately to defame or compromise the farm's good name. Or, as he put it, to play a practical joke on the farm's occupants. The evidence for believing they had simply didn't exist.

Instead of making spurious legal threats, Chris suggested I wrote a letter to the editor. For publication, naturally. Pointing out the distress and lost time suffered as a result of the confusion over similar addresses and urging advertisers to take more care in such matters in future. He suggested a light-hearted tone, not flippant by any means but strong on the humour to be derived from the situation I found myself in as occupier of the *other* Meadow Grange. What humour? Plainly Chris had not yet had guys turn up at his home asking for personal services. I believe I nodded and went along with it. Sam, you'll recall, hadn't seemed overly concerned about the confusion, so, you may ask, why should I be?

We drained our glasses on that note and, feeling duty bound, I offered to fetch refills for both of us.

When I got back to our table by the window two more cars, I saw, had pulled into the car park and were disgorging their occupants. A noisy lot, by the sound of it, who soon made their presence known at the bar. One noisy woman, in particular, looked and sounded so much like Mrs K that I turned to Chris and signalled to him, head down, that I knew this person walking past us with a glass of something in her hand but was pretending

I'd not seen her. In fact, it wasn't her. Mrs K had a doppelganger, believe it or not, who returned my gaze with one of her own, as if she too had set eyes on *my* double. What a small world, eh?

'It's not who you thought it was, then?'

Chris had a grin on his face. We all make mistakes. Now if Mrs V or her double had walked into the bar... Well, to start with, I would have been keen to see who she was with, naturally. Not churchgoing types, surely, pubs being against their rules, remember. I expect the woman would have been taken aback to see me there, in any case, and would have promptly taken herself and her companions off to a corner of the lounge where they could be assured of some privacy. I'd be a source of embarrassment to her, in short. Especially if she had only the one companion, and he was male, say. At least I'd get to see what type she went for.

By now Chris, I saw, was fishing more documents out of his folder in search of something which he told me had almost slipped his mind to mention. Did I know, he wondered, that Gordon Verity had kept some sort of diary?

Now why should Chris of all people ask me a question like that? What documents did he have in his possession that would prompt such a question? 'I was told he kept a diary of some kind,' I said warily. 'A journal, I think he called it. Why do you ask?' No point in saying any more at this stage. Especially if I was about to discover that mine wasn't the only copy. That there were multiple copies in various people's hands and anyone in search of the guy's diary didn't need to get their hands on *my* copy when so many others were willing to part with theirs.

Chris located the sheet of paper he was after and handed it over for me to read. 'I found this the other day among some of my students' work handed in for marking. I assume it got there by mistake. Don't ask me how. Reads very much to me like a final entry in a much longer account. Or it could be a suicide note, I suppose, when you bear in mind what happened. What do you make of it?'

Well, the handwriting certainly matched the scrawl I recognised as GV's handiwork. An authentic document then, as far as I could tell. The paper, too, was torn from the same book of lined A4 sheets. But how had Chris, who didn't know GV's handwriting for a start, traced it so conclusively to *my* erstwhile student? I scanned the page for evidence of his name and found it, tucked away in the text where Chris must have spotted it, too. Well, we *were* both teachers, accustomed to searching written work for clues as well as errors. But I had the edge when it came to spotting those quirkily encrypted characters of GV's. Take a look for yourself:

> 'This could be my last page as this is as far as I want things to go. If you don't speak up, people think it's very likely your fault for not speaking up, when really I can't find a way of putting a stop to things. I've tried and it hasn't worked. God decides where to lay blame in the end, that's what I've always believed, and it's right, nobody can hide things from Him, no matter who they are, and nobody else has the right to judge anyone or any of it, not even me.
>
> 'It's one thing writing things down like this, in my diary, under my own name, as Marcie would say. But some things are hard to put into words, or just not possible. The words won't come because if they do somebody may get hurt and it's not for me, not for Gordon Verity, like I say, to judge people for being who they are. That's His job, when the time comes. So you see, I have to find some other way to bring things to a stop. And I hope people will understand. I know some will say God will not forgive if you choose to take a route they think is wrong, but God as I see Him is so much more understanding than many people believe. Do please forgive me, Marcie. You too, Mo.'

Now, as I see it, if it's put together like a suicide note, reads like one, has all the giveaway hallmarks, turns of phrase, etc. then I guess it's perfectly reasonable to consider it as one. Hard not to see this as the kind of document a coroner, if he'd had it to hand at the inquest, would have quoted as pretty conclusive evidence that GV's final act was a premeditated one. It even included his signature, in a manner of speaking. What it didn't do was give any hard details of how exactly he proposed to bring things to a close, or indeed whereabouts. Nor did it offer a clue as to what those *things* were that he proposed bringing to a stop. Too confidential to go into detail, supposedly. And far too personal to disclose them to his tutor. Full marks, then, to GV, for taking absolutely no one into his confidence; and for leaving behind nothing but a trail of encrypted clues.

'Not sure what to make of it, to be honest,' I told Chris. 'What do *you* think?' Playing the perplexed tutor to the end, see, eager for light to be shed from any reliable quarter.

Chris had taken the opportunity to reduce his second pint substantially whilst waiting for my verdict. I couldn't tell him about the other pages, could I? Not without admitting I knew about the journal and had the rest of it in my possession. Mind you, for all I knew, more pages might be out there, dozens of them possibly, waiting to be discovered and reunited with the ones I had in my folder. So I kept quiet.

'Well, he hasn't dated it,' Chris pointed out. 'So whether a coroner would have considered it relevant, in the circumstances, I don't know. It could amount to a piece of fiction, for all we know. Was the youth a bit of a fantasist? You were his tutor. Was he often away with the fairies?'

Away with the fairies, eh? I had never had GV down as a dreamer, or a guy who filled his head with fanciful ideas or who exaggerated or distorted the truth. Those characters in his diary, whatever their quirky names, were real people, I was convinced. I was represented in there myself, remember. Steve too. And

Mrs K's disclosures were borne out faithfully by what I'd read. No, as far as I was concerned, Gordon Verity told things as they were, and this latest offering, unnumbered like the rest, simply highlighted something he felt unable to cope with, or talk about.

Chris felt the same. 'Something was troubling the youth, obviously,' he said. 'But fucked if any of us know what it was. Didn't his family have a clue?'

'Search me. Did you want to hang on to it?' The suicide note. No knowing if Chris had designs of his own on delving into GV's troubled history. 'In case any other pages come to light? You never know.' Who was the fantasist now?

'I brought it for *you* to look at. I thought it might mean more to you, as his tutor. If you want it, you keep it, by all means.'

A sensible move. Chris had his moments. He finished the rest of his drink, then gathered up his things and announced he was off to visit a friend of his who'd come out of hospital recently. The bloody fool, as he called him. Lucky to be alive after an accident on his motorcycle. No life-changing injuries, fortunately, but the bike was a write-off. 'Then it's back home to watch the match,' he added. 'Wouldn't want to miss that, would we?'

Not likely. Rugby – I assumed that's what he was talking about – was being played somewhere across the globe, very probably a test match featuring a South African team. I stifled a yawn.

As we left The Dog and Duck guess whose eyes followed me out and all the way to my car.

PARTY TIME

Never mind Mrs K's lookalike, blow me, the real thing greeted me at the kitchen door the minute I got back. No kidding. I should have spotted her Mini in the yard, but I missed it. However, there was no mistaking the figure in the open doorway, giving me a wave as I climbed out of the Astra. How, you may well wonder, had Mrs K contrived to gain entry to my kitchen? I felt sure I'd left the place locked up. Don't tell me Hilary was back. Either that, or the woman had a key of her own and could come and go as she pleased.

Hilary *had* to be back. *She'd* let her friend in. Only there was no Land Rover visible. No sign of luggage at the door, either. So, what was the occasion?

'Surprised to see me, eh?'

You bet I was surprised. And not a little irritated. 'Has something happened?' I wanted to know. 'What's the problem?'

There wasn't one. How about that? Basically, the woman had no good reason for being here. All I got was a lame excuse, something along the lines of today happened to be a special occasion, something she called her *official* birthday, a bit like the Queen's, so she said, where anyone can join in and celebrate. A load of rubbish, in other words. 'Thought you'd never show up. Now you *are* here, finally, come on in and join me,' she entreated. 'There's sandwiches galore, and a choice of drinks. Oh, and a slice of my home-made Madeira cake. Very yummy.'

Now you're here, finally. Like she'd been here a while, waiting for me. Not a word about how she'd got the door open. Now I don't know about you but the idea she'd let herself in while I was out, then proceeded, as I saw with my own eyes, to take plates from my cupboards, knives and forks from my drawers, and spread her foodstuffs across my table (okay, they were Hilary's cupboards and things, but you know what I mean), it all left me a little stunned. Rather light-headed, in fact. My sister, I felt, should have warned me about this woman.

It occurred to me she had maybe brought Boyd along too, and any minute I'd hear my loo flush and the guy would appear. Okay, she'd not raided my larder by the look of things, not if Madeira cake was on offer; she'd simply used my kitchen to lay out her very own feast. And talking of banquets, it was all there

– sandwiches, sausage rolls, pies, cakes, mini this and mini that. A choice of wines, too. Enough of a feast, then, to make a guy feel compelled to at least sample *something*. Especially if the guy in question hadn't eaten anything since breakfast.

Accordingly, I saw no harm in helping myself to a salmon sandwich and took the opportunity to ask about Boyd. You don't celebrate your birthday, even your official one, surely, without your married partner present. Well, not unless you've fallen out, or he's in no condition to attend. Even then, why choose *my* house? Hilary's house, sorry. I was missing something here, obviously.

Boyd was back home, apparently, and not up to celebrating. Not today at any rate. 'He can be a miserable sod at times,' Mrs K informed me. 'Such a shame to waste all this food and drink, don't you think? What's your tipple, then? How about a drop of this Italian red?'

I nodded whilst attempting to get my head round the way she'd gained entry. She must have read my thoughts, for no sooner had she poured me a drink than she put the bottle down, leaned in closer, and held up a key under my nose – and winked! Like I was the other party in this cosy conspiracy, whether I owned up to it or not. 'Courtesy of your sister,' she confided. 'In case you were going to be late. Came in useful, didn't it? Anyway, you're here now, that's all that matters. Another sandwich?'

Okay, I know, Hilary had a perfect right to hand out keys as she saw fit. My argument, if I had one, was with this friend of hers for taking my acquiescence, along with my good nature, for granted. I didn't feel particularly in a party mood, if I'm honest. And I did wonder what Boyd might have to say about it, assuming he knew what was going on.

So here we were, the two of us, me, still at a bit of a loss, she, inviting me to sit at my own table and partake of another of her sandwiches. Meanwhile, she'd topped up her own glass to overflowing and pushed a couple of sausage rolls into her mouth (there was plenty of room for them, believe me!). Setting an example, as she called it, to celebrate the occasion. *What occasion again?* Hilary would hardly have chosen to go away a couple of days before her best friend's *actual* birthday. The occasion had to be a pretext to get away from Boyd, didn't it, and make hay with this new caretaker guy. The table, I could see, was laid expressly for two. It struck me Hilary probably had no idea her friend was going to pull a stunt like this in her absence. The woman had clearly gone to a lot of trouble. How tell her she was wasting her time?

She raised her glass. 'Here's mud in your eye, Adam. You know, I did wonder about you, whether you'd agree to look after this place while Hil's away. Whether you had the balls, for one thing. But here you are, you made it, there's more to you than… Shit! Did you see that?'

She'd wobbled and most of her wine missed her mouth and went down her front. Down into her bra, to be precise. She offered *me* the serviette she had in her hand, indicating that *I* should do the honours and mop up.

From the flush on her face and the almost empty state of the bottle she'd poured from, I concluded she had to have downed a few glassfuls prior to my arrival. That would explain the directness of her invitation, along with the theatrical pose she struck as she told me, 'Get on with it then. I won't look if you're going to be shy about it. Quick, I can feel it running down between my boobs. What are you waiting for?'

By now she was leaning in close to my face with those enormous buffers of hers, and waiting for me, presumably, to go to work with the serviette. I did my best, dabbing here and there, trying to look casual about it, before finally screwing up the serviette and heading for the pedal bin with it. 'I think I'll make myself a hot drink,' I told her. And take a breath of air, whilst I gather my thoughts, and think of somewhere else I urgently need to be.

'No harm done. It'll wash out,' I heard the woman say as I filled the kettle. She'd washed red wine out of her clothes on numerous occasions before, apparently. I admit I half expected the woman to throw caution to the wind, and strip off there and then and bundle her bra into Hilary's washing machine. Instead, she grabbed another serviette from the table and completed the job I'd started.

*

Outside in the yard, looking up at the ancient stonework, cigarette in one hand, a mug of coffee in the other, I remember asking myself if perhaps Hilary had departed for good. Got sick of the place. Eloped, if you like. Pushed off with Steve to make a fresh start somewhere else. Leaving me to cope with the fallout by way of consoling Mrs K, disposing of the farm, sorting out Ted's grazing rights, dealing with Sam and Luke, in short doing the right thing by everybody. A letter was probably on its way to me right now, outlining all this and wishing me the best of luck.

'Why didn't you say you were dying for a smoke, you crafty sod, you? You've hardly made a start on this food. Or your wine.'

Glass in hand, beaming hideously (she'd declined my offer of a strong black coffee herself), Mrs K stood watching me from the kitchen door. Awaiting my presence, once more. Okay, for all her faults, here at least was the woman most likely to have some meaningful comment to make if I showed her GV's suicide note. She was the one most likely to suggest what might have driven the youth over the edge. Why Marti, now I thought about it, was missing from the list of farewells. All I had to do was take advantage of the genial mood she was in and ask her opinion while the mood lasted. Which it wouldn't do, you could bet, if I made an excuse to take off again and left her standing there. A woman scorned and all that. Her psychic self was probably at work right now scanning the wine dregs for evidence that the man she'd invited to her party might have just lost interest. I had some reassuring to do.

I finished my cigarette, stubbed it out, and started my trek to the door. That's when the cavalry came into view. In the shape of Ted Shimwell, of all people. Unbelievable, I know. Sure enough, his familiar figure limped its way across the yard from the direction of the fields where his cattle grazed. 'You again. That's twice in two days,' he called out. 'Still, you did say as you were lookin' after the place while the boss is away.'

'Fancy a cuppa, Ted?'

The least I could do. I owed him one, remember, in return for that swig from his flask. 'Or a glass of something stronger?' Seeing as there was wine aplenty inside, not to mention the odd bottle of beer Hilary had left me in the fridge. I felt an understandable surge of goodwill towards the guy for his impeccable timing.

He pushed back his cap for a quick scratch and glanced at the sky before nodding his acceptance and making for the figure still standing at my door. 'How are you keeping, Missus Kendrick? Don't like the look of them clouds. Reckon as it'll rain before long, don't you?'

Mrs K didn't say. It was clear to me these two knew each other, but equally clear that Mrs K hadn't counted on another guest at the party. I'd go so far as to say she resolved there and then to move Ted on as quickly as possible, having decided that the quicker she got the kettle on, the sooner she'd see the back of him. None of the hard stuff for him, though. Tea was what the man had been offered, and tea was what he'd get. The wine bottles and the glasses stayed where they were. If anyone was going to get merry, it wasn't Ted. It was left to me to find him a seat and offer him a beer. No thanks, tea would be fine, he insisted.

'What's all this in aid of, then?' he asked, nodding his head towards the array of drinks and foodstuffs alongside him. 'Somebody celebrating somethin'?'

'Do help yourself to a cake or a sandwich,' I suggested.

Mrs K gave an impatient grunt or two as she waited for the kettle to boil, then asked him, 'You finished for the day then? That's it, is it? Off home now?'

'Me? My job's never finished, missus. I'll just have a biscuit, if that's all right.'

I brought the plate within his reach. 'Seen her yet, 'ave you?' he asked me.

'Seen her? She's not back yet.' I assumed he meant Hilary. 'Not for a few more days.'

'Not *her*. The one I told you about. The woman I can't do anything right for. Tells me I don't keep the gates fastened tight enough. Doesn't want my beasts roamin' everywhere.'

Oh, *that* woman! Luke's mother, the woman Sam had assured me rarely showed her face at the farm, but who somehow had managed to put the wind up Ted.

'He's talking about Trude,' Mrs K informed me as the kettle came to the boil. The name didn't register. Too much whistling, and I'd already started telling Ted I'd not seen the woman around the place yet.

He's talking about Trude. Now it registered. Or rather it didn't. If you're like me, your instinct is to assume the other guy has got the wrong end of the stick, on account of they haven't been listening hard enough. 'We're talking about Luke's mother,' I insisted.

'That's her, Trude Verity. Christ, didn't you know that?'

No, I didn't. And I didn't know whether to believe it or not either. To my mind it didn't make a lot of sense. The eloquent smart-suited businesswoman and the gruff silent farmhand, they were no way mother and son to my way of thinking. They weren't cast in the same mould, cut from the same cloth, sprung out of the same pod, however you like to put it. Somebody was pulling my leg.

Ted munched on his biscuit, and I saw him still eyeing

the banquet laid out next to him. 'Missus Kendrick here is celebrating her birthday,' I explained.

If he had a notion of what was really afoot, he kept it to himself, and soon he was slurping the mug of tea Mrs K put in his hands. 'Get it down you, Ted,' she urged him, 'then off you go. I don't want your missus accusing me of detaining you when she's ready to put dinner on the table. That would never do, now, would it? I'm the same with Boyd if he's late for his meal.'

Behind Ted's back she gave me another of those winks of hers. I did wonder if Mrs K might be one of the women Ted had had a crack at in the past and I decided no, even Ted had his standards. 'Take another biscuit,' I urged him. His dinner could wait. My need was greater.

'Don't mind if I do.'

What was it he'd told me about Luke's mother? That she seemed to think the farm would soon be hers? I turned to Mrs K. 'Ted tells me Luke's mother has an interest in the farm. That can't be true, can it?' Time to settle this once and for all.

Mrs K drained her glass of wine. 'Trude's probably a bit uptight making sure everything's okay for this weekend. No big deal. Ted's taken it the wrong way. That's right, Ted, isn't it? She just wants to make sure the big field is left clear, doesn't she? No stray cattle in there, for instance. No walls or fences down. Not a problem, I'm sure.'

Ted nodded but didn't look convinced. Eventually he muttered something about how rude the woman had been to him. As for the weekend's do in the ten-acre field, he hadn't a deal of time for it, to be frank. 'A funny lot, if you ask me. What do they want to meet up in a field for, of all places? What's wrong with a fine old church building, and a proper roof over your head? And singing good old-fashioned hymns like, instead of that awful modern stuff they go in for?'

'My feelings exactly, Ted,' said Mrs K, looking to take his empty mug away from him. 'But live and let live, that's my motto. They're not doing anyone any harm. Ready for home now then?'

Ted turned to me. 'She's wantin' me out the way, I can see that. Did you get to the Barn, then? The way I showed you?'

I told him I'd not found Luke there. I didn't tell him I'd returned later and found the place somewhat crowded. I tried a shot in the dark, though. 'Whose is the sports car? The silver one?'

I don't think Ted knew much about cars and their owners. He started scratching his head again. In the end Mrs K came to his aid. 'That's his mother's car. She drives a silver hatchback.'

'Your friend Trudi's car, you mean?'

I didn't want to leave room for doubt this time. And there wasn't any. Mrs K gave me an emphatic nod.

*

Ted departed at the sight of Sam's Fiat pulling into the yard. On cue, as it were; I couldn't fault him. One in, one out, anything to keep Mrs K on her toes. I believe Ted had more than a shrewd idea I was playing for time and needed a third party as a distraction, if you follow my drift. Men spot these things, you know. It was not yet four thirty by the kitchen clock. Early for Sam, definitely, but a welcome sight all the same.

Or I thought it was. Except something wasn't right. I heard Mrs K take a sharp intake of breath as she pushed past me on her way to the car. Sam had climbed out and dropped her handbag, and now seemed in two minds about whether to pick it up. Mrs K picked it up for her, and with her arm round Sam's shoulder, led her past me and into the kitchen. That's when I saw how bruised Sam's face was, how swollen. Like she'd walked into something unforgiving. Tears were rolling down her cheeks and she was shaking.

Mrs K produced a wet wipe and started dabbing at Sam's

face. 'I *knew* this would happen sooner or later. I just *knew* it! Turn your head this way, darling. A bit more. That's it. How does that feel? Let's get you into a chair, shall we, and take a look at the damage? Oh shit!'

She'd lowered Sam down onto my chair and knocked my glass over in the process. Wine shot across the table, engulfing the biscuits I'd offered Ted. 'I reckon we've spilt more of this stuff than we've drunk,' she muttered for my benefit. 'One of us must have been tipsy to start with.'

Oh yeah? Any guesses? I mopped up the mess, then took down Hilary's first aid box from one of the shelves and opened it for Mrs K to help herself. She seemed to know what she was doing. 'Looks painful,' I commented, helpful as ever.

Mrs K nodded. 'This was bound to happen sooner or later. You saw what happened with Steve.' She turned to Sam. 'It was *him,* wasn't it? Couldn't keep his hands to himself. Worse than having a loaded gun round the place. A bloody menace! Sorry, darling, but some things have to be said.'

Him? Luke, presumably. There'd been a row and it had ended like this. A bit of a shock, but not such a surprise, as they say. Except hadn't Sam just come from work? Perhaps she'd done what I did and called in at the Barn on the way, having had her own suspicions about what Luke got up to on the other side of the farm. Not so blind after all, my niece, it would seem. Unlike me, however, she'd clearly suffered more than a push in the back for her trouble.

I did wonder about taking matters out of Mrs K's hands and summoning some serious medical help at this stage. And calling the police. I mean, I *was* Sam's uncle, I *was* family, and I did have concerns about her injuries, and her safety. Mrs K insisted there was no need. Sam would be fine as soon as the swelling subsided, and we'd allowed time for the pills to take effect. Pills? What pills? Mrs K held up the pack of paracetamol tablets Hilary kept in her first aid box.

Looking at Sam's face, I could be forgiven, I suppose, for thinking I'd got off lightly. From the sound of it, however, Mrs K had seen it all before. 'Not the first time, is it? And it's no good him keep telling you he's sorry. That won't wash any more. Not after this it won't, my girl.' Spoken like she'd witnessed countless previous rows between the pair and decided she needed to put her foot down this time, before things got any worse.

Sam kind of nodded. Not easy, I imagined, with a badly bruised head. I could see she'd by now spotted the food and wine, and I had the impression that, if her bruised eyes could have opened wider at the sight, they would have done.

'Quite a feast, wouldn't you say,' Mrs K explained to her. 'Your uncle's put on a fine spread. Somebody's birthday, I believe.'

Oh yeah? Time for the wink treatment again, in case I should object to being cast in the role of accomplice, though frankly, I doubted Sam could have cared less who had invited whom. I'm sure neither of us was her ideal choice of desirable company. We just happened to be first on the scene, and the first to offer help and, if need be, protection, in the event the threat wasn't over yet.

To be perfectly honest, the thought of Luke turning up in pursuit made me thankful Mrs K hadn't pushed off yet to look after Boyd. The woman had her uses, certainly. She made excellent tea, for a start. She decided Sam would benefit from a brew and in no time at all had put a fresh mug in her hands. She handed out tissues like we'd all got bruised faces, without regard for where the next roll might be found. She suggested I move the food to one end of the table and rebuked me for plying my niece with unhelpful questions whilst I went about it.

'Stop pressing the girl! Can't you see she's still in shock? She's not one of your college students, you know, that's just had a nosebleed. She's your niece, for Christ's sake, looking for a spot of sympathy and understanding. Am I right, Sam, or is he always like this?'

The question brought another painful nod from Sam. And got me wondering how Mrs K foresaw the rest of the evening unfolding. Did she expect the three of us to remain where we were, for instance, spending the night together in my part of the house, for Sam's sake if nothing else? Did she expect Boyd to go along with that idea? Or would Boyd get suspicious and send a search party?

Not for the first time Mrs K appeared to read my thoughts. 'Boyd will be getting worried, poor bugger, if I'm not back for his tea. Won't hurt him to wait for once.'

When Sam muttered something to her that I didn't catch, she told her to forget it, then explained for my benefit, 'She's worried Luke might turn up here. Not tonight he won't. Take my word for it, sunshine.'

I guess I didn't have an alternative. So where would Luke be likely to spend the night? Mrs K thought the Barn and pulled a face, when I suggested the Barn would be too risky for him. That soon changed to a grin as a penny or two dropped. 'You mean he needs permission? Who's he going to ask? You?'

Well, maybe not. The Barn did seem the obvious place for the guy to spend the night. Tomorrow would be different. I'd have to look at things afresh, put myself in Hilary's shoes, and perhaps take a stroll over there. Tomorrow, too, Sam might see things differently and not want a fuss made. For now, though, groggy as she was, Sam had a phone call to make. She wanted to call her friend Jasmine. On Hilary's phone. Fine by me, it wasn't my bill.

Jasmine's place, I learned, was where Sam would be spending the night. Oh really? I jumped at the chance to drive her there. Whenever you're ready, I told her, whatever the distance. 'You're in no fit state to drive yourself,' I pointed out. Well, any excuse to flee the farm in case, you know, come the middle of the night, I should find myself woken by one or other of these two fruitcakes, the angry farmhand or the amorous psychic.

In the event, Mrs K trumped my offer. Jasmine's place lay on her route home, she announced, and as she was late already, the sooner the pair of them left, the better. Adam here, she proclaimed, would keep an eye on the Fiat. Adam nodded, overjoyed at his luck. He even helped load the considerable bulk of unwanted wines and foodstuffs into the back of the Mini. Mrs K's neighbour kept a dog apparently, which would soon make short work of the uneaten sandwiches. Bully for him. The remaining Madeira cake was offered to Sam, only Sam didn't feel hungry. She wasn't keen to pack an overnight bag either, despite Mrs K's offer to go upstairs to the flat with her to collect a few belongings.

The light was fading on the final preparations for departure when a large car drove into the yard and pulled up with a screech. I saw it bore two, maybe three occupants, all of them young men. For a moment I imagined Luke had turned up with reinforcements. Mrs K shut the boot lid of the Mini and stepped forward for a word with the driver. I saw him lower his window and no, it wasn't Luke at the wheel, though they all look alike, don't you find, these young people today?

'You've got the wrong farm,' I heard her tell him. Directions followed.

As they manoeuvred the car to drive off again, Mrs K turned to where I stood at the kitchen door and shook her head before squeezing herself behind the wheel of the Mini. If only cars could speak, eh? This one would do its share of groaning, I swear. There was a brief moment as the motor struggled to start, then they were off out of the yard and down the lane.

*

Back in the kitchen I took a couple of paracetamol tablets myself. The day had left me shell-shocked, shall we say. One thing for sure: Hilary wouldn't lose sleep if today's developments signalled the end of Sam's liaison with Luke. The circumstances might concern her somewhat, but she'd regard Sam's bruised face as a price worth paying. Like Mrs K, she'd feel the rift was bound to happen sooner or later. What she'd make of her friend's birthday party was something else, of course, assuming news of it ever came to Hilary's attention. I didn't plan on raising it with her myself, let me make clear. Who'd believe me, for a start?

Talking of things being hard to believe, I still had difficulty accepting that Mrs V had any connection with Luke. Somebody had to be kidding. If it *was* true, it meant Luke was yet another Verity, didn't it? A product of the union between his mother and whoever the guy might be. Some kind of Heathcliff, if you ask me, but not so good-looking, not if Luke was anything to go by. The solicitor's letter, I recalled, had referred to Sam's partner as Luke *Beresford*. So was that the name Trudi had dropped in favour of keeping the family name as her own? I decided it was too late in the day to be pursuing the matter, it wasn't helping my headache.

More interesting to contemplate the weekend's Sahara Street shindig. It began to look as if Luke's mother had the job, according to Mrs K, of ensuring the whole thing went ahead smoothly. Like the woman was some kind of fixer, and that meant, surely, that she wouldn't just be attending the event, she'd be helping to *organise* it. With any luck our paths would cross, and she'd learn how my role had changed, how *I* was in charge at the farm, and not Ted, or her friend Mrs K. Imagine it – the two of us meeting on *my* patch for a change and putting our heads together to make the weekend go with a swing. Things were looking up.

*

The day wasn't over yet, it turned out. This was the day that began, you'll recall, with a visit from the rector. How long ago was *that*? How long, for that matter, since Chris Lambertson had sat down with me at The Dog and Duck and we'd talked about the law? Anyway, I'd shut the hens away and was preparing to retire for the night when the phone rang. Ten thirty, according to my kitchen clock. Who could be calling at this hour? It had to be Sam. She'd forgotten her clean underwear; would I be so kind as to collect it and bring it over right away. Hilary wouldn't ring so late. Or my family. So who else could it be? A wrong number, by the sound of the voice on the other end. A woman's voice, not Sam, not Mrs K, asking if I was Mister Goodman, and telling me, when I confirmed I was, that she was (wait for it) Gertrude Verity. A practical joker at large again? 'What do you want?' I blurted out. Caught off guard, you see. Well, it was stretching credulity a bit, don't you think? A call from a woman I'd so recently had uppermost in my thoughts. What is it they say about the power of telepathy? Must read up on it. She'd obviously been thinking about *me*.

Where was the call coming from? The footwear shop? At this hour? For some reason this detail seemed to matter to me more than the purpose of the call. And when I did ask again what the woman wanted, I did wonder if she might be calling to enquire if I was happy with the shoes I'd bought. 'Can I help you?' I finally put it to her.

She had to be ringing about preparations for Sunday's big day, I realised. To ask for my approval, perhaps. Better late than not at all. Or to apologise for upsetting Ted. Maybe she wanted me to have a word with him for her, to make it clear she wasn't the monster Ted thought she was. I knew that much, of course, and saw myself as the obvious choice to speak up on her behalf.

I tried picturing the woman on the other end of the line, but all I could see was the tall figure of her as I'd seen her in the shop, at the till, counting coins, a paragon of elegance in her clingy skirt and heels. Given the hour, I realise, she was more likely to be wearing something a lot less formal, and much less of it.

Quite a shock, therefore, when she spoke, to hear it was Luke she had on her mind. The son I was hoping wasn't really her son at all. A misunderstanding on somebody's part. Her opening words, in fact. 'There's been a dreadful misunderstanding,' was how she described it. 'With your niece, I mean. This afternoon. Luke is very upset about it, as you must have heard.'

One way of looking at it, I suppose. It sounded an all too familiar cry to my professional ear. So familiar that I knew what was coming. I'd been there before, more than once. The parent pleading for her boy to be given another chance, to be reinstated on the course, to prove he wasn't the total arsehole others perceived him to be, for the sake of his career if nothing else. What did I just say about the reason for this call? Now it struck me. Sunday could be in jeopardy for her if I was to take my niece's side against the Veritys and lock the farm gates. The woman needed my goodwill. She needed me to smile on her and her son, maybe even intercede on Luke's behalf to keep Sam onside. What a turnaround! Forget GV's journal, here was a much more immediate way to get this woman's attention.

I felt myself become quite calm. 'He can't be more upset than my niece,' I pointed out. How best to play my advantage? Lay it on a bit thick, maybe? To start with, at any rate. 'She's considering bringing a charge of assault. It was touch and go whether I rang for an ambulance for her.' Okay? A bit threatening, but accurate all the same. Sam *had* taken quite a punch in the face. In anybody's book, a reportable offence.

'I'm sorry to hear that,' came back the response. 'Naturally I haven't had the chance to speak to your niece and hear her side of the story. I hadn't realised it was being taken quite so seriously, to be perfectly honest. Let's say I was rather hoping we could manage to sort this out between us, Mr Goodman. Before it gets to a stage where we both lose control of what's happening. Salvage what we can between us, if you understand my meaning.'

Excuse me? Was I being propositioned here, for want of a word? Offered a tacit recompense in return for my complicity in a bid to restore relations between Luke and Sam? Let's say I think I could see the wood for the trees here. We'd sort it out between us, me and Mrs V, like sensible grown-ups who only want the best for all concerned. Fine by me. I wanted to suggest we drop formalities right away and use first names, but I guess *Trudi* would have sounded a trifle presumptuous, not to say inappropriate at this stage. Though she was welcome to call me Adam, of course, whenever she liked.

'I see no reason why an effort shouldn't be made to sort things out amicably.' I agreed. No harm in that at all. And no shortage of goodwill on my side. Where did she expect me to begin?

She continued to Mister Goodman me, probing for the extent of the pressure I might be willing to exert to get Sam to agree to take Luke back again. Laughable how much influence she thought I had over my niece. Clearly, the woman didn't know the first thing about relations between me and Sam. In her eyes I was a teacher, an authority figure, a tutor at a prestigious college, with a touch of class about him and a persuasive manner. Well, well.

Something else struck me as she spoke. Something I'd already half realised but now the impact hit me firmly in my loins of all places and made me almost gasp out loud. This woman actually *needed* me to intervene to salvage her stake in the farm. She sounded desperate. 'Adam, isn't it? I'd appreciate it very much if you would have a word with your niece and explain to her how sorry Luke is for what happened. He's a good hardworking boy really. You're a teacher. You understand young people like him. I'm sure your niece would listen to you.'

She'd appreciate it very much, eh? So, what sort of thing had she in mind by way of appreciation? Were we talking personal favours? 'Er, this could be tricky,' I made out.

'How do you mean?'

Yes, what *did* I mean? Well, Stage One, now she'd Adam-ed me, was surely to arrange to meet the woman. Face to face, the two of us. This had to be, after all, a joint affair. You scratch my back, and I'll see what I can do about yours, sort of thing. One good turn and all that. 'We need to get together on it,' I replied.

'Sorry?'

You heard me. I wasn't making myself awfully clear, was I? I tried again. 'I'll do what I can where my niece is concerned, but, Mrs Verity,' – there'd be time enough to call her Trudi, for the moment I had the upper hand and needed to stress the magnitude of the favour she expected of me – 'it's a big ask, and I do need to discuss some details face to face with you. About the problems likely to be encountered. The help that *you* can give. What we can do together, I should say, to help, you know, patch things up between the two of them.'

There, my cards on the table. Well, some of them. Otherwise, quite simply, she could forget it. I could hear the data being crunched, I swear, as the woman went over what might be involved in agreeing to conspire with a man she barely knew, but one who'd made the acquaintance of both her son and her nephew on one level or another. My educated guess, shall we say, was that she'd drop in to see me at the farm some time tomorrow. With Luke in tow, I shouldn't wonder, for me to see for myself what a remorseful authority-fearing young man he was, the image of his mother, and how indebted to me his mother would be if I could deliver an equally contrite Sam to them.

When the woman eventually resumed speaking, it was to remind me that it was Saturday tomorrow, the start of an extremely busy weekend for her, what with the Convention to organise and all it entailed. I had an urge to point out that her precious Convention was taking place on *my* doorstep but felt she must know that much already. 'I'll be on hand, to make sure the lane and the yard are kept clear,' I told her. 'Can't have access to the field obstructed, can we?'

'How right you are,' she conceded. And added, 'I dare say we'll run into each other at some time over the weekend. Things can get a bit hectic, though, believe me. But fingers crossed, eh?'

Not 'I'll make a point of knocking at your door in the morning. Coffee time, shall we say?'. Or 'I'll get Luke to polish and valet your car for you.' But hey, it was a start. We knew where we stood. More to the point, she knew how much she'd be relying on my co-operation to make her weekend a success, in more ways than one.

I believe I came off the phone feeling quite light-headed. My final thought that evening, as I recall, having remembered to lock the door and leave an outside light on (well, this was my first night entirely alone in the place, with not another soul for miles) was about whether Sam could be expected to show up again at the flat over the weekend and what I should do about it if she didn't.

SEVEN

DAY THREE

I woke up early. From a dream in which I was a waiter, curiously enough, carrying a stack of dirty plates in the direction of the kitchens and struggling with them, and ultimately failing to prevent the lot from toppling over and shattering at my feet, spilling gravy, custard, and God knows what over my shoes and trouser legs. All in plain sight of a roomful of guests. What was *that* about?

The time: seven thirty, by my watch. Had I knocked something over? As I gathered my wits, I thought my dropped crockery sounded more like a collision. You know, one vehicle running into another. That awful crunch they make. Then an engine revved. Outside my window. Like someone was trying to get away but hadn't let the clutch out fully. Except car revs aren't generally *that* noisy. Then another crash. Definitely from outside. From the yard below my window. If someone was driving across the yard, they were doing an awful lot of damage in the process, and I ought to take a look before they hit anything else.

It was Luke. At the wheel of Philip's old tractor, reversing away from Sam's car which he appeared to have run into. Twice, now, if my ears weren't deceiving me. He'd stopped for a moment and seemed to be engaging gear to drive the tractor forward again. He wasn't going to ram the car again, surely? For a third time? That's when, sensing I was there probably, he looked up and saw me watching. Saw me mouthing through the glass. And pointing at the damage to the Fiat.

My intervention worked. With a swing of the wheel, he steered the tractor away from Sam's car and accelerated off through the gate and down the lane in a cloud of smoke. As the fumes cleared, I saw that Sam's car had been pushed bodily into the side of mine. What a pillock! He'd managed to damage *two* cars! In a fit of rage, presumably, having found Sam wasn't at home to welcome him back.

So where had he spent the night? At the Barn? Or did his mother have a spare room she kept aired for him? And where, in that case, did *she* live? I supposed Luke could have ridden over on a motorcycle and started up the tractor. Maybe his mother had sent him. Told him to come and apologise to me, following our phone conversation of last night, and he'd made the journey like she asked, only hadn't felt able to go through with the apology bit. Now it looked as if I was going to have to phone his mother again and explain how much more difficult her son had just made my job. How much bigger the favour had become. How much greater the debt. At this rate payment looked like having to be made in instalments, with interest.

After breakfast, still thinking of making that call, I went out to take a look at the damage to the cars. You didn't need to be an expert to see that the Fiat was a write-off. The engine had been pushed out of position, one front wheel was buckled, and you couldn't get behind the steering wheel as the door had been pushed into the driver's seat. Sam would be heartbroken. She needed the car for her job. If I told her *I* was responsible, would she believe me? If I told her I'd had too much to drink last night, and had reversed into her car at some speed? If I offered to replace the car for her (at Mrs V's expense of course, but Sam didn't need to know that), did I think she'd look kindly on the idea of getting back with Luke? Hmm. Worth a try, wouldn't you say?

My own car looked dented and scratched on the passenger side but was still drivable. Look, it started straight away. And moved when you let the clutch out. Provided you took the handbrake off, I mean. A purely cosmetic job, repairing this one, I'd say. But throw in replacing the Fiat and you were looking at a substantial first instalment towards repaying the favour. Still, not a problem for Mrs V, I imagined.

*

I decided to wait for the woman to turn up rather than try and reach her on the phone. Nobody arrived till after eleven. No, I tell a lie – the postman brought me a card. It bore an unreadable postmark and depicted a coastal scene I didn't recognise. From Hilary? When I checked, I saw it was addressed to a Mr and Mrs Summers at *Far* Meadow Grange. Here was the evidence, if any was needed, that the postman could get it wrong; or else it showed the guy had a twisted sense of humour. I rushed out to call him back, but his van had gone. Never mind, at least I now had a pretext to go over to the Far Meadow place and have a word.

Like I said, the first arrival wasn't till after eleven. A black Toyota pick-up truck with a number of passengers aboard swung into the yard, drove past my window, and pulled up in front of the gate to one of the fields – the ten-acre, presumably. Another, almost identical, pulled up behind it. Both towed trailers loaded with, among other things, a portaloo cabin apiece. They could have been travellers, for all I knew, looking to move onto a patch of land they'd earmarked for a lengthy squat. No attempt to pause by my kitchen door and check themselves in. Not so much as a glance in my direction to see if the owner was at home.

I stepped out into the yard, expecting they'd wait for me to come along and open the gate for them, and give me a chance to see who they were and let them see me, sort of thing. Normal practice in my book, establishing credentials, exchanging greetings, looking newcomers in the eye. And soon, yes, a figure did alight from the lead vehicle and head for the gate. A woman. Unmistakable, the outline. In shapely blue jeans and quilted gilet, wearing a bobble hat and wellies. At the gate she must have heard my footsteps and turned her face. And blow me, if it wasn't *her*. Trudi Verity. In person. Looking for all the world like she'd turned up for a photo shoot for *Horse and Hound* magazine. I believe my jaw dropped at the sight.

She looked calm and elegant as ever, the woman did, whereas I must have been dressed in my least flattering, least attractive outfit. Certainly not attired the way I was at the shop. 'Mr Goodman, isn't it?' she queried. Who did she think I was?

'Good morning.' I had to think hard for a moment about how to proceed. 'I didn't recognise you. You *do* look dressed for the occasion, I must say. And you've picked a lovely day for…' For *what*, exactly? 'For whatever it is you've come to do. Let me open the gate for you.' Should I seize the moment? Make my point? 'By the way…'

'Yes?'

Crunch time. Think compensation. 'I was wondering if you saw the damage to the parked cars in the yard as you drove in.'

She looked round. 'Cars? Where? What about them?'

It wasn't an ideal angle from which to view the damage, to be honest. Too late anyway. I'd unfastened the five-bar gate by this time and her driver was on the move. I got a good look at him. In case, you know, it happened to be Luke. It occurred to me I could easily have put a padlock on the gate and obliged the woman to knock at my door for the key. From there she would have had a much better view of the cars, certainly. 'I need to point it out to you,' I told her. 'Is Luke with you?'

She cupped a hand over one ear, then shook her head. 'Later,' she shouted back. 'Can't stop now.' And with that she climbed back into the truck and left me holding the gate open as both vehicles bumped their way over the stony ground at the entrance to the field.

I thought she might at least have produced Luke for me to have a word with and show him the results of his handiwork. Where was the guy, anyway? Okay, he could have been aboard one of the trucks, out of sight somewhere. Sam too, for all I knew. The pair of them could have been sitting together, acting as though yesterday's episode had never happened. It crossed my mind that they could have had a good stiff talking to from the Grand Inquisitor himself, Mister Bartholomew, telling them that rows were one thing but separation between couples was another and was forbidden by the Church once the two parties had slept together. In any event, it felt as though I could have seriously over-rated my role in all of this, and that was the reason for Mrs V's coolness towards me this morning. Maybe she didn't need my services after all.

*

During the rest of the morning more trucks filed through the yard and into the field. I stopped counting. If Sam had been on board any of them and had bothered to look in the direction of the Fiat, the damage to it would have been obvious, and it would have been my fault, almost certainly. I was the one who'd promised to keep an eye on it for her. She would expect a replacement, no less, but in the meantime the loan of my Astra would have to do.

It was lunchtime when I looked out and saw one of the pick-up trucks coming in the other direction – emerging *from* the ten-acre and trundling slowly across the yard before stopping beside the Fiat. It was *her* again. Definitely the same woman. At the wheel this time. I recognised the bobble hat. Come to take a look for herself. I saw the wellies touch down behind the opened door; watched the jeans as the legs inside them straightened up, saw her shift weight from one leg to the other as her gaze moved over the damage, then watched as those same legs began a trek my way, towards my kitchen door.

For the past hour or so I'd been looking through more pages of GV's journal. In anticipation, you might say. I'd left the opus open on the kitchen table whilst I started preparing some lunch. Now here it was, the moment of truth. The knock on my door. And there she is, eyeing me keenly from under her bobble hat as the door opens, then looking past my shoulder at the state of my kitchen, the food on my table, the open journal.

'Mister Goodman, so sorry to bother you.' What, no Adam today?

I hastened to assure her we'd left the formalities behind, surely. 'Not at all. It's Adam, please. Welcome to my parlour. Won't you come in? Trudi, isn't it?' Of course, it was, and now seemed to me to be the ideal moment to demonstrate my willingness to get down to business.

She shook her head and declined the offer, keeping her eyes unblinkingly on mine. 'Another time maybe. Sorry if I'm disturbing your lunch. I'll come straight to the point. Did I understand you to say Luke was responsible for the damage to the two cars?' She pointed a finger back in the direction of the wreckage, as if I might not be aware she'd stopped to take a look.

I nodded. Time for *me* to come to the point, too. 'He drove at them with the tractor. Deliberately rammed them. Early this morning, just below my window. I saw him do it.' I resisted the urge to add, 'The noise got me out of bed.' I'd no wish to bring my sleep habits into this. 'One of the cars is a write-off.' I was going to say which one, but she raised a hand to indicate she'd seen all she needed to see.

'Have it attended to,' she told me, 'and let me have the invoice. I see no reason to let it get in the way of restoring the status quo. Do you?'

The *status quo*, eh? I fancied this was as close as we were likely to come to a cosy tête-à-tête this weekend, she not wishing to leave her workforce to spread rumours about her off-peak activities, so to speak. Next week maybe, once I'd had the car repairs sorted and had a bill to wave under her nose, things would be different. There'd be some serious bargaining to do. Behind the scenes. Confidential stuff. By then I'd have had chance of a word with my niece and – who knows? – a word, too, with the boyfriend. The way forward would be clearer.

'I'll get onto it right away,' I promised. Well, on Monday, obviously.

She nodded, then stepped back on her heels. Audience over, I thought, she's on her way again. But to my surprise she whipped the bobble hat off, shook her hair about a bit and put the hat back on. For my eyes only, sort of thing. A special treat. In response I opened the door a bit further. 'Are you sure you won't step inside and let me fix you some lunch? It's no trouble, I assure you. You must be famished after such a busy morning.' I was nothing, you'll gather, if not persistent in my offer of hospitality.

We gazed at each other for a moment as if intent on reading the other's thoughts. At this range, face to face, I had my second close look at those features I continued to find so striking, and I found myself comparing them to Julie's. The eyes were larger. The nose straighter. The mouth more open, more generous. Julie had shorter curlier hair and didn't look great in a bobble hat, to be honest. This woman looked great in anything, it seemed, and chose her hairdresser well. *Julie should consider changing hers,*

I thought, and at the same time should grow her nose, and try and look more like this woman looked.

So, what about that offer of mine, the invitation to join me for some lunch?

'Thank you, but I have a schedule to keep,' went the reply. She laid on a sigh, as an indication of how much she regretted having to turn me down, and smiled at me properly, for the first time as I recall, opening her lips wider than I'd dared imagine, revealing teeth far whiter than mine and lips I fancied other women might die for. 'Right now, as I'm sure you can understand, I have to be elsewhere,' she explained. 'It is a very busy time for us, this Convention. I expect your niece will be along at some point. Tomorrow maybe. Is she at home, do you know?'

Was she? I wanted to point out that my niece was her own person and just as likely to be nursing her wounds right now as Luke was his, but all I heard myself say was, 'I've not seen anything of Sam so far today.'

The woman raised her chin imperceptibly in acknowledgment, then stepped away from my door, turned her back, and legged it back to the pick-up, affording me, as you can imagine, a man's eye view of how well she filled the back of the outfit she wore and how well she moved inside it. *She would have looked good on a horse*, I thought. Would have looked good astride anything, in that outfit.

I shut the door and watched through the kitchen window as she moved to intercept a second pick-up that had emerged from the ten-acre. She spoke to the driver, inclining her torso at an interesting angle before straightening up and heading back to her own vehicle.

It struck me that I'd not seen or heard anything yet to confirm that these people were on a mission to celebrate their Maker. Unlike the buses I'd once seen in the Caribbean proclaiming Jesus Saves Sinners, their vehicles bore no slogans, nothing to identify who they were or what they were about. Tomorrow would be different, right? For now, people appeared to be knocking off for lunch and some of them, like Mrs V, were heading off to the chippie or wherever it was they gathered for their loaves and fishes. My table wasn't good enough, it seemed.

After lunch, while the yard was still quiet, I locked my door, lit a cigarette, and headed off into the ten-acre to see for myself what they'd been up to. Nothing wrong with being curious. At the entrance gate, because of the lie of the land, you had to take a few steps before the view of the field opened up. The first thing to catch my eyes was an enormous marquee, with some sort of stage partially erected on one end of it. A large area of the field had been roped off, presumably as a car park, and the portaloo cabins they'd brought with them extended in a row down the far side. One or two vehicles remained on the site, and a few hardy souls, the kind that don't bother with fish sandwiches for lunch, were still at work carrying things about and generally looking busy. They could have been getting ready to stage a pop festival, that's how it looked.

What, you may well ask, was Mrs Verity's role in all this? She didn't look the part, frankly, not to my eyes. Okay, she ran a shoe shop, but didn't this kind of event call for somebody in overalls, a hard hat, and with hands like Ted Shimwell's? This was a building site, surely. Luke wouldn't be out of place here, and, for all I knew, Luke *was* here somewhere, erecting things, installing things, doing his mother's bidding, playing the remorseful son.

Assuming they'd both gone for lunch, what might the two of them have to say to each other? Well, I dare say mother would be cautioning son to turn on the charm in my presence, just as she planned to do herself once this prayer-fest was over. She had already as good as written a cheque to cover the damage to Sam's car. Money didn't seem to be an issue, did it? *Get the matter attended to and let me have the invoice.* Presumably, if the Fiat was a write-off, I was to go ahead and replace it. She didn't want to hear the details. In that case Sam could have the Astra, as I'd suggested, and I wouldn't mind settling for the Scirocco myself. Hmm, we'd see.

Gazing at the partially finished stage and the marquee behind it, I did wonder if the people who go to the trouble of erecting and dismantling a temporary place of worship like this are the same people who actually turn up and do the worshipping. Would a different crowd roll up tomorrow, for example? Would the Veritys be replaced by others far more devout? Mother and son didn't seem to me to be the genuine churchgoing kind, if I'm honest. Not in the way GV, for instance, had shown himself to be (I'm talking about his journal, clearly). On the other hand, I hadn't read anything by these two, had I?

A passing thought: would Hilary be okay with what was going on here, on her land? I found it impossible to say, one way or the other. As I retraced my steps towards the gate, I wondered how Sam must be feeling right now. Tomorrow she'd put in an appearance, I felt sure. She wouldn't want to miss out.

*

Vehicles came and went that afternoon, and I gave up trying to keep a tally or look out for familiar faces. No good asking me to tell you what time Mrs V returned from her lunch break, or whether she returned at all. I had GV's journal still open on the table and it seemed a good opportunity to continue searching for anything I could find on Marti and the guy who'd fathered Luke. Once I'd been to the bathroom, that is, and played at being that guy for a while. Nothing wrong with a wish to emulate some of the things he might have got up to whilst detained at Mrs V's pleasure, is there? A harmless enough pursuit, surely.

I must have looked through a dozen or more pages from my Unread folder before coming across a paragraph headed MR

AND MRS B. If memory serves, I'd come across the old couple before and decided they had something to do with Marti's past. Now here for the first time was a younger man living in the same house and referred to as C. C for what? Cousin? Something ruder? Your guess is as good as mine.

> 'Marti seemed surprised to see him and asked him what he was doing home so early. He wore overalls and boots and looked like he'd been at work digging or something grubby. There'd been a big row, he said, and that was the reason he'd come home early. Only he swore a lot as he talked about it and Mrs B was embarrassed, you could tell, and tried to change the subject. That's when I heard C call her Gran. He told her to stay out of it, Gran, and mind your own business. When Marti told him to go and take a shower, he went without saying a word to anybody, and after that I didn't see him again.
>
> 'I remember Mr B lay ill in bed upstairs at the time and that must have been the reason we went to the house to see them. Marti had just reopened the shop, but she still found time to go and visit and talk with Mrs B about what the doctor had said about the old man. I remember he got worse, and Marti went over there a lot to help out and sometimes she didn't come home till after I'd gone to bed.'

Okay, let's take stock. C sounded very much like an early version of Luke to me. The job, the surliness, the rows. As for Gran, that had me thinking of Mr and Mrs B as the parents of Mister Fancy Pants Luke Senior, for want of a name. I pictured a guy not unlike Luke himself, to be honest. Couldn't help myself. A complete reprobate, the sort who would drive any woman to religion and make Sahara Street seem to her like a welcome refuge. Am I making sense here? Yes, I know, I'm doing my utmost to bend the evidence to my working hypothesis, and casting round for an indication that Luke Senior might still reside in the neighbourhood and might make efforts from time to time to see his son, and – who knows – maybe the mother of his son, too.

I read on and found not quite what I wanted but an interesting piece nonetheless:

> 'It was soon after Mr B died that we started seeing a lot more of Mrs B at church. She got very frail and bent and had to use a stick to get about. It made me think about what happens to people, the way they look and talk, when they get old. They held a funeral service and a lot of people turned up and that's where I saw C again. He was dressed up in clothes that didn't fit him very well but looked right for the occasion. When Mrs B nearly fainted during the service, he held her upright till she felt better again and he called her Gran again, saying I've got you, Gran, you're not going to fall, you're fine.
>
> 'A month or so later, because she was so busy at the shop Marti gave me something in an envelope to take round to Mrs B's and because she hadn't sealed it very well, I blew on it and opened it to have a look. There was '79' printed in big letters on a card and Marti had signed it To a Darling Mum with all my Love, Many Happy Returns. When I asked Marti about it, she said Mrs B was special and meant a lot to her, but her real mum wasn't around anymore and she didn't really want to talk about it. That's what I mean as people grow older, they hide things from you and change the subject because they don't want to talk about their lives. It's the same when we go to see Marcie.'

Welcome to the grown-up world, sonny. Clearly, GV had started to see his elders for what they were – frail, hypocritical, and inclined to pretend life's fine as long as you kids don't ask us too many awkward questions about it. Like why the secrecy about your past, Aunt Trudi? Why not come clean about the people in your life?

Anyway, let's assume we've got the story straight. Person C (aka Luke) lived with his grandparents (Mr and Mrs B) in the house Mrs V (aka Marti) lived in before moving out to look after Marcie's son, aka GV. Right? The said grandparents (Mr and Mrs B) now looked to be the natural parents of the guy (Mr Luke Senior) who got Mrs V pregnant with a son by the name of C (short for cousin Luke, we've assumed). With me so far? There is the question of why Mrs V should keep the two cousins under separate roofs. I'm working on it. The one person able to confirm if I'm right or not about any of this would be Mrs K, of course. Apart from Mrs V herself, naturally.

I read on a few more pages and this time got bogged down in GV's trips to see Marcie. The poor woman was still detained, with no prospect of returning home. Nothing at all about the lothario who'd taken advantage of his aunt and put her in the family way before doing a runner. A reprobate, did I call him? Make that the Invisible Man who, so far as I could see, seemed pretty skilled at avoiding a mention in the journal. The number of GV's pages I still had to read was diminishing fast. A couple of days and at this rate I'd have read the lot and still found nothing that could be considered either enlightening or compromising. Nothing to explain GV's suicide, or to embarrass his aunt.

The other thing that went through my head as I put the pages away was whether Luke might end up the same way as his cousin. Sorry, couldn't help it, just a thought. His state of mind was certainly worrying to *me*, if to no one else. I'd no idea what must be going through the guy's head. He'd trashed Sam's car under my nose, after spending the night brooding about it, God knows where. What next? My promise to do what I could to restore him to my niece's good books seemed rash, now I thought about it. Far too ambitious. And maybe not all that desirable. Add the fact that my motive in all this was rather suspect, if we're being honest, and you have a bit of a witches' brew, wouldn't you say? And I still hadn't sounded out Sam's feelings on the subject. She'd show up sooner or later, I told myself.

SAM AND JASMINE

Like I said, vehicles came and went that afternoon, so when a large limousine rolled past my window, I took no notice till a toot on the horn grabbed my attention. *It had to be her back again, Trudi, in a more appropriate vehicle this time, and dressed to kill*, I thought. *Come to tell me she'd rescheduled her day and had an hour or so to spare, could she come in?*

No, it wasn't her. But it *was* my niece, back home finally, as I'd hoped. She stepped out of the limo and stood with her back to my window, waiting whilst the driver, a young black woman who had to be her friend Jasmine, parked the car next to mine. Somehow the Astra must have hidden Sam's view of the wreck of her Fiat, for she didn't appear to give it a second glance, having more important things on her mind, evidently.

Next thing the two of them moved off towards the front door, giving me no chance to check the state of Sam's face.

I gave the pair of them time to open up the flat and settle down before leaving my kitchen and climbing the stairs behind them. Noisily, so they'd hear me coming. Whistling as I went, something I imagined Luke never did. I didn't want them mistaking me for *him*, now, did I? I figured Sam would be keen to impress her friend and was therefore less likely to ignore my knock at her door or my friendly request to come inside.

Her friend let me in. 'You must be Jasmine,' I beamed, as she held out a limp hand for me to shake or kiss; I wasn't sure which response she expected.

'Nice to meet you, sir,' she greeted me, dipping her head imperceptibly before lifting it again and giving me an enormous flash of teeth. Yes, that's right, she called me *sir*. Just like a student. 'You must be Sam's Uncle Adam. I've been hearing about you.'

A polite young woman, indeed. Caribbean, would she be? Or West African? She wore a floral dress that went down to her ankles. Mrs K's type of dress, only much more pleasing on the eye. In appearance this girl was not unlike a former student of mine from Nigeria. Serena, I believe she was called. Wanted to be a doctor, or was it a dentist, but hadn't got off to a good start, shall we say?

I turned to Sam, aware that she'd be waiting to hear the purpose of my visit. 'That eye still looks rather swollen. I hope it didn't stop you getting a good night's sleep.' I could see she'd been generous with the make-up this morning. Unlike her friend, who didn't appear to need any. I took a deep breath. 'I have a confession to make.'

'You forgot to shut the hens away and a fox has killed the lot.'

At Sam's very suggestion, Jasmine looked from her to me and burst out giggling, then clapped a hand to her lips and opened her eyes as large as they'd go.

'Take another guess,' I said.

This was it, I decided, the moment for launching Operation Two Hearts. Starting with the admission that I was the one to blame for wrecking the Fiat. 'I ran into your car. Don't know if you noticed the damage just now, when you arrived.' No response from Sam or her friend, so I continued with my pitch. 'No excuse, I'm afraid, apart from the wine I'd drunk. Blame Mrs Kendrick for bringing so many bottles of the stuff. I went out for a spin after you'd gone, and, well… your car ended up a bit of a wreck after I hit it trying to park. Naturally, I'll get it sorted for you, and paid for, as soon as the weekend's over. No worries on that score.' Take three guesses, my girl, I felt like adding, as to who will be footing the bill at the end of the day.

Sam stared at me for a while, taking in the significance of my admission, but searching too, I could see, for signs it might be one of her uncle's send-ups; she'd come across them before. 'You can use my car while yours is being repaired,' I added, in an effort to convince her this was not a joke.

'If you'd told me Luke did it, out of spite and for the hell of it, I'd have found that easier to believe. I wouldn't put it past him.'

At this insight of Sam's, Jasmine gave a few nods, clearly of the same mind in the matter. I assured them both it had been all my own handiwork.

Sam wanted to know if I'd seen Luke or his mother.

I shook my head. 'If they're here, either of them,' I replied, 'they'll be over in that field, won't they? The ten-acre, as you call it. Just don't ask me to put names to everybody who's driven through the yard so far today. It's been like a main road past here, I can tell you.'

Okay, I was messing a bit with the truth, so what? I had my reasons. The main thing was to find something positive to say about Luke. No easy business. 'I took a look earlier at what's happening in the field, and Luke could have been out there, I suppose, helping assemble things. He's pretty useful that way, isn't he?'

Sam remained silent. Impossible to tell what thoughts she had about Luke or his mother. Jasmine changed the subject and wanted to know if I thought the weather would stay dry over the rest of the weekend. 'Farmers know these things, don't they?' she queried, and immediately put a hand to her mouth. 'Sorry, I didn't mean to say it like that, like you're a farmer or anything, cos I know you're not.'

'He's a teacher,' Sam reminded her.

'And teachers are generally not much good at forecasting the weather,' I added.

Sam thought they were not much good at anything. 'Watch out, Jaz, in a minute he'll be suggesting we pray for the weather we want. He thinks we get preferential treatment, you know. From above.'

Jasmine ignored the remark and switched on her smile for me again. 'I think it's great to be a teacher. Passing on all that knowledge and stuff, helping young people sort out what they want to do with their lives.'

Sam did her best to roll her bruised eyes. 'Gordon Verity was a student of his,' she informed her friend. Like that explained what happened to him and why. 'Now he's going to tell me I did the right thing by giving Luke his marching orders. That's about it, isn't it? That's what you came to tell me.'

Well, not quite. 'It's not for me to pass judgment. I hardly know the guy, do I?' Okay, now for the guy's good points, there had to be a few. 'There's good in all young people,' I conceded. For Jasmine's consumption, this stuff, more than Sam's; the young woman was lapping it up. 'And teachers have the job of finding it and helping it along. A bit like your ministers or whatever you call them, in your church, wouldn't you say?'

Jasmine had to think about that one. Before she could reply, Sam informed me that her friend was none other than the daughter of their church leader, a man by the name of Jacob Something-or-Other – not a name I'd heard before, and not an easy one to pronounce. Ammo Wally, it sounded like. Not a native of Willsborough, then, by the sound of him. And guess what, the big man would be coming along tomorrow to address his flock. And get this: would *I*, Sam's uncle – Jasmine wanted to know – be interested in going along and listening to what the man had to say? When I hesitated, she went into a lot of unsolicited detail about what sort of speech he'd be making, what message he'd be conveying, giving me the impression that she was the one who'd actually written the speech for him. Well, she *was* his daughter and had probably received a far better education than he had. Now she sought my approval, seeing as I taught English and what's more, *was* English, and so congenial to boot. She didn't want her old man making a fool of himself, in short, not if I could help it.

Well, I did my best for the girl. Listened intently, advised against the use of too many quaint expressions while acknowledging that their congregation most likely knew their New Testament inside out and loved to hear the cadences and the quirky language. I learned in the process that some unfortunate was due to be shamed and chastised publicly for their transgressions, as an example to the rest. Now where had I heard that before?

'Do you still have a Mister Bartholomew presiding over proceedings of this kind?' I enquired. It seemed a good time to ask. One way of checking the veracity of GV's account of these quaint rituals.

Sam ignored the question. But Jasmine's hand flew to her mouth again, as if the idea of Mister Bartholomew presiding over anything was rather a hoot. There had to be a joke here somewhere, I gathered, but I'd missed it, evidently.

Jasmine was still thanking me for my help with the speech when Sam's phone burst into life. Sam made it clear she'd no intention of picking up. 'If it's *him*, I don't want to know!'

She watched as Jasmine picked up and said, 'Hello,' quietly into the mouthpiece before shaking her head for Sam to see. It was the girl's father, the big man himself, no doubt checking on his daughter's whereabouts and the company she was keeping.

I took the opportunity to ask my niece what sort of message I should give Luke if I came across him. A daft question, by Sam's standards.

'A message? What makes you think Luke would expect me to ask *you* to carry messages?'

Young people, eh? So infuriatingly predictable at times, don't you find? I speak as a parent twice over and tutor to hundreds of youngsters over the years. Time to bring my niece down to earth, point out to her the value of her bond with the Veritys. 'Tell me,' I said, trying to keep my voice out of Mister Ammo Wally's hearing, 'who do you think pays the lawyers to stop your mum from selling the farm?' And added, before she came back with an answer, 'I don't need to ask, do I, because you already know that that money would dry up if you finished with Luke for good.'

'What are you talking about? The farm is already on the market. You've seen the For Sale boards.'

I think Mr Ammo Wally had to be deaf not to start picking up some of this. Jasmine had by now put a finger in one ear. 'Oh, come on!' I chided my niece. 'Not for sale with vacant possession, it isn't. Your tenancy, yours and Luke's, keeps it from being sold as a vacant farm. If Luke goes, so does the tenancy. And that leaves your mother free to sell up.'

Sam recoiled. 'What's it to you? Any of it? Nobody asked you to stick your nose in. You're as bad as Luke's mother, you are. A fine pair, the two of you make, has anybody ever told you you deserve each other?'

Not in so many syllables, no. Nor with such venom either. I had to wonder if Sam had contacts who'd already started tongues wagging. By this time Jasmine had come off the phone. She tapped Sam on the shoulder. 'Have you told your uncle we'll be staying here tonight? My dad wants to know. I told him you had.'

I tell you, I warmed to this young woman, I really did. A long time since I'd come across such old-fashioned deference in a young person. Sam dismissed the question with a wave of her hand. 'No need to bother. He already knows.'

That's when, in my urge to look indifferent to the question of where these two would be spending the night, I felt drawn to a framed water colour painting that hung at eye level close by Sam's head. 'Not seen that before. Where did that come from? Done by anybody I know?'

Sam declined to turn her head. After all, I'd done what I came up the stairs to do, hadn't I? I'd satisfied my curiosity about her friend Jasmine; I'd taken the blame for the damage to her car; I'd pointed out the wisdom of restoring relations with Luke. Now I was admiring one of the pictures on her wall, wasting my niece's time and definitely trying her patience. For support I turned to her friend: 'What do *you* think of it?'

The painting had no particular merit, as far as I could see. But then, I'm no expert. Someone had stood outside in the yard and looked up at the house and painted Sam's window from there. From more or less the same spot where I had stood and looked up days earlier. *And seen the same face.* Unbelievable! Had actually gone to the trouble of painting it. Obviously, I wasn't the only person to have spotted a face at that window. Now here it was again, gazing back at me from a painting on Sam's wall, and it was still no one I recognised.

Jasmine shook her head, didn't know what to think. 'Ignore him,' Sam told her. 'He's only asked about it because it's one of Luke's. Don't know what his game is but you were just on your way out, weren't you, Uncle Adam?'

Not before Jasmine had taken a closer look. She professed to having no idea Luke dabbled in watercolours. Our heads all but collided in the search for a signature, some initials, anything that would show it was a genuine original the pair of us were gazing at. The girl stepped back in some embarrassment and apologised profusely. I was reminded again of my student Serena.

'Can't make it out. Some initials I can't read, down in one corner. CB, is it? Is that Luke, then?' I queried.

Sam gave an almighty sigh. 'Beresford. Thought you knew that. And that's his way of doing an L, not a C.'

Of course, it was, silly me. 'A talented guy,' I pointed out. 'Which side of the family does he get that from?' Like there could be any doubt in my head. I walked over to the window, from where the person he'd painted must have gazed out, and looked for myself. That person was a woman. Had Sam posed for it? It didn't look like her. It was an older woman's face, but not one I recognised. 'Who is it supposed to be?' I asked Sam.

'Don't ask me. Who knows what goes through Luke's head? Who does it look like?'

Frankly, I didn't want to speculate. Hardly the right time or place to bring up, say, the woman in the shower, the one with the painted toenails. Maybe Sam knew her better than I did. But like I say, now wasn't the time. I asked if there were more of Luke's paintings to take a look at and suggested they could be valuable. At least I'd found something of his to praise.

But Sam wasn't having any of it. She sniffed. 'I don't think Luke's the type to bother if they're valuable or anything, do you? He didn't even want that one framed.'

I wagged a cautionary finger. 'I didn't imagine Luke was the type to bother with water colours, full stop. Not everyone has that kind of talent. I might be able, if you have any more of these you don't want, to get the college to take them off your hands. They're always looking for new stuff to hang on the walls.'

Oh yeah! Who was I kidding? Not Sam, by the look of it. She eyed me suspiciously before conceding that one or two more of Luke's paintings had been framed and put away somewhere, and she thought probably his mother had those. 'After all, she paid for them to be framed,' she told me.

This became more fascinating by the minute. Maybe Trudi had some paintings of her own on her walls. Or knew an art dealer who was crying out for stuff like this. My cue to offer to take the matter further. 'I must have a word with her,' I suggested. Immediately Jasmine offered her services. 'I shall see her tomorrow,' she beamed. 'I don't mind at all. Really.'

If only my niece had this girl's charm, her manners, her willingness to please. Naturally, I declined the offer and made for the door, only for Jasmine to call me back. 'Oh, Mister Goodman, before you go…'

She held out a hand for me to grasp. Such a warm limp hand. A gesture of appreciation, apparently, on behalf of herself and her father, in return for my generosity. *Me,* generous? In what way? Well, I'd not raised any objection, had I, to their Convention going ahead? I'd not complained about the traffic going back and forth past my window, not made a fuss. Her father, she insisted, would want to thank me in person tomorrow if I'd be so good as to make myself available, as she put it. I nodded.

Sam's face, meanwhile, was a picture. Luke could have done it justice with his water colours, I felt. She had her mouth tight shut, her eyes on the ceiling, and her fingers quietly drumming on the arm of her chair. 'Careful, Jaz,' she warned, 'or his head won't get through the door.'

On the stairs I remember trying to picture Jasmine's father, the Ammo Wally guy, but couldn't separate him, frankly, from the picture already in my head of the phantom Mister Bartholomew. Maybe tomorrow I'd get to meet both these guys. Assuming they weren't the same person.

EIGHT

CONVENTION DAY

I woke up next morning to the sound of laughter overhead. Shrieks of it, along with a few thuds and bumps. A pillow fight, by the sound of it. Well, it made a change from the heady rhythmic stuff I'd been treated to before. These two young women were obviously the best of friends, and maybe I should be leaning more on Jasmine and her father to steer Sam and Luke back into line. Hmm, we'd see what the day would bring.

I'd gone through my customary routine – bathroom, breakfast, chicken feed time – and had just sat down on the doorstep for my first smoke of the day when the phone rang. Mrs V again, was it? With an offer to drop by and discuss progress with me over coffee? It was a wrong number. A guy asking for Betty. What had *she* been up to then, on a Saturday night? He didn't sound too pleased and hung about on the end of the line, as if expecting me to confess it was all my fault Betty wasn't there with him. A busy line, Hilary's, I was finding.

The first of the day's traffic rumbled by as I sat and relit my cigarette. For some reason I took it that Sam and her friend must have passed my door already and made their way into the ten-acre. Pausing on the way, of course, to check my story about the damage to the Fiat. Jasmine's car, a Lexus if you please, still stood next to mine. Ever had that feeling you're in danger of missing the action? That it's all happening over there, over the brow, only yards away, but out of sight? From my door, I could hear loudspeakers start pumping out some happy-clappy music to welcome worshippers still trundling through my yard. What exactly was I in danger of missing? The least I could do was show some interest and go and take a look.

There had been no rain overnight, and none was forecast, despite the dullness of the sky. I took my wellies out of the car boot and put them on, then grabbed an umbrella, just in case. After yesterday's encounter with the pick-ups, I considered I wouldn't have a problem being recognised round the place as the guy from the farm. Enough people knew my face by now, surely. From the gate I counted three marquees in all, erected across the bottom end of the field, while the top end, as I'd expected, served as the car park, and was filling up rapidly. I'd been obliged to step aside several times already, but so far wasn't aware I'd given way to Luke, or his mother.

Now the loudspeakers were inviting people to take their seats, and I saw groups converging on the largest of the marquees. Some of these people might well have been yesterday's construction workers dressed today in their Sunday best. I swear nobody looked older than I did, but everybody looked considerably smarter. You wouldn't mistake this gathering for a hippie festival, that was for sure. Matting of some sort had been put down to prevent cars from churning up the softer slopes of the field. Very sensible, eh? I guessed they'd done this before, on somebody else's land, and knew how to avoid cars getting stuck. Mind you, they could always call on Luke to fetch Philip's tractor to the rescue if need be.

It occurred to me that a few miles down the road people would be congregating in similar groups outside St Michael's, and no doubt Ted and his missus would be among them. As far as I knew, the Reverend BL-C didn't see a need to deploy security guards at the church door. Nor had the rector mentioned that I might be stopped and asked to identify myself if I turned up for his morning mass. Here, in the ten-acre, though, things were different. A couple of heavyweight types in uniform were patrolling the car park area together and, as our paths crossed, one of them buttonholed me and asked which was my car.

'I'm from the farmhouse,' I told him. 'Just checking to see if my niece and her friend are here yet. Only I don't see them.'

'Which car are we talking about, sir?'

Excuse me? Did these guys not recognise the landowner's agent when they saw him? Did I have to wear a badge or something? 'I'm with Jasmine,' I told him. 'And Sam. Their car is in the farmyard. The Lexus. Back there.' I jerked a thumb in the direction of the farmhouse.

One of the guys produced a walkie-talkie phone and spoke a few words into it, including those magic words Ammo Wally. He waited for a reply, then shook his head. 'Out of luck, mate,' he told me. 'She's not here. Not yet, at any rate.'

By this time his buddy had heard someone shout from the direction of the gate. He turned back to face me. 'Is your name Goodman? I believe you're wanted. Over here.'

Wanted by none other than Jasmine herself. On her own, waving frantically as she came down the field to tell me that my phone was ringing. Behind her, just coming into view and in no hurry at all, came my niece, struggling to put a coat on by the look of it. 'We saw you walk across the yard,' Jasmine explained. She had to catch her breath and stood panting for a moment, hands on hips, which, if truth be told, were not slim hips. The girl was a lot broader than I'd realised. We watched the security guys move off in search of someone else to hassle, and eventually Sam drew level, shaking her head. 'We thought you might be down here. Didn't we, Jaz?'

Jaz looked at me as if to see my reaction. I think I nodded. At one time Philip had installed a bell on the wall of the milking parlour so that when the phone rang inside the house you could hear it clearly from down the fields. It probably hadn't worked for years. I began my trek back to the house, wondering aloud if it was going to be another call about Betty. 'It'll have stopped ringing by now,' Sam called out after me. 'No need to hurry.' Helpful as always, bless her, my niece.

*

The call had been made from Mrs K's number. What could *she* be after? Maybe Boyd wanted to invite me to *his* birthday party for a change, and would I bring my own booze and sandwiches, and keep my hands off his missus? I resisted the urge to call back. I took the view that the Kendricks, if they had anything important to tell me, were welcome to try my number again later. I might not be in, but they could try.

I was on my way out of the door again when Mrs K rang me back. Seriously out of breath. Like she'd waddled up several flights of stairs to reach the phone. 'Sorry, darlin'. Just got back to my place. I rang earlier from Trude's, but you didn't answer. Looks like she's not been home. The bed's not been slept in. No sign of her. Don't know if she's turned up at the farm yet. Has she? No, I thought not. She's got me worried this time. Can't think what's happened, but something's wrong, I know it is. She wouldn't behave like this otherwise. I reckon as—'

'Just a minute!'

Wha*t was* she on about? Ringing to tell me she'd no idea where Trudi spent last night. Was she having a laugh? If the woman hadn't slept in her own bed, I'd say it was highly likely she'd slept in someone else's, wouldn't you? None of my business, or Mrs K's. The woman certainly hadn't slept in *my* bed. Is that what Mrs K suspected, hence the call? I'd seduced her friend and not told her about it. What kind of scoundrel did that make me? I suppose I should have felt flattered that someone should link the two of us in that way. Instead, I couldn't help myself, I denied it. 'Not seen anything of her here,' I declared. 'Should I have done?'

'You tell me, darlin'. Like I said, her bed's not been slept in, and that's not like Trude. She could be down the field by now at your place, of course, but somehow, I doubt it. Would you be a darlin' and check for me, before I really start worrying about what's happened to her?'

Somehow, I doubt it. Where else would the woman be? 'I'll call you back,' I promised, and hung up.

Now I'd heard it all. Suspected of having lured Trudi into my bed, I was now being asked to go and locate the woman and report back to her friend. Or do I mean her guardian? What on earth was it to Mrs K that her friend hadn't spent last night in her own bed? And how did she know that? All the way across the yard I kept telling myself it really wasn't any of my business what sort of relationship these two women had with each other. But I couldn't help feeling aggrieved all the same, feeling I was being used as part of an understanding I wasn't privy to.

I did a quick scan of the car park to check for the Scirocco and found myself shaking my head. No luck. Maybe she'd had a lift again in one of the pick-ups. Or in *his* car, you know, the lucky guy she'd spent the night with. By now just about everyone had disappeared inside the big marquee and, in spite of myself, I felt hesitant about gate-crashing proceedings without a more legitimate purpose than to catch sight of Mrs V. Did I even know what she'd look like on this occasion? I doubted she'd be dressed in yesterday's outfit. More likely she'd be wearing something smart, the same as everyone else. But would she be standing, or seated, or on her knees? And would I recognise her from the back, assuming that I found a way in at the rear of the marquee? I spotted one of the security guys. Or rather he spotted me, and we made a beeline for each other. This time he knew who I was. Out came the walkie-talkie once again and a lengthy exchange ensued before he gave me a definite no, Mrs V had failed to show as yet, but did I want to leave him a message for her?

I shook my head. Any message of mine wasn't for the security guy's ears. Back on the phone Mrs K sounded like she'd known all along what answer I'd bring. 'I knew it! Didn't I tell you something was wrong. She'll be at the Barn, I just know she will. That's where you'll find her. Check it out.'

Was she suggesting I go over there and check that place, too? 'What would she be doing there?' I asked. Lord's Barn didn't strike me as the sort of place Mrs V would be frequenting, today of all days, considering the ten-acre was where it was all happening for her and her crowd.

'That's where Luke will be as well.'

'Why would Luke be over there?'

'You do ask a lot of questions, Adam. I'm telling you that's where they'll be. Both of them. If you don't believe me, go and see for yourself. It's *your* place after all. You're in charge.'

'Hmm…'

I'd no idea, to be honest, how much of this to take seriously, how much of it might be a ruse. Psychics sense things, don't they? They rumble your plans, see what you're up to before you even know it yourself. Was that what was happening here? Mrs K *knew*, didn't she? She knew all about my arrangement with her friend and expected me to come clean about it and bring her in on it too. Well, two could play at that game. I'd check the Barn out, as she wanted. I'd even invite her along, so she could keep an eye on Luke while Mrs V and I got down to some serious haggling over how exactly *our* little arrangement was going to work. If the Barn was deserted and Mrs K's plan was simply to get me there under false pretences, for another of her wild parties, say, then you could bet your month's salary I'd drive off again quicker than she could drop an aitch or put two expletives together.

'Okay,' I announced. 'Since you put it that way, I'll drive over there and take a look. I don't hold out much hope, though. A shot in the dark, if you ask me.'

'Aren't you forgetting something?'

An invitation to come along with me, did she mean? 'I don't think so. I have my car key, and I know the way.'

'Won't you need a key to get *in* the place?'

Not if the Veritys are in residence, I won't. When I pointed this out to Mrs K, she sort of hissed (a wink wouldn't do it, come on), and told me there are no flies on the Goodmans. But by then she'd given the game away, hadn't she? She wasn't expecting her friend to be at the Barn, or Luke for that matter. It was a ruse.

The woman insisted she wasn't kidding. 'Listen, Adam, I've told you, I'm bloody seriously concerned for Trude's safety. I just know something's wrong.'

I should have said fine, in that case off you go and let me know in due course what you find, as I'm not convinced it won't be a total waste of my time and yours. But we were talking about Hilary's property, when all's said and done, a corner of it that nonetheless in a court of law might well be deemed to be my responsibility in Hilary's absence. Moreover, there was a young man at large, a rejected young man who, for all I knew, might have done himself an injury and wanted Mummy to come and sort him out, hence Mummy's absence from the main event. A far-fetched scenario, maybe, but should I ignore the risk it could be really happening?

I relented. 'I guess we should both go,' I conceded. 'There's no harm in checking it out. Better safe than sorry.' Not short of a platitude or two for the occasion, you'll notice.

Nothing for it then but to fire up the Astra and drive over to Briar Lane. Assuming the car would respond once again after the battering it had received. I did hear a few groans and creaks I'd not heard before as she moved off down the lane, but hey, with any luck I'd be driving a newer model soon enough.

I did wonder what approach to take in the event both Luke and his mother should be in residence. What was it Chris had told me about the *Agricultural Holdings Act*? Ask the pair of them for rent and you make tenants out of them – that seemed to be the gist of it, and I didn't imagine Hilary would thank me for that. On the other hand, I couldn't very well throw them out. I didn't have the authority, for one thing. Ask them to leave maybe, but if they chose to ignore me, what then? I didn't have answers. Perhaps they'd listen to Mrs K. We'd see.

As I pulled off the road to find a parking spot, I became aware of the contrast between this end of the farm and the ten-acre. A pretty stark one, it struck me. On one side of the farm cars stood in rows soaking up the sunshine as prayers and thanksgiving were being offered, whilst at the Barn the trees put everything in more or less permanent shade, the place looking as gloomy and deserted now as it had the first time I gazed down on it from the high ground. No sign of the Mini. No tractor, either. And no Scirocco. No sign of life at all.

MISSING PERSONS

The term 'fool's errand' passed my lips, I confess, as I sat in the car staring out at the empty scene. I looked at my watch. If Mrs K was going to arrive, she wouldn't be long. It looked as though I might have been played for a sucker. Not much point getting out of the car. I could see there was no one in residence here. I'd be better driving back via the shop. I needed more cigarettes, I found, as I took one out of the packet and put it between my lips.

I gave the horn a blast and watched for a face, any face, to appear at one of the windows, or for the door to open. The obvious candidate was Luke, and *he* could have walked here from wherever, being a fit, active type. Or he'd come on his motorbike and left it under cover somewhere handy. Over in that lean-to maybe, where, look, there was a wheel with a tyre on it under a tarpaulin, that *could*, now I focused on it more closely, be the wheel of a motorcycle.

It struck me that if I got out of the car to take a look, Luke, if he was by any chance hanging around the place, would be bound to put in an appearance, if only to accuse me of trying to steal it. The sensible thing to do was to keep my back to the Astra as I made for the lean-to. Don't make a target of yourself, in other words; remember this guy's M.O., and don't rely on him recognising who you are. I may have nodded at the wisdom of my own advice as I climbed out of the car and lit my cigarette. Time to go and check things out.

A winged creature shrieked and shot up into the air as I started moving. A pheasant, of all things, more terrified than I was. As it was, it startled me so much that my cigarette fell from my lips, and I had to retrieve it from my shoe before starting out in earnest for the tarpaulin. Sure enough, a complete Honda machine, of uncertain vintage as far as my knowledge went, was hidden under it. Some careful exploring in the region of its exhaust baffles (okay, I'd seen it done on TV – *Morse*, I think) told me the bike hadn't been in use in the last hour or so. As for the owner's whereabouts, your guess would be as good as mine. He could have been anywhere. Watching me, maybe, from behind one of the windows. I walked tentatively across and found, as before, that the blinds were pulled down inside so intruders like me couldn't peer in. I moved to the door and tried the handle. It opened, just as it had done before, and I stood there, reluctant understandably, to step over the threshold again without an invitation.

That's the moment the Mini arrived. With a screech of brakes and a toot on the horn to signify I'd been spotted, and reinforcements were here. Good old Mrs K to the rescue. Uncertain whether to feel relieved or not, I waited for the woman to park and join me.

'Got the door open already, I see. No sign of anybody about, then? Let's take a look inside, shall we?'

Fine, as long as *she* took the first step. 'Anyone inside?' I called into the gloom. 'We're coming in.' Well, Mrs K was, and she didn't wait for an answer. Leaving me behind, she made straight for the shower room, waddling her way between chairs and the coffee table I'd fallen against. She seemed remarkably familiar with the layout of the place, if you ask me, acting as if she'd been here before, and more than once.

Certainly, somebody had been here. Living here, I mean, by the look of it. Eating meals and leaving dirty plates and an empty mug behind. A pair of trousers too, *and* a pair of dark grey briefs (definitely menswear) over the back of a chair, along with a towel. Hardly the evidence Mrs K was looking for though, was it? Hardly proof her friend was here as well, trying to talk her son into tidying up after himself. How this situation struck Mrs K I found hard to tell. She kept her thoughts to herself as she came out of the shower room, head down, and went into the kitchen.

Aside from the general air of untidiness and the whiff of discarded garments, I had to admit all over again that Luke had made a cracking job of turning the old barn into a cosy retreat, at least as far as the ground floor went. Assuming it was all his own work, of course. The shower room came equipped with toilet *and* bidet, if you please (I took a look in there myself, for old times' sake). The kitchen looked better equipped than Hilary's, to be honest.

As for the sleeping quarters, well, they did seem to suggest work was still in progress. The staircase looked newly installed, with no support rail in place as yet. And the foot of it was as far as Mrs K felt able to go without calling on my help. Would I oblige her by going up there and taking a look? What, you may well ask, was I supposed to be looking for? We'd already established that Luke had taken up residence in the place. We'd discovered nothing to indicate his mother had done the same. Did we need to go through every room like this? Wasn't standing on the bottom step and calling up the stairs good enough?

'Are you expecting somebody to answer?' Mrs K wanted to know.

I shrugged, aware that the woman was waiting for me to lead the way. Luke knew my voice by now, you'd think, so he'd know this time, wouldn't he, that the person who proceeded to stomp up the stairs wasn't a burglar and didn't intend him any harm, merely wanted to check on the progress made in converting the place for Mrs Pope's future use.

'Anything up there?'

Like what? A whiff of Trude's perfume? A discarded negligee? By the light from a bare skylight window, I saw there was a double bed, and it had certainly been slept in, and garments lay where they'd been left. But they weren't *her* garments. They weren't a woman's garments, that was for sure.

'Luke's been sleeping here,' I called down.

I was standing in what obviously served as the upstairs bedroom, aware there wasn't a great deal of head space to move about without risk of injury. This part of the Barn's conversion, I remember thinking, needs more work on it if my sister is going to move in here any time soon. I couldn't see Hilary climbing up and down a flight of stairs with no handrail, for a start.

'Nothing else?'

Or did she mean *nobody* else? Like she didn't expect Luke to be here alone, he had to be here with a woman – either his mother, or Miss Painted Toenails. Some female or other. And it looked like the birds had flown. At the sight of cars arriving, would that be? The likelihood the place had a back door hadn't occurred to me till now. So, were Luke and his companion hightailing it across the fields right now, or wheeling the Honda silently onto the lane while this odd couple rifled through their dirty laundry? A likely story. Couldn't a guy hole up here quietly for a few days without having his possessions and his lifestyle turned over as though he was a common felon?

*

Outside again, I found myself looking to see if the motorcycle had gone. It hadn't. By now Mrs K had a distracted look in her eye, like those TV detectives have when their ducks are not lined up in a nice, neat row. Not a look I'd noticed before. This was a different Mrs K from the mad driver, or the party animal. For a moment she seemed at a loss for where to search next and asked for one of my cigarettes as she'd overlooked to bring her own.

After a few drags she stood shaking her head. 'This isn't looking good, you know. Something bad has happened. I mean *really* bad. I just know it.' She looked round, shielding her eyes, scanning the lean-to, the heaps of building materials, the row of trees on the far side of the yard, the ridge of higher ground beyond (the spot where I'd stood previously) as though expecting to catch sight of something that wasn't quite right, I guess.

'Let's take a look in the outhouse over there,' she suggested. 'Me, I mean. *I'll* go. No need for the two of us, is there? You take a look down the well, see if we can find anything between us.'

Anything? Like what, for Christ's sake? What was it she expected to find? 'What are we looking for exactly?' I asked. 'A body?'

She didn't hear me. She'd reached the outhouse and was rummaging among a pile of discarded pieces of furniture, by the look of it. Was she serious? Being guided by your vibes is one thing, but wasn't she carrying the act a bit far? No need for the two of us, eh? She didn't say that at the foot of the stairs just now, did she? So, what was I doing out here with her, scouring the place, when it was clear to me the place was deserted? They'd gone, Luke and whoever might be with him; they were probably over in the ten-acre right now, having a laugh.

Take a look down the well, the woman said. She'd assumed I knew where it was. I didn't recall seeing a well, or a sign of one, on my earlier visits. Wells have walls round them, don't they? And a device on top for hauling buckets up and down? Like this one here in front of me, large as life, as I turned the corner of the house, in plain sight of my vantage point on the ridge. How had I missed spotting it?

Here was the missing back door, too, on this end of the house. Now what was I supposed to be looking for down a well of all places if not something thrown down there? See if we can find anything between us, the woman had said. Like more of Luke's dirty laundry, would that be? Or his mother's bobble hat? The idea of spotting anything but water down a well like this one seemed remote as I stood and leaned over to take a look. Why was I even bothering? A pointless exercise, I thought. It suggested Mrs K had run out of ideas about why the two of us were here. Run out of all pretence, too, of wishing to impress with her psychic powers the guy she'd talked into meeting her here. She was beginning to look and sound like a crazy woman. And the guy she'd tricked into coming along was beginning to feel rather bored with it all.

At first, I couldn't see a thing down the well. Not surprising really. Don't they tell you to give your eyes time to adjust to the gloom? Okay, I did that, I gazed down the well and waited for things to take shape.

I'd never gazed down a well before, funnily enough. They weren't a fashionable feature in gardens on my side of town. I expected this one to be an example of the real thing, an original if you like – you know, containing water for use in times before piped supplies came along. Not much use for feeding your modern shower or refilling your lavatory cistern, though, was it? Not much use any more at all.

Well, this particular well didn't appear to have any water in it. A stone I dropped into it fell with a thud on something solid. Could be it hit a body, of course. Or at least a bundle of discarded clothes. But some way down (don't ask me the depth, I'm hopeless at gauging this sort of thing) I could finally make out something I certainly hadn't expected to come across. This well was occupied! Yes, that's what I said. I mean there actually *was* a person down there looking up at me, as if I'd startled them, or alarmed them by peering over and dropping stones. Perfectly understandable. What's more, as my eyes made out more details, this person's face took on a familiar aspect till I saw it was actually Luke's face gazing back at me. 'Sorry,' I called out. 'I didn't know you were down there.' Didn't realise it was you, sort of thing – the excuse he'd given me after pushing me in the back.

I guess in his place I would have been alarmed, especially if someone had begun dropping stones on me. So, this was where he was all the time, and perhaps he'd not heard us arrive. He remained looking up at me, sort of waiting for me to explain myself, tell him what I was up to. He appeared to be seated, legs outstretched, and leaning back against one wall, his head tilted up towards the light.

I remember wondering how he'd climbed down. There was no dangling rope he could have used, and no ladder visible. The possibility he'd fallen and injured himself crossed my mind. People do silly things, don't they, and then sit waiting for help to come along.

'Are you okay? Luke, can you hear me? Do you need a hand?'

The fact that he didn't respond, didn't appear to react in any way, should have told me, shouldn't it, that something was not quite right. When the light suddenly grew dim in the well and the figure of Mrs K loomed up alongside me, I should have realised. Even before I heard her speak and felt her grip my shoulder.

'That's Luke all right. You're not wrong, darlin'. That's him.'

'Can you hear us, Luke?' I shouted. 'How did you get down there?'

I didn't *need* to shout, actually; only the way he failed to react led me, not surprisingly, to think he didn't hear me too well. He just kept on looking up at us, staring, making me start to feel uneasy, if you want the truth.

Mrs K stepped back from the well and pulled me aside, shaking her head rather vigorously. 'Take it from me, sunshine. Luke's not going to give you an answer. Not now. Not in a month of Sundays.'

I guess I knew what she meant but I hadn't the words to say so, or to utter anything meaningful at all. In the circumstances I must have looked rather blank and, let's face it, rather silly. I do recall turning over the unspoken thought in my head that this woman couldn't possibly have seen Luke's face clearly because she'd not given her eyes time to adjust like I had.

'Shouldn't we take a closer look, I mean. Just to see if…' If we've jumped to the wrong conclusion, been a tad hasty. Surely, we had to *do* something to help, rather than just stand about discussing things.

I directed my gaze once more down the well, focusing hard on the figure seated down there, though I found it difficult to see him clearly now she'd blocked out so much of the light. I really wanted to prove this woman wrong, to show her that somebody needed to check the guy out – for a pulse, a heartbeat, his breath on a mirror, that sort of thing, any sign at all that Mrs K could be wrong. And since *she* wasn't likely to be the one to volunteer to go down the well herself (remember the unguarded staircase just now), I started fiddling with the winding mechanism in the hope that between us we could devise a way for me to be lowered down to the guy. Or else I'd fetch a ladder. There had to be one lying around the place.

'What are you doing? It's too late for that, believe me, Adam.'

'All the same…' It struck me as just not right to abandon the guy, treat him as if he really was beyond help.

Mrs K looked very stern all at once, as though she was going to wag a finger and shake me like she would a wayward child. 'Listen, Adam.' See what I mean, she was Adam-ing me. 'The only thing we can do for him now is get to a phone and get the police and the fire brigade up here. It's *their* job now.'

'Well,' I insisted, 'I'll stay here and find a ladder, while *you* go and phone them.'

I could have thrown a tantrum or stamped my foot. No way, at any rate, was I going to accept being the errand boy before satisfying myself she was right. Look at it this way. She'd been wrong, hadn't she, about finding her friend out here? She'd been convinced all along that Trude was the one who had come to grief. Not a word about finding it would be Luke instead. If her clairvoyant skills were so reliable, why hadn't we gone straight to the well? Why all the head-scratching?

Okay, I'll admit I'd not seen a dead person before, if that's what Luke was. Certainly not from a vantage point so far above where he sat and without the benefit of decent lighting. Mind you, that's not quite true. I'd seen my father laid out in his coffin in a darkened room, looking like he might still be alive. But that's not the same thing, is it, as coming across a familiar person, in the course of an otherwise normal day, who looks back at you as if he's going to speak and looks every bit as alive as the woman at your side trying to tell you he's dead.

That's when Mrs K locked her eyes onto mine and got even more serious. She told me to watch her lips (not a pretty sight at the best of times, especially when they opened, believe me!), as she – was – not – fooling. 'If you find a ladder and climb down there,' she said, 'you'll end up like him, I'm flaming telling you. You'll pass out and that'll be it. It's very likely Luke didn't fall or do himself an injury, he ran out of air, simple as that. There's no nice way to say this, Adam: there'll be *two* dead people if you go down there, and I don't want to be responsible for that, so let's get to a flaming phone, shall we? For fuck's sake!'

She had a hand on my arm as she spoke, the way you do with a child that won't take no for an answer. Only you don't swear like that at a child, do you? And she had that look in her eyes again, the one she'd had at the farm gate while separating Steve and Luke. I had a strong suspicion I was likely to be frogmarched back to the car if I didn't nod my head and agree with her.

'Okay, if you feel so strongly about it,' I conceded, 'maybe we should report it and get help.'

I felt my arm released, and I stepped away from her, the better to deliver my own last word on the matter. 'But *I'll* go. I'll drive back to the farm while you stay here. With *him*.'

*

Back behind the wheel of the Astra, I found I was shaking. Not surprising, was it? Not one of my dreams this time. I'd witnessed something that put the other things – events in the ten-acre, the damage to the cars, Ted's fears for his livelihood, to name a few – into a kind of feeble perspective. I'd witnessed something far more real and immediate. So demanding that it had to be reported right away, and other people had to become involved, the sooner the better.

How do you know when somebody has run out of air? Don't they turn blue or something? Don't they look like they're gasping for breath? Not easy to make out if they're at the bottom of a well, I guess.

He ran out of air. There'll be two dead people if you go down there.

The woman had spoken as if she knew a thing or two about bad air at the bottom of old wells. Like maybe it had happened before to somebody she knew. Or if it hadn't, like *she* could detect its presence, smell it perhaps, like those sniffer dogs they use to find drugs or explosives. Or she'd read up on the subject, come across a report in the *Gazette* about a fatality somewhere. For all I knew, she could have played round here as a child and seen some poor kid climb down and suffocate. That's how much I knew about the woman.

With the mobile phone not yet invented, I had no option but to drive back to the farm. To report finding a body, or what? People might want to know why, as the first arrival on the scene, I'd not made an effort to rescue the guy. *Ask* her, *officer*, I'd have to say. *Ask my psychic companion. I'm merely reporting an emergency here. She stopped me mounting a rescue on the grounds there was bad air at the bottom of the well. Don't ask me how she knew that, officer. What sort of bad air are we talking about, sir? Carbon monoxide? Hydrogen sulphide? If the latter, she'd be bound to recognise the smell, wouldn't she? They burnt women like that at the stake in times gone by, you know, sir. For being too smart for their own good, too knowledgeable by far. Not nice, sir.*

The possibility Mrs K would have vanished from the scene when I got back with reinforcements, along with the likelihood the well would be found to be empty, went through my head more than once. I could hear myself declaring, *Beats me, officer, I swear I left her here. And Luke was definitely down there. The guy must have recovered and climbed out by himself. Or she helped him. No, I assure you I'm not in the habit of making hoax calls or wasting police time, being a public servant myself. Check out my credentials, by all means.*

Imagine my surprise, on driving into the farmyard, to find a police vehicle already parked there. My first thought: Mrs K had located a phone at the Barn and rung ahead of me. The police vehicle was parked in my space, leaving me no option but to park behind it. As I climbed out, two uniformed officers approached from the direction of the ten-acre field, closely followed, I saw, by Sam and Jasmine. The girls spotted me and pointed me out, no doubt indicating that here he was, the man in charge, the man they were all looking for.

'Mister Goodman?'

I was being addressed by the shorter of the two officers who happened to be a woman. They wanted a word with me, if I didn't mind.

'It's about Luke's mother,' Sam informed me, while Jasmine hung back, saying nothing. 'Nobody's seen her all day. They think you might know where she is.'

The missing Mrs V. She was proving to be quite an elusive person today, and not only Mrs K had noticed her absence, clearly. Mind you, these people hadn't heard *my* news yet about the woman's son, but then Sam's presence made me think twice about the wisdom of mentioning it in front of her.

I got the impression that the other officer (male, and a former bouncer by the look of his build and his broken nose) was keen to separate me from the girls, in case they fed me more information than was good for his line of questioning. 'Alone, sir, if you don't mind,' he insisted, and shut the kitchen door behind him, leaving Sam outside with her friend.

His colleague kicked off the questioning. 'We're trying to locate Mrs Gertrude Verity, sir, and wonder if you can tell us where we might find her.'

I ran through the list of places I would try if looking to find the woman. They'd tried the lot, of course – the shop, her home, the Convention. They hadn't considered Lord's Barn, though, presumably because they hadn't had the benefit of hearing Mrs K's opinion of it as *the* most likely spot to look. That's when I put it to them that I'd just driven over from there to report finding a body. Only I didn't say whose body it was. 'Less than an hour ago we came across it,' I told them. 'Over at Lord's Barn, on the other side of the farm. Could that be the missing woman you're talking about?'

Okay, I know. The person in the well was not Mrs V. And I'd intended, as I said, to report the person as still alive and in need of rescuing. But I'm sure you'll agree that an unexplained death, and the suggestion it might be a woman's, surely trumps a missing person enquiry where police priorities are concerned. In this instance, happily, the officers weren't slow to put two and two together and soon started contacting base for fresh instructions on how to proceed.

I suggested the fire brigade might be required to recover the body, as it was at the bottom of a well. I said I feared the air in the well might be toxic. I didn't mention Mrs K's part in all of this as she could speak for herself as soon as we got there. Yes, *we*. I was going with them. No way was I being left behind to speculate about whether Luke would be pronounced dead or not. I could explain later my confusion over the way one body resembles any other when looking down a well.

I was offered a lift in the patrol car and took the opportunity, while they waited, to move the Astra and park it back in its usual bay. The girls, meanwhile, had disappeared – returned to the ten-acre, presumably, where activities continued as normal, and why not? I didn't want to start explaining to them where we were off to and why. Not yet, at any rate. Not till I'd seen for myself how the law would deal with what awaited us on the other side of the farm.

*

What did I tell you? Mrs K was nowhere to be seen as we pulled in beside the Mini. 'That's her car,' I said. 'She must be about somewhere.'

The male half of the police duo, Wayne (I'd overheard them talking, see) pointed towards a heap of builders' rubble. 'Isn't that her?' A woman appeared to be on her knees, with her back towards us, looking for all the world like a boulder left stranded after the glaciers melted. Mrs K, who else? But what on earth *was* she doing? While his colleague went over to have a word, Wayne followed me as far as the well. His torch beam picked out Luke's face with no problem; it still gazed up at us, and I must confess I still had my doubts. 'Is he…?' I wondered aloud. Wayne shook his head. 'Nothing we can do for him, believe me. The fire brigade will be here soon. They'll fetch him out. I'll tell you one thing, though. That's *not* our missing Mrs Verity down there, now, is it?'

He didn't go so far as to accuse me of deliberately misleading him. But he did ask me whose face I thought it was.

'Mrs Verity's son, eh?' He looked puzzled. 'Why do I get the impression that you and your lady friend over there know far more than you're telling us? I think it's time we established who you both are and what exactly your business is at this end of the farm. I'll get Angela to take a statement from you.'

Angela, eh? The scribbler. She couldn't wait. She'd already jotted down Mrs K's side of the story. Routine procedures were Angela's thing, I sensed, and she knew a bit about shorthand, too; she had most of my version of events down on paper by the time the fire brigade arrived. I watched as these guys confirmed the air in the well was suspect and they would need breathing equipment to send someone down. By this time Mrs K had joined us. 'You were right,' I told her. 'About the air down there. They're not taking any chances.'

She sniffed. 'If they've any sense, they'll keep looking. Trude's around here somewhere, I know she is.' But not under that pile of glacial debris you've been looking through, I presumed.

An ambulance rolled up. You have to hand it to these fire and rescue guys, don't you? They don't mess about. Somebody donned a spacesuit and breathing gear and disappeared over the lip. Next thing Luke was on the surface, laid flat out and being examined by one of the ambulance crew. A shake of the head, and that was it, he was zipped up. Cause of death: asphyxia. No doubt about it. Poor air in the well. Foul play? No obvious evidence for it, apparently, but then again, Luke didn't bear the kind of injuries to suggest he'd fallen or been pushed. How he'd got down there was open to question. The state of his clothing and footwear suggested he may have climbed down, using his back and feet to brace himself, though the reason for choosing that method of descent wasn't clear. A bit of a mystery in effect, one for the coroner to sort out. With the help of forensics, of course, Estimated time of death: some time the previous evening, say around 9pm.

That was the last I saw of Luke. The ambulance crew left as soon as they'd strapped him on board. I dare say the firemen would have departed too but for Mrs K's insistence that clues to the whereabouts of the missing Verity woman had to be close by; obviously no one had yet searched the area thoroughly enough. She seemed convinced the nearby pond could hold the answer. It lay behind the lean-to, out of sight of the Barn and overshadowed by several large trees. So, while the firemen set about draining it, and Wayne quizzed Mrs K more closely about her relationship with Mrs V, Angela cornered me for some information about Luke, and his relationship with my niece.

I got the impression she had me and Sam down as her leading suspects. Her questions developed a bit of an edge to them, that's how I knew. Soon, I thought, she'll be reading me a caution. Anything you say, sort of thing, may be used in evidence, especially if you choose to remain silent. Consequently, I gabbled rather a lot, stumbling over my replies in the process, and I may have misheard her at one point because I became aware of being asked what I meant by suggesting that any number of people might be considered to have had a motive if foul play was suspected.

'Sorry, I'm rambling,' I assured her. 'It must be the shock. I still can't believe it, coming across him like that at the bottom of the well. He was renovating this place, you know, doing it up for my sister to move into once the farm is sold. At least, that's what I've been told. Not by my niece, no. She suspected he was using this place to see someone else. That's what they had their big row about, as I've already explained.'

The woman kept one eye on me all the time she was jotting stuff down, checking doubtless to see if my face would tell her anything my voice didn't convey. Part of the training, I guess. The psychology module. What does this guy's face tell us, everyone? Study it carefully. Is it twitching? Or blinking a lot? Look where his eyes are focused. If he's miles away, don't believe a word; and step on his foot, to remind him to concentrate.

'Was that a yes or a no, sir?'

I was miles away, though she hadn't stepped on my foot yet. I was back at the well, if you must know, peering down and seeing *her* face, Mrs V's, peering up at me out of the gloom. 'Sorry, what was the question?' Through her increasingly mean lips (a habit of mine, I notice these things), Angela wanted to know if I thought Luke was likely to have made his home at the Barn after Sam threw him out of the flat.

'That's what it looks like to me,' I said. 'Take a look for yourself. Somebody's been living here. And that's his motorbike over there, under the lean-to.'

'We'll check it out.' But not until Wayne has finished talking to your psychic friend. Meanwhile, the firemen were busy draining the pond. After that they'd be calling it a day, probably, and driving back to base, leaving the police to continue their investigations as they saw fit.

"Fit" in this case meant a search sooner or later of the Barn and a call afterwards, if that produced no result, for reinforcements to widen the hunt for the missing woman. If you ask me, they were staking a lot on Mrs K's hunch that the woman was still on the farm, somewhere close by, waiting to be found. I believe Wayne and his colleague had their doubts. But since they had no alternative leads to follow, they went along with orders from base.

I could see the two of them expected me to join in the search, but frankly, I'd had enough. Not for me the prospect of coming across *her* face staring back at me the way Luke had stared. Not for me the job of finding her stuffed under some wretched tarpaulin or half buried in a shallow grave somewhere on the farm. Wayne gave me a dubious look when I told him I had somewhere else to be. Clearly, he subscribed to the school of thinking that interprets fleeing the scene as evidence you've something to hide.

'What about transport?' he asked. Try and trump that, sir, in other words.

He had a point. I needed a lift. Or did I? It occurred to me I could walk across the fields, as I'd done before, back to my car and off somewhere for a bite or a pint. Never mind where, exactly. Anywhere basically, so long as it wasn't a converted barn with a well outside or a packed marquee in the corner of a rented field.

Wayne acceded with all the reluctance of a police officer wanting a reason to detain a suspect. I was reminded that CID would almost certainly be wanting a further word with me. A word, too, with my niece, in case she had plans to leave the country.

I don't know if Mrs K noticed me climb the fence and make my way up to the top of the ridge. She had other things on her mind, I'm sure, and in any case, I'd no intention of looking back to see.

RECOIL

My way home, in case you're curious, didn't have to involve crossing the ten-acre field, so I avoided it. Instead, I came back past the wall Ted had been rebuilding. No sign of him or his cattle. Well, it *was* Sunday. As I climbed the last hundred yards to the farm, I was debating with myself how to break the news to Sam if I should see her, and hoping I wouldn't need to, she'd find out from other people. Police officers do this job all the time, don't they? It comes with the territory. How Sam would take it was another matter, of course. Bereavement advice was something she'd be needing in due course, though not from her uncle, you could bet. Make yourself scarce, Goodman, I told myself, as the Astra came into view.

The yard was deserted, which suited me fine, except I found myself looking round. Looking round for *her*, funnily enough. The missing Mrs V. As if suspecting the woman had taken refuge hereabouts, away from the hurly-burly. Wasn't she a *missing* person after all, not necessarily a deceased one? And on the run, if I'd understood the report correctly? A farm is not a bad place to hide out, when you think about it. Particularly a farm like Foolsmeadow Grange. The outbuildings were no longer in use; the owner was away; the caretaker was, you might say, an easy touch. What had the woman to lose? I may even have glanced up at Sam's window before climbing into the Astra. The sight of a face up there would have been more than enough to convince me my hunch was correct, but there was nothing. She'd turn up sooner or later, I felt. For now, though, I was out of here, in search of less challenging surroundings.

Mater was having a nap when I turned up on her doorstep. She'd long since eaten and cleared the table, and I had to raid her larder for a few scraps.

'What's made you so hungry?' she asked, seeing me tuck into a hastily assembled cheese sandwich.

'I've had a very busy morning at the farm. They've got this religious do going on in one of the fields; and now the police are looking for a woman who's gone missing. Oh, and Sam's boyfriend has had some sort of accident down a well. You couldn't make it up. Not good news, believe me. Enough to give a man an appetite.'

'You're not joking, are you? Who do you say the police are looking for? Not Samantha, is it?'

'No, Samantha's fine. But she doesn't know about the boyfriend yet. His condition, I mean. Luke didn't make it. Or have I told you that already? He's dead is what I'm trying to say. At least he wasn't breathing when they fetched him out of the well. She's going to be devastated.' Or so I assumed.

'Haven't you told her?

'I haven't seen her to tell her, have I? She's with her friends at this do. You know, the Sahara Street crowd I was telling you about that she's mixed up with. They've rented one of the fields and put tents up in it and parked their cars there. Some big get-together.'

'Good job it's not raining then, isn't it?'

'I don't think the rain would bother them particularly. It's one of their people the police are looking for. Luke's mother. Only they found Luke instead. Don't ask me what's going on, I'm as much in the dark as you are. I don't know what Hilary's going to say about it all when she gets back.'

Cheer, probably. Congratulate me on taking out the two people causing her the most grief over the sale of the farm. I don't want to hear how you did it, Adam, she'd say, but I owe you, big time. As for Steve, well, he'd be bound to say it couldn't have happened to two nicer people.

'Dead, did you say? A fine thing, that is. Whose fault was that, then?'

Mine, Mater seemed to be suggesting. On my watch, at any rate. Blame the guy in charge. He's a teacher, you know, and you don't put a teacher in charge of a farm, now do you? Any more than you'd put a farmer in charge of a classroom, for Christ's sake. What's the world coming to? 'Not quite the vacation I had in mind when I agreed to take the job on,' I confessed.

'Funny place to be, down a well, isn't it? There isn't a well at the farm, anyway, not as I remember. I've never seen one.'

'It's over at that place they call Lord's Barn, on Briar Lane. The other side of the farm. About as remote as you can get, if you ask me.'

'What was he doing over there?'

Having his bit on the side, you might say. But I didn't go into detail, I told Mater he'd been renovating the place, making it into a holiday let or something.

'So how did he get down the well? Somebody push him?'

'Don't ask me. I told you, it's been a weird morning. The police are trying to sort it out. I've left them to it. I needed a change of scenery, frankly. And a bite to eat.'

Not to mention a familiar face, and someone to listen to my side of the story. Mater fitted the bill – up to a point. It wasn't long, however, before she was reminding me that I'd made my bed, and I had to jolly well lie in it. I should have been holidaying with my wife, moreover, instead of playing at looking after my sister's place. Not once in her entire married life had Mater failed to share a holiday with the man she married. Yes, how about that? It was the same with my sister, apparently, at least while Philip was alive. 'I wouldn't have dreamed of going off anywhere without your father,' I was told. 'Now look at the two of you. Your sister's gone away with the first man she meets, and *you* can't wait to turn your back on your wife and kids.'

Like that, was it? Not a word about the favour I was doing my sister, or the opportunity I was giving Julie and the kids to take a well-earned break from my company. Nothing about the way I was looking out for my niece's welfare. It was distressing, yes, but hardly my fault Sam's boyfriend had come to grief. Either I was jinxed, shall we say, or the farm had a curse on it.

Mater wasn't slow to blame both. 'You've got your own reasons for staying behind while your family are away. From what you tell me, though, Hilary's place has brought you nothing but a hard time. And you've not been there a week!'

So much for finding support and comfort in the parental homestead. I think Mater expected me to announce I'd given up on the farm for good and would be sleeping in my own bed from now on. Had I heard from Julie or the kids at all, she wanted to know? Charlotte had been thoughtful enough to send her gran a postcard; and Adrian had stopped requesting more cash. No doubt I would learn in my own good time how much the family missed their old man.

*

It had gone dark by the time I got back to the farm. I'd remained at Mater's for the rest of the day, talking endlessly about this and that, me doing a few jobs round the house for her, she making me drinks and sharing her food. Finally, we'd watched some evening telly together. Like old times, you might say.

Driving into the yard, I felt everything looked reassuringly normal. The PIR lights snapped on, revealing absolutely nothing new or different. The wreck of Sam's Fiat still stood there, with no other car in sight, no limousine this time to tell me Sam and her friend were in residence tonight. And definitely no police car. No sound either, except for a breeze that now and then stirred a few branches in the trees nearby. I appeared to have the place to myself again. The Sahara Street crowd had gone, I presumed, driven away in their cars, vanished, their big day over. The Barn was out of sight, out of mind. My bed awaited.

I found two messages pushed under the kitchen door. The first was inside an envelope addressed to Mr Adam Godman, (that's right, one "o" to my name; next stop sainthood, if I wasn't careful). With it was a cheque for an inordinately generous sum made out to the same Adam Godman and signed by one Jacob Amoako (at least that was the name printed under the man's appalling scrawl). Jasmine's father, wasn't he? The Ammo Wally guy? In charge of the accounts, too, by the look of things.

The message was a note from Jasmine, written in capital letters and informing me that her father wished to thank me for my 'extreme generosity in the matter of the provision of one of the fields for use by the Sahara Street Mission Church of Our Lord'; he had intended to thank me personally but had not found me at home to do so. The cheque, it was hoped, would go some way to covering my 'personal inconvenience and unavoidable domestic disruption in the matter'.

Notes don't come much quainter, do they? Plainly, Jasmine hadn't asked for Sam's help in writing it. I imagine Sam would have told her that hire of the ten-acre was not in her uncle's gift and that he had absolutely no right to the money being offered.

The note made no mention of Luke, his mother, the police presence, the discovery at the Barn, the search – why would it? Not clear, then, was it, if Jasmine and her father knew any more about the day's developments than I did? Maybe Mrs V had turned up in the end and been told the bad news about her son and was being comforted somewhere – by her good friend Mrs K, probably. Or else she'd been detained for questioning in connection with whatever misdemeanour she was wanted for and was awaiting developments in a police cell in town. Who knows?

The other message was a calling card from the *Willsborough Gazette*. One of their reporters, a senior correspondent by the name of Ollie Marchant, had dropped by and not found anyone at home but would like to have a chat with me about 'today's events', as the message said. Nothing to do with the day's events in the ten-acre, you could bet, otherwise they'd have made a beeline for Mr Ammo Wally or his daughter.

My version of events had to be important to these people, I concluded. If that was the case, they'd be back. But not tonight. Even senior correspondents need their sleep, don't they?

PART **4**

NINE

AFTERMATH

Next day was Monday, and I could only guess what sort of day it was going to be.

I lay for a while in bed, reflecting on yet another of my vivid dreams. Quite an addiction, eh? In it I'd been watching a woman read the news on one of the TV channels. Nothing odd about that, right, except her face was in shadow, and the minute the lights came up it turned out to be none other than Mrs V doing the announcing. All glammed up too, looking fabulous in a new hairdo and low-cut blouse. The news items had no relevance, as you might have guessed. Far more significant was the way the camera started moving back from her so that she became progressively smaller and more distant till eventually, like Alice, she'd shrunk to no more than a diminutive face peering out from the other side of a square frame, a window, if you like, and you could no longer hear a word she said.

When a different camera picked her out, she'd returned to her normal size, but it wasn't her anymore, it was the mother of my children, Julie no less, reading out not the news anymore but the weather forecast, and having fun with those sticky clouds they used in those days that kept falling off the map behind her and making a farce of the whole business.

I must have switched channels after that, for in place of the newsroom came clips from a natural history programme. An Attenborough special, all about blind creatures that live in caves, and similar dark places, and making the point that if humans dwelt in that kind of environment for long and had no recourse to fire or artificial light, they too would go blind. A natural evolutionary process, apparently. Here was a case in point: a man, lost for decades in a labyrinth of underground passages, had developed antennae when people found him, so the story went. Only by now, as you've probably guessed, I was watching a horror movie and Attenborough had been replaced by a slithering, ugly, hairy, naked creature that couldn't face the glare of sunlight and fell flat on its face in front of the people who'd discovered its lair. It growled too, having lost the power of speech as we know it. And it spat at people.

Given the right circumstances, it could happen to any of us – that seemed to be the message on the screen. I guess you don't have to be that guy Freud to spot the way my dream picked up on my experience at the Barn and replayed it as a series of rather bleak and ironic images. Luke in the well – he had to be the creature from the underworld, wouldn't you say? And Mrs V and her diminishing face, that suggested the action of falling down a well, right? To which I'd been a witness (in my dream, I mean). And what about her face looking out from behind a tiny window? That certainly rang bells.

I sat up in bed, shaking my head and wanting to believe yesterday had never happened. Maybe I'd dreamed the whole thing. I actually shouted Luke's name across the bedroom, then carried on a conversation with him in the shower, asking him, among other things, what he'd been doing in the well, for

Christ's sake, and did he know where his mother was? One thing for sure: my days at the farm weren't going to be the same without the guy. He'd become a fixture in the short time I'd known him, so much so that, in spite of everything, I still found myself expecting to hear him moving about above my head. Or driving the tractor across the yard.

At breakfast, it was the same. At one point, over my cereals, I believe I implored Hilary to come back and take over before things got any worse. I ended up accusing her of dropping me in it *deliberately*. It seemed natural to assume she'd been forewarned of these disturbing events by her clairvoyant friend. Where was Mrs K right now, I wondered. On her way to start another week behind the counter at the charity shop, presumably. After leading the police a merry dance at the Barn, no doubt.

The thought that Mrs V might have met the same fate as her son didn't make much sense to me. She was a missing person, nothing more, as far as I was concerned. She was bound to turn up somewhere before long. I found myself insisting that the greater likelihood was that right now, as I finished my breakfast, Mrs V was in the act of unlocking her door on the High Street and opening up the shop. Hardly, I decided on reflection. That was the last thing she'd be doing. Either she'd be on her way to the morgue to identify her son's body, or she'd be at the station answering those questions the police wanted her for in the first place. Or she'd be still on the run, and her shop was the obvious place the police would look for her on a Monday morning. More likely Lucy would be opening up the shop for her and telling officers she'd no idea where her boss could be found. Dumb little Lucy, what was *she* going to do when the truth came out?

What truth was that, then? I shelved my thoughts and stepped outside to let the hens out for the day, and to take another look at the damage to Sam's car. I had my promise to keep, didn't I? Get the Fiat repaired or replace it. Okay, the circumstances had changed, and it looked increasingly unlikely that Mrs V would be honouring her side of the bargain and reimbursing me. There is no bargain to honour any more, she'd say, unless you're offering me a new one – my protection, say, in exchange for a new car for your niece and the Scirocco for your good self. How does that strike you, Mr Goodman?

I was still considering this scenario when one of those familiar pick-up trucks drove into the yard and pulled up next to my door. At the wheel was one of the Sahara Street security guys I'd met in the field. And beside him, in the act of opening the passenger door to alight, was a woman I dared to think for a minute might be *her*, the missing Mrs V, in her wellies and with a scarf over her head. As she shut the door and stepped away from the vehicle, however, I could see it was Jasmine. Come to have words with me about something. That cheque, perhaps. They'd offered me too much money.

'Good morning, Mister Goodman. Can I ask if you found my father's note?' She was beaming at me, all lips and teeth. Should I feel guilty?

'I did, thank you, but there was no need. For the cheque, I mean. It wasn't as if we had a business deal or a contract, or anything. It's not my field to hire out anyway, as I'm sure my niece must have told you. In the circumstances I really can't accept the money, tell him.'

Her face dropped. I was looking her father's gift horse in the mouth, I realised. 'I'm sorry, I've no wish to offend him,' I added.

Jasmine insisted, in case I hadn't understood, that it was my personal kindness and generosity her father wished to repay, and he would, yes, be most offended if I didn't accept. She too, by the look on her face.

I relented. I could always tear up the cheque later. 'Tell him I'm most grateful. Who's this then? It looks as if we have company.' Another of the pick-ups had pulled up. It turned out more were on their way, Saturday's lot back again, so Jasmine informed me, come to dismantle and take away the stuff they'd installed earlier. 'Where's Mrs Verity then?' I asked. Couldn't help myself, could I? She'd been in charge of this lot, remember.

Jasmine shrugged her shoulders, opened her eyes wide, and looked genuinely at a loss. 'Mrs Verity? Didn't you go with the police to find her? Nobody has seen her since Saturday. Except you, maybe, and the police.'

I swiftly disabused the girl of the notion that I was privy to the woman's whereabouts. 'We didn't find her,' I assured her. 'I assume she's still a missing person.'

Along with Luke, I assumed, at least as far as Jasmine was concerned. It appeared news hadn't travelled as far as this end of the farm. These people lived in a bubble of their own, oblivious to events outside. Absences must have been noticed, though, surely. Sam must have been aware Luke didn't turn up, and questions must have been asked about why that was. Where was Sam now, I wondered. At the pastry shop? Jasmine confirmed as much; she'd dropped her off there that morning.

'I'll let you get on with your job,' I said. 'We're holding up the traffic.' I stood back to allow the convoy to proceed. No point trying to get more out of Jasmine while we stood at the head of a queue. She appeared to have taken over the job in Mrs V's place, more or less running the show. I'd maybe catch her again later.

I followed the trucks to the gate, then decided against taking a look at what state the field might be in. A bit of a mess, I imagined. Understandable after a day of spreading the gospel and feeding the multitude, but at least I could count on Jasmine to get the site cleared and left tidy again. It could have been worse. It could have rained for two days and turned the field into a quagmire.

I still had Sam to break the news to, I told myself, as I walked back across the yard. I had the Fiat in my sights at that point but found myself distracted by a flutter in my peripheral vision, some movement off to my left, high up, from the direction of Sam's window. No face gazing out this time, but I felt convinced someone *had* been gazing out and must have stepped back to avoid being seen. You know that sense we all have at times of being watched, only to find, when we turn to look, that we're too late, no one's there anymore.

What to make of it? It was the sort of trick Sam would pull – step back before he sees you, avoid acknowledging him, don't give him an excuse to make something out of it. But Sam was at work, dropped off there by the person I'd just been talking to. So, who was up there if it wasn't Sam? Well, it couldn't be Luke, now, could it? But it just *might* be his mother. If you're on the run from people who know your movements, a sensible ploy is to do the unexpected and move into your son's empty flat. Especially recommended, I would imagine, when his girlfriend is staying over with friends.

The woman had to have used Luke's key to get in. Would she let *me* in, I wondered. As a recent but trusted acquaintance, say. Better still, as GV's erstwhile tutor, a professional listener accustomed to hearing all sides of any story, especially when the odds seem stacked against you. The last thing I wanted to do was *confront* the woman. Or shop her to her pursuers, whoever they were. I might even convince her she'd be safer in *my* part of the house; explain to her that, sooner or later, Sam would be back to reclaim possession. I would be doing the woman a favour, surely, by going upstairs to tell her so.

I tried the phone first. I mean I picked it up and thought about it, before deciding it perhaps wasn't the cleverest move. She wouldn't answer it, of course she wouldn't. Neither would I, not in her position. Her safest bet would be to lie low and stay out of sight, out of contact altogether. And my most sensible approach would be to go up there and tap on the door and announce myself, then make clear I wanted to help. With that plan in mind, I climbed the two flights of stairs to the flat.

Before knocking, I attempted to peer through the keyhole. For signs of a key in the lock, I mean, nothing pervy, if that's what you're thinking. But I found the mortice lock had been abandoned in favour of a Yale type that was certainly a recent addition. Luke's handiwork, most likely. Right, here goes, I thought, and gave a couple of taps; then, in the friendliest sotto voce I could muster, I announced myself and asked if I could come in. I did this a couple of times before trying the door handle and deciding I was getting nowhere. There was not a sound in response. Not a scurry of feet or the slam of a door. The feeling I might be making an ass of myself did occur, I must admit, especially when I heard myself call out the words, 'Go to the window, and I'll talk to you from outside. Just give me five minutes.'

Was I being delusional? There had to be some explanation for the movement at the window, I kept telling myself. One thing I wasn't going to do was try and force the lock or fling my shoulder against the door. I didn't want Sam thinking I got off on systematically wrecking her property in her absence. Maybe she kept a spare key concealed close by. Under the doormat, say? I checked (without success) on my way back to the yard.

Looking back, I was crazy, wasn't I, to entertain any hope that Mrs V's face would appear at the window as soon as I stepped into the yard? Instead of coming to my senses, however, I made excuses for the woman. I convinced myself that the window was open a notch or so because that's how she'd left it, after watching me cross the yard earlier. If I could climb up there, I thought, I might open the window wider and talk to her. It looked feasible. All I had to do was fetch a ladder from somewhere. Luke obviously kept one handy for his work on the roof. I managed to locate one of those extending aluminium jobs and was manoeuvring it into position when the postman's van arrived in the yard.

'A bill for Mrs Pope,' he called out.

Too much to hope he'd offer to help me raise the ladder. 'Just leave it inside the kitchen door,' I told him. 'I'm busy at the moment.' In case he hadn't noticed.

'Okay, mate. Did Mrs Pope drop the idea of a post box at the gate then?'

Excuse me? So, *that* was the story Luke had given the postman – the box at the gate was all Hilary's idea.

'She's still thinking about it,' I made out.

The postman's van had no sooner gone from the yard than I decided my plan with the ladder was not such a good one after all. It was highly likely, I thought, to scare both parties. Think about it – I had been known to suffer from vertigo at such heights, and my face at any woman's window could have induced the kind of panic that I imagine midshipmen experienced when attempting to repel boarders. I was returning the ladder to its former resting place when the Mini swept into the yard and out got Sam, followed by Mrs K.

*

The sight of these two turning up together signalled an obvious development as far as I was concerned, namely that Mrs K must have done my job for me and told Sam the news about Luke. Sam's demeanour bore it out. She was distressed and hurried off towards the front door without so much as a glance in my direction. Mrs K saw me and hung back, waiting for me to put the ladder away.

'Doing repairs for your sister, I see,' she remarked. 'After a few brownie points, are we? You can come over and do some jobs for me if you like. Boyd, bless him, doesn't climb ladders these days.'

I saw no point going into detail about what I'd been up to. I was more interested in what would happen the minute Sam walked in on whoever might be lurking inside her flat. She wouldn't be expecting to find Luke there. Or would she?

I saw Mrs K's mouth open but got my word in first. 'You told Sam, I take it? About Luke.'

Mrs K fetched a bag out of the Mini and slung it over one shoulder. 'Somebody needed to tell her. She's upset, understandably, so I offered to bring her home. No good leaving her there, was it? Anyway, I'm going to make us a coffee and keep her company for a while. If you've finished arsing about with that ladder, you can always come up and join us.'

Sam would love that, of course. Me coming up to join them. One way of seeing who *was* up there, though, no doubt about it. Maybe, too, I'd get to witness Mrs K's reaction. Maybe she was in on it and wanted me in on it as well. Join them? I couldn't wait.

Sam sat in an armchair, not saying a word when I followed Mrs K into the flat and made a beeline for the window. As I suspected, it wasn't latched securely. While Mrs K went to put the kettle on, I told Sam how sorry I was about the news she'd been given.

'What are you looking for? Cobwebs?'

Mrs K had spotted me eyeing up the place for doors to rooms and closets behind which an extra guest could be lurking. Sam dropped a used tissue into a nearby bin and sat up, her face a mess from bruises and wiped tears. 'He's looking for that painting I took off the wall,' she called out. 'One of Luke's. He took a fancy to it. That's what he's after.'

'Yes, what have you done with it?' Sam had given me the excuse I needed to look round the place. There were only two possibilities, I decided – the bedroom off to the left, and the bathroom next to it, both with their doors firmly shut. 'You've taken it into one of the other rooms, I'm guessing. To wrap it up for me?'

Mrs K overheard me. 'You after Luke's possessions already?

My, you don't waste any time, do you, Adam? Anyway, what were you doing with that ladder just now? Trying to break in and rob the place while nobody's here?'

Sam stared at me from her chair for signs I might be guilty as charged, then called out to Mrs K, 'He got some kind of fixation with this window. Reckons Luke painted it with a woman standing there looking out across the yard. A woman he thought was me. How weird is that?'

'It takes all sorts.' Mrs K pitched her voice knowing I'd hear. 'Teachers, eh? They do get some funny ideas at times. Spend too much time with their heads in their books, if you ask me. Right, sugar, anyone?'

By the time the woman emerged with the coffees, I'd started telling Sam about my latest encounter with Jasmine. I said nothing about the cheque, for obvious reasons, but I did mention Jasmine's new role of organising things the way they'd been done on Saturday by, er, someone else. Luke's mother, I was about to say. Only Mrs K got there first. From where she stood behind Sam's seated figure, she fixed her eyes on mine and shook her head rather vigorously, her lips shaped into a silent but unmistakable "no". Not a name she wanted airing right now, clearly. Not in Sam's presence. So I dropped the topic, and found myself a chair and another less comfortable one for Mrs K to join us.

The woman eased her weight onto it and said, for my benefit, 'Sam's car, I see, is still out there, looking very sorry for itself. Didn't I hear you promise her a replacement?'

I nodded. The sort of nod that meant these things take time, you know, but I'm on it. 'Meanwhile, Sam,' I asked, 'can I have the keys? They'll be needed.'

Sam pointed to a hook behind the door to the stairs, where I could pick them up on my way out. Would Sam have the use of the Astra in the meantime, Mrs K wanted to know. A promise was a promise. I bowed to the inevitable. 'If that's what she wants, I'll drop the keys off later. I have to go out first. There are a few things I need.' Were there? Well, there might be mail to collect from home, for a start, and a few more cigs wouldn't come amiss.

Mrs K pulled a face. 'Watch you don't run into the news and TV people on the way. I think they're setting up camp on the lane. Haven't they paid you a visit yet?'

'I must have been out. They left a card, though.'

'They didn't waste much time descending on Fletcher's shop this morning. Ask Sam. That's why we came back here, to escape the questions. I'm surprised they haven't bothered you yet. You've got that pleasure to come, sunshine.'

Sam got up at that point and headed for the bathroom. At the door she stopped and coughed rather loudly, as if to warn someone behind the door to stand clear. Or at least make themselves scarce. Didn't these old houses have secret panels at one time? And hidden staircases connecting one floor with another? For all I knew, our intruder could be making her way down some creaky steps this minute and emerging via a sliding panel into, of all places, my bedroom. I've dreamed stranger things.

With Sam out of the room Mrs K lost no time telling me she would be taking Sam to identify Luke's body later. The police also wanted a statement from her.

'Don't tell me they regard her as a suspect.'

'Nah, just routine. Poor girl, she's nearly out of her mind, what with this shit coming on top of her falling out with Luke. She thinks it's all her fault. Not easy getting her to see it differently. Anyway, what happened to *you* yesterday? You scarpered pretty sharpish.'

'Did I miss much?'

'I saw you cutting across the fields, you sneaky sod. I called out but you ignored me. Late for your lunch, were you?'

'Something like that. Did I miss much?'

'Guess where—'

Mrs K got no further, as Sam reappeared at that point, and I didn't get another chance to raise the matter of how the search went or ask if the missing Mrs V had turned up anywhere near the Barn. As for that elusive third person in the flat, I'd given up on finding her by the time I left. A strong suspicion, as I'm sure the police would agree, does not amount to anything more than that, a suspicion. It's proof we need, laddie. Show me a body and I'll show you a case. The words of some sleuth or other. Scottish, probably.

LAST DAY

My house, as I pulled up outside, had that look about it that told the world nobody was at home. You know, the neglected look: an overgrown garden, windows all tightly locked against burglars; curtains open twenty-four seven; a deserted driveway. Okay, nothing an hour or so with the Astra parked on the drive, a noisy mower at work on the lawn, and the windows thrown open wouldn't put right. At least there wasn't a police car standing outside the gate. Or a horde of cameramen and reporters at my door.

'You back home, I see.'

My neighbour, old man Greatorex, from the semi opposite, shuffled up to his gate to give me the time of day. Didn't miss a trick, Harry. He was the one safe person in the street I'd informed about our holiday arrangements, the one person I could trust to keep an eye out for anyone tempted to take advantage of the family's absence.

'I'm starting to feel homesick, Harry,' I told him.

Or was I simply in need of familiar faces to talk to? Anyway, Harry knew the feeling. He'd served all over the globe in HM Armed Forces. If it was dead bodies and missing persons I needed to talk about, Harry was the guy. So I indulged myself. I told him a friend of the family had died over the weekend. My niece's boyfriend, to be precise. A weird business, I called it. Some kind of freak accident at the bottom of a well, the sort of thing they put on TV to entertain you, but not the sort of thing you expect to come across while you're doing your sister a favour and looking after the farm for her while she's away on holiday. That sort of weird business.

None of it surprised Harry. He told me he'd heard about it on the local radio station that morning. 'I didn't realise it was your sister's place,' he confessed. 'They said they were looking for somebody else as well. A woman. They said she'd gone missing from a weekend rally or something.'

Yeah, something like that. I imagined getting back to Foolsmeadow later to find a media circus moving into the ten-acre as Jasmine and her crew left, bringing their own portaloos and trailers, erecting structures of their own in anticipation of a lengthy stay. I pictured them still around to welcome Hilary and Steve back on the day of their return.

Harry hadn't forgotten GV's demise and the media flurry over *that* story when it broke. 'You do seem to land in the thick of it, Adam. Not been your year, has it?'

I started telling him how GV and my niece's boyfriend were related, and the missing woman was their mother (near enough), and was agreeing with him that yes, on the face of it I did seem to be caught up in that family's misfortunes one way or another. Only, I didn't get to finish. Harry had unbelievably sharp hearing for his years, let me tell you, and picked up the sound of my house phone ringing from his front gate! 'Are you sure?' I asked him.

I couldn't hear it myself till halfway up the drive. It was Lorna on the line, JR's secretary, speaking from the principal's office. She'd been about to put the phone down. Apparently, people who take an inordinately long time to pick up were the bane of her life today for some reason. It turned out the matter of that folder had arisen again, the one containing GV's written work that I'd told her I couldn't find. It seemed Mrs Verity was convinced I had it in my possession and had insisted on having it returned to her. Would I have another look for it?

As you can imagine, I was taken aback. Lorna never got things wrong, so the question to ask was *which* Mrs Verity could she be talking about? Except I didn't ask Lorna, heavens no, as she would have told me to stop wasting her time. But I couldn't help asking myself, could I? With one Mrs Verity missing, presumed to be on the run, and the other shut away in a psychiatric unit, what part could GV's journal possibly play in either of their lives? Was I being set up? Made the victim of somebody's practical joke here, by any chance?

'Are you still there, Mr Goodman?'

An irritable and impatient secretary, this one, do I need to point out? 'Sorry, yes. I was just wondering when it was that Mrs Verity got in touch with you about it, actually.' And wondering if you people in the office have tuned into your radios lately or watched the local news on TV and, like me, asked yourselves if there isn't something odd about this request to have the journal returned.

'If you must know, she called in at the office this morning. Does it make any difference?'

Did it? It told me that *someone* badly wanted to get her hands on the journal, or else wasn't averse to playing elaborate tricks on GV's erstwhile tutor.

'She's coming in again on Wednesday,' Lorna informed me. 'And Mr Langtree doesn't want her making a wasted journey this time, if you get his meaning.'

No more excuses, in other words, for failing to produce the goods. 'I'll do my best to ensure the work is on Mr Langtree's desk by nine o'clock Wednesday morning. How does that sound? Better still, I'll turn up and see the woman myself.'

See exactly which Mrs V I was dealing with. See if she knows or not what happened to Luke. See if she knows more about GV's journal than I do! Oh, and see, if it's Trudi who turns up, what my chances are of being reimbursed for the cost of replacing Sam's car. Probably not the most exciting piece of news to reach Lorna's ears that day but she made a note of it nonetheless, the bit about my returning the work in person. And that was it. I had an appointment to keep. The Verity saga wasn't over, folks.

I promised myself that back at the farm I'd take a last look at the pages of the journal. For old times' sake, more than in any hope of coming across anything new. Meanwhile, I phoned my garage about the state of Sam's car and asked them to pop over and take a look at it, then collected the modest pile of mail from behind the front door. Mostly bills, a few sales brochures, and, lastly, a postcard from Julie that told me the weather was mixed and the sea rather choppy off the coast of Malta but gave no clue as to the date she and Charlotte would be home. The weekend would be my guess.

*

I arrived back to find, blow me, a recovery truck already in the yard and the driver taking a stroll round the Fiat. How's that for prompt service? The Mini, I noticed, had gone. I presumed Mrs K had taken Sam downtown, as she'd said she would, to make a statement and identify the body. Hmm. Sooner them than me.

The garage man shook his head. 'This is the sad old lady, I take it. Somebody drive a bulldozer into the side of her, did they?'

'Something like that. I'll get the keys.'

I went and fetched them from the kitchen table. Time to remove any items of Sam's that were still in the car. Outside again, I braved dust and tumbleweed blowing across the yard in the wake of one of the Sahara Street trucks as it drove past and disappeared down the lane.

'That's the second one of those things to come through here since I arrived,' the garage man observed. 'A bit like attending a breakdown on the hard shoulder. Have I come at a busy time, or what?'

I agreed that it looked that way and proceeded to empty the Fiat of a rolled-up umbrella, a solitary glove, a box of Kleenex, and two pairs of sunglasses – nothing particularly personal, you might say. I then watched as the man went about winching the car onto the back of his recovery truck. Such a fascinating procedure that I didn't hear the arrival of a vehicle behind me till a door slammed and a voice called out my name.

It was Jasmine, bless her, beaming as ever, come to tell me the work of clearing the ten-acre was over and things had been left as they'd found them. I remember thinking she would have made the ideal niece. Failing that, a student worthy of my tutelage When I asked her if she'd seen anything more of the police, she shook her head. Any reporters? She seemed more hesitant about that, and I had to wonder if she was under instructions from her father to say nothing. I told myself that if she didn't know yet what had happened to Luke, another night in my niece's company would put her right. For the moment, for all Jasmine knew, Sam was still behind the counter at the pie shop.

The garage man knew all about the police presence on Briar Lane. Having made a final check on the safety of his load, he turned to me and said, 'That's where all the coppers are, mate. I passed them on my way here. Up the old road. Don't know what's gone off, but you can't move for them.'

You don't know the half of it, matey, I could have told him. This is my sister's farm, where absolutely nothing happens till I move in. Then all hell breaks loose. Have you tried Far Meadow Grange by any chance? It's much quieter there, I believe. More accommodating.

Job done, he gave a cheery wave, climbed into his cab, and off he went, with Sam's car in tow behind him. The last time I'd see the Fiat, I told myself. 'I'm supposed to be getting Sam a replacement,' I told Jasmine. She'd climbed aboard her chauffeured pick-up by this time and gave me a parting smile.

Back in the kitchen it struck me that Jasmine didn't seem at all curious to know what had befallen Mrs V. Was that normal, I asked myself? Or a silly question?

*

I sat down once more with GV's manuscript and resumed my search through the remaining unread pages. If the journal contained nothing remotely incriminating, nothing particularly scandalous or saucy, no state secrets, nothing that could potentially unseat a minister of the crown or defrock an archbishop, what *was* the hold it continued to exert on whichever Mrs Verity was insisting on its return?

Whatever the hold, I found my own interest in its pages had waned. It no longer had any useful bargaining power for a start. Events had moved on, priorities had changed. And it didn't shed as much light as I'd hoped it would on the reason GV chose the path he chose. If somebody else wanted to pore over GV's memoirs, so what? They were welcome to them.

Anyway, determined to finish the thing, I read on and after a while a new reference to Mo caught my eye. The student friend, the one who found Marti so attractive, you'll recall. I picked the piece up somewhere in the middle of it, having looked and failed to find a beginning. Missing pages again, I guess. It appeared Mo had suggested the two of them leave home and rent a house. It wasn't at all clear how they would pay their way, though Mo did seem to have a part-time job and saw no reason why GV couldn't do the same. Marti was the fly in the ointment, apparently. She didn't want GV to leave. They had rows about it, and she fell ill and took to her bed. Really? Mo called that emotional blackmail. Astute kid. See for yourself:

> 'Mo said parents were known to play that trick. That's what he called it, a trick to make you feel guilty about leaving home. His parents weren't like that, they thought it a great idea to stand on your own feet. When I told him Marti needed me to look after her, he laughed. He thought Marti one of the smartest and healthiest people he'd come across. Your mother is kidding you, he told me. She's not really ill. Tell her to stop pretending. I told him I'd try.
>
> 'But how do you tell someone like Mo that the love of your father and mother is one thing, but it isn't the same with Marti? Not the same at all. Marti stepped in to look after me when all seemed lost. That's real love, she says, the kind you don't walk away from or throw back in someone's face. Come here and show me you understand, she says. Hug me, and take hold of me properly, like you mean it. How do I tell Mo why Marti pretends to be ill? Mo wouldn't understand.'

No, I didn't suppose Mo would understand. I wasn't sure I understood myself what exactly GV was trying to say here. I know what my imagination was suggesting, but I needed more evidence, more hard detail, more words on the page, before I could accept what my imagination seemed to be saying. The rest of the page concerned itself with Mo and where he felt the pair of them should look for accommodation. Marti wasn't mentioned again. The pages after that didn't allude to her either. Typical, I thought. I reached the final sheet with the realisation that I'd read all there was to read, and I wasn't really any wiser. *How do I tell Mo why Marti pretends to be ill?* What precisely could GV be referring to? And how did Mo, you have to ask, read the situation?

Feeling cheated, short-changed, and totally exasperated by the way this collection of personal experiences and reflections kept me guessing, I believe I did let fly with another Nigel Cartwright tantrum as a way of venting my frustration. In the end I decided to withhold that page about Marti. I wanted time to reflect on its significance, maybe read fresh meaning into it later; maybe even, given the chance, ask the woman herself to clarify it for me – if the right Mrs V turned up, of course. Whoever turned up, I resolved to hand over all of it except for that particular page. Oh, and the suicide note, of course. I decided that it didn't belong with the rest. This is all of it, I'd tell her. The pages aren't numbered, as you can see, but they're all there, in the order I received them. My apology for hanging on to it for so long. Do please be careful not to lose any of it. Ha ha.

If she spotted that page was missing, and asked for it, well, that would suggest she had something to hide, wouldn't it? Let's suppose for a minute that both Mrs Veritys, Marti and Marcie (Trudi and Claire, in case you've forgotten), knew the reason for GV's suicide and where the blame for it lay. And suppose both of them suspected GV of recording the reason in his journal, of setting it out there in some detail. In that case, surely, both women would have a reason to want to get their hands on it. One would be after the evidence, the other would be seeking to suppress the evidence. Am I making any sense here?

Okay, I never claimed to be the town's smartest detective. I teach for a living, remember, and GV was a student of mine. A fairly articulate student, as you can see, when it came to putting some of his life's experiences down on paper, but not an organised one where sequence and chronology were concerned. Rather rubbish at it, in fact. I could have helped him with it if he'd given me the chance. Helped him get matters off his chest, even those matters he didn't seem to want to mention in any great or graphic detail because, perhaps, they were just too personal, too intimate. I was GMan, remember, someone he looked up to for guidance and support. He could have taken me safely into his confidence before things reached the pitch they did. And maybe I could have averted the end tragedy, who knows?

*

That night I lay in bed listening, despite myself. Listening intently, I confess, for any giveaway sounds of movement from the rooms above. Sam's bathroom could be particularly noisy, as I've already said, especially when anyone took a shower or flushed the loo, and anyone up there would have to use the facilities sooner or later, wouldn't you agree? I'd dismissed the likelihood that Sam and Jaz would be back before morning. If Mrs V (or anyone else) was up there by any chance, I'd hear them.

I'd no sooner fallen asleep than I was awake again. Another dream, vivid as ever. This time Ted Shimwell was the star. Swimming towards me, with no cap on his head, pursued by his cattle, all of them struggling to stay afloat as they crossed a swollen river or something to reach me. Then the scene changed, and the river became an ocean, and I was on board a cruise liner that was sinking. There was pandemonium. People were pushing and shoving in their attempt to flee the vessel. I was behind someone who looked very much like Mrs V, following her down a rickety rope ladder to get aboard a lifeboat that seemed very cramped to me but would take two more people at a squeeze, with no room for Luke who was supposed to be with us but was now nowhere to be seen. I followed the woman onto the boat but it quickly foundered and capsized, and I had to grab hold of one of her legs in order to stay afloat. She kept kicking at me wildly, trying to shake me off. The last thing I remember was losing the hold I had and being bashed against the side of the ship. One of the ship's portholes came into view and I could see a stricken face peering out at me from behind the glass but wasn't sure whose face it was. One moment it looked like Luke, the next it was more like a woman. Except his mother could hardly be in two places at once, I remember thinking.

If I told you that same face has haunted my dreams ever since, I dare say you wouldn't be surprised. That face, along with the image of the sinking ship. Next morning, when I went out to open up the chicken coop as usual, I confess I wandered into the yard to take another look at Sam's window. Okay, just checking, nothing to actually see there. No stricken face at least. I did wonder about the Mediterranean, though. That cruise of Julie's. She and Charlotte together. Victims of a disaster at sea or something of that magnitude as yet unreported in the news media. I dismissed the thought as the ramblings of a man who has spent too long in the company of a mad clairvoyant and a delinquent farmhand.

I was about to go back indoors when, blimey, who should show up but Ted Shimwell himself. Not out of his depth on this occasion, though, and with his cap firmly back on his head. He seemed to be limping more than usual and looked tired, like he'd not slept. For all I knew, he could have had the same dream I'd had and was here to admonish me for not lending him a helping hand out of the water.

'Morning. Mrs Pope due back this week, do you know?' he asked, after lifting his cap for the customary scratch.

'I imagine so, Ted, but your guess is as good as mine. Anything wrong?' The limp, I meant.

'My arthritis, it gets me some days worse than others. It's all right for you young uns. Mrs Pope won't know about the business over at the Barn then, will she?' What *was* he about to say? 'Couldn't make it up, could you? That's what my missus says, and she reads a lot of books, you know. Crime and bodies and all that stuff.'

Ted had his sources, obviously. 'It'll all come out in the wash,' I told him.

'Not a nice thing to 'appen though, is it? Not on your own doorstep. I know how I felt the day my Spot got knocked down.' Not *that* tale again, surely. 'No sense trying to figure out a reason for it, is there? That's the way it is and it's no good fretting about it. Like you say, it'll all come out in the wash.'

I don't know why I mentioned the "p" word, but I did. 'I expect the police will be wanting a statement off us both, Ted.'

Perhaps I just wanted to hear if Ted had been approached already. Then wasn't surprised to learn that he had, and had told the police all he knew, which wasn't a lot, he admitted. 'There's not much I can tell them, and that's the honest truth,' he explained. 'I knew, like, as some funny business went off at the Barn every now and then, but I keep my nose out of business that doesn't concern me. Best that way, I find.' Wise fellow. He'd known all along what Luke was up to, it seemed. 'They asked me what I knew about *you*, the police did. If I knew where you were, like, yesterday. I told them if you weren't at the house and your car had gone, you must be out. Not my business to know where everybody goes, is it? Not as I'm interested, like, at my age.'

But if I cared to tell him, like, he'd do his best to keep it to himself. According to Ted, the police had called on me in my absence. Doubtless, they had also by now had a word with Sam, and Mrs K. That left *me* as the one person they'd not yet ruled out of the picture. Presumably, they'd be back.

Hilary's phone rang at that point, and as I came into the kitchen to answer it, Ted went limping off down the fields. My sister finally, was it? To tell me she and Steve were on their way home. Or was it the police? It was neither. The man from the garage wanted me to know he'd taken a good look at Sam's car and decided it definitely wasn't worth repairing. Did I want to consider a replacement? Their sales people just happened to have something that might interest me.

*

On my way down the Drovers Road, I tried looking at things from a police detective's point of view. Someone had been found dead on my sister's land in suspicious circumstances, and that dead person's mother was missing. What was going on? Was a crime involved? If so, who were the suspects? We could *all* be suspects, I concluded. Even Ted. We all had our motives for wanting Luke out of the way. Even me. Think about it. I could be acting on Hilary's behalf to rid her of her unwanted tenant while she pushes off to Scotland. Would the police seriously see me in that light?

And what about the missing woman? I'd overlooked to ask Ted just now if Luke's mother had put in an appearance at the Barn. He would have been certain to know if she had. Could *she* be the guilty party? Could she have got rid of her own son? If she wasn't hiding out on the farm somewhere, where else could she be? At the Kendricks' house, possibly, the two of them being close friends after all. What about co-conspirators to boot? Mrs K had to be suspect number three. The search at the Barn was all a stunt, shall we say. Humour me for a moment while I explore this angle. With Trude's help she'd by then disposed of Luke's body in the well. Now I thought about it, Mrs K hadn't seemed too surprised at my finding Luke in the well; she was the one who'd directed me to look there, you'll recall. Maybe I'd be seen as an accessory myself, the guy who'd pushed Luke over the edge knowing he'd die down there one way or another.

Like I said, I never claimed to be a smart detective. I just wanted to clear my name, give my own account of events, allay any suspicions the police might have that I was in any way implicated. With that in mind, I made the police station my first port of call. I would volunteer a statement and leave the detective work to the professionals. They could weigh up where I stood in the order of suspects, along with how much of my evidence to take at face value. If not exactly in charge of the case, DI Patrick Merriman, as he announced himself, was happy to take it upon himself to hear what I had to say.

'We've already had a statement from Miss Samantha Pope. Your niece, I believe. I'm told you have something new to tell us, Mister Goodman.'

Disappointingly, he didn't seem to see the need to switch on a tape recorder or caution me, or even ask if I wanted a solicitor present. None of the formalities you associate with police procedurals on TV. Nothing like that. 'I thought I'd save you the trouble of coming out to the farm again,' I explained. 'I gather you called yesterday while I was out. Or someone did. Sorry they missed me. I assume you have some further questions for me. In addition, that is, to the statement I gave one of your officers on Sunday.'

In other words, here I am, Inspector, at your service. I'm nothing if not your helpful, public-spirited citizen willing to do all he can to assist in the fight against crime.

'I have it on file that Police Officers Gardner and Adams both had a word with you soon after you reported the discovery in the well. That's right, isn't it?'

Gardner and Adams? That would be Wayne and his colleague, no doubt. 'I didn't catch their names,' I confessed. 'But yes, there were two of them.'

'And are you wanting to change what you told them? Or add to it in some way?'

Well, did I? Damned if I could remember what exactly I'd told Angela. Asking to see a copy of my statement didn't seem right. 'Not really. Except to make clear that it's my sister's farm and she's still away on holiday in Scotland somewhere. She and Mrs Kendrick are good friends, but I dare say Mrs Kendrick will have told you that herself. She's the one with the psychic powers. It was her idea to look for Mrs Verity at the Barn.' So she's the suspect you need to concentrate on, Inspector, if you don't mind me saying. And no, there's nothing going on between me and Mrs K, never mind what it looks like.

The DI sat back, narrowing his eyes and pursing his lips,

in that way TV detectives have of crunching the data while considering the various possibilities and permutations. Then he asked me when was the last time that I'd seen Mrs Verity. Not exactly a *coup de bombshell* but there you go. 'Saturday morning, and again at lunchtime. She seemed to be in charge of preparations for Sunday's religious festival being held in one of my sister's fields. Well, that was the impression she gave – that she was in charge. We spoke in the farmyard, but only briefly.'

'It says here you didn't know her very well.'

'I didn't. I mean I don't. I know she has a shoe shop in town, but I've only recently learned that she's Luke's mother. A bit of a surprise to me, that was. Mrs Kendrick knows her far better than I do.' And she can tell you a lot more than I can about the family history and about Luke's father, in particular, what sort of a guy he is, for example. Have you tried asking her? 'Anyway,' I said, 'has she turned up? Mrs Kendrick seemed convinced we'd find her at the Barn.'

The DI rubbed his hands together and leaned forward, as if to let me into a secret. 'I think you'll find events have moved on, Mr Goodman. Rather rapidly, I'm pleased to say. I wish all our cases were resolved as swiftly.'

All our cases? I took it the crime rate in Willsborough was way above the national average for a provincial town of its size, and the Foolsmeadow case was just one of dozens on their books. 'So you've figured out what happened, have you? To Luke Verity, I mean. And located his mother?' Not to mention arrested somebody for wasting police time?

'Mrs Kendrick helped us close the case.'

Of course. They'd rumbled her, seen through the smokescreen she put up. The DI expressed his surprise that Mrs K hadn't kept me informed. The woman's assistance at the scene, he confirmed, had proved invaluable in enabling them to locate the second body and piece together what had happened.

The second body. He had to be talking about Mrs V. 'So you found her then? I asked. She must have been in the area all the time. 'You found the woman you were looking for? Mrs Verity? Luke's mother?' I didn't want them making a mistake and confusing her with someone else's body, obviously. My voice sounded odd, like I'd pitched it too high but was struggling with the volume.

'Her body, yes.' The DI paused a moment and looked at me as if I might want to contradict him, then added, 'Yes, there's no doubt about it. Mrs Kendrick herself identified the body. It was found under the rubble that had been tipped into the well by her son before he… well, you know the rest of the story. A distressing business, I must say. A very sad case. And most upsetting for your niece. And for you, of course.'

TEN

HILARY'S RETURN

I thought *upsetting* was hardly the right word to use. *Shocked*, more like. About what had happened to Mrs V, certainly. And *intrigued*, shall we say, at the part played by Mrs K. The police couldn't thank the woman enough for her services, it seemed. Okay, my views on Mrs V's whereabouts had been way off the mark. More a case of wishful thinking than anything else, I guess. One thing for sure: my chances of getting the woman to pay for Sam's new car had been finally and irrevocably dashed. Not surprising then, was it, that my enthusiasm for calling at the garage had dimmed by the time I climbed back into the Astra and had vanished altogether on nearing the forecourt. I promised myself I'd look at that new car for Sam another day and drove on out of town without stopping.

My head was still turning things over as I pulled into the yard. There I found, would you believe, parked in my spot, a vehicle that looked very much like Steve's Land Rover. It was all happening, it seemed. The honeymoon couple were back. And there was the man himself, clad in T-shirt and shorts, in the act of climbing back into the cab and starting up the motor. If I'd known Steve was on his way out again, I'd have wound the window down and greeted him there and then. Hilary could have been sat alongside him for all I knew, I never thought to look. Anyway, before I could finish parking the Astra, he'd driven off, disappeared through the gate, heading God knows where down the lane. Impossible to tell if he'd spotted me.

Hilary hadn't gone with him. I found her in the kitchen. With Mrs K. The two of them engrossed in exchanging news across the table. Plenty of stuff to go at, by the sound of it. And I might well have been the invisible man for all the notice they took of my arrival. 'Where's Steve off to?' I asked. No reaction. The two carried on talking. I heard the kettle start to boil and, seeing both of them ignore it, I stepped forward to finish making tea. 'I'll have coffee myself,' I announced, and added, 'It's nice to welcome the two of you to my kitchen,' as I reached into the cupboard for an extra cup.

Hilary looked at me and gave a shrug. Her luggage, such as it was, lay strewn across the floor and it looked as if she'd pulled up a chair and simply flopped into it, too exhausted.to start unpacking. 'We can tell you're pleased to see us,' she remarked. 'Do join us.'

I nodded in Mrs K's direction. 'I see Pauline has beaten me to it. Been bringing you up to speed, has she, on what's been happening here while you've been away? Anyway, like I said, where's Steve gone, dashing off like that?'

Hilary gave another shrug. As though she'd heard me but couldn't be arsed. Pauline's account was far too interesting. 'Unbelievable,' she kept saying. 'You couldn't make it up, could you?'

I tried a different tack. 'It's nice to see you back home again, Hilary. Had a great time in Scotland, did you?'

She turned to me briefly. 'I wouldn't say that. Nothing like as exciting as what's been going on here. Pauline was just telling me about the bodies in the well.'

'Adam here legged it across the fields after we found Luke down there,' Mrs K pointed out. 'Couldn't face coming across another body, not down a well, at any rate That's right, isn't it, Adam? No stomach for a second stiff, eh? Admit it.'

My turn to shrug. Hilary meanwhile shook her head. Several times. 'Is that it then?' she wanted to know after testing her tea for flavour. 'Have the police finished sorting out what happened? Are they going to charge anybody for…?' She shrugged her shoulders again. 'For dumping two bodies down a well?'

Mrs K had clearly been briefed by sources close to DI Merriman. 'They're not looking for anyone else, so I gather. They've more or less finished their work at the Barn. They'll not be wanting a statement off you, Hil, don't worry, and nobody's going to be arrested. Not even Adam here.'

I pretended to look relieved.

'What about Sam? How's she taken it?' Hilary wanted to know.

Mrs K thought Sam would be hanging out at Jasmine's. 'She's cut up about what's happened. Understandable, really. She thinks she's to blame. I've tried telling her it wasn't her fault. She's not in a listening mood at the moment, though.'

Hilary gave a long sigh. 'So, what happens now? Besides two funerals, I mean?'

Mrs K winked in my direction; God knows why. 'You sit back and read all about it in this week's *Gazette*. I gave them the story so the news people wouldn't be banging on your door the minute you got back.'

Such a thoughtful soul. I turned to Hilary. 'I'm wondering how you got on with your ankle. Was it a problem? And where's your tan?'

Hilary didn't look to me as if she'd been away enjoying herself. Not for the best part of a week, with the new man in her life. She looked tired and glad it was over, frankly. I guessed things had not worked out as she'd expected. Was that why Steve had shot off like that?

Hilary wasn't giving much away. 'Not been all that sunny really, not where we've been. Plenty of midges though. Pauline tells me the weather has been glorious here. Far better than we had.'

'The luck of the draw, I guess. You missed the Sahara Street do, their religious festival, over the weekend. I thought you must have okayed it, so I let them use the ten-acre field. They were very grateful. Tidied up after themselves, too. I assume you knew about it before you left.'

Hilary nodded. 'Sam may have mentioned it to me. She usually lets me know about these things beforehand. I must have forgotten to tell you.'

Huh? Was I hearing right? This was for Pauline's consumption, I decided. 'Anyway,' Hilary went on, 'you've had a memorable time. Put this past week down to experience, Adam. It could have been a lot quieter for you, yes, and more relaxing, but never mind, at least it wasn't dull.'

I made a note to count my blessings and went over to the drawer to retrieve Mr Ammo Wally's cheque. 'They gave me this for the hire of the field. They insisted. They seemed to think it was *my* field. Do you want me to make the same sum out to you?'

Hilary took a close look at the cheque before handing it back. 'Generous with their money, aren't they? I'll give them that. But no, you keep it, Adam, for your trouble.' She wanted Mrs K to hear that bit, definitely. 'Did they offer you a price for the farm while I was away? It wouldn't surprise me.'

She didn't bat an eyelid on hearing that Barker Liddell had withdrawn the farm from sale because of the alleged tenancy agreement. The one that had lapsed on Luke's death, I reminded her, though I wasn't sure she understood. She turned to Mrs K once more. 'It's a nightmare trying to sell this place. But Adam thinks I should offer it to Sam's church, seeing as they're so keen on having it. I thought they might have made an offer while I was away.' She permitted herself a wry smile at the thought of it before asking me if Sahara Street were expecting to have the use of one of her fields as a burial ground. 'You know, for those two, Luke and his mother,' as if I'd already been approached and had given my consent.

'I think you'd better ask Sam. Nobody has spoken to me about it.'

*

Sam turned up later that day. In a smart limousine, with her friend Jasmine, and their very own chauffeur. A guy who knew his place, I'd say, for he stood to attention as they got out, then took a couple of holdalls out of the boot and carried them to the front door. Not sure if he carried them all the way up the stairs as well, the obsequious chump, but by the time he returned, he needed to mop his brow and lean against the car before resuming his place behind the wheel and driving off down the lane.

'What was that all about?' Hilary wondered aloud.

'Sam's friend is the daughter of one of Sahara Street's bigwigs,' Mrs K informed her. 'I assume that was his personal limo and chauffeur.'

Did Sam notice that her mother was back? Of course, she did, only I imagine she wasn't in the mood for an exchange of pleasantries. Right now, I imagine the last thing Sam wanted to hear about was what went on between her mother and Steve in bleeding Scotland. Not like me then. I was after hearing chapter and verse, except Hilary wasn't in the mood to oblige, and told me, when I cornered her again about his departure, that Steve was the best person to ask.

'He can tell you better than I can where we went. I know

we went across to one of the islands one day. And drove along Loch Something-or-Other. Loch Ness, is it? The one with the monster they're always talking about. Couldn't see a hand in front of your face most of the time, never mind spot a frigging monster half a frigging mile away.'

Okay, a start, but not exactly forthcoming, was she, on how much she'd enjoyed Steve's company? A rather irritable response, too, if you ask me. When I suggested a repeat trip for the pair of them to give them the chance to see more of the country, Hilary's face twitched a bit and she pushed her now empty cup towards the middle of the table, like it might have come from north of the border. 'We'll see. Put it this way, Adam. You've had a far more exciting time here at the farm while I've been gone, believe me. Anyway, are any of your family back home yet? I'm sure they'll have plenty to tell you about what they've been up to.'

You could sense she wanted to open up about her wild nights north of the border, couldn't you? When I told her Steve had shot off like a rocket without so much as a greeting for his old mate and that really wasn't like him, she sniffed. 'Are you sure you know Steve as well as you think you do?' I'd missed a thing or two about him, in other words. Well, I dare say Steve and I didn't cover quite the same ground together that I expect he and my sister covered, but our relationship went back a lot further. It had had time to grow and mature. We knew each other's moods, and we knew each other's foibles. We got along just fine, whether my sister understood us or not.

Mrs K thought Hilary must be hungry and suggested making a meal. 'For the three of us, eh? Why not? I bet you've had nothing to eat since breakfast, Hil. I know what you're like, trying to keep your weight down. I'll do us some chips, eh? With some of Adam's fish fingers. He won't mind. I bet he was planning on eating them today anyway. Rather than taking them home with him.' These being Adam's last hours under his sister's roof, she's reminding me, seeing as the woman of the house is back and has now relieved me of my caretaking duties.

In fact, the fish fingers were part of the stock of frozen food Hilary had left in the freezer for my consumption while she was away. I'd say the size of the stock suggested Hilary had planned on being away rather longer than a week. Or else she'd seriously misjudged my appetite. Anyway, no keeping the contents of my freezer from Mrs K's eyes, it seemed.

I suggested extending the invitation to include the two women upstairs. Have a family gathering round the kitchen table, in other words, a kind of last supper before taking my leave, if you like. But hey, Hilary wasn't about to change the habit of a lifetime, was she? She and her daughter didn't get on, remember. They hadn't got on for years, and that was why they lived apart under the same roof. Never mind that they had both just suffered a serious setback in the romance stakes (I'm presuming so, in Hilary's case); never mind one of them was in mourning. Let's face it, there was nothing to celebrate either upstairs or downstairs. Except my departure.

'Best leave them to it,' was the way Mrs K reacted to my suggestion. 'Sam has Jasmine with her. She'll be all right.'

A meal for three it was, then. So, while Mrs K got to work with grill and frying pan, I set an example to Hilary by giving her not exactly a blow-by-blow account of my days in charge at Foolsmeadow but a pretty detailed rundown of my experiences all the same. Needless to say, when it came to her turn to reciprocate, she did an excellent job of making me feel I'd wasted my time.

'Been having a word with Ted, have you?' was one of her comments. 'What did he have to say for himself? Been moaning about hard times again, has he? Or trying to convert you? That's what he did with me once. Saw it coming, didn't I? He's never tried it since, has he, Pauline?'

Mrs K shook her head in agreement. She'd donned an apron

by now, one of Hilary's that was several sizes too small for her and wouldn't fasten round the back. 'His missus is a keen temperance campaigner,' she told me.

Hence Ted's reluctance to accept the beer I offered him. He didn't want word of it getting back to his missus, understandably. I reckoned if there was one person happy to see the back of Luke and his mother, it had to be Ted Shimwell. 'I think he feared Luke's mother would end up running the farm and put an end to his grazing rights,' I pointed out to Hilary. 'He said he'd have a word with you about it as soon as you got back off holiday. Looks like that won't be necessary now.'

'That sounds like Ted all right.' Hilary flapped a wrist at me. 'What is it they say about an ill wind? You know what I mean. Ted doesn't want me to sell the place, I've known that for a while. Anyway, he's entitled to put in an offer for it like anybody else. They're not exactly paupers, you know, Ted and his missus.'

No more than Sahara Street, I thought.

*

I let myself out after the meal and took my cigarettes and lighter with me for a smoke and a stroll in the yard.

Time to reflect. On whether anything, anything at all, had changed for the better on my watch, during my few days in charge. Time to reflect, too, on what those same few days had done for the likes of Steve. Where was *he* right now, and what was going through *his* head? Was the relationship with Hilary as fraught as it appeared? Steve would no doubt fill in the gaps for me when I had a chance to speak to him, probably tomorrow. And what of that other unhappy soul, the one upstairs, my niece? *Her* plans for a future at the farm had really come unstuck in a way nobody could have foreseen, not even Mrs K. And I'd been working so well, hadn't I, towards ensuring she and Luke got back together? I could have done it too, I felt convinced, and in the process forged a promising relationship with the guy's mother, the one Mrs V I'd come to know as so much more than a coded name in GV's journal. Why had everything gone so badly wrong?

I heard myself voice that same question out loud as I paced across the empty yard, so bewildered did I feel in the face of events. I was just getting to know the place, getting to know GV's family when wham, what do you know, two of the family turn up dead in one day and on the same patch of land! Luke's demise I guess I could come to terms with. But the woman was something else. Women like her don't end their days down a well, for Christ's sake. It was only the other day I'd spoken with her in the yard, on this same spot where I now leaned over the five-bar gate and blew smoke at the skyline. I didn't deserve to lose a woman like that. I'd done nothing wrong, nothing to warrant such a meaningless twist of fate. We'd been destined to meet and get on, surely.

I didn't even know how the woman had come to be lying where they found her. Oh, there'd been an argument, a disagreement of some kind with her son, so Merriman had told me. But over what? Some disagreement to end in that way! Pure speculation on Merriman's part, if you ask me. How did he know it wasn't an accident, say, that Luke simply didn't know afterwards how to deal with? And couldn't Luke's own death have been accidental, too? Two terrible accidents in one afternoon, rather than anything more sinister. A coroner would have to decide, of course, based on the available evidence. I didn't envy him the job.

Let's face it, there was no guarantee that even a coroner would arrive at the truth. If the evidence isn't there, you decide on the basis of probability. You speculate, in other words, the way Merriman had done. As for why the police wanted a word with Luke's mother in the first place, I admit I hadn't got round to asking. I still wonder about it. And to this day. I ask myself would the awful business at the well have occurred if Hilary had stayed at home? Had *my* presence at the farm in some way precipitated matters and brought them to a head?

One can go on in this vein, I find, and become quite pathologically obsessed with the thought of one's own impact on the world. I switched to thinking instead about the *other* Mrs Verity, the one I was due to meet, the one who'd spent time in a psychiatric unit and who was now, presumably, fully rehabilitated and asking, not for the first time, for her son's written work to be returned to her, GV's biological mother, Claire, aka Marcie. Had she, I wondered, heard the news of what had befallen her sister-in-law and Luke? Or was *I* to be the bearer of the bad tidings? Two more premature deaths to add to the family toll. Here was one story Claire wouldn't be reading about in her son's journal.

I stubbed out what remained of my cigarette and started back towards the kitchen. After a sneaky last glance, that is, at Sam's window, for old times' sake. Surprise, surprise, there it was again, the face. Honestly. Jasmine's face this time, beaming at me, dazzling me with her teeth. Seeing me look up, she opened the window and waved, calling out my name, my title. 'Mister Goodman. Hi. How are you?'

I waved back and told her I was fine.

'Have you got a minute? Sam would like a word. If you wouldn't mind.'

She being such a delightfully innocent creature, I went along with her request, and hung about while she disappeared from view, leaving the window wide open. I heard her and Sam laughing together about something, followed by what sounded like furniture being dragged across the floor. Something to stand on, it turned out. I watched as Sam proceeded to climb on top of it, not without a wobble or two and that look of concentration on her face that trapeze artistes wear as they weigh the odds against falling. Eventually, as she stood up to her full height, I couldn't see her head at all. Just the dress she wore, and her bare legs below that.

'What are you doing?' I called out.

She'd turned now, with her back to me, her head still out of view. She had her arms down by her sides, her fingers close to the hem of her dress. A risky manoeuvre, it struck me, in front of an open window, at a worrying height above a cobbled farmyard, and balanced on a chair.

'What are you trying to prove?' I repeated. She had a card or board of some kind fastened to her back, with letters scrawled on it that read BOG. That's right, Bee Oh Gee. Meaningless stuff. I feared she was about to perform some crazy acrobatic stunt, involving a backward somersault or something equally suicidal. Sam had never been what you'd call an athletic child, so what was she up to?

If I moved closer, I told myself, I could try catching her if she fell. Like heck I could! More likely she'd fall on top of me and do us both a serious injury. Alternatively, I could…

No time for alternatives. By now Sam had bent forward and lifted her dress all the way up to her waist to reveal clearly what she wished me to see – two bare cheeks with the highlighted letters OF drawn in black across them, O on the left, F on the right, to be precise. A spelling error, did I take it? Meant to be OFF? Jasmine's handiwork, if I wasn't mistaken. But a very unambiguous message, wouldn't you say? BOG OFF. Not really a surprise though, just an unnecessary stunt to pull when I was about to depart for home anyway. On second thoughts, it was hardly Jasmine's style. Sam must have tricked her into it.

I'd be lying, wouldn't I, if I claimed that the sight of my niece up there made me sick to my stomach. I feared for her safety, naturally. But it was over in a couple of minutes. Sam, as I have already made clear, had blossomed in recent years into a shapely young woman capable of turning most men's heads.

Clearly, however, it wasn't her uncle's admiring eye she was after by affording him the sort of view not generally afforded by a niece to an uncle. Yet that is exactly how I chose to react. I put my hands together and applauded. Loudly, and without irony. To show my appreciation, what else? And to convey that I understood her message. 'Ten out of ten,' I called out. 'Now get back inside before you fall, and I have to pick up the pieces.'

It worked. Sam let her dress fall back into place and disappeared inside, leaving it to Jasmine to close the window. Polite to the end, the girl waved merrily to me from behind the glass as I made my way back to the kitchen door.

CLAIRE

That evening I duly took my leave and my luggage and drove home. Taking two lasting images with me. Not difficult, when you think about it, to guess what they were. Luke's face gazing up at me from the bottom of the well was one – I believe that image would have haunted anyone who saw it. At least now I know the reason for the tradition of lowering the eyelids of the recently deceased. 'I'm sure if it had been me, I'd have nightmares about it, too,' Hilary confided. 'For the rest of my days, believe me.' Mrs K's comment by way of reply: 'He'll get over it, Hil. The first one's always the worst.' As though she'd seen corpses by the truckload, having been a death camp commandant in a former life.

The second image had to be that face at the upstairs window, the one I *thought* I saw. The same one Luke had seen and painted. Two faces then, in all, that I wasn't likely to forget in a hurry, both of them reminders in their way of my niece's unhappy situation in that house.

I made no mention of Sam's antics when I got back to the kitchen. I wouldn't have traded places with her, I remember thinking, not for all the pies in Fletcher's shop, considering what she'd been through during my brief stay at the farm. Her home had been put up for sale; her car had been trashed; her boyfriend had cheated on her, then gone on to commit the unthinkable; she'd been given the job of identifying his remains. If you put aside the antics I'd just witnessed at the window, I could only guess at the effect all this turmoil was having on her, the same as I could only guess at how much Luke had really meant to her. For all his rough edges, his infidelity, and whatever differences he'd had with his mother, he might still have been *the one* as far as Sam was concerned. The one person who'd assured her of a future at the farm. The truth was I didn't know, did I, exactly how she felt. Except towards me, of course, and she'd made that plain enough.

And maybe the same went for Hilary; she seemed to be hurting, too. On the one hand she'd returned to find Fate had intervened and miraculously removed a couple of obstacles from her path, enabling her to think in terms of going ahead and selling up. On the other, something appeared to have happened to put her relationship with Steve in doubt. Like daughter, like mother. They were both all over the place with their lives and their feelings right now, and I guess it was something of a relief to be gathering up my things and packing my bags at this stage.

'Are you off then?' Mrs K wanted to know. I thought that much looked pretty obvious myself. 'This has been one hell of a holiday you'll not forget in a hurry, eh? He even found time, Hil, to look after your hens for you. And serve up a banquet for *me* while he was at it. You couldn't have left the place in better hands. You should do it again some time.'

'I'll pass on that, if you don't mind.' The banquet, too, the cheeky cow. The farm wouldn't be Hilary's for much longer anyway, I predicted. 'I dare say I'm going to find my old homestead rather dull for a time. By comparison, I mean. Till the family get back, at least.'

Hilary thought I'd had enough excitement to last me the rest of the year. Well, till my new term started. Mrs K went so far as to suggest I would find myself suffering withdrawal symptoms at home, having become addicted, as she put it, to the pace of life at Foolsmeadow.

Hilary gave a snort. 'If I know my brother, Pauline, he'll be fine. Won't you, Adam? Anyway…' She got to her feet and cast an eye over the pieces of luggage lined up, hers and mine together, on the kitchen floor. 'Let's not get these bags mixed up, eh? Give me a hand, Pauline, and we'll get my stuff upstairs. Adam, if you're going, shut the door after you, will you, and give my regards to your family when you see them. To tell you the truth, it's not going to be long before I'm off to bed myself. I feel like crap at the moment, to be honest.'

She'd missed her soulmate, I could see that. As for whether the two of them would be sharing the place for the night, and what their precise sleeping arrangements might be, I'd no intention of hanging around to find out. I did wonder briefly how Mrs K came to be in the house in time to greet Hilary on her return. Her psychic powers at work again, were they? Or had she planned to spring another party on me, and Hil's return had taken her by surprise? For all I knew, Steve could have objected to the woman's presence and given Hilary an ultimatum: it's that woman or me, sort of choice, and been disappointed with the response.

I discounted the idea of ringing Steve's number that evening. I guessed he'd feel like crap, too, after a long day at the wheel and so soon after the flight from Hilary's kitchen. If they'd had a tiff, nothing more serious than that, they'd need a day or so to cool down and get over it. *Better to leave it for later*, I thought. Till after I'd met with Claire, let's say.

*

What sort of Mrs Verity would Claire turn out to be? Another stunning-looking woman? Or a fragile, worn-out, little creature, not quite herself? Considering the woman was on my mind last thing before bed, I suppose it was inevitable I'd dream about her. But you knew that. My bed for the night was the old matrimonial divan, mine and Julie's. Far more comfortable than Hilary's iron bedstead and lumpy mattress. The bed Hilary actually slept in (I took a peek, didn't I, that first day) was the same four-poster, believe it or not, that she and Philip had honeymooned in on their wedding night. Never you mind how I knew about that.

The thing is, when it came to picturing Claire, I couldn't do it without seeing Trudi. The same went for my dream, so no surprise that the two of them appeared in it as identical twins. Because of a change of plan, I'd gone not to JR's office but to Lord's Barn to meet Claire and hand her the pages of GV's manuscript, and I remember finding myself once again inside that gloomy ground floor room and coming across garments, a woman's under and outer wear, strewn in a line that led, yes, to the shower room where, yes, I could hear the shower running, and yes, it seemed to be a replay of my earlier experience and any minute, if that was the case, Luke would pop up in the doorway behind me and I'd be violently pushed in the back. Well, he didn't, and I wasn't. Instead, I heard myself call out, as you do, in an attempt to get whoever was in the shower to identify herself.

No answer. She hadn't heard me, presumably, for the noise of the shower, so I knocked on the door, and this time called out the name Claire. Immediately the shower stopped running. I called out again, and announced who I was, in case she imagined I was some reprobate loose in the house. In my experience people need a moment or two after showering to grab a towel or a bathrobe before emerging. That's when a voice behind me, a woman's voice, asked if I was looking for *her*. It startled me, I can tell you, and I spun round to find the other Mrs Verity, Trudi no less, standing at the door, wearing the outfit I'd last seen her in, looking tall and elegant as ever. But get this: right behind her, following on her heels so to speak, stepped her twin, a woman identical in her face, her hair, her height, her every detail down to her matching outfit. I honestly could not tell the two of them apart.

By now the door to the shower room had opened and I got yet another shock. For it was Julie who stepped out. Starkers. Nothing around her at all, no robe, no towel. She walked straight past me, without a word. Suddenly we weren't in the Barn anymore, we were back at my house, and I was asking Julie how long she'd been home and wondering whether she'd caught sight of the two Verity women. She couldn't have missed them. That's when the doorbell rang – in my dream, I mean.

Julie, now with some clothes on, turned and told me she had a good idea who was ringing it. 'Those two girls,' she called them. Yes, *girls*! Apparently, they'd called earlier, and I'd not been at home. 'Two students of yours,' she called them. Wanting some written work that I'd promised to mark and hand back. But I couldn't lay my hands on it. It turned out Julie had thrown it out with the rubbish. Unbelievable. And guess where the rubbish was to be found? Next thing I was back at the Barn, heading for the well (yes, *that*'s where) to retrieve it. Only I never arrived. I woke up, sweating, and not happy at all at the prospect of having to climb down into the depths after those missing pages.

Did I seriously expect Claire to look exactly like her sister-in-law? Of course not. I was just at a loss to know what the woman would look like. As GV's mother, she had to have some of her son's looks, didn't she? Naturally, she wouldn't know me from… well, from anyone else on the staff payroll. My part in the handover of her son's manuscript would be a side issue, a distraction if you like, if JR had anything to do with it. In his eyes I didn't need to meet the woman face to face at all. My appearance, my demeanour, my attitude, were all bound to risk letting the college down.

In the event I didn't make it in time to meet the woman. Fate intervened, probably at JR's behest. I set off in plenty of time, but then the Astra was involved in a shunt at a set of traffic lights on the way across town. Not my fault. The woman behind me failed to stop and pushed me into the guy in front. A big enough setback in itself, it goes without saying, what with all the attendant formalities. But Fate didn't leave it at that, oh no. Back behind the wheel, checking my watch and realising I was now cutting it rather fine. I soon began to experience the feeling my car wasn't rolling as smoothly as it should. At the next set of lights, a cyclist pulled up alongside me and pointed to the rear wheel. The tyre, it turned out, was flat.

In the end I rolled up at JR's office a good hour or so late. Lorna answered my knock and told me I'd missed the action. 'Didn't you see the ambulance leaving as you drove in?'

I did, but since its blue lights weren't flashing or its siren wailing, I'd ignored it. I'd also failed to spot the police vehicle standing in the car park.

'What exactly have I missed?' Apart from the chance to meet GV's mother.

I'd missed a weird encounter, according to Lorna. She found it hard to stop shaking her head at the thought of it. 'You could have warned us. No good waving those papers at me now, is it?'

'So I've had a wasted journey, have I?'

The chance to meet GV's mother and hand her the journal, as I suspected, had come and gone. I must have looked disappointed, for Lorna set about poking me in the ribs (metaphorically, I'm talking about, let's not get excited) and told me to be grateful I'd escaped the ordeal John had had to endure. Yes, John. Not JR. She forgot herself, still caught up in the emotion of the encounter she'd been party to, I imagine. John, she explained, was giving the police a statement right now, and she didn't know how long it was going to take.

Something seismic had happened, clearly. For one thing,

she had never let me stand this close to her before, as I recall. As though she badly needed a hug, someone to hold her tight and comfort her. Someone with more courage than I had, I guess. Don't get me wrong, Lorna was not an unattractive woman, far from it. A bit horsey for my taste, but hey, quite a feisty one and talk about loyal, she wouldn't hear a word said against JR. Wherever he went, she went, and she was always well turned out on those occasions. There was talk of a *Mr* Pritchard in her life, though I never set eyes on the guy. He could have been another Boyd Kendrick for all I knew, a housebound invalid who maybe encouraged his missus to do all she could to please her boss, as long as she didn't bring anything or anyone home by way of evidence. As far as I could see, she and JR made a very discreet and a very well-behaved couple, all credit to them. A model to the rest of us, if I'm honest about it. Right now, however, Lorna stood alone and bereft; she'd clearly had a fright, and, realising she wasn't going to receive a hug from the likes of me, seemed intent on blaming me for the state she was in. 'You might have warned us what she was like,' she accused me.

I told her I'd never met the woman, and added, 'I was looking forward to making her acquaintance, actually. Now I suppose I have to be glad I didn't. Only nobody has told me yet what happened.'

'Heather will give you the details. I must get that.' *That* being JR's hotline, the phone that rang in the admin office which Heather had clearly been told to ignore if Lorna herself was present to take the call.

*

Not the same, is it, hearing the story from somebody who didn't actually witness what took place? Heather was the one who'd called the police. And called the caretaker too, he and his dog being the best the college could muster in the way of security.

Only it happened to be their day off. The emergency call was made at Lorna's bidding. She had stuck her head round the interconnecting door and hissed at Heather to get help.

Not only that. Soon after the call was made, Lorna had reappeared, apparently, and gone over to the sink to rinse blood out of a handkerchief before grabbing a first aid box off the wall and dashing back into JR's office. 'It was very noisy in there,' Heather confided.

Throughout the summer vacation the college was pretty well deserted, as you'd expect, and the office was manned by a few *essential* staff, I guess you'd call them. This morning it was Heather's turn to be on duty. 'That's what I said. I could hear the woman shouting,' she explained when I queried the kind of 'noisy in there' she meant. 'I could hear all this bad language. From *her*, I mean, not from Mister Langtree. You didn't think I meant Mister Langtree, did you?' She giggled at the possibility I might have.

'So what was the blood all about?'

'The woman did something to herself. On purpose. Cut herself or something. With some scissors. And then threatened Mr Langtree with them. That's what Lorna told me, at any rate.'

'What set that off then?' JR's abrasive manner, at a guess. He wasn't known for his people skills.

'Lorna reckons the woman mistook Mister Langtree for *you*.' A pause for another giggle, this time at the picture I presumed Heather conjured up in her mind's eye of JR insisting he wasn't me. Okay, faintly amusing but not *that* hilarious, surely. No accounting for what this girl saw through her mind's eye, though. I nodded understandingly.

She went on to tell me that Mrs Verity had got quite stroppy with JR for not being straight with her about the written work she wanted returned. She accused him of not wanting to return it because of what was inside it. 'What did she mean by that?' Heather wanted to know. 'What was she on about?'

'It's a long story.' Well, I wasn't going to go into detail about the journal, was I? Not with the office junior, come on.

I wanted to ask her what the woman looked like, but of course Heather hadn't seen the woman, and even if she had, would I have been any the wiser for hearing Heather's account? Heather didn't do accurate or reliable descriptions – you know, the kind the police ask for from witnesses, and she certainly didn't do the kind *I* wanted. Did Mrs Verity look anything like her son, for instance? You know, round the eyes, the chin, the expanse of her forehead, the shape of her nose. How was she dressed? Like she'd just absconded from one of those safe units they keep them in? Or did she look like a prosperous woman from, say, the Brookfield end of town? And was she alone? Or was there someone with her? A carer, perhaps? Or even a gentleman friend, one with designs on turning GV's work into a TV documentary drama of some kind. No, Heather assured me, Mrs Verity had turned up entirely alone. That much she did know.

Eventually I got the story from JR himself. He beckoned me into his office for a briefing after a uniformed officer had picked up his hat and left. Job done, you know, villain apprehended, witness statements taken, normal service resumed. JR looked at his watch. 'What time did you tell Lorna you'd be here?'

He knew the arrangement as well as I did but was due an explanation, I guess, though he sniffed a lot on hearing it. You'd think I'd turned up late on purpose in order to embarrass the guy. The way I'd embarrassed him before, remember, by not making it to the station in time to stop GV from bringing the next through train to an unscheduled stop. We were dealing with the same family, see, who in his eyes were nothing short of inadequates who I should have spotted and kept at arm's length, certainly kept outside the college gates and off my register from the outset.

'Were you aware Mrs Verity had been detained in Sweetlands?' he asked.

I shook my head. Denied it, on the grounds that what I learned about the Veritys through gossip or by way of anecdote was simply that, gossip and hearsay, not to be taken too seriously. Anyway, was *he* aware that another Mrs Verity had been found at the bottom of my sister's well only the other day? And that *her* son had topped himself too? No, I refrained from mentioning the subject, for fear JR would fail to see its relevance to what he had to say.

'She was discharged from there only a few weeks ago, so I'm told,' he went on. 'She was assessed and considered no longer a threat either to herself or to others. Now she's back inside, and rightly so after this morning's episode. A good thing you weren't here in the thick of it, that's all I can say.'

That wasn't all he had to say, mind. He proceeded to describe how Mrs Verity had been aggressive towards him from the start. For reasons of his own he left out the bit about her mistaking him for me, before rolling back the cuff of his jacket and showing me the tear in his shirt sleeve where the woman went for him with a nail file, so he said. He and Lorna had managed to disarm her between them, but only after she'd slashed herself with the file. No scissors, apparently – don't know where Heather got that from. 'Definitely a bit of a fruitcake, that one,' was JR's verdict. 'I guess it runs in the family.'

Did I tell you I was never JR's greatest fan? I discovered that, in my absence and faced with having no journal to hand over, he'd insisted the woman had to be mistaken as there was no written work to return to her and never had been. He'd made out she'd imagined it and was wasting his time, in effect. Told her he'd been given that message by yours truly, over the phone. He'd done it to get rid of her, supposedly, as he had more important matters to attend to that morning.

Naturally, JR didn't tell me this to my face. I learned of it later through another source. So there was an understandable innocence to my question when I put it to him, 'Didn't you explain to Mrs Verity that I'd been delayed, that I was on my way with the written work she'd asked for?'

The tone of my question may have been sharper than I'd intended, for JR stared at me for a moment in what looked to me like disbelief. As though I'd overstepped the mark and needed reminding of who and where I was. His reply, when it came, bore this out and might well have been accompanied by words to the effect of *I shouldn't need to remind you of this, my dear Adam, but you leave me no option.* 'If you put your mind to it, I dare say you'll understand that we, in the office, were completely in the dark about what could have happened to you. None of us had the benefit of knowing how long Mrs Verity would have to wait. In the end a decision had to be made and I decided to deal with the woman myself. You've heard what happened. The woman, I assure you, was in no mood to wait. Or be reasoned with.'

'She would have listened to *me*.'

Spoken, I realised, as if I knew this woman personally from way back, knew all about her family history, her time in Sweetlands, her need to be reunited with her late son's memory, and to have in her grasp his collection of reminiscences. As if I knew her far better than JR did, who stiffened at my words and set about fixing me with those icy blue eyes of his.

'What makes you so sure of that, may I ask?'

'Because I have her son's written work.' I held up my briefcase in front of his face. 'This is what she came for. It's all she wanted. It's a bit like a diary, full of memories for her. It may even throw some light on the reason her son did away with himself while he was a student here, and…' My voice died in my throat. Had I over-egged the pudding? Leaked information to him that JR would have preferred not to hear about or be reminded of?

He gave me an odd look, as if that was exactly what I'd done. Then he recovered himself and went on, 'In the circumstances I think her son's written work would have been neither here nor there. The woman came here intending to cause trouble, full stop. You weren't here to see it for yourself. Nothing either of us could say would have made a scrap of difference. Being rational with her didn't cut it. You don't seem to understand the nature of the episode you've been fortunate enough to avoid. Consider yourself lucky you weren't involved.'

The image flew through my head of Luke swinging his toolbox into Steve's crown jewels and I permitted myself to imagine my briefcase performing a similar arc in JR's direction. 'I really feel you should have waited,' I heard myself insist. 'You're not exactly the best choice of person to deal with a parent, especially a grieving one like Mrs Verity, now, are you?'

The colour drained from JR's face at this outburst from a lowly member of his teaching staff. He eyed me intently, presumably for signs I might do a Mrs Verity of my own and lunge at him with my nail file. Having decided that I didn't pose that kind of threat, he cleared his throat and sort of nodded his head. 'It's been a regrettable incident all round,' he conceded. 'Thankfully, it's over, and no amount of argument about why things weren't done differently can alter that. Now if you don't mind, I'll take that written work from you and do what I can to see it's put in the right hands.'

The binman's hands, if I knew JR. Or Lorna's, with instructions to consign it to the shredder. Without a word more, I took the folder out of my briefcase and handed it over. I couldn't think of a good reason for withholding it. I felt resigned at that stage, I guess, to the prospect of not getting to meet Mrs Verity after all. Ever. Not this Mrs Verity. Not GV's real mother. The game was over, it seemed, and I'd no wish to risk my job by chancing my luck any further.

STEVE

It turned out that Steve knew someone with a relative in Sweetlands, a delightfully barmy old dear, apparently, who wouldn't hurt a fly. He'd not mentioned it before because he'd had no reason to, so he said. I'd reminded him of it by telling him the tale of GV's mother and how JR had dealt with her.

'End up in there, mate, and you never get out alive, so they say.'

That was Steve's verdict on Sweetlands and its residents. Not a word to say in support of my stand against JR. Or in support of the woman claiming to be GV's mother. Parents were bad medicine where Steve was concerned; given the chance, he would have dispatched several he knew to the nearest psychiatric unit. When I told him about events at the Barn and told him that the two characters involved in *that* little drama also went by the name of Verity and were in fact members of the same extended family, he accused me of pulling his leg. 'That *is* weird, mate,' he concluded.

We'd arranged to meet in the bar of The Cavalier, our regular watering hole. Its rooms attracted types like us – blokes of a certain age, seeking refuge from the daily grind of life. This was where I'd first heard Steve mention the way he felt about Hilary. 'Didn't think it would ever be my turn to get smitten, mate. Not at my time of life. Fancy, eh? There's hope for mankind yet.'

He'd found it hard to believe his luck. Women were from another planet, he'd always believed, one whose orbit did not intersect his as a rule. Women made him feel ill at ease and his instinct was to keep them at a distance. Hilary was different. He could be himself in Hilary's company, so he told me; with her he didn't have to watch his language or mind his manners. I guess in that respect he appealed to Hilary in much the same way as Mrs K did. There was evidently a side to my sister I'd not been aware of during the years we'd spent growing up together.

Like Hilary, Steve thought I'd had a far more interesting few days than he'd had. To be honest, he didn't look as if he'd had a great time, considering he'd just been away with the woman of his dreams. The weather hadn't been brilliant, for a start; they'd stayed in some grotty bed and breakfast places; and, what's more, he'd had some grief with the Land Rover. All in all, he'd really rather not talk about the trip to Scotland, if I didn't mind. Instead, he preferred to hear more about *my* experiences. He seemed particularly taken by my distaste for Mrs K's attentions. 'Lucky you, eh? I bet you led her on at the start, mate, then found her too much of a handful. Couldn't cope with her, could you? I reckon Pauline spends more time in Hilary's kitchen than she does in her own. Finds Boyd's company a bit of a drag these days, I reckon. Then you come along, eh?'

'Did you know she has psychic powers? Hasn't Hilary ever mentioned it?'

'You mean she knew all along you'd be leaving your door unlocked for her at night? And you a happily married man, with a wife and two kids, and a respectable job in town.'

Yeah, how about that? 'Odd, though, don't you think, that she seemed to know there were bodies to be found over at the Barn? So why invite me to meet her there? And why ask me to be the one to look down the well like that? It frightened the life out of me, I can tell you, seeing Luke down there, staring back at me like he was still alive.'

Steve wagged a finger in my face. 'Ask yourself this, mate: why do women do the things they do? It looks to me like Pauline wanted you over there as her alibi. And you fell for it.'

'What do you mean?' Fair enough, I could see where this was headed. I guess I just wanted to hear it confirmed. 'You think Pauline did it, do you? Got rid of both of them?'

'That's what it looks like. The police just haven't tumbled to it yet. Women, eh, they can be so devious, so cunning.'

'You're speaking as a man of experience, of course.' Well, in this case as one who appeared to have struck choppy waters in navigating the ocean of amorous relationships, and who might, given the right encouragement, be persuaded to go into detail about what exactly had happened to sour things with Hilary. Assuming relations between them *were* sour.

'They can be hard as nails, I'm telling you, mate. Never trust a woman, that's my advice.'

'Are we talking about my sister here, by any chance?'

Wrong question. Steve gave me a look and shook his head. 'I'm talking about Pauline. It was what you told me about her, that's all, that got me thinking things aren't always what they seem. Especially where women are concerned.'

'You've just spent a whole week in the company of a woman. Was it so bad? The holiday, I mean. It went okay, didn't it?' Nothing like perseverance, I've found. And a direct question. The worst Steve could do was tell me to ask Hilary for the answer.

Steve took his time, draining his pint and giving his head another shake. 'Is that what Hilary told you?'

No need here to choose my words with care, the point was straightforward enough. 'Hilary hasn't told me anything. Nothing whatsoever. On the day you came back from Scotland she was far too busy listening to Pauline's account of what went on at the farm. Wasn't even inclined to tell me why you dashed off like you did. I haven't seen her since.'

That's when Steve broke with the habit of a lifetime and offered to buy me another drink. The lengths some people will go to, eh, to duck the issue. When he came back from the bar with fresh drinks, I opened my mouth to try again but he stuck a cigarette between my lips and went on about my failure to tell him about the male side of the Verity family. Wasn't there a *Mister* V at large somewhere? The guy responsible for fathering my erstwhile student, say, not to mention the one who'd sired Luke, now he thought about it. 'Or did the men bugger off after they realised what nutters the women were?'

'One did emigrate to Australia,' I pointed out. 'Gordon's father, as far as I know.'

Steve nodded approvingly. 'Sensible bloke. Did you know they're advertising for skilled tradespeople over there? Single blokes like me, who can teach youngsters a trade. I'm giving it some serious thought.'

Huh? 'Sounds interesting. Thinking of taking Hilary with you, are you?' *Interesting*? It sounded positively *over* to me – as though his love life was definitely shelved or had become a lost cause, as if Hilary was the last person that he'd be taking with him. There had to be some way of getting him to unburden himself and spill the whole can of beans. I could hazard a guess as to what had gone wrong, but that wasn't good enough, was it?

Steve took the opportunity to make a big impression on his latest pint. 'Are you going to light that cigarette?' he asked eventually. 'Or worry it to death?'

Time to come to the point. 'Why don't you start by telling me why you shot off rather smartly the other day. Showing me a clean pair of heels like that, I thought there must be a Land Rover rally in the neighbourhood, or something. Or did you and Hilary have a row?'

A mistake, if ever there was one, mentioning the words Land Rover to a guy like Steve. An invitation to reminisce, reflect on the old days, the days before ever Hilary came over his horizon. I should have known better. He and I had spent days together in that vehicle, negotiating some of the most unforgiving tracks and terrain we could find. Now he chose to remind me of it. 'Do you remember that time we came across that couple stuck in a farmer's gateway? In a Hillman Imp, for Christ's sake. Been for a picnic or something, so they said. A snog, more like. Wanted us to haul them out before the farmer spotted them.'

I knew the incident well, but I'd no wish to relive it. I wanted to hear Steve talk about how he and Hilary had got on while cruising along those long, lonely Highland roads. How they'd maybe got lost in the mist, say, miles from anywhere, and had to bed down together in the Landy? Okay, he wasn't going to give me *those* details, but how about a word or two about how they'd coped with so much time spent together in the cab. Initially, it seemed, in Steve's own words, 'all had gone well'. Then the weather had closed in, and soon after that the Land Rover had given him grief on a number of occasions which he said he'd managed to fix. When I quizzed him about Hilary's navigating skills, you might say that's when the wheel nuts really began to come loose.

Traditionally it had been *my* job, whenever seated alongside Steve in the past. He'd grown accustomed to having me direct operations and had relied on me to pinpoint where we were, or at least where we ought to be. We're talking pre-satellite days here. No on-board sat-nav, no global positioning devices, nothing like that. We used maps. And still got lost. All part of the fun, of course. But now I was being made aware that Hilary hadn't measured up in the route-finding department at all, and the experience had proved a source of irritation to them both. It had definitely spoilt Steve's fun, and probably hadn't done much for Hilary's temper either. Women and geography, eh? I could have warned Steve at the outset not to trust Hilary's map-reading skills, nor expect her to enjoy riding in a Land Rover at speed on unmade single-track roads.

'I thought everyone at least knew where north is on a map,' Steve complained.

Everyone except Hilary, apparently. Hilary also felt uncomfortable, he'd learned, travelling on roads that wind across large expanses of open moorland – you know, the sort you find plenty of in Scotland. Steve called it "agriphobia" and felt perhaps I should have warned him about that earlier.

'I thought maybe she'd grown out of it by now,' I pleaded.

Steve pulled a face. He wasn't likely to accuse me of deliberately misleading him about the extent of my sister's shortcomings, but he did wonder how such a woman could end up marrying a farmer. 'Don't you have to love open spaces to be a farmer's wife? I would have thought so, mate,' was his opinion on the matter.

I told him I didn't know, for instance, that Julie had a fear of being made fun of till after she and I had been married for a while.

'Is there a name for that?' he wondered.

'It's called regret.' Okay, not my most amusing remark, but never mind, Steve had been known to laugh at far worse. 'Anyway, how did Hilary get on with that ankle of hers? I don't suppose she could walk very far on it. I thought she should have let it heal first, before heading off to somewhere like Scotland. A bit much for her, I thought. But you know Hilary. She doesn't listen to advice, especially not her brother's.'

'Don't think it would have made much difference, mate. She didn't care for those big open spaces, like I said. Too empty, Scotland, she reckons.'

'Well, whose idea was it to head that way?' Not Hilary's, I'd wager. 'You could try somewhere different next time.' Assuming there'd be a next time, which on the face of it looked more and more unlikely. 'How about Morocco, and the Sahara?'

'You're taking the piss now, mate, aren't you? You're the one who's been sampling the Sahara. That church of your niece's put you in mind of it, I bet. Paid it a visit, did you?'

I told him briefly about the gathering in the ten-acre field and the cheque they'd handed me for my services.

Steve's eyes twinkled. 'Thought it was *your* farm, did they? Hilary mentioned she was thinking of putting it on the market. Sounds like she already has a buyer.'

'Luke's mother was interested, apparently. Did you ever meet her?'

So far as I knew, Steve had never set eyes on either of the Mrs Vs. So, no surprise to hear him tell me he couldn't bring Trudi to mind. 'A classy woman, you say. With a son like Luke? You can't be serious.'

'She ran her own shoe shop in town. You probably bought your latest lace-ups from her.'

'Not me, mate. This pair came all the way from a market stall north of the border.' Steve pulled up a trouser leg to show me his latest purchase. 'See. Hilary thought I should buy them.'

'She didn't offer to buy them for you then?' I had to be joking. Hilary didn't do gifts, especially not spur-of-the-moment ones. I seized the opportunity though. 'So, Scotland wasn't a total disaster? You had your moments, you and Hilary, while you were away?'

He shrugged. 'A few, I guess. Anyway, what did Luke's mother want with the farm if she already had a business in town?'

'She wanted Luke to take it on as the sitting tenant. Co-tenant, that is, with Sam. That way she'd have a stake in the farm without having to actually hand over any money. And that way, seeing as all three of them were Sahara Street worshippers, their church would be the winner. QED, matey.' Not a bad summary, even if I thought so myself.

Steve wiped beer from his chin and pursed his lips. 'Neat, eh? And Pauline saw through their plan and got rid of them both. Dumped them in the well. It makes a lot of sense, mate.'

'Except Pauline and Trudi were the best of friends. They'd gone to school together.'

That counted for nothing, according to Steve. Best friends can end up as worst enemies, though he had no specific examples in mind. 'Real estate, mate, that's what it's about,' he insisted.

'Are you saying Pauline is after the farm?'

'You're putting words in my mouth. I'm saying she may have acted to prevent others from grabbing the farm. Out of loyalty to your sister.' *Your sister*, see. Not Hilary. 'Luke and his mother, they weren't exactly everybody's favourite people, now, were they?'

Just a minute, not so fast, matey. 'I didn't see anything wrong with Luke's mother myself. Rather a good business head on her, actually.'

'You mean she caught your eye, don't you? Maybe Pauline got jealous. Real estate *and* jealousy, that's a powerful cocktail, mate. Maybe you were the fuse that set it all off. Have you thought about that?'

Several times. 'Funny you should say that. Do you think Hilary will ever have me back again? To look after the farm for her, I mean.'

Steve shrugged his shoulders. He'd given up second-guessing Hilary. I think he felt I was more likely to be invited back than he was. 'Who's organising the funeral?' he wondered.

Sahara Street was the obvious candidate. You could rule out Claire, and most likely Lance, too. Sam would attend, of course. And Mrs K. When I told Steve about Hilary's fear that Sahara Street might want the two Veritys buried in the ten-acre field, he grimaced. 'Is that what Sam wants?'

I told him I'd lost touch with what Sam wanted now Luke was no longer in the picture.

Steve sighed. 'Women again, eh? Impossible to fathom. Not just me then, is it?'

For a minute I was tempted to mention Sam's farewell prank at the window but decided the incident might be misconstrued, seen as lewd, or even as evidence of forbidden goings-on in the hay barn. Steve had his standards, I'd no wish to call them into question. For the same reason I kept quiet about my one-time arrangement with Mrs V. Whether she would end up in the ten-acre, along with her son, was a detail I felt happy to leave to members of her church. Up to them to decide how best to dispose of and remember her, though I felt pretty certain Hilary would put her foot down and deny them the use of her land.

'What about *you*?' Steve enquired. 'Will you be going to the funeral? To pay your respects, I mean, to that woman, the one that caught your eye?'

I shook my head. 'I don't think so. I have a wife and children to think of, remember. Besides, I think I've had more than enough of the Verity family for the time being. I won't stop you from going though, if that's what you've a mind to do.'

Steve gave a snort. 'Not my scene, mate. Not my crowd either. You know I've no time for those church people. If Luke's the best they can produce, then God help them. I think you'll find your sister feels the same.'

'You could be right.' I gave him a nod and a nudge. 'I'm quite prepared to acknowledge that you know my sister's mind better than I do at the moment. After all, you have been seeing rather a lot of each other lately.'

I sat back sharply as a beer mat hit the table edge and landed in my lap.

'I've told you, mate, I've had it up to here with women. Can't get on with them.' Steve tapped his forehead to indicate the level of his disenchantment. 'Now what do you say we have a day out in the Landy, you and me, for old times' sake? Friday suit you? I'll even let you choose where we go. Can't say fairer than that, now, can I? And don't tell me that your diary's full. It'll give us both a chance to clear our heads of some of the stuff we've had to put up with over the past week.'

*

It was to be a re-run of an earlier jaunt. Over familiar territory. Along lanes we'd travelled many times before, enjoying the views, the discomfort and, if I knew anything about Steve's Land Rover, the day-long aroma of burnt diesel. Only this time I had it in mind for us to drive out of town via Briar Lane. That way we could stop briefly at Lord's Barn. For a quick look, nothing more. To point things out to Steve, show him a corner of the farm I assumed he'd not been aware of till now, show him where *it* had happened, where the discoveries in the well had been made, and Luke and his mother had met their untimely end.

But first I suggested we pick up a copy of the latest *Gazette*, along with more cigarettes. I wanted confirmation, something in print to show Steve (and convince myself, I dare say) that it had all been for real, that it wasn't just another of my colourful dreams. And there it was, in black and white, several pages of it, with a photograph of the Barn on the front page beneath a banner headline that read:

DOUBLE TRAGEDY AT REMOTE FARM

There was a smaller photo of DI Somebody-or-Other holding a press conference. Not my man Merriman, though.

'Who the fuck is Ollie Marchant?' Steve wanted to know. The name appeared at the start of the opening report. 'I used to teach somebody with a name like that. Hopeless at carpentry, he was. Must have decided to have a go at journalism instead. Does he mention you and your part in the death of the Verity family?'

No, in a word. I couldn't find my name anywhere. Mrs Pauline Kendrick, on the other hand, featured just about everywhere. She, not me, had been looking after the farm while Mrs Pope visited relatives in Fife. *Fife*? And she, not me, had led police to the bodies after having a premonition that something sinister was afoot in the vicinity of the old barn. She knew Mrs Verity, she claimed, as the mother of the young man who'd been helping with work around the farm. Had known her since childhood and couldn't believe what had happened to her. Yeah, how about that?

Sam got no mention either, I noticed. Perhaps as well. But Ted Shimwell was quoted briefly as saying farm workers like Luke Verity were hard to come by. 'An unlikely compliment if ever I heard one,' I said to Steve. 'I think he's been misquoted.' Steve thought I could be right.

I read him bits from OM's report. Luke's body had been discovered lying (not *sitting* then) on top of rubble freshly thrown into the well (I could easily have spotted that clue, couldn't I, if I'd gone ahead and climbed down there myself). They'd found Mrs Verity's fully clothed body buried under this same rubble. A post-mortem showed she'd died from a blow to the head, her son from carbon dioxide poisoning (yes, okay, give Mrs K a pat on the back for spotting that). No one else was being sought in connection with the deaths. The DI wouldn't be drawn on the question of motive but confirmed that a report was being prepared for the coroner.

'They're guessing,' said Steve. 'How does anybody know what really went on? Mind you, it didn't take much to fall out with Luke, did it? You could do it with your eyes shut. Look at that business at the gate, when I told him to take the intercom away, or else. Anything in there about how his mother came by her blow on the head?'

A spade, apparently, had been recovered from where Luke had been sitting on it. *Lying* on it, according to Ollie Marchant. No details given as to its use.

By this time, I'd taken my eyes off the road and Steve, inadvertently or not, had taken the Old Drovers Road instead of the back route leading to Briar Lane. Too late to correct our course, so we agreed we'd leave it for now and call on the way back. 'Isn't it still a crime scene?' asked Steve. If I didn't know him better, I'd say he appeared less than enthusiastic about seeing the place. 'Are you worried we might disturb vital evidence or something?' I asked him. More like he feared bumping into Hilary.

'If you reckon the police have finished their work there,' said Steve, 'then I guess that's good enough for me. I'm just a simple teacher, you know. One of the good guys, wary about stepping on other people's toes, or wandering onto other people's land.'

I tapped his shoulder. 'This is Hilary's land we're talking about, matey. The woman you've just been on holiday with. You're hardly a trespasser.' Any more than I was. Better not to mention to him, however, that Hilary had been planning on turning the Barn into a cosy retreat for two. Steve was liable to name Mrs K as the lucky contender.

Steve's face took on a knowing look – the look that suggests you don't know the half of it, mate. 'All the same, let's just say I'm not one to count my chickens. Now which way at the next crossroads, did you say? Come on, get the map out. Start doing your job, mate. I need a navigator, not a marriage counsellor.'

I produced the map and unfolded it. 'If this was Scotland, you know, I'm not sure I'd be any better at this game than Hilary.'

Steve gave one of his snorts.

*

Over lunch, we found time to read more of the *Gazette*'s coverage of events at the Barn. Steve thought the police had been too quick to wrap up the case, too quick in his view to rule out the involvement of a third party. 'Surely, they were suspicious of Pauline?' he suggested. 'Weren't *you*, for that matter?'

'Are you being serious?'

'Look, mate, your sister and Pauline are thick as thieves, you know they are. It's not a secret. Like I said, Pauline might have thought she was doing your sister a favour by getting rid of Luke and his mother. An ideal opportunity, don't you think?'

I sighed. 'I'm no good at this detective lark. If you think about it, we all of us had motive and opportunity, even *me*. If you want my opinion, the police don't look for complications if a simple solution is staring them in the face. Yes, *I* was surprised how quickly they wrapped it up, but I suppose they have a budget to stick to, targets to meet, that sort of thing, like everybody else. It's not a television audience they have to satisfy after all, is it? One murder case a week, and a whole glamorous team on standby to solve it.'

'And here's me thinking what a fine story for a TV drama!

Morse would have had a field day sorting this one out.'

I reminded him this wasn't Oxford. Later, after setting off for home, my reminder to make for town via Briar Lane afforded Steve the opportunity to bring up the subject once again. He thought the police could have missed a clue or two in their haste to wrap up the case. 'For all we know, mate, they may even have their eye on someone, may even be waiting for that someone to revisit the crime scene.'

'Someone like us, you mean?'

I believe he would have welcomed any excuse not to call at the Barn. As we cruised down Briar Lane, he thought it likely we'd find a police patrol car lurking inside the entrance to the place. Sitting in wait, just in case. But before we could find out if he was right, something else intervened. The Land Rover suffered a serious coughing fit – the second one that day, as it happened, the first having occurred just before lunch and been identified, with a shrug from Steve, as either fuel starvation or an electrical fault, and which he expected would continue to give us trouble till it was fixed. Meaning sorted out at home later, with the help of his garage mechanic neighbour. 'It'll get us home. If I coax it. Treat it like a woman,' he promised.

I thought he'd had it fixed after the Scotland trip. At this rate I began to wonder if we'd make the remaining few hundred yards to the Barn. But we did – just. And there the engine gave a final splutter before it died completely.

'Just my luck,' said Steve. 'It was going fine yesterday.'

We'd coasted to a standstill and were pretty well blocking the entrance. From inside the cab, I could see we weren't alone. Another vehicle stood on the hard parking area, not a patrol car as it happened but a pick-up truck, that looked to me as though it could have been one of Sahara Street's Toyotas. It was parked under the trees and the driver, I saw, was still in his seat behind the wheel. At least I assumed it was a guy. Not always easy to tell, is it? At the sight of us he acted as if *we* were the police, and on patrol in the area. I heard him start his engine. Next minute he'd squeezed past the back of us and turned onto the lane where he sped off the way we'd come.

'Who was *that*?' Steve had got out to lift the bonnet.

'Well, it wasn't the police. I've seen that pick-up before. If he'd come past the front of us, I dare say I would have recognised the driver.'

Doubtful, actually. The sun was getting low and casting long shadows. Of course, it *could* have been one of the security guys I'd spoken to in the ten-acre. He *could* have had a passenger with him. And the passenger *could* have been female. It *could* have been Sam, even. Or Jasmine. Hell, it could have been *anybody*! *Get a grip, Goodman*, I told myself. It was far more likely to have been a local farmer and his missus. They drove pick-ups. Or a couple taking advantage of a quiet spot to get more intimately acquainted. Not a very reliable witness, was I?

Steve hadn't paid much attention. Having decided it wasn't the police, he'd stuck his head under the bonnet and was busy tinkering. 'Get me my toolbox, would you?' he said. While I hunted for it behind the seats, he went across and had a pee where the pick-up had stood. It occurred to me we'd missed an opportunity to ask for a tow. Or a lift. A closer look round the empty Barn seemed out of the question now; a guided tour had to be the last thing on Steve's mind. Unless I persuaded him to give the engine more time to cool down before he started taking it apart.

In the circumstances he thought the suggestion made a lot of sense. So I lit a cigarette, and made my way towards the Barn's by now familiar front door, on the assumption Steve would join me. If I expected the place to look any different – more like a crime scene, say, than a cosy retreat – I was not disappointed. The obvious new feature was the heap of earth and rubble next to the well. Yellow sand mixed with clay and broken stone for the most part. Looking every bit as sinister as I thought it would look, frankly. They'd left it there, like the earth you see heaped beside an open grave, suggesting work in progress, come back in a week, folks, and it'll be gone, sort of thing.

I couldn't imagine how the bottom of the well looked right now and I wasn't particularly keen to walk over there and find out. Whatever they'd found under the rubble, it wasn't Mrs V, I told myself. It couldn't have been. Not the woman from the shoe shop, or the one by the gate to the ten-acre, and definitely not the woman who'd stood in my kitchen doorway in her wellies shaking her hair at me. Women like her don't, as I've said before, frequent the bottom of wells. If hers had been the face staring up at me out of the gloom, I guess I would have had a total memory blackout or something and been found later wandering the lanes in a traumatised state. I considered I'd done well to keep my head as it was. Clearly, Luke's face hadn't quite the same effect.

I turned my gaze towards the windows. Then changed my mind, in case, you know, I saw something I really didn't care to see. Like someone moving about inside, fresh out of the shower. Or the reflection of somebody's face next to mine, peering over my shoulder. Silly things like that, for hey, this place had the power to spook me, in case you hadn't noticed. I felt like the kid who watches the telly from behind the settee and then bawls if you switch his creepy film off.

As Steve caught up with me, a breeze sprang up, that shook the trees overhanging the place, and lowered the temperature noticeably.

'Looks more like a building site. Anyone at home?' Steve took a peek through one of the windows. Clearly, he needed to take his mind off the Landy and for the moment the Barn fitted the bill. Any old barn would have done it.

'Luke hadn't finished doing up the place,' I pointed out. 'This is where he was living after Sam threw him out of the flat.'

'And this is where Pauline asked you to meet her, is it?'

Steve nodded knowingly. 'At the crime scene, eh? You're lucky she hadn't got you lined up as the third victim, mate.'

'I know. I was her alibi, wasn't I? So you said.'

Steve grinned. 'You get the picture, mate. You'll look at Pauline through different eyes in future. Is that the crime scene over there?' He nodded towards the well. 'You don't see many of those about these days. An original, is it?'

'As far as I know.'

'What's under there?' He pointed to the tarpaulin under the lean-to.

'Luke's motorbike, if it's still there.'

'A bit risky, isn't it, leaving a bike where thieves can get at it.'

'I don't think Luke's going to worry about that just now, do you?'

'We may need to borrow it to get home. Keep your fingers crossed.'

After several more minutes spent strolling round the place and peering at various items of interest, Steve announced he was going to give the Landy another whirl. 'The sun's disappearing, look. It'll be dark soon.'

I'd already put my cigarette out and now followed him back to the road. There were tyre tracks and litter everywhere. Not surprising, was it? The place had seen a lot of activity in recent days and, being uninhabited, it attracted its share of uninvited visitors. A couple of cars went by. I remember thinking again that if it came to the worst and the Landy refused to start, we could thumb a lift. We weren't exactly in the middle of nowhere.

Steve had left the bonnet up, and I saw him look under it and then step back and wave his arms in the air the way you do to scatter a swarm of flying insects. Except it was steam he was trying to disperse, or smoke, to be precise, rising from the engine and curling skywards. We both watched it thicken and darken and climb higher, before I heard Steve gasp (or it could have been me, I guess) as a mighty whoosh turned the smoke to flames and the engine compartment became an inferno that forced us to step away and shield our faces. In no time at all the flames had spread to the cab. I remember thinking that if there *were* police patrol cars in the area, this blaze was guaranteed to bring them to the scene. On reflection though, I imagine it probably caused no more alarm in the neighbourhood than a garden bonfire would have done. You had to be there, standing next to it, to appreciate the scale and intensity of this particular bonfire.

Your first thought, as soon as you realise that you're not in any danger yourself, is how on earth to bring a blaze like this under control. I knew Steve kept an extinguisher handy inside the cab; I also knew the device was beyond his reach or mine at this stage, as well as being fine for tackling an overturned camping stove but not much else. We needed a hose pipe and a supply of water, and we needed both right away.

Steve beat me to it. He'd spotted a reel of hose pipe over by the Barn, only now he wanted me to point him in the direction of an outside tap. I remembered I'd seen one on the wall behind Luke's bike. By the time we had the hose connected to it and the water turned on, the blaze, let's face it, had done its worst. True, our efforts produced a lot of steam, but as the flames died down, we found ourselves gazing at the burnt-out shell of Steve's pride and joy. Not only that; the few items we'd left inside had gone up, too – coats, maps, sandwich box, flask, sunglasses, a cardigan, a torch, my copy of the *Gazette*, and, most seriously of all, Steve's copy of *The Land Rover Story*. Not a page of it left untouched.

I turned the water off, and we stood and stared together at the sorry scene. Steve shook his head and started muttering to himself. 'I don't believe it. I Don't. Fucking. Believe. It. Tell me I'm dreaming. It can't be real. What in Christ's name caused *that* to fucking happen?'

I believe my own mutterings dwelt rather more on the

question of how we were going to get home now, followed by the thought that another car was bound to come along soon, and we should flag it down and ask for a lift. Only Steve had other ideas.

'What about that bike?' He began walking towards the lean-to. He reckoned he could hot-wire it to get us home, provided the tank had fuel in it and the tyres had air in them. This was an emergency, he reminded me, never mind the machine's roadworthiness, or the matter of its tax or insurance cover. He'd once owned a bike of his own. He'd no intention of not returning this one to its lean-to in due course. No reason for anyone to look outraged at the idea of borrowing it.

In the end it wouldn't start. The tank, he decided, must be empty. By that time a car *had* gone by, more than one, actually, and the sensible next option seemed to be to start walking in the expectation that another would soon come along and stop for us. If we reached a house first, we'd ask to use the phone and call Steve's neighbour to come out and collect us. This, remember, was before everyone had a phone in their pocket, and before ever a phone mast went up on Foolsmeadow land.

The Mitchells, if my memory served, occupied the next property down Briar Lane. Not a family I'd ever had occasion to meet. In fact, for all I knew, they could have sold up and gone. A number of farms in the area lay vacant. One of them, you'll recall, had been converted into an adult entertainment venue. Others struggled to make ends meet (sorry about that, ignore me, I'm not myself).

We'd covered several hundred yards on the lane when finally, its lights on, a vehicle overtook us and pulled up a short way ahead. I'd stuck my thumb out in the time-honoured fashion and the driver obliged. I thought he looked vaguely familiar, though in the gathering darkness I couldn't be sure. I reminded him who I was. 'Hilary Pope's brother, eh? Is that where you're headed? Her place? Foolsmeadow Grange? That's not far at all.' He sounded surprised when I denied that's where we wanted to be.

He was, I remembered now, George Palfreyman from distant Moor Farm, on his way to his local, the Last Judgment. I'd heard talk about the pub but had never set foot inside. I'd met George for the first and only time at Philip's funeral. I told him the pub would be fine, we'd phone for a taxi from there. By this time Steve had decided against calling his neighbour after all.

George had clearly been reading his copy of the *Gazette*. 'An upsetting time, eh, for Mrs Pope? An awful thing to happen to anyone, two bodies turning up like that. Don't know what to make of it myself. You know Ted Shimwell, do you? Well, Ted told me it was all because of a row over who should run the farm if Mrs Pope sold up. Some say she'll sell, others say she won't. She'll decide in her own time, I say.'

Unless I told him differently, of course, me being family and likely to know my sister's mind before he did. 'Put it this way,' I told him. 'I'll be surprised if it isn't put on the market pretty soon.'

'You in the farming business, too, then?'

The notion I might be would have struck the pair of us as hilarious for sure, given happier circumstances. As it was, neither of us felt particularly light-hearted. 'Adam here is a teacher,' Steve told him. 'Me, I'm just getting started in the scrap business. That was my Land Rover back there, what's left of it. You passed it.'

George muttered something I didn't catch, before assuring us it wasn't the first vehicle to be torched and abandoned at that spot. He had the same problem to contend with on his own land. 'You never know these days. I'm always finding vehicles parked or abandoned in my gateways. Folks with motor caravans, they're some of the worst. They never ask permission. They think you've no right to tell them to move on either. Did somebody pinch it from you then, the Land Rover?'

Steve gave me a puzzled look before deciding he'd been misheard and, with a shake of his head, let it go. One man's pride and joy, was clearly another man's joyride. I couldn't be bothered to ask George if he'd spotted a Toyota pick-up truck in the vicinity lately. I think the fact he was driving a pick-up himself and had found room for us in the cab alongside him may have had something to do with it.

The landlord at the Last Judgment did the phoning for us. A favour for a mate, he called it. His mate ran the local taxi service. While we waited, I bought Steve a pint, in an effort to lift his mood. He took it over to a seat by the door and sat there without saying much at all. Not even to query the name of the brew in his hand. By the time the taxi man put his head round the door, Steve had drained his third pint and come as close to tears as I'd ever seen him. Talk about maudlin. Or about one man's shitty summer. A hug from me, and I dare say he would have sobbed his heart out on my shoulder.

'Need a hand, mate?' the driver asked me.

I nodded. 'Let's get him to the car.'

EPILOGUE

Julie seemed curiously unmoved by the account I gave her of my time at Foolsmeadow. It was as if she'd already heard about it from somebody else. Hard to tell with Julie just how much of it she judged to be shameless exaggeration on my part, though she didn't dispute the *facts* as reported in the *Gazette*. The nub of the matter was she had a tale of her own to tell me, if only I'd listen: a woman had fallen overboard at sea and been found, when the body was recovered, to have expired *before* hitting the water. Killed by a single gunshot, apparently. How about that for high drama? A Poirot or a Miss Marple case if ever she and Charlotte had heard one. Small wonder my own account made so little impact. Nothing like high-octane Mediterranean shenanigans for giving the cruise fans their money's worth. God knows what tale Adrian and his girl were going to bring back from the Far East to top that one. Charlotte told me I'd at least acquired a tan to match theirs. I told Charlotte to pull the other one.

It didn't take Julie long to notice I was on the phone rather more than usual. I told her there were developments to keep up with, loose ends to tie up, things didn't come to a stop, you know, just because members of the family returned home from their holidays. When Adrian eventually staggered in with his enormous backpack, I remember I happened to be on the phone to Hilary at the time (or it could have been Steve, I forget), and I distinctly overheard him say to Julie, 'I see Dad's pleased to see me back.'

Quite honestly, I was pleased to see the lot of them. An empty house, not to mention an empty bed, is no great fun once the novelty of being back home wears off, I find. Okay, since we're being totally honest about things here, I confess I may, just may, have indulged in a spot of fantasising under the duvet after Julie resumed her place alongside me. For a while Julie could have become *her* – you know, the MILF or whatever they call them these days, the woman I would have loved to try for size. No surprise that as time passed, I felt an inevitable sense of relief that the situation had resolved itself in the way it had, and I no longer needed to ask myself how far things would have gone. Nowhere near *that* far, I like to think.

I read in due course the report in the *Gazette* of the inquest into the deaths at Foolsmeadow Grange. Unlawful killing, in Mrs V's case; accidental death, her son. Well, I guess that came as no surprise either. There was also, I noticed, a brief piece about the 'disturbance' at Willsborough College, but no names were mentioned. That would have been at JR's request, I didn't doubt.

When I announced I might attend the funeral of Luke and his mother, Julie questioned my motive. 'You hardly knew them,' she pointed out. When I in turn pointed out that Luke had been my niece's boyfriend and his mother had been, well… the mother of my niece's boyfriend, Julie sniffed. The kind of sniff that accused me of ignoring her point.

She went on to query if I meant the same Mrs Verity who ran the shoe shop in town. Now why should I be surprised to learn that Julie knew the name of the woman who ran the shoe shop? My wife rarely bought new shoes. Moreover, at the time of GV's death, she'd never asked me if GV was related to the woman at the shoe shop. Yet it turned out she *knew* the two were related! And that piece of information put a different slant on things, at least where the funeral was concerned. I dare say Julie might have gone so far as to suggest coming with me if I'd insisted on attending.

In the event I didn't bother. Not after Hilary informed me it was to be a strictly Sahara Street affair. Sam would be there, naturally. That was all she could tell me. I'd have to speak to Sam if I wanted more details. And Sam was rarely at home these days. As for her car, I'm happy to say I eventually honoured my pledge to replace it for her, though I think happy might be the wrong word to describe how I felt about it. Julie didn't like the tale I told her about it being entirely my fault and therefore my responsibility. That's what insurance is for, she insisted. Sam, like I said, wasn't available to give me feedback on whether she liked the car or not. I gathered she was spending a lot of her time at Jasmine's. On occasions Hilary said she had spotted a different car in the yard, but you couldn't rely on Hilary to provide sensible details.

Sadly, relations between Sam and her mother didn't improve. Unable to get Sam to speak to me on the phone, I wrote her a letter but received no reply. Julie told me I was expecting too much – young people these days didn't bother with letters, reading or writing them. And anyway, my niece had her own life to lead, she didn't need her uncle telling her how to lead it or, for that matter, choosing her next car for her.

Julie did show enough interest to ask me one day what I thought would happen to the farm now Luke wasn't around to do odd jobs. I told her I felt sure Hilary would go ahead and sell, and in due course that's what happened. The farm was put up for auction (without a request for help or advice from yours truly this time, I should add) and the highest bidder turned out to be someone acting on behalf of Sahara Street. No surprise there then. If you want my view, I think Hilary was past caring who bought it, as long as it made her reserve price, and she kept the Barn for herself. Ted put in a bid, I heard. An unsuccessful one, as it happened, but he kept his grazing rights. Sahara Street were only interested in the buildings, and as expected, they went on to submit a planning application to convert and extend them into a course and conference centre, with an accommodation block and car park sited (yes, you've guessed it) in the old farmyard, with an overspill into part of the ten-acre field. You might say they were intent on restoring the Grange to something close to its original purpose, as a monastic retreat.

Sam kept her flat, so I learned. She and Jasmine became resident custodians, if that's the term, with responsibility for looking after the site while building work took place and the centre took shape. Mrs K told me this after I dropped into her charity shop one afternoon. Some other girl, meanwhile, took over Sam's job at the pie shop.

'Out of touch, are we?' Mrs K teased. 'Mind, you'll have a lot on your plate now your students are back at college, won't you? Day off, is it? Hil and me, we were only talking about you the other day, and saying how you'd all be back at work now, you teachers. What's it like then, being in charge again? Bet you don't stand for any nonsense from *your* students.'

Some people, eh? I refrained from asking her if the police had had her in for questioning yet. 'How's Boyd these days?' I asked instead, and immediately regretted mentioning the guy. If anything, he was worse, I learned, and I found myself saying how sorry I was whilst praying the subject of that meal with the Kendricks wouldn't be raised. 'Give him my best wishes,' I said.

Mrs K had been to Trude's funeral and chided me for not attending. The remains of both mother and son lay buried in Dale Park cemetery, I was told, in case I wanted to pay my respects. No mention was made of Foolsmeadow land as a final resting place for either of them.

Months later I popped into the charity shop again for

some reason and was regaled with details of the improvements and alterations my sister was having done to the Barn. The staircase, for instance, had been made safe at last. A separate garage was being built. And a porch. As for the well, it had gone, understandably. Filled in and bulldozed. Obliterated entirely. If I saw it now, I was told, I'd never know there had been a well on that spot. An electric gate, too, had been installed at the entrance. To keep out undesirables, obviously, some of whom would drive in and torch their vehicles and leave them for others to remove.

I checked this out with Steve. He assured me the remains of the Land Rover had been taken away within days. Naturally evidence would have been left behind in the form of ashes and charred debris, but not enough to enable someone to trace it back to him. Someone like Hilary, say. Still the last person he wanted to talk about, despite the passage of time. On one occasion, when I raised the subject with him, he put a finger to his lips and told me to ask my sister. Sound familiar? Fair enough, I raised it with her, in the course of one of our phone conversations. 'How's your love life these days?' I asked her.

'If you mean Steve,' I was told, 'we don't have any plans to see each other. Not at the moment.' The cue, if she needed one, for my sister to wax philosophical about life's little tribulations. 'You enjoy what you have at the time, and you move on, don't you? That's life for you, Adam, I'm afraid. Nothing lasts for ever, don't they say? A good thing, too, if you ask me.'

No regrets, then. During another of our chats she raised the subject of the walking stick we'd borrowed, telling me her friend Pauline had told her to just forget about it. By then, of course, Hilary had long since got over the need for a stick, if there ever was one. Her ankle was fine. Did *I* have a use for a stick, by any chance? I could have tried returning it, dropping in for an excuse to have a word with Lucy, but by this time the shoe shop had closed its doors for good and was up for sale.

What of the other Mrs V, the detained mental patient, Claire? The encounter in JR's office remained a talking point for a while at the college, coming as it did in the wake of GV's suicide, with its reminder that not all families succeed or conform in the way educators would like. Some enlightened members of staff thought I should thank JR for so heroically putting himself in the firing line. It was clear to them that *I* had been the intended target. I'd been GV's tutor after all, and didn't tutors have a responsibility to ensure their students stayed alive and did well on their course? Needless to say, Claire made no further attempt to contact me – none that I was aware of, at any rate.

And what of GV's journal? JR never mentioned it to me again. He could indeed have consigned it to the bin. I very much doubt he tried reading it. It wouldn't have made much sense to him, now, would it? All those coded references and the absence of page numbers. JR was many things, but he was not a patient man. Our disagreement over the way he conducted his encounter with Claire was never alluded to again. If I knew JR, he was glad to see the back of the Veritys. As far as I was aware, he had no way of knowing that what he read in the paper about the deaths at Foolsmeadow involved members of the same family, or that it involved a member of his staff. Or, if he did, he chose to ignore the connection. College principals do have to get their priorities right, I realise, if they are to keep on top of their workload.

As for my new crop of students, there wasn't a Verity among them; nor did I come across a Claire, a Trudi, a Jasmine, nor indeed, a Luke. I dropped the idea of trying to guess which of my hopefuls might be compiling a journal of personal reflections on life at college. Likewise, I resisted the temptation to inquire if any of them had connections to Sahara Street. Steve did confide to me at one point that he'd taken to calling one of his new students 'a bit of a Verity, lad, aren't you?' on account of his attitude. The same lad didn't last long on the carpentry course, oddly enough.

Steve drove a borrowed car for a while – till he got his hands on another Land Rover, a neat second-hand job which I'm happy to say acquitted itself perfectly the first time we went out together in it. 'Just don't ask me to pull in at *that* place,' he insisted. Needless to say, to my knowledge Steve never again visited any corner of Foolsmeadow land, either behind the wheel or on foot. And Hilary never asked after him. As for talk of moving to Australia, forget it. Steve didn't mention it again.

It must have been some five years later when I learned that my sister had put Lord's Barn on the market. By then she'd renamed it Briar Cottage and made it extremely comfortable for herself. I did wonder if Mrs K played any part in her decision to move, or if the location proved just too remote. Or too spooky. 'You don't think the place gives off the wrong vibes then?' I teased her.

'Adam, you know me well enough by now to know that kind of tittle tattle doesn't worry me in the slightest. I make my own decisions, thank you very much. In my own good time. I just fancy living nearer town, that's all.'

Oh yeah? She had her eye on a terraced house that was located nearer town. Not far from where the Kendricks lived, as it happened. Apparently, Boyd needed round-the-clock care by then and Pauline was finding it increasingly difficult to spend time away from him.

When I told Julie the news she shrugged. 'Can't say I blame her. Who'd want to live in a spot like that anyway? Enough to give anybody the creeps.'

'You've never been there! Not with me, at any rate.'

I'd told her all about it though, hadn't I? Drawn her attention to the report in the *Gazette*. And the photos. Enough to convince her, apparently, that converted barns, even the most lavish and sympathetically appointed ones, don't make for the most tranquil living space. 'You know what I'm talking about,' she said. 'You still have nightmares about the place, even now. Or hadn't you realised?'

Did I? I tried telling her it wasn't so much the place as the family that I'd found unsettling. But Julie was having none of it. 'Ask Steve,' she said. 'Ask him what he thinks of the place, the Barn, as you call it. I bet he's thankful he didn't end up living there, with your sister.'

I let the subject drop. Everyone, after all, is entitled to their view.

For writing and publishing news, or recommendations of new titles to read, sign up to the Book Guild newsletter: